BRIGHT SPEAR
TRILOGY

H. L. Macfarlane

COPYRIGHT INFORMATION

For Scotland, and for faeries.

PRINCE ØF FØXES

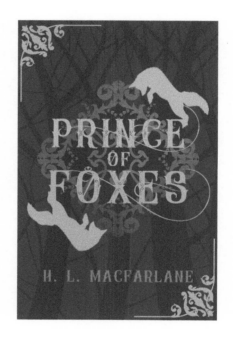

FŎX SLEEP

When someone has wakened to what is really there
is that person free of the chain of consequences
and I answered yes and with that I turned into a fox
and I have been a fox for five hundred lives
Fox Sleep (W. S. Merwin; 1992)

PRØLØGUE

Names were important. They always had been, from the moment man first developed language to understand the world around him. They were important, but the intense popularity of a particular playwright's work in the South of England suggested otherwise. When hoards of Londoners leeched into Scotland in search of good hunting grounds, golfing estates and other leisurely pursuits that they could not find at home Sorcha became unwillingly familiar with Shakespeare's plays.

But Sorcha and her family knew better than to take his words to heart. A rose by any other name would *not* smell as sweet, for once it lost its name it was no longer a rose as one knew it. And names weren't important simply for their superficial usage in eliminating the need to wordlessly point at things.

All her life Sorcha had the rules of names drilled into her. Do not call a person by their first name if you are not familiar with them. Take your husband's surname when you marry and leave your own behind. Bear a son to pass on his father's name. Give your children names full of luck, strength, wisdom and beauty, for they would need such traits when they grew up.

But these mantras all paled in comparison to the one rule the infuriating English tourists liked to laugh at most. They would not laugh so loudly if they knew the truth. Nobody who knew the truth laughed about it. This rule was the very reason Sorcha often went by Clara, an anglicised version of her first name that she despised but eagerly used nonetheless.

She had witnessed first-hand, as a child, what happened when you did not follow this one, most important rule. You disappeared – sometimes forever, sometimes for no time at all – but if you returned you were changed, and almost never in a good way. Sorcha had seen calm and even-tempered folk go mad, and the loudest, brashest of her father's friends retreat into their own minds, never to speak another word.

Tourists often thought the locals were crazy when they came to visit the little town of Darach. It was nestled between large, sweeping forests and breathtakingly beautiful lochs, so it was a popular place to visit away from the hustle and bustle of Glasgow and Edinburgh. Locals warned them against conversing with anyone they might meet roaming beneath the trees, or wandering along the shores of the lochs, especially at twilight. The tourists, without fail, never heeded their advice.

So they disappeared, in one fashion or another, and they only had themselves to blame. They had been warned, after all, and they didn't listen.

Never, ever give your real name to a faerie.

CHAPTER ONE

Lachlan

Today was the queen's funeral and Lachlan, her only child and heir to the throne, was deliberately avoiding the ceremony.

His mother would understand, he was sure. He'd never been one for mournful occasions; most of the Seelie folk weren't. Their lives were long enough to be considered immortal by the humans who largely lived, unknowing and unseeing, beside them. If Lachlan allowed himself to be truly sad he'd spend centuries feeling that way.

It was the last thing he wanted.

So Lachlan was currently whiling away his morning following a human girl who was collecting early autumn brambles on the outskirts of the forest. She lived in Darach, the closest human settlement to the central realm of the Scots fair folk. The people who lived there were, in general, respectful and wary of Lachlan and his kind. They saw what members of the Seelie Court could do fairly regularly, after all. The rest of the British Isles was another story entirely, though it hadn't always been that way.

Everybody in the forest knew things were changing.

The advancements made in human medicine, and human technology, and human ingenuity, meant that humans were beginning to forget what it felt like to fear 'otherness'. They believed themselves above tales of faeries, and magic in general, though Lachlan knew there were humans capable of magic, too.

Not here, though, he thought, creeping from one tall bow of an oak tree to another to trail silently after the girl. She was happily eating one bramble for every two she placed in her basket, seemingly without a care in the world. *Not on this island. Not for centuries.* Lachlan knew this was largely because his mother, Queen Evanna – as well as King Eirian of the Unseelie Court far down south, in England – spirited all such magically-inclined British children away to the faerie realm, to live for all intents and purposes as faeries themselves.

That's certainly better than being an ordinary human, especially now, when they've forgotten about us.

A stiff breeze tearing through the oak tree caused Lachlan's solitary earring to jingle like a bell. Adorned with delicate chains and tiny sapphires, and spanning the entire length of his long, pointed ear as a cuff of beaten silver, the beautiful piece of jewellery had been a gift from his mother from a time long since passed. Back then Lachlan had been enamoured with the blue-eyed faerie, Ailith, and had been convinced the two of them would marry. The earring was ultimately meant as a gift for Ailith, he'd decided. His mother would never be so direct as to give it to Lachlan's beloved herself. It wasn't in her nature.

But then Queen Evanna had married the half-Unseelie faerie, Innis, who was the Unseelie king's brother. He had himself a grown son, Fergus, who came with his father to live in the Seelie realm. The two were silver where Lachlan and his mother were gold, and Ailith had become betrothed to his new-found stepbrother instead of him.

So Lachlan lost his love and, now, he'd lost his mother. The earring was all he had left of both.

I should go to the funeral, he decided, turning from the girl as he did so. *I am to be king, after all. I should –*

Lachlan paused. He could hear something. More chime-like than his earring in the wind, and clearer than the sound of the nearby stream flowing over centuries-smooth stone.

The human girl was singing.

"The winds were laid, the air was still,

The stars they shot alang the sky;

The fox was howling on the hill,

And the distant echoing glens reply."

Lachlan was enamoured with the sound of her voice. The words were Burns; the melody unfamiliar. He thought perhaps she'd invented the tune herself and, if so, she was a talented girl indeed. He peered through the yellowing leaves of the oak tree, intent on seeing what the human with the lovely voice truly looked like.

She was not so much a girl as a young woman – perhaps not quite twenty – though since Lachlan himself had lived for almost five times that long she was, for all intents and purposes, still simply a girl. Her skin was pale and lightly freckled, though her cheeks held onto some colour from the fast-fading summer. Her hair was a little darker than the oak trunk Lachlan was currently leaning against. It flashed like deep copper when it caught the sunlight and hung long and wild down her back, which was a sight rarely seen on a young, human woman.

A cream dress fell to her ankles and sat low on her shoulders. Small leather boots, made for wandering through forests and across meadows, were laced across her feet. A cloak of pine-coloured fabric was slung over the handle of her almost-full wicker basket. *Well-made clothes*, he concluded, *but nothing elaborate or expensive. Just an ordinary girl.* She dithered over the correct words of the next verse of her Burns poem as Lachlan merrily watched on. *Fair to look at, for a human. But it is her voice that is special. Special enough to ask her name.*

He delighted over thinking how his stepfather and stepbrother would react when he brought back a human girl, enchanted to sing for him until the end of time. *I wonder what Ailith would think. Would she be jealous? Would she mourn for the loss of my attention?*

Lachlan was excited to find out.

He stretched his arms above his head, causing his earring to jingle once more. Below him the girl stilled. She stopped singing, dark brows knitted together in confusion.

"Is somebody there?" she asked, carefully placing her basket down by her feet as she spoke.

"You have a lovely voice," Lachlan announced. He was satisfied to see the girl jump in fright, eyes swinging wildly around before she realised the voice she'd heard

9

came from above. When she spied Lachlan standing high up on the boughs of the oak tree she gasped.

"You are – it is early to see one of your kind so far out of the forest," she said. She struggled to maintain a blank face, to appear as if she wasn't surprised in the slightest to see a faerie standing in a tree.

Lachlan laughed. "I suppose it is. Today is a special occasion; we are all very much wide awake."

The girl seemed to hesitate before responding. Lachlan figured she was trying to decide if it was wise to continue such a conversation with him. "What occasion would be so special to have you all awake before noon?"

"The funeral of the queen. My mother."

"Oh."

That was all she said. Lachan had to wonder what kind of reaction he'd expected. Certainly not sympathy; he had no use for such a thing.

"You are not at the funeral?" the girl asked after a moment of silence. "If you are her son –"

"I shall get there eventually," Lachlan replied. He sat down upon the branch he'd been standing on. "Tell me your name, lass. Your voice is too beautiful to not have a name attached to it."

To his surprise, she smiled. "I do not think so, Prince of Faeries."

Clever girl.

"You wound me," he said, holding a hand over his heart in mock dismay. "An admirer asks only for a name and you will not oblige his lowly request? How cruel you are."

"How about a name for a name, then?" she

suggested. "That seems fair."

Lachlan nodded in agreement. The girl could do nothing with his name. She was only human.

"Lachlan," he replied, with a flourish of his hand in place of a bow. "And you?"

"Clara."

"A pretty name for a pretty girl. Is there a family name to go with –"

"I am not so much a fool as to give you my family name," Clara said, "and I think you know that."

He found himself grinning. "Maybe so. Come closer, Clara. You stand so far away."

He was somewhat surprised when she boldly took a step forwards, half expecting her to decide enough was enough and run away.

Even careful humans give in to the allure of faeries, he thought, altogether rather smug. *It won't be long until I have Clara's full name.*

When Clara took another step towards him Lachlan noticed that her eyes were green.

No, blue, he decided. *No, they're –*

"Your eyes," he said, deftly swinging backwards until he was hanging upside down from the branch. Lachlan's face was now level with Clara's, though the wrong way round. She took a shocked half-step backwards at their new-found proximity. "They are strange."

"I do not think my eyes are as strange as yours, Lachlan of the forest," she replied. "Yours are gold."

"Not so uncommon a colour for a Seelie around these parts. Yours, on the other hand...we do not see

11

mismatched eyes often."

Clara shrugged. "One blue, one green. They are not so odd. Most folk hardly notice a difference unless they stand close to me."

"Do many human boys get as close to you as I am now?" Lachlan asked, a smile playing across his lips at the blush that crossed Clara's cheeks.

She looked away. "I cannot say they have."

"Finish your song for me, Clara. I'll give you something in return."

"And what would that be?" she asked, glancing back at Lachlan. Her suspicion over the sudden change of subject was written plainly on her face.

He swung himself forwards just a little until their lips were almost touching. "A kiss, of course."

"That's...and what if I do not want that?"

"Then I guess I leave with a broken heart."

Clara's eyebrow quirked.

"You do not believe me," he complained.

"With good reason."

"You really are a cruel girl."

The two stared at each other for a while, though Lachlan was beginning to grow dizzy from his upside down view. But just as he was about to right himself, Clara took a deep breath and began to sing once more.

There were four verses left of her Burns poem, about a ghost who appeared in front of the poet to lament over what happened to him in the final years of his life, and it was both haunting and splendid to hear. Lachlan mourned for the spirit as if it had been real, and wished there was more to the poem for Clara to sing.

But eventually she sang her last, keening note, leaving only the sound of the wind to break their silence. When Lachlan crept a hand behind her neck and urged her lips to his Clara fluttered her eyes closed. The kiss was soft and chaste – hardly a kiss at all – but just as it ended Lachlan bit her lip.

The promise of something more, if Clara wanted it.

The girl was breathless and rosy-cheeked when Lachlan pulled away. A rush ran through him at the sight of her.

"Tell me your last name," he breathed, the order barely audible over the breeze ruffling Clara's hair around her face.

She opened her eyes, parting her lips as if to speak and –

The sound of bells clamoured through the air.

Clara took a step away from Lachlan immediately, eyes bright and wide and entirely lucid once more.

"I have to go," she said, stumbling backwards to pick up her forgotten basket and cloak before darting away from the forest.

No matter, Lachlan thought, as he dropped from the branch to the forest floor. *I shall see her again. I will have her name next time.*

But he was disappointed.

Now he had to go to his mother's funeral alone, with no entertainment to distract him from his grief when evening came.

CHAPTER TWO

Sorcha

"Have I lost my senses entirely?" Sorcha cried. "Singing for a faerie. Their *prince*! I must have gone mad!"

She passed Old Man MacPherson's farm in a haze of scurried footsteps, dropping brambles from the basket clutched to her chest as she went. The man's son was up on the roof; he waved to Sorcha when he noticed her, and she nodded in response. He was replacing a slate tile which had come loose and smashed upon the ground in the middle of the night. Soon the mild weather would turn and the farm would need to be as watertight as possible to avoid the coming rain, which arrived hand-in-hand with the darkest months of the year.

But Sorcha was happy with the promise of wet, cold days and wetter, colder nights. For though the creeping autumn weather and the inevitable winter that followed caused damage to roofs and fields and sometimes livestock, it also signalled a blessed end to the slew of tourists that had bombarded the tiny town of Darach since April.

Good riddance to them, Sorcha thought with vicious pleasure. *Let them return to their cities and their pollution.*

She paused by the loch-side to pick up a pair of empty glass bottles and a filthy handkerchief. Sorcha scowled; only a city-dweller would leave behind such a mess on the shore of the most beautiful loch in the country.

I'm biased, of course, she thought. *All lochs are beautiful. But Loch Lomond is...special.*

Sorcha skipped a stone across the water's surface, watching as it leapt once, twice, three times. On its fourth skip it fell beneath the dark, shimmering surface of the loch, never to be seen again.

She rearranged the basket and cloak in her arms to make room for the rubbish she had picked up, tossing the offending items into a large receptacle behind her parents' house when she finally reached it. The house was handsome to look at, and finer made than the nearby farmhouses. Red stone and slate, with painted windowsills and a sweeping garden that circled all around the building. Sorcha loved it; it had been in the Darrow family for as long as anybody could remember. Now it was almost all that remained of their wealth.

Generations ago the Darrows had been far richer than they were now. They were the landlords for the area, owning the very ground Sorcha walked upon right up through the forest and along the shore of the loch. The farmers in the area were all tenants of her father, and nobody could so much as cut down a tree or keep a boat on the loch without his permission.

But Sorcha's father was a kind man, and an understanding one. Despite outside pressure from the cities and an increased cost of living, he never raised the rent for the people who lived on his land. It was part of the reason the Darrows were much poorer now, but Sorcha was happy for it.

She could never forgive her father if he sold his principles for a more comfortable life.

Though I have to wonder why he's agreed to meet this Londoner for the third time in as many months, Sorcha thought as she crept into the kitchen as quietly as possible. She dumped her basket of brambles on the table, hung up her cloak, then used the large window overlooking the back garden to check her reflection. She looked just about as windswept and bothered as she felt, with wild hair, red cheeks and a dishevelled dress.

Sorcha knew she really should have put her hair up before going outside. She knew this, but it hadn't stopped her keeping it long and loose down her back instead. She ran her fingers through it in an attempt to tidy her appearance, wincing when she met tangle after tangle. She smoothed out her dress, splashed cold water on her face from a basin by the sink, then left the kitchen to walk down the corridor towards the parlour room.

She could hear both of her parents inside, as well as the stranger they had insisted upon Sorcha meeting today. Of course she hadn't wanted to; she had no interest in Londoners. But she was an obedient daughter, and she knew she was lucky to have parents that had not once pressured her into marriage, though Sorcha would turn twenty at the end of the month. She could be polite and lovely for this *one* Englishman.

16

The very notion of being lovely caused Sorcha's thoughts to return to Lachlan. It had seemed like a dream, to meet the Prince of Faeries. Sorcha had met her share of his kind before, though they tended to slip from her vision just as easily as she had laid eyes on them. On the occasions they had spoken to her they quickly gave up trying to charm her once they realised she would not give them her name.

I nearly gave it to Lachlan, though. This wasn't quite true, of course; Sorcha hadn't given him her real first name. Had she told him her surname was Darrow he could have done nothing with it. And, even then, if he knew her first name was Sorcha, he did not know her middle name.

Her father was a smart man. He had raised a clever daughter. Sorcha would not be caught be a faerie so easily.

I wanted to be caught even just for a moment, she thought despite herself, dwelling longingly on the memory of Lachlan's warm, golden skin and molten eyes. Even his braided, bronze-coloured hair had seemed to be spun of gold when the sunlight shone upon it. The silver cuff adorning one of his inhumanly pointed ears had seemed mismatched against it all, though the sapphire-encrusted piece of jewellery had been so beautiful Sorcha thought she might well have died to possess it for but a minute.

She brought her fingertips up to her lips, committing the feeling of Lachlan's mouth on hers to memory. *He kissed me like it was nothing at all. Does he go around kissing every young woman he sees whilst hanging upside down from a tree?*

It struck Sorcha that she had not taken notice of

17

Lachlan's clothes even once, though he had said he was going to a funeral. *Were they black?* she wondered. *I do not think so. Would faeries wear black to a funeral? What are faerie funerals like? And this was their queen. Lachlan's mother. He did not seem all that sad. Just how did she –*

"Sorcha Margaret Darrow, if you do not get in here this instant I will lock you in your room until the end of the year!"

Sorcha flinched at her mother's voice reverberating through the door. The woman had the uncanny ability to know when her daughter was lurking where she shouldn't be – which was often – and was quick to scold her. She sighed heavily, forced all thoughts of Lachlan away for another time, then fixed a smile to her face before swinging the door open.

"I'm sorry, mama, I was cleaning up by the lochside," Sorcha apologised. Her mother clucked her tongue.

"It is not befitting a young lady to go around cleaning up filthy bottles and – look at your hair! That is no way to appear in front of a guest! Go and –"

"It's quite alright, Mrs Darrow," interrupted a low, gravelly voice. Though it was largely smoothed over with the typical accent of upper-class London that Sorcha had come to resentfully recognise from tourists, there still existed a trace of local, melodic Scots that she liked the sound of.

Out of the corner of her eye she saw her father, a mild expression on his face that suggested he did not care what Sorcha looked like. He was simply glad she had shown up at all. He inclined towards his guest with a hand.

"Sorcha, this is Murdoch Buchanan, a gentleman who grew up not ten miles from here before moving down to London when he was twelve. Mr Buchanan, this is my lovely daughter, Sorcha."

She withheld a wince; Sorcha did not like her real name revealed to anyone but her closest friends, despite the fact her mother thought this silly. But the lessons her father had instilled in her from a young age – to be wary of strangers, for they might be faeries – very much filtered into her attitude towards tourists. And this man, Murdoch Buchanan, had already heard her full name.

Thanks, mama, she thought dully as she turned towards the man with an apologetic smile on her face, curtsying as she did so. "I am truly sorry for my appearance and my lateness, Mr Buchanan. It was an accident."

"No need to be sorry for wishing to keep the loch-side clean. It is a truly beautiful place; those responsible for sullying it ought to be ashamed of themselves."

Maybe this Londoner isn't so bad. He was born around here, after all. He might not be detestable.

Sorcha allowed herself to look at the man properly for the first time. Murdoch was tall and dressed impeccably in a white shirt, dark grey tail coat with matching waistcoat, ebony trousers and shiny leather boots. His black hair grew in loose curls around his head, and his face was clean-shaven. His eyes were dark.

Not just dark, Sorcha thought. *They are as black as his hair.* They were the most striking thing about him, though Murdoch was, by anyone's measure, a very handsome man.

His impossibly dark eyes watched Sorcha intently as

she watched him. She did not know what to say; she had the most unsettling feeling that something bad was about to happen.

"Mr Buchanan is going to be staying with us for a few days, Sorcha," her mother said, dragging her daughter out of her own head.

"Why?" she asked, though she knew she could have worded the question a little more politely.

"You know things have been getting harder for us around here," her father said. "Something has to be done to preserve the area so that nothing bad can happen to us, or to the farmers. I don't want what's happening in the Highlands to occur here."

Sorcha nodded. Everyone knew about the Clearances. An icy chill ran down her spine.

"What does this have to do with Mr Buchanan staying with us?"

It was her mother who answered. She sounded excited, which was a bad thing. Margaret Darrow being excited was a very, very bad thing indeed. "Why, Sorcha," she began, standing up to envelop her daughter's hands within her own. She smiled brightly. "You are going to marry him!"

Sorcha's mind went blank. She could only stare at Murdoch Buchanan in horror. He was a Londoner. A stranger. She did not know him, nor did he know her.

Yet he had already agreed to marry her.

She took a step towards the door, then another and another.

"No," was all she said, before fleeing for her bedroom.

No, no, no.

CHAPTER THREE

Lachlan

"Lachlan, where have you been?! The ceremony ended five minutes ago!"

Ailith came rushing towards Lachlan just as he pushed open the heavy, ornate wooden doors to his bedroom, her breathtaking face full of genuine concern. When she touched his shoulder he shrugged her off.

"I consider it a blessing to have missed it," he told her. "We both know my mother herself hated funerals. Who do you think I learned to loathe them from? But she looked forward to the feasts that followed them and I'm here for that, at least."

"You didn't answer my question."

Lachlan rolled his eyes, pouring a goblet of wine from the bronze pitcher on his bedside table when he reached it. Wordlessly he handed it over to Ailith before pouring another for himself. "Here and there," he finally replied. "Nowhere of consequence."

"Lachlan –"

"The outskirts of the forest. I sat in a tree and watched the world go by. Are you happy now?"

Lachlan didn't look at the beautiful faerie as he lied. Well, it wasn't exactly a lie. Faeries could never truly lie. The human girl Clara *was* part of the world, but he hadn't simply watched her. That was a secret he had no desire whatsoever to divulge to Ailith.

I want Clara's full name, he thought longingly. *I want it now.*

"You don't seem affected by Queen Evanna's death at all."

Lachlan was struck by the sadness in Ailith's voice. Most faeries didn't wear such negative emotions on their sleeves for everyone else to see; the blue-eyed creature in front of him was different. Perhaps it was because her father died almost a decade ago, and she was yet to get over it. Perhaps she was just as emotionally impulsive as humans were. Perhaps it was something else entirely.

Either way, it was one of the reasons Lachlan had loved her so. Now, because he couldn't have her, it was one of the things he could stand least of all.

"I shall deal with my grief however I like," he said before swallowing a large mouthful of wine. He glanced at Ailith out of the corner of his eye. "Shouldn't you be consoling my beloved stepbrother, anyway? Or your future father-in-law? I'm quite certain they are both missing your company."

Ailith grimaced. "Lachlan, don't talk about your family like –"

"Those two? My family? Don't make me laugh, Ailith. Innis and Fergus are no more my family than you are."

"You don't mean that."

Lachlan lay back onto his bed, careful not to spill his wine as he did so. Ailith *wasn't* his family, but it was a cruel thing to say nonetheless. She stood in front of him, close to tears, though even in her misery she was beautiful. It was as if her pale, elegant face had been carved to display such an emotion.

His own expression softened. "You're right. I apologise. You're all I have left in the world. You know that. I'm merely...handling my grief in my own way. I didn't mean to snap at you."

Being polite was the only way the two of them managed to deal with their intimate past, though ultimately all that meant was that they ignored how they'd felt towards each other before Fergus stole her away. But that suited Lachlan just fine.

Give it a few decades and I'll forget I loved Ailith altogether.

"Speaking of Fergus," Ailith said, though her tone suggested she was bringing him up reluctantly, "he and his father were looking for you. There's a lot that needs prepared before your coronation ceremony."

He made a face. "It is still two weeks away. If they wish to speak to me they can find me themselves."

"Lachlan –"

"Alright, alright," he sighed, swinging up from his bed and waltzing over to the large, gilded mirror hanging on the opposite wall. Lachlan fiddled with his hair, inspecting the braid that crawled across the left-hand side of his scalp. After hours spent climbing in the forest he knew he could do with unravelling the braid to comb it out, but he resisted. He liked having his hair styled this way; it ensured his mother's earring was on full display. Despite this, Ailith seemed determined never to notice it, as if she knew exactly for whom it had been intended.

In the mirror Lachlan could see Ailith walking towards the door. She sighed when she saw Lachlan watching her. "You do not have to be king if you don't want to, remember."

Lachlan scoffed at such a notion. "Where did you get that idea? If I'm not king then my half-Unseelie step family will have the crown. That's almost as bad as allowing the creatures lurking deep in the lochs to take over our court."

Ailith laughed softly into her hand. "That your mother named you after the thing you so hate never fails to amuse me."

"You and me both. Though it's not the *lochs* I mislike," Lachlan corrected, fitting on a chestnut-coloured tailcoat over his loose white shirt and dark breeches. "Merely what lives in them. You know every dark thing in there hates Seelies."

"And we hate them right back," Ailith said. "Perhaps it's time to reassess such feelings. After all, both the forests and the lochs are having to fight humans nowadays."

Lachlan said nothing. He knew Ailith was right, of course, but that didn't mean he wanted to let her know she was right. Humans really were becoming a growing problem with every tree they felled, every badly-extinguished bonfire they left behind and every broken bottle abandoned upon the forest floor.

"Come find me after you've spoken with your stepfather," Ailith murmured when Lachlan joined her by the door, brushing her elegant fingers along his sleeve before leaving his room. He touched the fabric where her fingers had been.

Another few decades, Lachlan reminded himself. *Another twenty or thirty years and Ailith will not matter to me at all.* And so Lachlan left his room, once more alone, to venture down the palace corridor with his wine goblet in hand. He veered in the general direction of his mother's old chambers, where Lachlan knew he'd find both his stepfather and stepbrother.

The building wasn't so much a traditional palace as it was a network of connected rooms carved into the very forest itself. The fair folk were a vain and prideful race, so the labyrinthine home of the royal family was painfully exquisite to look upon. The very walls were aglow, lighting the way to Queen Evanna's chambers in soft, golden tones the colour of Lachlan's skin. The tunnels and hallways were perfectly curved; not a single sharp angle existed anywhere within the palace. Some days Lachlan adored this – it was beautiful, after all. Other days he detested it, for there was nowhere to hide.

Nowhere to cry, or scream, or keep secrets from one another.

"Lachlan, there you are!"

Lachlan resisted grimacing at Innis' voice. It wasn't that he hated the faerie – he hardly bothered to hate any faeries at all – but rather that Lachlan simply did not have the patience to deal with him. Innis and his son were always scheming and plotting, their silver skin and hair stark and obvious against the gold of the Seelie Court. When his mother first announced her engagement to Innis, Lachlan had been convinced the marriage was somehow a scheme concocted by the faerie

26

himself.

But my mother would never have been so stupid to fall for an Unseelie plot. Lachlan knew this. He *knew* it, but it didn't stop him indulging in his paranoid beliefs, either.

"We didn't see you at the funeral," Fergus said, smiling slightly as he patted Lachlan on the shoulder. Lachlan hated the way he tried to act brotherly towards him. It was all a lie, that much he was sure of. After all, had Fergus ever felt even vaguely brotherly towards him then he'd never have orchestrated a betrothal to Ailith.

Lachlan was still unsure how the faerie had managed it. Ailith certainly never told him.

Perhaps she was enamoured by his silver countenance, Lachlan supposed. *It certainly looks better against her fair skin than mine does.*

"I was grieving in my own way," Lachlan replied, giving both faeries the same answer he'd given Ailith.

Innis nodded in understanding. "Whatever you need to do, I support you. We all do. In two weeks you are meant to be king, after all."

Lachlan said nothing. Fergus' hand was still on his shoulder; when he tried to shove it off his stepbrother instead moved his hand to the silver cuff on Lachlan's ear.

"This was meant for Ailith, wasn't it?" he asked, removing the piece of jewellery before Lachlan had a chance to protest. "It truly would look beautiful on her. Have you ever considered giving it to her as a betrothal gift? Or a wedding gift, perhaps?"

"I'd rather keep it to remember my mother by," Lachlan replied, on-edge from the drastic change in subject. Something was off. Wrong. He didn't know what.

Fergus held the earring up to the light, his mercurial eyes transfixed by the way the sapphires shone. "A shame," he muttered. "It really doesn't suit you. Neither does being king."

Lachlan froze. A terrible shiver ran down his spine. "Excuse me?"

"Now, now, Fergus," his father said, shaking his head in disapproval, "you can afford to be more delicate with the boy. He just lost his mother."

Lachlan bristled. "I'm not a *boy*. Fergus is barely two decades older than me."

"And it shows." Innis' face grew stony, all previous sympathies gone. "Lachlan, you must know that you are not fit to rule. You despise the Unseelie Court –"

"I do not *despise* it," Lachlan interrupted. He made to snatch his mother's earring from Fergus but he easily glided out of the way. "I merely disagree with the Unseelie King's brother being married to the Seelie Queen."

"Come now. My mother was Seelie, or have you forgotten? I spent most of my life growing up off the coast of your own land! I have always been closer to your kind than I have been to Eirian or our father."

"And that's beside the point, anyway," Fergus added on, smiling widely at Lachlan to show his vaguely pointed teeth. "Ailith and I are to be married before the month's end. The two of us would make far greater rulers than you, Lachlan."

And then it clicked. Fergus was marrying Ailith because the court adored her. He and Innis had been

28

plotting his ascension to the throne for months.

"You killed my mother," Lachlan said, staring at Innis with all the hatred he could muster.

But the faerie shook his head. "That I did not do, nor did my son. It was Evanna's time. That Fergus would be better on the throne than you has nothing to do with your mother's death."

"So you mean to kill *me,* instead."

His stepfather shook his head once more. "Others would ask what had happened to you, and we could not lie about it. No, Lachlan, you must disappear."

He bristled at the suggestion. "As if I would leave of my own volition!"

"Oh, that we already knew and had prepared for," Fergus said. He wrapped his hand around the silver earring; Lachlan clutched at his stomach and dropped his wine glass, sending it clattering to the floor. He watched with unfocused eyes as the dark liquid within it spilled across the cream-and-gold carpet, soaking the fibres as if it were blood. Lachlan fell to his knees, then collapsed on his side; the shiver from before had become full-on convulsions, rending his insides into tiny little pieces.

He glared at the two of them, though his eyes were watering and he could barely see. "What have you – what is this? What have you done to me?!"

"Just a little magic," Fergus said, grinning. "You know, I think I'll give Ailith your earring myself. I'll tell her it's all you left behind before you ran from the forest to escape your mother's shadow. She would believe that. I think she'd even cry for you. Would you like that, Lachlan? To know she's crying for you?"

"I –" But Lachlan couldn't verbalise the rest of his sentence through the pain. His body was changing – shimmering and twisting and cracking into something else entirely. When the convulsions finally stopped Lachlan felt altogether much smaller that he had been before, and Innis and Fergus much taller by comparison.

Innis stared down at him with a grave expression on his face. "I'd suggest you run while you can. Nobody will ask if we killed a stray fox, so we will not need to lie about it."

"A fox?!" Lachlan cried out, though the words were strange in his new throat. He bolted for the closest mirror, dismayed beyond reckoning to see russet fur, dark, pointed ears and a white underbelly. His eyes were small and beady, though his golden irises remained. There were no two ways about it; his new appearance wasn't a glamour or an illusion or a trick of the light. Lachlan really was a fox. "How did you –"

"You underestimate the power of Unseelie magic, you fool," Fergus sneered. "Now run off or we really will kill you. But who knows? Maybe an owl will do the job for me."

Lachan swung his head from Innis to Fergus then back again, too shocked to feel anger or disgust. But then fear began to creep in – the kind of deep-set instinct all animals had for anything bigger or more predatory than themselves.

He ran.

Lachlan fled the palace, winding through the corridors so quickly that even the spare passers-by who weren't yet at Queen Evanna's funeral feast did not know what to make of him. He ran out through the forest, stumbling over rabbit holes and fallen branches

30

and loose stones until he reached the very outskirts of the trees. And then he ran some more, for good measure.

When finally Lachlan slowed to a halt to fill his lungs with much-needed air he found himself in a garden to the back of a handsome red-stoned house. Though it was by the tree line it was so close to the loch that Lachlan had never ventured near it before. When he saw the shape of a human shifting behind a window he crept closer to see what they looked like, despite the fact that he was a fox and they might throw a rock his way if they saw him.

But then the figure turned to look out the window, and Lachlan felt his heart stop.

It was Clara.

CHAPTER FOUR

Sorcha

"For the last time, Sorcha, open the door!"

"Come on, dove, I know this is a surprise. Just let us explain."

"Explain what?" Sorcha demanded from her position slumped against the door. Her parents had spent the last fifteen minutes attempting to coax her out of her room; she didn't want to budge. "You've never brought up marriage before. Why now? Why so suddenly?"

There was a pause. Sorcha heard her father sigh.

"Please, Sorcha," he said, very quietly. "Let us in. This isn't a conversation to be had shouting through a door with a guest sitting two rooms away."

Sorcha bristled at the reminder. Murdoch Buchanan was indeed a *guest,* not a family friend or a man she had fancied from afar for years. So why did her parents wish for him to marry her? Realising that her curiosity was ultimately getting the better of her Sorcha dolefully got to her feet, unbolted the heavy iron lock on the door and swung it open.

Her mother's angry face greeted her; behind her mother stood her father, who looked resigned. He gave Sorcha a small smile as the two of them trailed into her room, Sorcha closing the door behind them.

"Thank you," he said. He sat on the well-made fir wood rocking chair by the window; like their dining table and the chairs that matched it, the piece of furniture had been carved by Sorcha's great-grandfather. She loved the chair dearly, though it was beginning to creak in protest whenever someone sat upon it.

Her mother fussed for Sorcha to sit on the bed, then located a brush and began untangling the knots in her daughter's hair. Sorcha knew better than to protest, so she sat in dull compliance whilst her mother went to work.

"Why now, then?" Sorcha asked again. "And why... him? Why Mr Buchanan?"

"Do you not like the look of him?" her mother cried, offended on the man's behalf. "He is so handsome, and so gentle and well-spoken! London has been very good to him. And he's *wealthy*, Sorcha –"

"So I am to be bought, then?"

Her father shook his head. "You know it isn't like that, dove. Mr Buchanan is an investor. He informed me that there are many people in the same position as him who are interested in acquiring our land and moving the farmers off it. Mr Buchanan is from here, Sorcha. He doesn't wish for that to happen. But I didn't want him to outright buy our land, either. I want to keep it in the family."

Sorcha rolled her eyes. "That *does* sound like I'm being bought, papa. You won't sell him the land but you'll give him it by selling me to him."

"Don't speak to your father like that!" her mother chastised, dragging the brush through a tangle in Sorcha's hair far harsher than necessary to drive home her complaint. "He is doing the best he can!"

"But what about what's best for me, mama? I don't want to get married! You only wish for me to marry him because you're besotted by every city-dwelling tourist who plagues –"

"Sorcha, don't speak to your mother like that."

She winced; it was rare for both her parents to admonish her in the same conversation. But Sorcha was *angry*; how could she not be? She was to be married to a stranger.

Her father looked out of the window at the dazzling afternoon sun. "Sorcha, my health isn't what it used to be. Everyone knows that. I was always planning to pass over the land to you upon your twenty-first birthday. I would feel much better if you were financially secure and in a position to look after the farmers for many years to come."

"Papa –"

"We will not force you to marry Mr Buchanan," he interrupted, voice firm. He stood up and moved to the door. "But you can at least put in the effort to get to know the man over the next few days. Your union may not be one of love, but it could be. You have to give it a chance. He is a kind one, dove. I would not wish for you to marry him if he was not."

Her father left her room then, leaving Sorcha with

her uncharacteristically quiet mother. Though her hair was smooth, shiny and tangle-free once more, her mother was still brushing through it. It was only after several more minutes of silence that she put down the brush and turned Sorcha round to face her.

"Sorcha –"

"I know," her daughter said, though her tone was miserable. "I know papa is right. I will get to know Mr Buchanan, if that is what you both wish."

Her mother smiled approvingly; she stroked the side of Sorcha's face with the back of her hand. "I know you disapprove of city folk, especially Londoners. But remember – I grew up in Edinburgh! And I didn't turn out so bad, did I?"

Sorcha averted her eyes. "Debatable."

"Such a rude daughter!"

"I wasn't aware that honesty was considered rudeness."

The two of them giggled softly. Though Sorcha and her mother were often at each other's throats they still loved each other dearly. She ultimately trusted the older woman's judgement, even if at times she did not like it.

"Come on, then," her mother said, taking hold of Sorcha's hands to pull her up from the bed and out of the room. "Mr Buchanan will be wondering what happened! I do believe that you will rather like him, once you get to know him."

"Again: debatable. But I shall at least try to act civil."

She smiled at the look her mother gave her, and kept that same smile on her face when she was brought back through to the parlour room and left alone with

Murdoch. He was sitting by the large bay window overlooking the loch, and did not notice Sorcha's presence until she nervously sat in the armchair opposite him.

"Miss Darrow," he said, eyebrow raised in surprise when he looked at her. "You brushed your hair."

Sorcha couldn't help but laugh at the comment. She ran her fingers through a lock of it, causing it to shine like burnished copper in the sunlight. "My mother did. I apologise for my reaction earlier. The news of our engagement was...unexpected, to say the least."

The hint of a smirk crossed Murdoch's lips. Sorcha thought he almost looked amused, though it could just as easily have been the man making fun of her.

Don't think like that, she thought. *Be nice. Papa likes him. He can't be that bad.*

She fidgeted with her hands in her lap, fishing for something to say. "You're from close by, then? Where did you grow up? How old are you?"

"Twenty-seven," Murdoch replied. He pointed out through the window towards the northern point of the shimmering loch outside. "I'm from further up the loch shore, where it gets narrow and deep. I used to spend all my days swimming – even when winter was approaching – but that all stopped when I moved to London."

"Why did you move?"

"My mother died, and my father took up a new position at a bank down there. He insisted I learn his trade, so it wasn't all that surprising when I ended up as an investor."

"And now you're looking to, what? Save the loch-side from other Londoners like you?"

Murdoch straightened in his chair, expression serious as he replied, "I do not think I am as similar to them as you think, Miss Darrow. If I were I'd have simply forced your father off the land, like what is happening in the Highlands as we speak."

Sorcha said nothing. It was a sobering thought, and not one she wished to dwell upon.

She looked at her hands. "So why marry me? That seems like an awful lot of effort to go to just to procure some land."

To her surprise Murdoch laughed, his voice rough and low and very much entertained by Sorcha's take on things. Sorcha still couldn't tell if he was making fun of her, which she did not like at all. "Are you implying that you mean to be difficult, Miss Darrow?" he asked, voice full of mirth. "That you will *be* a lot of effort? Because it is most certainly effort that I'm willing to put in, having now finally met you."

Sorcha darted her eyes up to the man's face, suspicious. He only laughed harder.

"You do not believe me," Murdoch said. He clasped his hands together and rested them in his lap; Sorcha watched him do so to give her an excuse not to look into his eyes. "Are you always so sceptical of compliments? You are of good birth, and bonnie to look at. You aren't afraid to speak your mind, which I like, and you clearly care deeply for the land on which you live, which I like even more."

Sorcha didn't know what to say. She'd had local lads attempt to woo her with sweet words before; it had been easy to ignore them. But she was supposed to *marry* Murdoch Buchanan. She could not ignore him, nor what he said.

"You are kind to speak of me in that way," she ended up saying, inclining her head politely. "But I must profess that I remain dutifully suspicious. I think, after a few more days of truly getting to know me, you will realise what a horrible mistake you have made."

Sorcha half expected Murdoch to laugh at the comment as he had laughed at her previous assertions. When he remained silent she raised her head to look at him. All traces of amusement had left his face, leaving only his dark, bottomless eyes staring at her with unknowable intent.

"I do not think so," he said, so quietly Sorcha wasn't sure if she had been meant to hear it. But the words unnerved her, as did Murdoch's gaze; she shot up from her seat.

"I am tired," she mumbled, averting her eyes as she curtsied slightly. "Today has been full of surprises. If you would excuse me."

Sorcha didn't give Murdoch an opportunity to respond before she marched back to her bedroom and closed the door firmly shut behind her. She began pacing upon the wooden floor, a frown of worry creasing her brow.

"He is not bad, but I don't want to marry *anyone,*" she said aloud, not caring if anybody heard her. The afternoon sunshine filtered through her window, lighting dust motes on fire and warming Sorcha's skin when she passed through it.

He is not bad, but there is something wrong with him.

That she didn't dare say aloud.

Several hours later, when the sun was low in the sky

and her parents had both come and gone to see if she was hungry, Sorcha was still pacing around her room. Something felt off. Awry. She felt like she was being watched.

Is Murdoch behind the door? she wondered. She wouldn't put it past the man, despite the fact she knew very little about him. *Or is he outside, spying on me through the window somehow?*

But when she moved over to look into the garden all she could see was the russet fur of a fox where the garden met the forest. The creature was quick to hide when it spied her.

"Strange to see a fox so far out of the forest," Sorcha yawned. She felt suddenly and inexplicably exhausted, as if she had ran for days on an empty stomach. She needed to lie down. She needed to rest. She needed sleep to help her sort through everything she had learned today. But Sorcha slipped on the flat-woven rug that lay beneath the end of her bed, tumbling over her feet with a panicked cry lodged firmly in her throat.

She was unconscious before her head hit the floor.

CHAPTER FIVE

Lachlan

He hadn't meant to knock Clara out. How could he have? Until that moment Lachlan hadn't known if any of his powers remained after being transformed into a fox. But after watching Clara pace her room for hours he had not been able to resist edging across the garden to get a better look at her, and then she'd seen him, and then –

And then she collapsed to the floor, Lachlan thought, clambering up onto the windowsill to look through the glass. The girl did not seem hurt; instead, she looked incredibly peaceful. *I only thought of her a little and she fell asleep. Does this mean I can reach her in her dreams?*

Lachlan hadn't sneaked into a human's dream for years. When he was younger he'd delighted in the pastime, seducing impressionable youths and frightening old men alike. But he'd grown out of the habit after he'd honed his skills in enchantment. Invading a person's dreams seemed pitifully easy pickings compared to manipulating them when conscious.

"I need the skill now, though," he said, muttering so quietly that if anyone had seen him they would not have been aware a fox was talking. He leapt down from the window to curl up under the rose bush growing beneath the sill, careful to ensure that nobody would be able to spy his orange fur as he lay hidden there.

He closed his eyes.

As easy as breathing, he thought, and just like that he made it through.

Clara was dreaming of sunsets.

All around her were golds and scarlets and deep, dark purples, bleeding into the horizon of her dream like ink upon a canvas. The edges of the world Sorcha created shimmered and danced in the corners of Lachlan's eyes, reminding him of the way Loch Lomond reflected the late-afternoon sun. He wondered how many thousands of sunsets across the loch Clara had seen for her dream to be such a vivid, startlingly beautiful rendition of it.

Lachlan looked down at his hands and was relieved to see he was no longer a fox. Within the realms of dreams he was once more the Prince of the Seelie Court, rightful heir to the throne.

A lot of help that is, within the head of a human girl.

He took a few steps towards Clara, whose thick, dark hair tumbled down her back far more elegantly than it had done when Lachlan spied her in the woods. The burnished copper in it was even more beautiful in the sunset than it had been in the morning light – it reminded Lachlan of the dying embers of a fire. But either Clara did not notice his approach or was blithely ignoring him; going by the stillness of her frame Lachlan assumed the former.

"Your dreams are as fair as you are, Clara."

Silence followed Lachlan's remark for the duration of a heart beat. Two. Three. And then –

"I knew I would dream of you today," Clara replied, voice soft and vacant. She did not look at Lachlan.

He took another step towards her. "And why do you say that?"

"You kissed me, did you not? I sang for you and you kissed me. To not dream of you after such a thing is impossible."

Lachlan smiled at Clara's admission. When he closed the gap between them to sit beside her she merely swung her legs back and forth from her invisible perch within the sunset.

"You are not truly dreaming of me," Lachlan said, turning Clara's head to look at him with a hand on her chin. Her mismatched eyes were lovely in the fiery light, though they remained cloudy with dream-induced confusion.

She frowned. "What do you mean by that, Lachlan, Prince of Faeries?"

"I mean that you are dreaming, but you are not dreaming of me. I invaded your dream to speak to you."

"And that is all you wish to do? To speak?"

Lachlan's lips quirked at the disappointment in Clara's voice. *Just what exactly were you hoping to dream of this evening?* he mused. Clearly the young woman's mind was far from innocent. Lachlan liked that. He liked that a lot.

He stroked the line of Clara's jaw with a gentle

thumb; she closed her eyes and sighed happily. "Perhaps in another dream, when circumstances are not so dire, we can do more than simply speak," he answered. "It's an idea I wholeheartedly look forward to exploring"

Clara froze. She opened her eyes and backed away, a frown once more returning to her face. She no longer looked to be in a trance.

"You are telling the truth," she said. "You have stolen into my dream."

"The Fair Folk cannot lie, as I'm sure you know. I'm indeed telling the truth."

Clara shook her head to clear it of its previous haze. She wrapped her arms across her chest as if they might protect her from what Lachlan was going to say next. "What circumstances are so dire you had to contact me in a dream?"

"I...hadn't meant to talk to you like this," Lachlan admitted, turning his head slightly to hide his grimace, "though admittedly if I'd spoken to you as a fox things likely would have turned out –"

"A fox?" Lachlan looked back to see Clara's face aglow with curiosity, all previous suspicion immediately cast aside. "What do you mean, a fox?"

"I mean precisely that. I seem to have found myself cursed and banished by my loving stepfamily."

Clara cocked her head to one side as she considered Lachlan's ridiculous-sounding claim. He knew the look she was giving him very well. It was the look anyone gave a faerie when they were trying to work out how they had spun a lie into something they could verbalise as truth.

"It happened exactly as I said, I swear it," Lachlan insisted, though he did not know why it was so important for Clara to believe such a thing. She could not help him, after all. "I went to see my stepfather and stepbrother after my mother's funeral and they worked Unseelie magic upon me. According to them I am unfit to wear my mother's crown, so they wished to be rid of me."

Lachlan laughed bitterly. Now that he was himself once more he had the space inside him for anger. More than anger. He was furious, and humiliated, and filled with a red-hot desire for vengeance.

Clara leaned towards him, lips parted in shock. She bit her lower one before speaking; Lachlan watched her do so with hungry eyes. Even now, when he had far more important things to deal with, he wished to control the human sitting in front of him. "So how are you going to break the spell cast upon you?" she asked. "If it is Unseelie magic then –"

"Why, my best bet is to kill them, of course," Lachlan cut in, grinning viciously. "Most any kind of curse breaks when the one who cast it dies."

"And how will you do that, when you are a fox? Can you steal into *their* dreams and smother their life from the inside?"

Oh, I really do like Clara, Lachlan thought. She hadn't tried to dissuade him from his murderous aspirations for even a second. All she wanted to know was whether he was capable of fulfilling said aspirations.

He shook his head. "I'm afraid dream-weaving on another fae is impossible. Can you imagine the havoc that would wreak?"

Clara thought about this for a moment, gaze fixed on some point beyond Lachlan's head. "What can you do, then?" she wondered aloud. "Do you have any magic left within you as a fox?"

Lachlan shook his head once more, feeling all the more frustrated as he did. "Not when I'm conscious, aside from putting little humans like you to sleep. I think I only have my full powers when I am my true self." His hand glanced against Clara's; she curled her pinky finger around his as if they were children trying to comfort one another.

"Then you need your body back," she said, so matter-of-factly that Lachlan burst out laughing.

"If I had my body back, lass, then I would not need to find a way to kill my stepfather and stepbrother."

Clara said nothing. She stared at him with her strange eyes, giving absolutely nothing away about what she was thinking. Then she looked down at her hand; Lachlan had unknowingly laced their fingers together.

"Why are you telling me what happened to you, then, when it seems neither you nor I can do anything about it?"

Lachlan leaned forward until his forehead rested against Clara's. He swept her hair away from her face, relishing the sharp intake of breath she took as he did so.

"Because you sang for me," he said. "Because you did not pity me when I told you my mother had died. Because I wanted to kiss you."

And then Lachlan moved away, standing up as if to leave. He couldn't exit Clara's dream like it was a room, of course – there was no door nor window nor opening to speak of through which to do so – but he wanted to fade out of the girl's consciousness as softly as possible so as not to rouse her from her sleep.

"You're leaving now, aren't you?" Clara asked, a disappointed look upon her face. "Will I see you again?"

"If I don't run out of time, you might."

"If you –"

"You should string rowan berries across your window to stop others like me invading your dreams," Lachlan interrupted. He didn't want to think about just how *much* time he had before he became a fox forever. "I'm surprised you haven't been spirited away into the forest already, given the proximity of your house to it."

To his surprise Clara shrugged, entirely unperturbed by the notion. "No fae who lives in the forest would dare take away a Darrow straight from their bed. We've been protecting the land here for generations. I'm somewhat surprised you didn't realise whose house you had come upon, *Prince* Lachlan."

Lachlan felt somewhat foolish. For it was true that Clara's house was considerably nicer than most others in the area. If he hadn't been a fox when he first saw it he likely would have worked out exactly which family Clara belonged to. "I have never been one to steal away the local folk before," he said, in an attempt to protect his dignity. It was true, so he could say it.

But Clara was not convinced by his cover-up. "I do not think you are as clever as you believe you are, Lachlan."

"Is that so, Clara Darrow?"

Clara's eyes did not glaze over the way they should have had Lachlan's imprisonment of her name actually worked. The smirk upon her face meant she knew exactly what he'd tried to do.

"You are clearly cleverer than I believed *you* to be," he laughed, genuinely delighted by this turn of events. Clara was certainly a worthwhile opponent. "I'm assuming there's a middle name I'm missing?"

"Something like that."

"You are lucky you can lie so well, Clara," Lachlan said. He was tempted to reside within her dream for longer, despite how precious every second of time now was to him. To wheedle Clara's full name from her – to watch her try her best to keep it from him but ultimately have it accidentally slip out – would be immensely satisfying.

Clara sighed. "Lying is the one thing I wish humans could not do." She brought her knees to her chest, staring out at the horizon of her all-encompassing, never-ending sunset. "If they could not lie then I'd know what he really wants."

Lachlan's pointed ears twitched. "He?"

"Never mind. I thought you were leaving?"

"Do you want me to go?"

"I imagine what I want doesn't especially factor into your plans, Prince of Faeries."

"I guess not," Lachlan snickered. He inclined his head towards Clara, though she wasn't looking at him. "Until next time, Clara Darrow."

"Until next time, Lachlan."

When Lachlan returned to his wretched fox body a low snarl filled his throat. It felt wrong – obscene, even – to be reduced to such a form. But his conversation with Clara had helped to clear his head and set things straight.

I need only kill Innis and Fergus. I don't need my magic to do that; all I need is my wit.

He could do it. He could craft a way to kill them.

Then he'd steal Clara's full name and ensnare her forever.

CHAPTER SIX

Sorcha

When Sorcha awoke everything was dark and silent. She could not hear the loch beat upon the shore, nor the hooting of wood pigeons and owls that ruled the skies at twilight. Even the trees were quiet, the breeze that ripped through the forest during the daytime having finally died down to nothing at all.

It is very late, Sorcha decided, rubbing her head as she tried to regain her sense of reality. It was only then that she realised she was no longer sprawled across the rug on her floor. She was in bed, securely tucked beneath the sheets.

She sat up abruptly, wide awake and hyper-aware of everything around her in the space of a moment. "Who put me to bed...?" she wondered, holding a hand firmly over her chest to calm her throbbing heart. Sorcha was still wearing the dress she'd had on when she fell asleep, suggesting one of her parents had found her lying on the floor and simply moved her over to the bed without waking her.

Or maybe they did try to rouse me and I remained asleep, Sorcha thought. *Dreams brought about by faeries are clearly heavy indeed, if I have been unconscious for hours.*

Then Sorcha remembered everything from her dream and leapt out of bed. "Lachlan," she gasped, skittering across her floor to the window. She was desperate to spy the orange fur of a fox creeping through the black of night. "Lachlan, where are you?"

But there wasn't a fox in sight, and Sorcha couldn't see a single flash of movement that might have been him, either. She collapsed into her great-grandfather's rocking chair with a heavy sigh. For all Sorcha knew Lachlan had been inside her dream for mere minutes before fleeing through the forest. He could be miles and miles away from the Darrow house by now.

I want to help him.

In truth Sorcha knew she shouldn't. The faerie clearly wanted her full name to enslave her forever, which was something she very much didn't wish to happen. Even if Lachlan was charming. Even if Lachlan was beautiful. Even if Lachlan was the immortal Crown Prince of the Seelie Court, though Sorcha knew that this was the most glaring reason of them all for why she should avoid him no matter the cost. Forever might not seem so long to a faerie; to a human it was unfathomable.

He said he was running out of time, though, Sorcha thought, burying her head against her knees as she focused on each and every word Lachlan had spoken to her. *Will his curse kill him? Will he lose all sense of himself eventually? Something else?*

But it didn't matter what would happen when his

time ran out; only that it would. Lachlan had to kill his stepfamily to break his curse, or so he believed, whilst he still had the ability to do so.

"And what if he doesn't?" Sorcha asked the air. She shivered at the notion. For what if Lachlan was wrong, and killing his stepfather and stepbrother did nothing at all? Or what if he wasn't capable of killing them in the first place? He was a fox, after all.

So he needs his body back, Sorcha decided, getting up to light the lantern that sat on her desk. She picked it up by its heavy iron handle and brought it over to her sizable bookshelf. *There must be some way he can return to his original form for long enough to break the curse.*

Sorcha ran her forefinger along the spines of each and every one of her books. Seelie magic clearly couldn't help Lachlan, otherwise he'd have simply gone to a faerie he trusted to help him. Unseelie magic might have been able to break an Unseelie curse, but Lachlan was unlikely to find a member of their kind close by who was willing to aid him.

"Which leaves the realms of other things," she muttered, brows knitted together in concentration as she tried to find the tome that would give her the answers she sought. "Beings more powerful than faeries. Darker than the Unseelie. Creatures like..."

Sorcha dropped her lantern as she realised exactly what she – or, rather, Lachlan – needed. It clattered to the floor with an enormous thud which echoed all around the room. Outside her door she heard a wooden floorboard creak; had the noise woken someone up? Sorcha dared not breathe as she waited to see if anybody would check up on her. After a tense minute of silence she exhaled, gently picking up the lantern and placing it on top of the bookshelf to prevent her from dropping it again.

"It must be here," Sorcha whispered, resuming her search for the book she needed. It was one of her favourites – a compendium of stories about all the remarkable, wondrous and downright terrifying creatures who lived beneath the water's surface – and yet, for whatever reason, it was missing. And then she realised where it must be.

Her father's study.

The two of them enjoyed reading together in the evenings. Last sennight Sorcha had insisted upon reading her favourite fairy tales, since she loved to hear her father's deep, sonorous voice narrate the stories. The book she was looking for was definitely on his bookshelf.

Grabbing the lantern and hoisting the hem of her dress up to her knees, Sorcha crept over to her door and carefully opened it. The hallway was dark and quiet, save for the soft sounds of her father snoring a few rooms down. Sorcha's gaze lingered on the door opposite hers; it led to the guest bedroom, where Murdoch Buchanan was most likely sleeping. The door was ajar, but she couldn't hear anything, so Sorcha tiptoed down the corridor towards her father's study.

He had an expansive collection of books; it was no wonder Sorcha had learned to love reading from him. The man spent as much time as possible with his nose in a book, whilst Margaret Darrow preferred the company of real, living people. It never ceased to amaze Sorcha that her mother read so little when her husband – and daughter – read so much.

Sorcha held the lantern up to the top shelf of the first selection of books, quickly dismissing them all when she saw they were alphabetised encyclopaedias. The next shelf down was full of atlases, then books about birds, botany, fishing and a whole host of other interesting topics.

Sorcha moved to the next bookshelf, which looked far more promising. But though she found her father's favourite collections of poems – missing three volumes of Burns' work which were currently sitting on Sorcha's desk – and a large collection of fiction written in Scots, she still could not see what she was looking for.

When she was halfway through searching the third bookshelf Sorcha was so engrossed in reading the spines that she did not hear the door behind her creak open, nor the footsteps padding towards her across the soft, lush carpet.

"Is this what you're looking for?" a low, gravelly voice asked, followed by an arm reaching over Sorcha's head to grab a book sitting on the very top of the bookshelf.

"M-Mister Buchanan," Sorcha stuttered, backing away only to hit the man's chest, for he was standing right behind her. She looked up and over her shoulder at him; his dark eyes watched her with interest. "I did not mean to wake you."

He smiled softly. "I was already awake. What are you doing up, Miss Darrow?"

"I couldn't sleep."

"You did not seem to have an issue with that earlier."

There was something about the way Murdoch spoke

– or, perhaps, the way he *looked* at Sorcha as he spoke – that informed her he had been the one who carried her to bed. The skin on her forearms tingled like it was being pricked by a thousand needles. She did not like the idea of such an unknowable stranger standing in her room, holding her close whilst she was completely unaware that such a thing was happening.

Sorcha turned on the spot to face Murdoch, though standing this close to him it was difficult to look him in the eye. He was much taller than her. *And taller than Lachlan,* she thought despite herself. *Broader, too. Stronger. If it came down to a physical fight Murdoch could probably overpower him.* It occurred to Sorcha that what she had been feeling towards Murdoch since first meeting him was fear.

"I – I do recall mentioning that I was tired," she mumbled, before attempting to side-step away from the man. Murdoch held out an arm to stop her, then waved the book he'd found in his other hand.

"This was what you were looking for, am I correct?"

Sorcha looked at the book – at the beautiful script of its title, and the haunting illustration of the most dangerous creature one could find in the darkest depths of a Scottish loch.

The Kelpie, and Other Aquatic Creatures, the title read. It was precisely what Sorcha had come into her father's study to find.

She glanced up at Murdoch, nervous beyond reckoning. "How did you –"

"That bookshelf was full of ledgers," he said, pointing behind Sorcha. "I didn't imagine you were wanting to read any of them in the middle of the night.

A book of fairy stories out of your line of sight seemed much more likely."

Sorcha said nothing. Murdoch's reasoning was sound. It made sense, so why didn't she believe it? With a slightly trembling hand she took the book from him, working hard not to recoil when his fingers brushed her own.

"Thank you," she muttered, keeping her head down and sliding out of the man's way when he finally allowed her to. "Good night, Mr Buchanan."

"And you, Miss Darrow," he replied. "I hope you fall back into dreams just as easily as you did earlier." Sorcha resisted the urge to look back to see how Murdoch was looking at her. Some part of her was deathly curious, as if she was a rabbit under the piercing gaze of a hawk, or a fox.

Lachlan, she remembered, as soon as she thought of foxes. His plight pulled Sorcha out of her terrified state like a hook in her heart. *I need to help Lachlan.* Sorcha all but ran from her father's study, leaving Murdoch to stand there in the darkness by himself. When she reached her bedroom she locked her door, planted her lantern down on the windowsill and dropped into the rocking chair, riffling through the heavy book in her hands until she reached the page she was looking for.

"This is it," Sorcha whispered, eyes bright and shining with amazement as she read every word on the page. "This is it."

For kelpies, the book said, *though their true form is akin to a large, black horse, are capable of changing their shape using their silver bridle.*

Who was to say the bridle couldn't do the same for

another creature?

Abandoning her book on the chair, Sorcha wasted no time in rummaging around her room for a bag. She filled it with clothes, a blanket, a small number of coins and some camping supplies her mother had stored beneath her bed when she hadn't known where else to put them. A tent. A pot. A canister of fuel to keep the accompanying lantern lit. Spare wicks for said lantern.

"I need food," she muttered, unlocking her door in order to peer down the corridor. But Murdoch's door was open even wider than before – a warning that Sorcha understood loud and clear.

I'm watching you.

And so Sorcha retreated back into her room, deciding that she could buy some food on her journey around Loch Lomond. She tied the bag closed, changed into a clean dress and threw on her boots, lacing them up before searching for her cloak. She ran a hand over her face when she realised it was in the kitchen.

"No matter," she said, very, very quietly. "It is barely September. I will not need it."

And then she moved over to her window, fighting against its protesting hinges to fling it wide open.

You're doing this for Lachlan, Sorcha told herself, over and over again. *If it happens that finding a kelpie takes so long that Murdoch has no choice but to return to London then that's a happy coincidence.*

Sorcha barked in amusement. Of course it would be no coincidence. It didn't matter that she understood why her parents wanted her to marry the man. It didn't matter that he was handsome, and wealthy, and clearly genuinely interested in her. When she'd looked into

Murdoch's dark, fathomless eyes and felt nothing but startling, all-consuming fear Sorcha resolutely made up her mind.

She jumped over the windowsill, deftly avoiding the rose bush beneath it. She would keep to the edges of the forest until the sun came up, then she would wander the shores of the loch. She could do this. Sorcha could find a kelpie and save Lachlan.

And she would not get married, no matter the consequences. Her father would have to find another investor, and Murdoch Buchanan another bride.

CHAPTER SEVEN

Lachlan

Lachlan had been prowling around the forest all night, counting himself lucky when he came across a sleeping pheasant near dawn just as his stomach began growling insistently. It had disgusted him to eat the bird raw, feathers and all, but when his fox body reacted greedily to every morsel he tore from the unfortunate creature Lachlan forgot to hate himself for doing so.

It is so easy to get used to being like this, he thought. *Too easy.* For after several hours of being a fox Lachlan no longer stumbled over his feet, or struggled with his new eyes and overwhelmingly keen senses of smell and sound. He'd always thought faeries had great eyes and ears; after becoming a fox Lachlan realised by comparison just how wonderful that eyesight had truly been...and how sub-par his hearing was. Now he could hear the whisper-quiet scurrying of a mouse through the underbrush twenty metres away.

"Is this how one loses themselves to the curse?" Lachlan wondered aloud, simply to remind himself that he still had a voice. "They give into the fox's base instincts and forget their own?" Turning a human into a fox was a fairly standard faerie curse, for the Seelie and Unseelie alike. It was an amusing way to punish or anguish a victim, knowing that they were running around desperately trying to free themselves from the curse whilst slowly succumbing to it.

But what about cursing a Seelie? Lachlan thought. *Turning a faerie into a fox is most unheard of.* Human princes, certainly. Kings, even. But never faerie royalty. Never faerie princes.

"When I get my teeth into Fergus..." he muttered, nose buried in the dirt as Lachlan followed the scent of...something. He wasn't sure what. He *was* sure, however, that Fergus had been the one to actually cast the fox curse, not his stepfather. So Lachlan would kill Fergus first, and Innis second. He wanted the wretched half-Unseelie to watch as his only child died in front of him.

"And it will be his own fault!" Lachlan growled viciously. "His scheming will be his downfall – him and bloody Fergus both!"

"Is – is someone there?"

Lachlan stilled, ruff bristling as his ears pricked up to identify the direction of the feminine-sounding voice. *To your right,* he decided, creeping beneath fallen tree branches and across the dense carpet of pine needles that covered the forest floor in search of the speaker.

"There is nobody there," another voice said. "You are hearing things." This one was definitely male – a gruff, assured kind of voice that would have convinced Lachlan himself that he was hearing things had he not known the human was wrong. For the pair of them *were* human, which was what Lachlan had been smelling. Human, not faerie, nor animal. But there was something else he could smell or, rather, sense, that was rarely found so close to humans.

Magic.

When Lachlan got close enough he used the very early morning light filtering through the trees to help him watch the strangers. The man was tall, with a heavy cloak draping over his shoulders that covered most of his frame. The woman was much shorter, with blonde hair that fell in an intricate braid to the small of her back. *Not just blonde,* Lachlan realised. *Gold. It has been enchanted.*

"Somebody *is* here," Lachlan called out, despite his fox senses begging him to run away. But he knew the pair of strangers would startle when they could not locate who had spoken, and Lachlan was still a faerie, after all. He could not resist playing with their heads a little. And he was curious about the woman's magic hair. How could he not be? It was beautiful, even to his inferior fox eyes.

But, to his extreme surprise, the man turned to face him almost immediately. Lachlan took a careful step backwards, realising that perhaps he had made a mistake trying to unnerve the strangers. "What kind of creature are you?" the man called out. "We mean no harm! We are searching for an enchanted fox. Might you be able to help us?"

"A fox?" Lachlan echoed back, even more surprised than before.

"Yes!" came the woman's excited voice. "Julian –"

"You do not give your name to their kind, you idiot!

How many times have I told you that?"

"But –"

"You are not from around here," Lachlan interrupted, before fighting his animal instincts once more to trot over to the pair. The woman's eyes widened in shock and delight when she spied him; the man – Julian – was unperturbed. If Lachlan still had eyebrows he would have frowned. "But you have dealt with my kind before?"

Julian nodded. "I have. My partner here has not. But you...are not the fox I am searching for." He laughed softly. "Tell me, how often do the Fair Folk turn their own kind into foxes?"

Lachlan tilted his head to one side and twitched his tail. "Our own kind? Never. It's always humans we curse in such a way."

"And yet you aren't human, are you?"

"Call me an exception."

Julian's lips quirked. "Which makes the fox I'm looking for an exception, too. He was definitely a Seelie."

"How long ago was this?"

"About...four years ago, give or take a few months," Julian replied, chewing his lip thoughtfully. "He had just been cursed. When he saw me in the forest I think he hoped I'd be able to help him."

Lachlan drew even closer, not daring to be excited but feeling his heart quicken nonetheless. "With your magic?" he asked. "Like the kind in the lovely lass' hair?"

The woman beamed at the compliment. "Julian is a

wizard from the mainland," she explained. "The strongest wizard in France. And –"

"And I was not able to help the fox," Julian interrupted, kneeling down to better look at Lachlan. His eyes had a glow to them Lachlan would have been wary of even if he'd been in his own body. "My expertise does not lie in curses, I'm afraid. The fox parted ways with me entirely disappointed. I was... hoping to find him, if I could, though I admit I likely cannot do anything for him even now."

Lachlan's spirits fell. "So you could not help me, either."

Julian shook his head. "I'm afraid not. I could try, but I might make things worse."

"Better not to do that. I hope you find your fox, wizard, and that he is not *just* a fox by now."

His female companion narrowed her eyes. "What do you mean?"

"I mean that, eventually, the one cursed succumbs to the fox's instincts," Lachlan explained. His own fate was truly beginning to sink in now that he was speaking of it out loud. "For a human it can take as little as a few days, and as long as several months, if their minds are strong. For my kind...I do not know."

"Oh, Julian, but that would be terrible!" she exclaimed, bending down to grab the man's arm in worry. Her eyes darted from his face to Lachlan's. "Can't you do anything at all to help him?"

Julian hesitated. "I...do not think it wise. Messing with magic is a dangerous business indeed, as our friend here can attest to, given his current predicament."

Lachlan snickered despite himself. "Well met,

wizard. In that case I had best be off. My time has become precious to me in a way it never was before. Be very careful exploring the forest; I'd suggest leaving if I were you."

"What do you mean by that?" Julian asked as both he and his partner stood back up, brushing off their knees as they did so.

Lachlan had already taken several steps away from them. He turned back for a moment and grinned as much as a fox could grin. "There has been a...change in management in the Court, so to speak. I should be proof enough that said management isn't particularly *nice.*"

And then Lachlan was off, darting through the trees just as he heard Julian mutter, "And this is why we can't use our names around here, foolish girl!"

I like them, he realised. *They are an interesting couple. When I get my body and my throne back I shall have to seek them out. I might even resist finding out their full names and allow them to remain as they are.*

It took Lachlan a moment too long to realise he had reached the outskirts of the forest once more, stepping out of the safety of the trees and onto the rocky shore of Loch Lomond before coming to a sudden halt.

"You could be shot!" he admonished aloud, skulking back into the trees with a furtive look around to make sure he was not seen. When Lachlan was sure he was safe he surveyed the loch with distaste. He knew the kinds of creatures who lived within it. Monstrous things which lured humans and faeries alike into its depths and consumed them. Beings with magic akin to his own, but who could lie, which made them terrifying. Even 'harmless' aquatic creatures could be dangerous – the shape-shifting selkies living along the coast of Scotland had drowned more than their fair share of humans and Seelies, who were heartbroken to discover that the one they loved had disappeared beneath the waves forever.

Then Lachlan heard a familiar voice singing and forgot about the loch altogether. *Clara!* Lachlan thought. He padded across the border between the shore and the forest until he spied her, close to the water's edge. *Just what is she doing?*

Clara clambered over a shelf of limestone, dropping down to a lower part of the beach with an ease that suggested she'd spent much of her life climbing. Her voice didn't falter over a single note of her song even as she hauled herself over the next rock and jumped across to yet another. Clearly she was enjoying herself, otherwise she would be using the path beneath the trees for a far easier journey. Lachlan had to wonder what she was doing up so early, and so far from home.

Wait, if she is so far from home then for how long has she been walking? She is miles from her house! Lachlan turned his nose up to the sky; going by the angle of the sun it was nearing seven o'clock. He'd exited Clara's dream almost eleven hours ago, with no idea when Clara herself would wake up. Considering the distance she'd travelled Lachlan had to assume she'd left her house at around three in the morning.

She is up to something, he decided. *I wonder if it has something to do with the 'he' Clara mentioned before I left. The one she didn't wish to talk about.* Curiosity firmly piqued, and with Clara's song filling his ears, Lachlan felt like he almost had no choice in the matter but to follow the girl.

I will follow her and find out what she's doing, then

get back to my own problems.

It did not occur to Lachlan even once that Clara might have left her house in the middle of the night on his behalf.

CHAPTER EIGHT

Sorcha

Despite the fact she'd been trawling along the edge of Loch Lomond since the early hours of the morning – and had, for all intents and purposes, run away from home – Sorcha was feeling surprisingly spry and good-natured.

The first few hours had been spent taking the easy path around the outskirts of the forest, with moss and pine needles beneath Sorcha's feet to soften her footsteps. But as soon as the sun had risen over the horizon she'd happily taken to the shore, climbing over rocks and dropping down to small pools caused by low summer rainfall and travelling sand drifts beneath the water. Sorcha did not care when her boots soaked through, nor when the bottom third of her dress soon followed suit. She had never cared for such things.

Sorcha lived to be outside, surrounded by the loch and the forest and the sky. It was her home. It was where she belonged.

And not with the caveat that I must have a husband, she thought, tingling all over at the memory of Murdoch pinning her against her father's bookshelf. Sorcha had wondered, at the time, whether the man could have overpowered Lachlan. She had not once considered the fact that he most definitely could overpower *her.*

"Well, he did not catch me leaving, so it doesn't matter," she said happily, nodding a greeting at an elderly couple who were sitting on a stretch of sand nearby to eat their luncheon. They watched her curiously; it was not every day that a grown woman was spotted flouncing about the loch shore, on her own, without a care in the world. Sorcha knew they were wondering who on earth her parents must be, or what her husband would think if he knew where his spouse was.

I do not care. I have more important things to think about. Like my stomach. For Sorcha was empty inside, having not eaten a single thing since the brambles she'd popped into her mouth the day before – when she'd first met Lachlan. *Has it really only been a day? It feels like weeks and months and years.*

And so Sorcha finally left the shore to venture towards a path she knew twisted through the forest to a small collection of houses about half an hour away. Though she used to accompany her father in his cart when he visited the nearby settlements in order to collect rent, nobody this far out had seen Sorcha since she was fourteen or so. She trusted they would not recognise her now.

"And if they do, so what?" she petulantly demanded of a nearby duck waddling down to the loch. It quacked in response. "By the time they send word to my parents that they've seen me I will be miles away."

As she neared the houses Sorcha was stopped more than once by passers-by; sometimes concerned, sometimes surprised, always curious. She brushed them all off by saying she was local, and knew what she was doing, then rushing away before they could enquire any further about her identity. Sorcha imagined she painted quite an unusual sight, with her heavy bag thrown over one shoulder and wet, muddied dress hitched up at the waist to avoid slapping her ankles with the sodden material. Her hair had grown wild once more, too, eliminating all suggestions that it had ever been tidy.

My mother would scream if she saw me, Sorcha mused. *Considering the fact that I am missing from the house she might well be doing so already.*

She managed to procure a few well-fired bread rolls, a couple of recently-cooked sausages and a water skin full of apple cider from a small crofting farm. The farmer's wife tried to convince Sorcha to stay a while and eat her luncheon inside, though by the look on the woman's face she knew that doing so would result in Sorcha being locked in a room until the farmer could work out who her parents were.

So she ate on foot, taking the same twisted path back to the loch-side that she'd used to reach the hamlet in the first place. It was late afternoon by then, with only a few, wispy horsetail clouds to break up the sun and the sky. *It may well be a cold night, if the sky stays this clear,* Sorcha mused as she took in the expansive blue above her. *I should find somewhere to camp sooner rather than later.*

She didn't want to have to regret not bringing a cloak with her.

Sorcha didn't want to stray too far from the loch to

camp – not least because camping deep within the forest was folly indeed. And she was seeking a kelpie, after all, which resided in the loch. She'd had no luck all day in finding one, though truthfully she had no idea how to 'find one' in the first place. *This is all guesswork,* she thought. *Guesswork and blind hope. It's not as if any of the books I owned told me how to contact such a creature.*

Eventually, after another hour or two of walking, Sorcha came across a nook at the edge of the forest that still granted her a clear view of the loch. It was a good place to set up camp: soft grass upon firm ground and tall, stepped shelves of sandstone sheltering the area from the worst of any wind or rain that might build up over the next few hours.

"I do not think I will have to deal with such things tonight, though," Sorcha murmured. The early evening sun was warm and wonderful on her face as she got to work setting up her tent; there was no foreseeable threat of bad weather. She would likely have a very pleasant night's sleep.

Despite the fact she'd eaten two hours prior, as Sorcha drove pegs into the ground and stretched out the canvas material of the tent her stomach began to grumble insistently. She knew she should have bought more food when she had the opportunity, even if people *had* asked too many questions about who she was or where she was going. Tomorrow Sorcha would have to get up early and go out of her way to purchase more. She wished she'd thought to bring a fishing rod.

Sorcha glanced back at the forest. Much of it was coniferous now that she was heading north; there would be no apples to find. She might get lucky and find some bramble bushes along the edge of the trees but it wouldn't be enough to keep her hunger at bay.

The fae have their own delicious fruit trees hidden in their realm, she thought, *but I would literally go mad if I ate from them.* Sorcha had seen it at work before – once with an unfortunate local child and twice with hapless tourists. Salt was supposed to dull the effects until the fruit was out of one's system, but in all three cases simply too much had been consumed. Only the faeries themselves could take away the hallucinations and giddy insanity brought on by the fruit, and they would only do so for a price.

A price all too often impossibly high to pay.

Will the kelpie be the same? Sorcha wondered. *I know little and less of their behaviour.* For Lachlan's sake, and for her own, she had to hope the kelpie was far more amenable than the faeries who lived in the forest.

With everything set up Sorcha unrolled her blankets and piled them into the tent with her. She didn't close up the front of it, instead choosing to keep it open in order to watch the sun set over the loch as she lay there. The water was darker here than it was back in Darach, where the loch was wide and shallow. It would only continue to get narrower and deeper than this far up the northern shore.

"I can't have walked more than six or seven miles, really," Sorcha mused, for nobody to hear but herself and the kelpie, if it happened to be listening. "It's slow going walking directly on the shore instead of on the path through the forest, you know. I'm going to a lot of effort to find you."

She sighed. If she chose to continue along the eastern shore at the rate she was going then she'd reach the most northern tip of Loch Lomond in a couple of days. After that, if Sorcha still hadn't caught sight of the kelpie, she would have to walk south along the western shore of the loch and hope to find it before she looped all the way back to Darach.

"Or I could cut through the forest tomorrow and try Loch Arklet, Katrine, Chon and Ard." She frowned at the water, daring the creature inside to respond to her suggestion. "You're not the only kelpie in the area. There's supposed to be one for every loch in Scotland."

"You are *not* searching for a kelpie. Tell me you're not that foolish, Clara."

Sorcha startled at the sound of Lachlan's voice, rushing to sit up so quickly that she knocked her head on the canvas above her. She stuck her face out of the tent and darted her eyes around, searching for the faerie in fox form. "Lachlan?" she called. "Where are you, Lachlan?"

When he crept around the side of her tent Sorcha had no doubt that Lachlan couldn't quite believe what Sorcha was planning to do. *I never knew foxes were so expressive,* she thought, watching him in wonder as he padded into her tent with a face that screamed of disapproval. Then he collapsed onto her pile of blankets as if he owned the place.

A typical faerie, to act in such a way. And yet despite the fact Sorcha knew he *was* a faerie – and a prince, to boot – rather than a domesticated animal, she still struggled to resist the urge to tickle the soft, white fur of his belly when Lachlan rolled onto his back for a moment.

"What does it matter if I'm looking for a kelpie, Lachlan?" she asked him, though now that she could see the fox shape Lachlan was cursed to possess she couldn't imagine his voice answering her through its mouth.

It did nonetheless.

"Of all the creatures to seek out, one *never* seeks a kelpie," Lachlan insisted, staring at Sorcha with gleaming eyes. They were lustrous, liquid gold – just as they had been when Lachlan was in his true form. "They lure humans to the loch and eat them, or have you forgotten?"

She didn't answer, choosing instead to gawk at the fox that spoke with Lachlan's voice and saw with Lachlan's eyes. It was discomfiting to watch. Bizarre. Uncanny. He stalked forwards and nipped at her heel until Sorcha yelped.

"What was that for?!" she complained, grabbing her ankle with a hand to massage the bite marks out of it. "Forgive me for finding the voice of a *faerie prince* coming out of a *fox* somewhat bizarre!"

Lachlan said nothing, instead patiently waiting for her to answer his question, and so Sorcha pushed aside how odd it was that she was talking to a fox and rolled her eyes. She settled into a cross-legged position a careful distance away from Lachlan and his teeth. "I do not mean to fall for the kelpie's tricks. I merely plan to _"

"To what? Ask it nicely to help you do whatever it is you want to do? What *is* it you want to do, anyway? Why have you run away from home?"

Sorcha didn't answer for a long, uncomfortable moment. She felt distinctly self-conscious about the fact she'd brazenly taken on the responsibility of aiding Lachlan's plight without so much as asking him if she could. She averted her eyes, looking out towards the loch as the last of the sun's rays disappeared beneath the very edge of the dark water.

"Clara –"

"I want its bridle," Sorcha answered, too quickly. "A kelpie can change shape using it, right? So if you had it then you could –"

"Tell me you are not seeking out a kelpie on *my* behalf, you stupid girl!" Lachlan cried, getting to his feet to hiss at Sorcha. All his fur stood on end, making him twice the size he had been before.

But Sorcha could only laugh, though she didn't mean to. Now she'd gotten over her discomfort it looked ridiculous to see a fox speak with the voice of a fae, standing inside a tent and trying to intimidate her. She reached out a hand to touch his head, knowing Lachlan would likely bite her but no longer caring if he did so.

"Don't touch – Clara, will you listen to me? Go home –"

But Lachlan's voice was lost to progressively louder yips and purring noises when Sorcha began scratching behind his ears. She knocked him onto his back, indulging her reckless urge to stroke and tickle his belly.

"You have no control over me in this form," she said, delighted. "You are just a fox with the voice of a prince."

"You – Clara, this is madness!" Lachlan just barely got out. "Stop this and listen to me!"

But Lachlan's back leg was twitching the way Old Man Macpherson's collie dog did whenever she bent down to scratch her; Sorcha knew Lachlan was enjoying the attention despite himself.

"I will be careful, I swear it," Sorcha told him. "And if you are so worried about me then stay with me whilst I search."

Lachlan looked up at her from his position on his back. It reminded Sorcha of how he had swung upside down from the oak tree, and her face flushed. But the growing darkness of night hid the colour that filled her cheeks, and by the time Lachlan spoke again Sorcha's skin had grown cold.

"Your journey is folly," he said, voice quiet and serious. "You must know this. Do not endanger yourself for me."

"You wish to imprison me forever in the faerie realm," Sorcha countered. "I am no less in danger with a kelpie than I am with you."

"And yet you have chosen to help me. I do not wish to *eat* you, at the very least."

"You're right; that makes you *far* more dangerous than the kelpie."

Neither of them said anything; they were at an impasse that neither was willing to back down from. Sorcha stopped scratching Lachlan's fur and backed away.

"I will not go home even if you wish me to, Lachlan. I was the one who decided to do this, not you. You can't make me go back."

Lachlan rolled over and got up to his feet, shook out his fur and moved over to sit by her side. "Why don't you want to go home, Clara?"

"None of your business."

"That hardly seems fair," he harrumphed. "You

know what troubles me."

"That doesn't count. You came to *me* to tell me of that. I did not seek you out to bore you with human problems."

Lachlan snickered; it was a bizarre sound to hear coming from a fox's mouth. "You are certainly an intriguing one, Clara Darrow. If you insist on keeping quiet then I shall have to work even harder to make you divulge your secrets."

She gave him a side-long glance. "Does that mean you're staying with me whilst I search for a kelpie?"

"I suppose it does."

"Then get off my pillow; I'm going to sleep."

Lachlan yelped in indignation when Sorcha unceremoniously tossed him off it, before laying down and placing her own head upon it. But then he settled down against her stomach; his fur tickled Sorcha even through the thick fabric of her dress.

Lachlan tucked his tail around himself and yawned loudly. "Sleep sounds good," he agreed. "It's exhausting being a fox."

She patted his head. "Good. That means you'll let me sleep instead of crawling into my dreams."

Sorcha fought hard to calm her rapidly increasing heartbeat when Lachlan didn't reply.

CHAPTER NINE

Lachlan

"So how old are you, Clara?"

Clara lurched in surprise before she turned to face Lachlan, eyes widening at the sight of his original form. "I told you not to sneak into my dreams tonight. You said you were exhausted."

"I am," he replied, grinning at the way Clara tried to hide how pleased she was that he'd ignored her request. "But I never promised not to bother you. You do not seem all that disappointed."

Clara said nothing.

Her dream was far more muted tonight – all dark, swirling greys and foreboding, murky blues. It imitated the shallow shore of the loch at night. *Almost, but not quite,* Lachlan noted. His keen eyes spotted the subtle yet impossible ways in which the water ebbed and flowed in Sorcha's dream. Real water never moved in such a way, though one would have to sit and look upon it for hours on end to realise this.

"Do you always dream of the land around you?" Lachlan asked as he walked over to stand by Clara, who was shifting her feet through the dark water as if it were truly real.

She shrugged. "Not always. But when you live in an area full of magical, mysterious creatures it's difficult *not* to dream of it."

"I suppose that's true. Do you know why you're dreaming of the loch?"

"Because of the kelpie, of course."

"This loch seems rather dark and dangerous."

"That fits the kelpie, then."

"Yet you did not seem at all bothered by it before you fell asleep," Lachlan countered, curious about what Clara was lying to cover up. "This loch does not fit the way you think of the real one, nor the idea of a kelpie."

Clara bristled at the comment. Lachlan hadn't yet seen her lose her temper; he was interested to see what anger looked like upon her fair face. "What is it you're wanting me to tell you, Lachlan?" she demanded, before collapsing to her knees in the false water. It swirled around her without ever getting her wet, though the skirt of her dress moved as if it really was beneath the surface of the loch. "Are you really that concerned about why this dream is darker than the last?"

"Not concerned," Lachlan said, sitting down beside Clara to trickle the mysterious water through his fingers. The stuff was insubstantial – he could not feel anything at all against his skin. "Merely curious. Why did you run away from home?"

Clara stared at her knees, expression glum. There was something about the trembling of her lips that suggested she was either about to cry or rant about something. "They want me to marry."

"Who? Your parents?"

She nodded. "They've never pressured me into marriage before. Even though I'm twenty at the end of the month –"

"Thank you for finally answering my question," Lachlan cut in, smirking despite himself when Clara threw a glare his way. He thoroughly enjoyed talking to her in his actual body – one which could frown and sigh and grin and laugh the way he wanted it to.

"Do you actually want to know what is troubling me or do you merely wish to poke fun at all my silly, mortal problems?"

"They are not silly to you though, are they?" Lachlan said. "You *are* mortal. Tell me the rest of your tale and I promise not to interrupt."

Clara looked at him as if she did not believe him, though she knew Lachlan couldn't lie. She exhaled loudly, closing her eyes for a moment before sinking onto her back in the dream water. It just barely tickled her ears, causing her long hair to wind and twist around her head like a selkie's.

"There are men down in London who want to *invest* in my father's land, though we all know what that means," Clara began. She did not look at Lachlan as she spoke. "They want the farmers and villagers gone so they can do what they like with the area – chop down the forest for farmland, or turn it into their own personal hunting ground, or use the loch for one large pleasure-boat experience. We're already overrun with tourists as it is, all of them obsessed with this romantic and mostly false notion of Scotland."

Lachlan watched intently as Clara's mismatched eyes shone too brightly with barely-contained passion and rage. Clearly she'd been holding back her opinions for a while. It was fascinating to watch; even Ailith in all her emotional fragility could never dream of matching a human in the throes of anger or sadness.

Clara continued on as if Lachlan was not there beside her. "They're all in love with our 'quaint' fairy stories, and they spend a fortune buying paintings depicting them all, yet what do they do when locals warn them to be careful? They ignore us! It serves them right when they disappear without a trace or come back completely changed."

Interesting to hear a human say that about another human, Lachlan thought. He twisted his fingers through Clara's ghostly hair without being able to ever quite touch it; the water of the loch she had created was strange indeed.

"My father doesn't want anyone to lose their homes and livelihoods like they are in the Highlands," Clara said, getting back to her original point. "But the Darrow family does not have the money it once had. So he met this man from London who grew up near here." Clara glanced around as if she was back in the tent. "As in, really near here, actually. Murdoch Buchanan. He said he lived ten miles from Darach. And this man is wealthy, and an investor, but he claims he wants what's best for the area."

"You do not believe him?"

"I don't know what to believe!" Clara cried out, smashing her fists into the water in frustration. They made no sound when they hit it. "My parents wanted me to get to know him. They like him. They believe him. But my father doesn't want Mr Buchanan to outright buy the land. He wants to keep it in the family, so he wants me to marry him."

Lachlan considered this for a moment. His hand stroked against Clara's cheek as if to soothe her, though he did not remember ever *deciding* to do such a thing. "You say your parents like this Mr Buchanan," he said thoughtfully. "Does that mean you do not?"

"I –" Clara faltered. She glanced at Lachlan's long, golden fingers when they moved from her cheek to her shoulder. "I do not know if I would ever like him. I'm... scared of him."

This is interesting.

"And why is that? Because he's wealthy? Because he lives in a city? Because he –"

"No, nothing like that!" Clara protested. "I'd never be scared of someone for such superficial things, especially not when my parents asked me to give him a chance. I *wanted* to give him a chance, just for them. But I...don't know. There's something about him that terrifies me down to my very soul."

When Clara shivered Lachlan felt the vibrations of it run right through his fingers. The girl was not lying about her fear, that much was true. But Lachlan had known humans and faeries alike to be scared of that which they most desired just as often as he'd seen them terrified of monsters.

"Maybe you truly *do* like him," Lachlan muttered, so quietly Clara didn't hear him. He traced his fingers down Clara's arm to her hand; it twitched as if she wished to hold on to him.

She didn't.

"I will let you sleep," Lachlan finally said, because he did not know what else to do. But when he stood up he looked down at Clara and grinned. "If you ended up marrying this man against your will would you consider giving me your full name *then*?"

He was pleased to see a small smile curl Clara's lips. "I know better than to promise a faerie anything."

"That wasn't a no."

"Good night, Lachlan."

"Good night, Clara."

When Lachlan found himself back in his cursed fox body he felt a twinge of regret. He'd wanted to stay in Clara's dream. He'd wanted to poke and prod her to find out everything there was to know about Clara Darrow, until the biggest, darkest secret she'd ever hold inside her was that the Prince of Faeries knew her better than anyone else possibly could.

I will own all of you, Lachlan thought, taking advantage of his furred form to burrow through the folds of Clara's dress to reach beneath it. She would likely be horrified to discover that he was lying against her naked skin, though Lachlan revelled in it.

But he'd be sure to extricate himself before Clara roused from sleep. In the morning he would hunt and bring her breakfast, and then eventually she'd come to realise that a life within the faerie realm with him would be far better than some miserable arranged marriage that would suck the life and soul and voice from her.

For now, though, Lachlan truly was exhausted, so with one final glance at Clara's face he eagerly drifted off to sleep.

CHAPTER TEN

Sorcha

Several days had passed since Lachlan had decided to join Sorcha on her quest. It was more than a little bizarre to travel with a fox – not least because of the looks she received from curious passers-by. Lachlan insisted on trotting along by Sorcha's heels, though she had tried to convince him to follow her under the cover of the forest instead.

He enjoys the odd looks, Sorcha could only conclude. *He is no stranger to attention. And he likes seeing me try and act as if having a pet fox is completely normal when I come across other people.* But venturing into hamlets and villages for food with Lachlan in full view had eventually become too annoying to deal with. Sorcha had subsequently taken to wrapping a blanket around her shoulders like a shawl and hiding Lachlan inside it – an arrangement he was more than pleased with. He chose to snuggle as close to Sorcha's skin as he could possibly get, nibbling at her collarbone, pawing at her breasts and constantly trying to bother her until

Sorcha yelled at him to stop.

He is a fox, Sorcha had to keep reminding herself whenever her insides coiled up like a snake and her cheeks grew red. *There may be a beautiful faerie inside but he is still a fox. Stop getting excited.*

Lachlan had not invaded Sorcha's dreams since their first night camping together. She reasoned that it was because their days were long and hard, and he roused earlier than her every morning to go hunting for rabbits and mice and pheasants. The fresh meat helped Sorcha out immensely, and saved her rapidly-dwindling supply of money. But the early mornings and long days meant the pair of them were often so exhausted by the time Sorcha pitched her tent that they simply fell asleep before the sun finished setting, collapsed in a tangled heap together.

I do not mind, Sorcha lied. *As a fox I can get to know Lachlan better without risking him being able to work any magic upon me. Our relationship is better this way.*

That didn't stop her day-dreaming about the golden faerie prince's hand against her face whenever she had a moment to herself. She wanted that hand to rove further. She wanted him to bite at her skin and paw at her breasts as a faerie, not a fox.

"What now, Clara?" Lachlan muttered from his position swaddled against her chest, startling Sorcha out of the beginning of her dangerous day-dream. He looked obscenely comfortable; she was tempted to tip him onto the muddy ground simply to disgruntle him. Above their heads the sky was grey and heavy with low-hanging clouds. All day they had been spattered with the beginning of what promised to be a wicked bout of rain, and there was a marked chill to the air that threatened the true death of summer.

"I want to buy some bread, eggs and apple cider," Sorcha replied, indulging the fox by scratching behind his ears. "And then we should find somewhere to set up camp before the rain grows torrential."

"It wouldn't be so much of a problem if you had a cloak."

"I don't have the money to buy one and I couldn't risk taking my own with me," she replied, sighing heavily. "I told you that already."

Lachlan popped his head out of the blanket, ears stiff and twitching with interest. "And why was that, exactly?"

Sorcha pushed his head back down and out of sight; they had reached the hamlet and couldn't afford any bizarre looks thrown their way. "It was hanging up by the kitchen door. To reach it meant leaving my room and... Mr Buchanan's door was open. He'd found me browsing through my father's library for the book about kelpies half an hour before I ran away. I think he was suspicious about me being awake so late at night."

"He suspected you might run off?"

"I don't know. It doesn't matter. He never saw me leave so he can't have known where I decided to go. Now *hush* and behave yourself so the people in the market do not find me odder than I already am."

Lachlan dutifully did as he was told, which was rare.

Sorcha moved from stall to stall, pleased that she had finally come upon a hamlet when they were running a farmer's market. She bought eggs – extra for Lachlan to eat uncooked – along with venison sausages, potatoes, onions and garlic to cook in her pot. A stew was exactly the kind of thing to eat in an early autumn downpour.

But when she reached a woman selling vats of apple cider Sorcha grew nervous. People were looking at her far more frequently than usual. She wrapped her blanket a little tighter around her shoulders, ensuring that it covered most of her hair and clothes. *If I had a hood or a hat I could pass as far more anonymous than this,* she thought, frowning when she spied a couple of men around her father's age watching her intently.

"...William Darrow's girl has been missing for days," she heard one of them say.

"You think she was taken by the f–"

"Maybe," the first voice interrupted. Sorcha did not have to hear the end of the second person's question to know to whom they were referring. Her heart battered against her ribcage; she felt Lachlan press an ear against it. "I've heard rumours she was to be married, though. Might just be that she ran away."

"What do you think that means for the land?"

"I suppose it all depends on whether they find her. She must be nearing her twenties, now. I remember William bringing her with him when he did his rounds! What was her name?"

"Ah, I think it was –"

"We need to go," Sorcha muttered, resisting the urge to look at Lachlan. She scurried away from the apple cider vendor without buying any, careful to avoid looking anybody in the eye. But one of the men who had been speaking noticed her rushing off.

"Miss!" he shouted, drawing the immediate attention of everyone around him. "Miss, won't you stay and –"

"Sorry, I cannot stay!" Sorcha called back, practically tripping over her feet in order to leave the hamlet. She made a beeline straight for the forest, picking up the pace until she was all but running through the trees. The area around her was unfamiliar – she and Lachlan had deviated from Loch Lomond in order to explore the smaller lochs to its right for the past few days, though they'd had no success whatsoever in locating a kelpie.

But Lachlan emerged from the blanket, darting his eyes around and twitching his whiskers before saying, "Go left here then keep going straight until the trees are all pine. There is a clearing hidden away there in which we can camp away from prying eyes."

Breathlessly Sorcha obliged his directions, not daring to look behind her to see if anyone was following the pair of them. It was only when Lachlan leapt down to the ground and nodded his head that Sorcha finally stopped. Above them the rolling call of thunder warned Sorcha she did not have long to pitch her tent before the sky heaved opened and soaked her to the bone.

That afternoon, despite her shaking hands and the fear of being caught, Sorcha set up camp faster than she had ever done before.

CHAPTER ELEVEN

Lachlan

It was raining down hard upon the tent and Clara could not sleep. Lachlan was buried in the blankets, watching her as she lay there, tense, with eyes wide open. He knew that, at this rate, Clara would not get any sleep at all.

He had to distract the girl from her restlessness until her brain finally shut off.

"You constructed this tent rather well, Clara," Lachlan said, crawling out from the blankets and over her legs to inspect each and every corner of the canvas. His claws bit into her skin whenever he lingered upon it, though Clara didn't tell him to get off. "It isn't letting any wind or rain in at all."

Clara was silent for a moment. Then she sighed, blinked away the vacant look in her eyes and said, "I used to pitch it in the garden by myself when I was younger, right by the forest edge. I loved to play at camping." She kept her gaze on the pointed roof of the tent as she spoke. The rain was heavy against the material, each drop a muted thud above their heads. Every so often a gust of wind howled around the tent, too, sounding as if the world was about to end. "I had no siblings," Clara continued on quietly, "though I was never lonely doing such things by myself. I liked learning how to do new things. And besides..."

Clara turned over onto her side to face Lachlan. He sat up straight, ears and nose twitching when she cocked her head to one side and smiled softly. "A few of the local children often joined me in the tent when my parents' backs were turned. It was fun. We felt like Highland rebels hiding from the evil men who wished to send us away from our homes."

She snickered at the thought, clearly finding it childish. In truth Lachlan knew it was not so childish; it wasn't only humans who lived further north for which Clara and her friends' fantasy was very much a reality. As forests were felled and the countryside destroyed to make way for large swathes of farmland all manner of magical creatures were being pushed out alongside the humans. It was a serious, dangerous problem for all involved.

Lachlan dismissed the sobering thought for now – there was nothing he could do about it, after all.

"You know," Clara said, laughing quietly before looking away from Lachlan, "I had my first kiss on one such night in the tent, to a fiery-haired, freckled boy."

"And what became of the boy?" Lachlan asked. He crept closer to Clara until he could feel her cheek against his whiskers. She blushed, and her eyes remained averted.

"Oh, he grew up to be a fiery-haired, freckled man,"

she replied, holding her hands above her head to twist her fingers around each other. "He asked me to marry him when we both turned sixteen. I declined, of course, though my parents would have dismissed the engagement had I said yes, anyway. We were still practically children. Old Man MacPherson's son. Gregor is his name. I saw him repairing the roof of the family farm just after I met you, actually. I wonder if he still fancies me now? I hope he has moved on."

Clara spoke as if Lachlan wasn't really there, her words flowing one after the other almost as a single sentence. He had asked her, that first morning in the forest when she'd been picking brambles, if she had allowed many boys to get close to her. Clara said she hadn't; Lachlan wondered if this Gregor MacPherson kissing her in a tent was all the experience she had.

Then Clara wrinkled her nose and swung up to a sitting position. Lachlan took a few steps back in surprise. "What is wrong?" he asked.

She picked at the hem of her dress. It was filthy and damp and, Lachlan imagined, rather uncomfortable to wear. "I was so concerned about the villagers that I forgot to change into my night dress."

If Lachlan had brows to raise he would have done so. "You haven't once changed into a night dress."

"That's because my normal dresses have been dry by the time I've gone to sleep," she replied, fishing through her bag until she found the piece of clothing she was looking for. Clara smiled as she held it up and shook it out.

Lachlan circled around the material, curious. "That's not so much a dress as an overly large shirt. Very inappropriate for young ladies."

"It is one of my father's old shirts," Clara said. "I like the feeling of it."

And then, without asking Lachlan to turn away to protect her modesty, Clara deftly unfastened the front of her dress and pulled it up and over her shoulders. She slid off her stockings next – which were even filthier than her dress – leaving only a chemise to remove. Clara wasn't wearing a stays, which somehow didn't surprise Lachlan whatsoever despite it being most unheard of for a woman of marriageable age.

He could only watch agog as Clara, finally, slid out of her chemise, and though his fox eyes were not as keen as his faerie ones during the day they were excellent in the darkness. There was not a single detail Lachlan missed of the woman kneeling in front of him: he noted the curves of Clara's hips and thighs; the length of her legs; the flat planes of her stomach and the way her long, unruly hair flowed over her shoulders and covered her breasts. Lachlan was rather familiar with them, of course, given that he hid against Clara's chest whenever they were amongst other people, but he was nonetheless disappointed that her hair obscured them now.

I want to be me, he thought. There was a hunger inside him that he could not satisfy as a fox. *I want to stop Clara putting on her father's shirt with my own hands. I want to push her hair back from her face and kiss her until she's begging me to do more. I want her to tell me her name and ask that I whisk her away to the Seelie Court forever.*

"What is it, Lachlan?" Clara asked, voice carefree as if she had no idea what was going on in Lachlan's head. She was clothed once more, though the shirt barely fell below her thighs. He almost choked when he saw how exposed her legs were.

"You are killing me," Lachlan muttered, padding over to Clara and sitting in her lap before she could protest. He reached up and placed his front paws on her chest. "Lie down," he ordered. "Lie down and think of where we are."

Clara laughed at the bizarre request. "And why do you want me to do that?" She ruffled his ears; Lachlan nipped her wrist with his teeth until she pulled her hand away, wincing. "Fine," she complained. "I'll do as I'm told. There was no need to bite me, Lachlan."

"Oh, trust me, there was," he said, once more under his breath. Clara eyed him curiously but dutifully lay down nonetheless; Lachlan moved from her lap to stand overlooking her face, dipping his head down until their noses were touching. He could see his fox form within Clara's green and blue eyes and fought back a grimace. "Think of the here and now. Think of us in the tent, and the rain upon it, and the forest we're in. Keep it all in your head."

"What are you trying to do?" Clara asked in a whisper. She had grown serious once more, for which Lachlan was glad. He did not wish to spend any more time joking around.

"Just do it. Are you thinking of it?"

Clara nodded, though she still looked as if she wanted to protest. Lachlan closed his eyes, inhaled deeply, then thought of Clara – the way he had done when he'd accidentally sent her to sleep in her bedroom.

When he opened his eyes hers were closed, and her chest rose and fell beneath Lachlan's paws as if she was deep in slumber. "Good," Lachlan murmured. "Good." He leapt off Clara to slink into a corner, curling his bushy tail around him before slowing his own breathing and closing his eyes once more.

This time, when he opened them, Lachlan was himself again, and Clara was dreaming. But the tent remained around them, and the rain fell hard above them, and the night air felt cool and real and full of thunder.

Lachlan's heart rate sped up just as Clara began to rouse from where she lay. How he had missed the excitement of being himself; of using his words and his looks and his magic to get what he wanted.

"You have a talent for keeping hold of thoughts," he said, wasting no time in creeping over to Clara's side to sit by her head. She stared up at him, eyes wide in shock at his appearance. "No wonder I failed to enchant you when first we met."

"Lachlan," she began, "what are you –"

Clara's question was lost when Lachlan ran a hand through her hair to pin her to the blankets. He bent down low over her face, revelling in the way she bit her lip and tried not to avert her gaze.

He grinned.

"I think you know what I am doing."

CHAPTER TWELVE

Sorcha

One minute Sorcha was conversing with Lachlan as a fox, wishing that he was himself once more, and then the next minute her wish came true.

This is still a dream, she reminded herself. *Even if Lachlan has decided to interrupt it, and we still seem to be in the tent, this isn't real. Remember that, Sorcha. Don't forget it.*

But it was so easy to forget, when Lachlan was looking at her like that.

"This is really a dream, isn't it?" Sorcha asked. Her heart beat erratically in her chest when Lachlan's hand smoothed back her hair. "Everything looks so real."

"And yet it is indeed a dream," he replied, golden eyes and white teeth alike glinting in the darkness. He watched Sorcha intently; she squeezed her thighs together and begged for her imagination to stop running so wild.

She wanted to touch the golden-skinned faerie

leaning over her. She wanted to run her fingers along the sharp planes of his face; the braid in his hair; the points of his ears –

"Your earring," Sorcha breathed, squinting as she noticed its absence. "It is gone."

A flash of something Sorcha couldn't quite understand crossed Lachlan's inhumanly beautiful face. "Yes. Fergus – my stepbrother – took it from me to give to Ailith. Proof that I had run off and left. The bloody bastard."

Sorcha had never heard Lachlan talk in such a way. "Who is Ailith?" she asked, though she had a feeling she did not want to know the answer.

"My stepbrother's betrothed. They are to be married at the end of the month. Ailith will be Queen of the Seelie Court by his side."

"Did she...did she know what your stepfamily planned to do to you?"

To Sorcha's surprise Lachlan barked in laughter; it did not sound all that dissimilar from a fox. He shook his head. "Ailith would never do anything to hurt me, besides break my heart."

"You love her."

It wasn't a question; Sorcha was certain of it.

"I *loved* her," Lachlan corrected bitterly. "And she loved me, or at least I always thought she did. If I still love her now I do not wish to. The feeling will pass in time, as with everything."

"That is tragic," Sorcha whispered. Her eyes were full of tears, though she did not want to cry. With a gentle thumb Lachlan brushed the moisture away.

"Do not pity me," he said. He curled a hand through Sorcha's hair, lifting her head up until their lips brushed against each other. "I do not need a human to waste their emotions on me – not when their lives are so short. There are much better things you could do for me instead."

Sorcha could feel her resolve fading with each and every beautiful, carefully-chosen word Lachlan spoke to her. She knew what faeries were capable of doing to humans even without knowing their names. A cleverly-woven sentence or two could convince a person to do something they would never normally do; to indulge a dangerous whim or lie with their neighbour's wife or give all their money away. Whether Lachlan *meant* to enchant Sorcha at this specific moment in time was another thing entirely – it was possible that his magic was always at play whether he wished it or not.

When Lachlan moved away from her Sorcha sat up to face him properly. She tucked a lock of tangled hair behind her ear, regarding Lachlan with curious eyes. The faerie was wearing a long, chestnut-coloured tail coat that flowed out behind him upon the blankets. Beneath it was a white shirt that hung lazily over his frame and dark, fitted breeches. He wasn't wearing any shoes.

"Were you wearing these clothes when I first met you, Lachlan?" Sorcha asked, changing the subject so suddenly that he laughed.

Lachlan flipped his hair over his shoulder. "Yes, but not the coat. You do not remember?"

"I was rather...distracted," Sorcha admitted. "It is not your clothes that one first notices."

"That's awfully honest of you, Clara," Lachlan said, grinning wickedly. "What did you notice first, then?"

"Your hair, perhaps. Or your golden skin."

Lachlan fingered the braid that ran across the left side of his scalp. "I should unravel it. I no longer have an earring left to show off."

Another lurch of sadness filled Sorcha's stomach. Without thinking of whether it was a good idea or not she reached behind Lachlan for her bag, rummaging through it until she found a comb. "How about I plait one side of my hair to match yours, instead? That way your braid won't remind you of what you lost anymore."

But Lachlan was not listening; his gaze was on Sorcha's thighs which, because of her position stretched out towards her bag, were no longer covered by her father's shirt. Sorcha thought at first that she should protect her modesty but something insistently stopped her.

Maybe I am enchanted. I wanted Lachlan to watch me undress earlier even though he was a fox. There is something wrong with me.

But the heat roaring inside Sorcha could not be denied. It made her forget all about the villagers who had recognised her and nearly revealed her name. It made her forget about the fact her parents were no doubt looking for her. Most of all, it made her forget about Murdoch Buchanan and her sham of an engagement to him.

Sorcha wanted Lachlan, the faerie prince, no matter how dangerous giving into such a desire could be.

She stared at him staring at her. "Lachlan –"

"Let me do it," he cut in, blinking focus back into his golden eyes before removing his coat. He reached out a hand for the comb Sorcha was holding. "I will braid it."

Sorcha wordlessly complied, hesitating for only a moment before sitting herself between Lachlan's outstretched legs. His thighs were all lean muscle beneath his breeches; Sorcha gulped when she imagined feeling then intertwined with her own. Lachlan raised the comb to her scalp, and then –

"Ow!" she complained, pulling away from the comb immediately. Sorcha rubbed her head, turning to scowl at Lachlan.

He shrugged. "What did you expect? Your hair has been a mess for days."

"You're supposed to start from the bottom! That way it doesn't hurt as much."

"If you say so," Lachlan smirked, amused, pushing Sorcha back around with a hand on her shoulder. "Staying still will make it hurt less, too."

And so Sorcha forced herself not to wince and smart away every time Lachlan hit a tangle. Neither of them spoke, the only sounds around them being the soft thudding of dream rain upon the tent and the whisper of the comb through Sorcha's hair.

After a few minutes that felt, somehow, entirely endless, Lachlan finished untangling the knots in her hair and urged Sorcha to face him so that he could braid it. But he brought his knees together, deliberately not leaving enough space for her to sit between them. Despite how outrageous it was, Sorcha didn't even blink before sliding her legs over his thighs.

I am practically straddling the Prince of Faeries as he plays with my hair, she thought. *Just what am I doing? Where is this going? It's just a dream...a dream. Even if something happens it will not have truly happened. Everything is fine.*

Despite the fact Lachlan had – just barely – kissed Sorcha ten minutes ago, she felt far more self-conscious being so close to the faerie's face now than she had been before. His fingers deftly wove through the right-hand side of her hair until a braid formed, pulling one of the laces from his shirt with his teeth in order to tie it off where it curled around the back of her ear.

The opposite side from his, she thought, eyeing up Lachlan's braid as she ran a hand across her own. *I like it.*

"Much better," Lachlan murmured, putting down Sorcha's comb in order to turn her head back and forth to inspect his handiwork. "Though I imagine you'll destroy it within hours of waking up – if the braid is present at all in reality."

A noise of indignation left Sorcha's throat as she made to move away from Lachlan. But he wrapped an arm around her, squeezing her close until there was no space left between them.

Sorcha gasped at the iron of his arms. "You are strong," she said. Her hands were on Lachlan's shoulders; it was the first time she had touched him in his true form with her fingertips. The fabric of his shirt was soft and impossibly insubstantial beneath them. She thought that she'd barely have to apply any pressure at all to rip right through it.

She wanted to rip right through it.

Lachlan grazed his lips against her ear. "You are surprised that I am strong, Clara?"

Unbidden she thought of Murdoch. A chill ran

98

down her spine, though she shook her head and ignored it. "Not surprised," she replied, somewhat breathless by Lachlan's proximity. "Excited, perhaps."

"A good answer. Would you like to see how strong I really am?"

Lachlan's eyes glinted as he raised himself up onto his knees, placing his hands beneath Clara's thighs to lift her up with him in the process. She wrapped her legs around his waist before she could stop herself; when his fingers squeezed into her flesh Sorcha bit her lip to keep in a moan of longing.

"You almost feel as good as you do awake, Clara," Lachlan murmured. He kissed her neck; her ear; her eyelids when she fluttered them closed.

"Almost?" she whispered.

"Almost. When I have my body back I'll be sure to teach you the difference between doing such things in a dream and doing them for real."

Sorcha pulled away just enough to stare at Lachlan's mischievous face. "And what if I do not wish to?"

"One day you will stop lying to me," he laughed, "and to yourself. Trust me, you will feel much better for –"

Lachlan froze. His eyes became glass and his fingers steel against Sorcha's thighs. She frowned. "What is it?"

"I do not know. I need to wake up."

He disappeared so quickly that Sorcha was viciously thrown back into consciousness with him, disconcerted by the fact she was now lying down on the blankets in the tent, alone. In the corner Lachlan-the-fox jumped to his feet, nose held high as he sniffed the air. He burrowed through the opening of the tent and did not return for almost half an hour.

When he came back his russet fur was soaking wet. "What is out there, Lachlan?" Sorcha asked, terribly afraid. "Did those villagers find –"

"Nothing," he interrupted. Lachlan's eyes were flat and distracted. "There was nothing."

"But –"

"Just go to sleep, Clara. If I said there was nothing there was nothing."

Lachlan could not lie, which meant there really was nothing. But Sorcha was not convinced.

There is something out there. Something that bothers Lachlan. But I cannot sense it. Just what is it?

It came as no surprise that neither of them slept that night.

CHAPTER THIRTEEN

Lachlan

Rain battered Lachlan and Clara for three days before finally letting up in a bout of glorious sunshine. It brought with it the last vestiges of summer heat, which was delicious upon Lachlan's fur in combination with the new-found autumn freshness of the air. The two of them had made slow, careful progress back through the forest towards the northern point of Loch Lomond, with the intention of travelling down the western shore to the shallow southern banks. With every step he took Lachlan became certain they would not find a kelpie; there hadn't been a single sign of one so far.

The kelpies in the smaller lochs would have known we were there, looking for them. They chose not to appear. The kelpie of Loch Lomond, however...

The loch was the largest expanse of fresh water in not only Scotland but the entire British Isles. It was entirely possible that the kelpie who dwelled within it was never close enough to where Lachlan and Clara were searching to notice their presence.

But Lachlan didn't believe that for a moment. The larger the body of water, the stronger and more dangerous the kelpie. The only reasonable way the creature could not have been aware of a solitary human wandering the shores of the loch – an otherwise perfect victim to drown beneath the surface – was if it was not currently *in* the loch itself.

The idea was not so strange; the dark and twisted creatures that resided in the depths of lochs and rivers and seas often delighted in tricking humans by looking just like one of them. In that respect they were not so dissimilar from the Unseelie, who more often than not had terrible, deadly plans for the people they beguiled.

Look out for humans wearing silver chains, Lachlan told himself, over and over again. He and Clara had thankfully passed nobody on their way through the forest, but now that they were reaching the open loch shore once more Lachlan knew they had to be on their guard. *Silver chains. Silver chains. A kelpie's bridle becomes a silver chain.*

For ever since Lachlan had so very nearly indulged his desire for Clara he had not been able to shake the feeling that they were being followed. Perhaps he was being paranoid; he certainly could not *smell* anything awry. There hadn't even been the scent of a lowly human nearby for the past three days. All Lachlan had sensed were deer and birds and rabbits and, occasionally, the presence of a faerie.

A kelpie following us through the forest of the Seelie Court is impossible, Lachlan thought, trying desperately to reassure himself. *It is possible I am merely on edge because my fox senses are beginning to grow more prominent.*

Lachlan did not like that at all.

In contrast Clara seemed decidedly carefree. Now that it was clear no humans were following them she had relaxed back into enjoying their journey, revelling in the ease with which Lachlan traversed the forest as if he knew every tree, which he did. *She does not feel the same way I do,* he mused, watching as the girl nimbly jumped over a burn whilst she whistled softly. *She can't feel what it is I sensed three days ago.*

Lachlan hadn't experienced the unexplainable sensation that had frozen his entire body since. But the memory of it was there, taunting him. The only time he'd felt anything close to it had been the moment he realised Innis and Fergus had cursed him.

They cannot be following me. They can't. Maybe they sent someone out to follow me in their stead? Or is it some kind of Unseelie magic? For if it was then Lachlan had to hope that Clara's harebrained scheme to borrow a kelpie's silver bridle would somehow, miraculously, work.

When finally they broke through the trees and into the gleaming, late afternoon sunshine Lachlan and Clara were faced with a stretch of perfectly golden sand, hidden from view on two sides by sloping shelves of sandstone.

Clara tilted her head down to look at him, face bright and enthusiastic.

"Clara, we shouldn't –"

"Lachlan, it would be madness not to enjoy the sunshine for a few hours. It may be the last good afternoon we get until next year. We can spare a few hours, can't we? And besides..." Clara's gaze wandered over to the loch. Even Lachlan had to admit that the wretched, dangerous water was beautiful in the sunshine. "I would kill to bathe properly in there. My clothes could do with a soak, too."

Lachlan did not want to stop and rest. But how could he say no to Clara's request, when she was so eager? She began pouring out the contents of her bag onto a strip of grass that separated the sand from the forest before Lachlan even had a chance to nod in assent.

"We should probably camp here," she babbled excitedly. "This cove is sheltered from the elements, should it rain once more, and it is not easy for folk to spot us from the forest path if they walk along it. We can set off early tomorrow morning."

Lachlan sighed. "As you wish, Clara. Just...be careful."

He didn't know *what* she should be careful of. At this point Lachlan had to admit he didn't know anything at all. He hated it.

Clara spent the next half an hour setting up the tent, tossing Lachlan an egg which he deftly caught in his jaws when she spotted him eyeing up the last of them. They'd need to venture into a village soon to purchase more supplies, and Lachlan knew Clara was dreading it. But he didn't bring up the subject of dwindling food; it could wait until the morning.

Once their camp was set up Lachlan settled onto the sand, revelling in the warmth it had absorbed from the sun. He rolled around in the stuff for the sheer delight of doing so, causing Clara to giggle as she watched.

"It is hard to think of you as the Prince of Faeries

when you act like that, Lachlan," she said, before pulling off her boots and unbuttoning her dress. Lachlan remained as baffled by the girl's lack of modesty as he had been three days ago, especially now that her stockings and chemise joined her dress on the sand. Clara was left standing naked upon the shore of Loch Lomond for all the world to see.

"Do you not care if somebody spots you, Clara?" Lachlan asked, genuinely curious about her answer.

She shrugged. "There is nobody around but you and me. And you are a fox. Why should I worry?"

"I am a fox *now*," he muttered, whipping his tail back and forth in frustration as Clara sauntered to the edge of the loch.

Despite Lachlan's assertion that she would ruin the braid in her hair in mere hours, Clara had ensured it stayed perfect. Perhaps it was to spite him. Perhaps it was because it had survived crossing over from unconsciousness to reality – a small, inconsequential fragment of Lachlan's magic capable of surviving a dream. It kept Clara's face clear when a gust of wind battered the beach, billowing the rest of her hair behind her.

In the sunlight Clara's pale skin looked even paler than it had done in the forest. It was the typical colouring of the Celts, including the burnished copper highlights in her dark hair. Lachlan wondered if she ever tanned at all or if the freckles on her arms and face merely absorbed all the sunlight beating down upon her. *How much sunshine would she need to be as dark as me?* The thought amused Lachlan to no end.

Clara turned back to grin at him. Water lapped at her toes, breaking against them in a wave of white foam.

"Care to join me, Lachlan?" she called over. She rubbed the length of her forearms with her hands – physical proof that the loch was, most definitely, very cold.

"Never in a thousand years shall I swim in there," he asserted. Clara rolled her eyes, shrugged her shoulders once more, then ran straight into the loch without a care in the world. "Madness," Lachlan muttered. "She is absolutely mad."

But Lachlan had to admit that it was fun to watch Clara swim in the loch. She was clearly enjoying herself, dipping below the surface only to leap back up to smooth her hair back and close her eyes to the sun. When she lay back to float on the water he remembered how Clara's hair had looked in her dark, dream loch. How it had swirled around Lachlan's fingers without ever touching it.

"If I had my true form now I would join her in there," he informed the sky, in direct contradiction to what he had only just told Clara herself. "I'd swim by her side and then Clara would know that I truly wished for her to join the Court."

But despite the fact Clara had responded eagerly to Lachlan's advances in her dream back in the forest, there was something holding her at bay from him still. *If she does not come with me willingly when I have my own body back then I really will have no choice but to seek out her name.*

For under no circumstances was Lachlan going to allow Clara to live out the rest of her life as a human. He couldn't fathom the idea of her living for a handful of decades – likely fewer years than Lachlan had already lived – only to die old and grey and miserable. He could give Clara a life worth the brightness she held within her.

Lachlan spent so long thinking about Clara that he did not realise he could no longer hear her splashing about in the loch. He stood up, shaking himself of sand in order to creep towards the edge of the water. "Clara?" he said, wondering where on earth she was. No doubt she had dived beneath the surface to see how long she could hold her breath; Lachlan knew humans often enjoyed challenging themselves in such a way.

A minute passed. Two. Three.

"Clara?" Lachlan shouted, uncertainty colouring his voice. Something was wrong. Dreadfully wrong. His body began to grow cold until he could no longer move it – the same feeling that had crept up on him in Clara's dream.

"Oh, no," Lachlan cried, before leaping into the loch without another thought.

Oh, no. Oh, no. Oh, no.

CHAPTER FOURTEEN

Sorcha

Sorcha revelled in the feeling of the loch upon her skin. The bracing water tingled and stung her every nerve at first; it was much colder in the northern, deeper depths of the loch than it was in Darach's shallow shores. But then Sorcha got used to the temperature and the tingling disappeared, leaving behind a feeling of clarity and contentment as she floated on the surface like the otters she had once witnessed on a trip to the coast.

How I have missed this, she thought, closing her eyes and smiling as the sun beat down upon her face. For Sorcha swam in Loch Lomond most days between late April and early September, and the fact she hadn't done so for an entire week felt like part of her very soul had been ripped away from her.

"Especially in the forest," Sorcha murmured. "I could not live in the forest forever whilst avoiding the loch."

For of course she had been thinking about what it

would be like to live in the Seelie Court as she and Lachlan carved their way through the forest. Between his advances in her dreams and the way he watched her every move as a fox Sorcha knew the faerie had every intention of convincing her to live amongst his kind.

"I should be flattered," she told a duck when it swam close to her. "It's not very often that adult humans get taken away to the faerie realm to live with them." It occurred to Sorcha as she watched the bird that most every duck and swan and migrating goose that lived around the loch knew all her secrets – not having any siblings ultimately meant that the wildlife in the area were her closest friends. The duck quacked at her, wondering for a moment whether Sorcha had any food, before paddling on by.

She sighed. Living in the Court would be dangerous indeed. If she went willingly then she would be bound by her promise to reside there and could never leave. And if Lachlan went ahead and found out her name...

Well, it would be him that would not let me leave. Just what exactly does he want with me?

That was the crux of the matter, of course. Sorcha could not possibly know what the Prince of Faeries wanted with a mere human. He liked her voice, and he liked the look of her, and clearly he found some amusement and interest in conversing with her. But was Lachlan really so shallow as to imprison Sorcha within the faerie realm for such superficial reasons?

"Absolutely," Sorcha muttered, dunking her head beneath the surface of the loch as if it could scrub her head clean of such thoughts. After Lachlan told her about Ailith she was left with no doubt that he was capable of deep, unrelenting love. But it was also apparent that Lachlan did not revel in such emotions. It did not matter that Sorcha longed for him to return to his original form – to hold her in his arms and allow her to get lost in them. Faeries were still overwhelmingly frivolous, hedonistic creatures.

Sorcha could not live among them.

I wonder if Lachlan will let me live as I am if I'm successful in procuring the kelpie's bridle, she thought. But what did that mean for Sorcha, ultimately? A marriage to a man who scared her in order to protect the livelihood of everyone who lived around the loch? Perhaps taking Lachlan up on his offer of living in the Seelie Court would not be so bad...if Sorcha could set some conditions for her living there.

"Do not do that."

Sorcha froze. Blindly she turned her head left and right in the water, trying to see who had spoken to her. The voice was masculine and soft. Low and impossibly clear. More melodic than anything Sorcha had ever heard before. Considering she was currently underwater she had no clue how she'd heard such a voice. Sorcha darted up to the surface, gasping back a large mouthful of air before diving into the dark, swirling loch once more.

"Who is there?" she asked, the question coming out as bubbles and garbled, incoherent fragments of words.

"You have been seeking me out. Why?" the voice asked her. Beneath Sorcha the water seemed almost solid for a moment – a huge, night-dark shape closing in on her until, in the blink of an eye, it was gone.

Sorcha held her knees to her chest in order to sink a little further into the loch where the shape had been.

The water was clear, for it was free of the silt and sand and peat that often clouded the southern shore. She could see as far as the sunlight above her was capable of illuminating, which meant Sorcha could see nothing at all, for nothing was there.

"You are the kelpie," she said with certainty, the words once more a stream of bubbles exiting her mouth. Sorcha's heart twisted painfully in her chest; she was scared, and excited, and torn between fleeing for her life and diving ever deeper into the loch. But if this truly was the kelpie then she could not afford to lose him, so Sorcha forced herself to stay exactly where she was.

To her left the water grew solid once more. "You need not waste your breath on speaking," he said. "I can hear your thoughts. You need my help to save a faerie?"

Sorcha nodded emphatically. *I need your bridle,* she thought in the direction of his voice. *Just for a day or two. I will give it back, I swear.*

The kelpie laughed. It was a beautiful, terrible sound, reverberating all around Sorcha until it filled her mind and blocked out everything else. "Why should I help a member of the Seelie Court? They hate anything that comes from the water. Don't you want me to help *you* instead?"

There is...I do not think you can help me with my problems, Sorcha replied. She was beginning to grow faint and light-headed; she needed to breathe. But just as she kicked up towards the surface the shadowy, indistinct shape of the kelpie slid past her skin, and Sorcha forgot all about her lungs crying out for air.

"You underestimate what I can do, human," the kelpie said. When he brushed past Sorcha again she saw a flash of silver and just a hint of his dark, fathomless eyes, but as soon as she tried to focus on them they disappeared.

Do not touch him, Sorcha thought, remembering the stories from her father's book whilst temporarily forgetting that the kelpie could hear her thoughts. *I will not be able to let go. I will die.*

"Only if I wish to kill you," he replied, laughing once more. Sorcha felt a nudge against her back; she twisted around to try and catch sight of the kelpie to no avail. "And I do not wish to kill you," he continued. "Just tell me what you want."

I want to save Lachlan.

All around Sorcha the water stilled. "...the prince? Lachlan, Prince of Faeries?"

Yes! Sorcha thought, excited by the kelpie's response. *His Unseelie stepfamily cursed and banished him so they could take the throne from him. They –*

"That changes things completely."

Sorcha lit up at the kelpie's answer. *You will help him? You will lend him your bridle?*

"...in a manner of speaking," he replied. "Tell me, what is this curse that has been placed upon the prince?"

He –

But then something sharp and vicious bit at Sorcha's wrist, pulling her out of her conversation with the kelpie. "Lachlan!" she cried out when she spied the fox's orange fur turned green in the water. His name upon her lips used up the last of the air in Sorcha's lungs; she scrabbled at her throat with her fingernails as she began to sink.

Lachlan glared at her with his golden eyes before

pushing at her chest with his head, urging Sorcha towards the surface. She was dimly aware of the kelpie's presence dissipating as she desperately kicked and clawed through the loch; when Sorcha finally broke the surface there was no evidence left of his presence at all. She drew in a shuddering breath the instant she could, the air stinging her lungs like a thousand knives. It warned Sorcha of just how close to drowning she had been.

"You *idiot!*" Lachlan barked at her, incandescent with rage as the two of them struggled back to shore. "You careless, stupid human!" Had he been dry his fur would have stood on end to punctuate his anger, Sorcha knew. As it was Lachlan looked small and drenched and pitiable.

"He can – help," Sorcha breathed, barely managing to crawl onto the sand before collapsing onto her chest. "Kelpie said he can...help."

Lachlan bit her shoulder. "Don't lie down here! Get back to the tent. For the love of the forest *get back to the tent.*"

It took Sorcha every ounce of effort to move forwards, the sand below her scratching and sticking to her skin as she slid across it. When she reached the strip of grass in front of the tent Sorcha could move no further. All her strength had been drained.

Furious, Lachlan shook out his fur and bolted into the tent, dragging a blanket behind him and throwing it over Sorcha using his teeth. "Dry off and get in the – Clara? Clara!"

But Sorcha couldn't move; she'd fallen asleep.

CHAPTER FIFTEEN

Lachlan

"What is wrong with you?!"

Lachlan wasted no time invading Clara's dream in order to drop his tirade down upon her. All around him the landscape was blank – grey and dull and nondescript. Had Lachlan not sneaked inside Clara's head she likely would not have dreamed at all.

She looked at him from her position kneeling on what Lachlan could only assume was the 'floor' of her dream, blanket wrapped around her shivering shoulders as she took several deep breaths.

"He will help us," Clara stammered, fighting to vocalise each and every word.

Lachlan went bug-eyed in disbelief, flailing his arms wildly in anger. "You almost *died,* Clara! Just how stupid are you? The kelpie tried to kill you!"

"It is my own fault I almost drowned," Clara replied in earnest. She stood up, shaking slightly on her legs before finally managing to straighten herself. Her braid had come undone, unravelling over her shoulder and dripping water down the blanket. Lachlan wondered if it had also come undone in real life or whether it was merely part of Clara's dream.

He took a step towards her. "The only reason you were drowning is because the kelpie had enchanted you. Would you have spent so long underwater had it not kept you there?"

But Clara shook her head at Lachlan's explanation. "He didn't enchant me! We were talking. He was going to help. He was –"

"If it was going to help it would not have brought you so close to death!" Lachlan spat. "How can you not see that? It was twisting you around its proverbial finger because that's what kelpies like to do. They toy with their food. Surely you must know this?"

"But we were only –"

"Talking. *Talking.* Do you know how easy it is for a creature of magical birth to bend a human to its will through mere words? I think you do, Clara. I think you know this perfectly well."

Clara said nothing. She turned away from Lachlan and tightened the blanket around her body, finally aware of how exposed she was beneath it. But Lachlan closed the gap between them, grabbing Clara roughly by the shoulders in order to shake her.

"Don't ignore me!" he demanded. "You know I'm right! You *know* I am!"

"You said yourself I am not so easy to enchant," Clara protested, though she kept her eyes on her feet. "Who is to say the kelpie had any more luck than you did at weaving its will around me?"

"Look at me and find out, you ignorant human."

At first Clara did not comply. Going by the set of her shoulders she was determined not to back down from her assertion that the kelpie was actually going to help them. But, eventually, she turned around to face Lachlan properly, staring hard into his eyes with her hauntingly mismatched ones.

"I did not try all that hard to enchant you when first we met," Lachlan began, settling into a steady, poetic rhythm that would burrow quickly into Clara's mind. "Usually it takes but a mere sentence or two to ensorcell a human. It is true that you are not so ordinary. It is true that I have to put more effort into enchanting you. But I can do it, and so can the kelpie. Your will cannot keep ours shut out."

In front of him Clara's eyes began to glaze over. Her frame swayed back and forth ever so slightly, waiting patiently for his next words. Lachlan cocked his head to one side and touched the index finger of his left hand to Clara's temple. "You *want* us in your head," he continued. "You want to see with our eyes, and listen to our voices, and eat our food, and dance our dances. You long to see the darkest, most mysterious corners of the world just as much as you wish to be engulfed by the light we can create. And even if, on an ordinary day, you might not *think* you want these things, all it takes is the suggestion of magic and you will fold. Magic is magic, and humans always want what they think they cannot have. Unlace my shirt, Clara."

Of course she did as she was told – all humans did in the end. Clara's delicate fingers pulled loose the remaining lace in Lachlan's shirt, for the other had been tied into her hair, until the impossibly light fabric slipped from his shoulders to fall to the grey, never-

116

ending ground.

"Touch me," he ordered, watching with savage delight as Clara swept her fingertips across his chest. Her eyes seemed to see right through him, or see nothing at all, as she moved her hands down to his waist. Lachlan's breathing accelerated until he could barely think.

He took hold of Clara's arms and slung them over his shoulders, causing the blanket protecting her modesty to fall. Her skin was cold and pale against his; he longed to warm it up. "Kiss me," Lachlan whispered against her lips. "Kiss me like it's all you've been thinking about from the very first moment we met. Kiss me like you want me to take you away from your dreary human life and its dreary human problems forever."

When Clara did so Lachlan eagerly dipped into the kiss. Her tongue was searing hot against his teeth, in stark contrast to her skin, and her hands crawled through his hair to pull on it, urging him closer and closer and closer.

But just as Lachlan was ready to get lost in the moment he caught sight of Clara's eyes once more. They were completely empty. Clear, lifeless glass where once her soul had been.

All her brightness was lost.

"Damn it," he muttered, pushing Clara away and bending down to retrieve her blanket. He tossed it over her shoulders before picking up his shirt and angrily putting it back on. "Damn you, Clara. Damn this farce of an alliance. Go back to your parents. I shall solve my problems on my own."

Lachlan left Clara's dream before she had the opportunity to blink life back into herself. When he returned to his fox form the sun had fully set, cooling the sand and grass and air to a decidedly autumnal temperature. Clara remained just outside of the tent, lying on the grass, covered in her blanket and so deeply unconscious Lachlan doubted even a torrential downpour could rouse her from her sleep. In his current form he was too weak to pull her back into the tent. Part of him didn't even want to.

"You are just a human," Lachlan told her, hating Clara but hating himself even more, and then he fled. Lachlan had been a fool to trust a mortal.

He would be sure never to make such a mistake again.

CHAPTER SIXTEEN

Sorcha

When Sorcha awoke it was morning. The sun shone pale and weak through a thin layer of perfectly white, even cloud, making her feel as if she hadn't quite made it back to reality yet.

"Lachlan," she uttered, though speaking his name was painful on her parched, agonised throat. Desperately Sorcha searched around for the water skin she always sat beside her at night only to realise that she was not, in fact, lying in the tent.

And she was completely naked.

"Oh my – oh my lord," she muttered, scrabbling for the blanket she had kicked off in her feverish sleep. Then Sorcha reached inside the tent and felt blindly for her water skin until her fingers found purchase on it. She drank the water down in one go, though much of the liquid escaped her lips to dribble down her chin instead.

Beads of sweat lingered upon her brow; Sorcha

wiped them away with a trembling hand. Despite the fact she was wide awake Sorcha found herself struggling to cling to her own consciousness. It unsettled her to no end that lucid, coherent thought seemed simply impossible.

Sorcha could hardly fathom what happened to her before she fell asleep, let alone what Lachlan had said and done within her dream. The whole enchanting, dangerous, alluring, wicked evening leeched away at her mind, insisting that she dwell upon it instead of the very pressing, very real issue of what she was supposed to do now that she was awake.

But one thing was for sure: Lachlan was gone.

A gust of wind carried several tangled locks of Sorcha's hair across her face. She moved them away, realising in the process that her braid had come undone.

"How was the braid even there in the first place?" Sorcha wondered, feeling stupid for not having asked Lachlan about this when she'd had the chance. He had tied it up in her dream, with the lace from his shirt, and when she had awoken the braid had remained. "He told me what happens in a dream is not truly real. So why do I have the lace from his shirt?"

Or had it, rather, Sorcha thought. She couldn't see the thin, dark strip of leather anywhere, which meant Sorcha likely lost it in the loch. She stared out at the water; it shimmered innocently beneath the weak sunshine. *Did the kelpie truly mean to kill me? He said himself that if he'd intended to do so then he would have. But I almost drowned nonetheless.*

Sorcha shivered at the memory. She never wished to experience such a raw, brutally painful experience again. Feeling her lungs collapse in on themselves was a horror unlike anything she could have ever imagined.

Lachlan was right. I'd never have stayed underwater for so long had the kelpie not enchanted me. But then...

"But then he did exactly the same thing!" Sorcha exclaimed, indignant and angry as she began to finally make sense of her dream in dribs and drabs. "He made me undress him! He made me kiss him! He – he –"

When Sorcha began to cry she detested Lachlan for what he had done all the more with each and every tear. She rubbed her hands up and down her arms over the blanket; the wool scratched her skin in the process. Sorcha wished the scratching was worse – painful enough to knock some sense back into her.

For even though she had been enchanted in her dream she had *wanted* to give in to Lachlan. She had wanted it, though the circumstances had been horrible, and he pushed her away. Something had stopped Lachlan from continuing with his dangerous game.

Sorcha doubted it was a conscience.

He told me to go home. He said he'd deal with his own problems and that I should deal with mine. I have disappointed him.

Sorcha ran her fingers through her hair until it wasn't quite so tangled for lack of anything better to do. It smelled of the loch, which twisted her insides into knots until she thought she might be sick. But it sparked the beginning of anger, too.

"The kelpie would have helped," she murmured, somehow certain of it despite Lachlan's overwhelming doubts. "He said he was going to help. I would not have been a disappointment to Lachlan had he heard our entire conversation."

121

But it was too late. Lachlan was gone, leaving Sorcha morose, alone and naked miles and miles from home. She knew she should get dressed and find the closest village in order to buy food – her stomach was painfully aware of the fact she had very little of it left to eat – but Sorcha did not have the energy within her to do anything. All she wanted to do was huddle beneath her blanket, feel the autumn wind in her hair and decidedly *not* think about how much of a failure she was.

So absorbed was Sorcha in her own helplessness that she did not hear the sound of hooves approaching, nor the whinnying of a horse as it was ushered to a stop mere feet away from her tent. It was only when the dark leather boots of its rider appeared before Sorcha's downcast eyes that she finally realised she was no longer alone.

"Miss Darrow."

Sorcha did not have to look up to know who had spoken, yet she was shocked nonetheless that the man in question now stood before her.

"Mister Buchanan," she said, very, very quietly. "I must confess that I'd rather not have to endure your company at present. Please leave."

Murdoch chuckled entirely humourlessly. "After spending four days searching for you it is highly unlikely that I'll listen to your request. The terrain around the loch hardly makes for easy riding."

"What were you hoping to achieve by finding me? It should be clear to you by now that I do not wish to marry you."

"And what were *you* hoping to achieve by childishly running away, Miss Darrow?" Murdoch countered, kneeling down upon the grass until his face was level with Sorcha's. She recoiled immediately; he squeezed her cheeks together with an iron grip that Sorcha could never hope to shake off, forcing her to look at him.

She did not want to meet his gaze. She didn't want to, but she had to. Murdoch's dark, haunting eyes were so obviously furious that Sorcha pointlessly tried to back away once more. He merely tightened his hold on her face until she gasped in pain.

"L-let go!" Sorcha stammered. "Let go! You're hurting me!"

"You want me to consider the pain I'm putting you through when you don't abide by the same consideration for others?"

"I'm *sorry* that I didn't want to marry you but there was nothing you could have said to me to make me change my –"

"I'm not talking about me!" Murdoch bit out, leaning closer to Sorcha as he spoke. She could hardly make out where his pupils ended and his irises began, but the whites of his eyes were apparent all around them. "I'm referring to your father."

Sorcha's insides froze. "My – my father? What about my father?"

"He collapsed when he realised you'd run off."

"He...is he alright? Is he –"

"I wouldn't know!" Murdoch yelled. "He was still unconscious in his bed when I decided to look for you myself. A doctor from the city was on his way to Darach when I left. Are you really so selfish that you hadn't thought of your father's poor health when you ran off? Or how your disappearing stunt would affect your

123

mother? And for what – to sit cold, penniless and alone on some anonymous stretch of sand miles from home? Either you are a feckless, blind fool, Miss Darrow, or you are a callous and cold-hearted woman. I do not know which of those is worse, all things considered."

Sorcha went slack against his grip. She couldn't breathe. Couldn't think. Even when Murdoch eventually let her go to collapse onto the grass beside her Sorcha's sightless gaze did not waver from where his eyes had been locked on hers.

She vaguely heard him sigh. "I thought you were more mature than this, Sorcha Darrow."

Sorcha perked up at the sound of her name. She had not heard her true first name spoken aloud in a week; to hear it now – from Murdoch's lips – was odd enough to drag her back to the present. She glanced at the man. Looking closer she realised that Murdoch clearly hadn't slept much over the past few days. His curly hair was dishevelled, his boots were dull and muddy and his clothes were, for lack of a better word, decidedly ruffled.

He cast his gaze over to his horse and let out a low whistle. "Galileo, come here," he told the stallion, who raised his head from the loch's edge where he was drinking to look at his rider. The man's horse was huge in stature, with a sleek, midnight-black coat and an enviably thick, flowing mane. He was undoubtedly the most beautiful horse Sorcha had ever seen. Murdoch waved an insistent hand towards Galileo when the horse did not move until, with an impatient flick of his tail, he trotted over to the pair of them.

"Galileo?" Sorcha wondered aloud when he stopped in front of her and lowered his head. She raised a careful hand to his muzzle, stroking the soft hair there when Galileo allowed her to do so. His eyes were a deep chocolate brown; Sorcha smiled when he blinked his long lashes across them. *If it wasn't for those warm eyes he could be mistaken for a kelpie.*

"My father named him," Murdoch said, turning slightly to face Sorcha. "He was fond of philosophers and men of science."

"Was?"

"He died last month."

Galileo nudged his nose against Sorcha's cheek insistently, only stopping when she placed her forehead against his long face. She glanced at Murdoch out of the corner of her eye. "You did not tell me he passed away."

"You did not give me the opportunity to tell you."

All the anger had disappeared from Murdoch's eyes, leaving only the emptiness Sorcha had witnessed back when she first met the man. She couldn't help but wonder what had caused such nothingness to fill a person's soul, though knowing that the man's father had so recently passed away went some way in explaining it.

"...I am sorry for your loss," Sorcha murmured, looking away once more as her face flushed in shame. "And I am sorry I ran away. I truly am. You are right; it was childish and selfish of me. But I – I had my reasons."

"Reasons more important than the love you hold for your parents? For your duty to your family and to the land you profess to adore so much?"

Sorcha bristled at the accusations yet she forced her anger away. For how was she supposed to tell Murdoch about Lachlan and his curse? She somehow doubted that, after all his years living in London, he would still believe in faeries.

When Murdoch raised a hand past Sorcha's face to stroke Galileo's cheek she instinctively flinched away. "Why do you do that?" he asked, frowning at her.

"Do what?"

"Avert your eyes and avoid my touch. What have I done to scare you so?"

"I...nothing." Sorcha had no words to explain how she felt towards Murdoch – especially not now that she was beginning to realise her first impressions of him may well have been wrong. "It is nothing. I'm simply not used to –"

"Men seeking to marry you?"

Sorcha's lips twisted into the smallest of smiles at his suggestion. She risked a look at Murdoch's face; he was watching her with the same intensity that had filled his eyes the night he'd found Sorcha in her father's study.

"Strangers," she corrected. "I am scared of strangers. Particularly those from London."

Murdoch scoffed at her answer. "I *am* from here! About eight miles from this exact spot, in fact."

"No local would go about wandering the loch-side *on a horse* in such fancy clothes," Sorcha said, pointing at his boots. "You have ruined those."

"I found you, though, so I'd wager it was worth ruining a pair of shoes. And besides, the advantage of being wealthy is that it is easy to replace that which has been destroyed."

"Not all things," Sorcha muttered, thinking of her parents and, despite herself, Lachlan. "There are some things money can never repair."

Murdoch sighed heavily. Then he brushed off his coat, stood up and held a hand out to Sorcha.

"You are right, Miss Darrow," he said. "Fortunately for you, a deep-felt apology can fix what you have broken with your parents. Now, would you allow me to escort you home or will I have to tie you to Galileo and drag you back?"

Sorcha laughed softly at the ridiculous idea but quickly grew serious once more. Lachlan had told her to solve her own problems. He was right, and so was Murdoch. She couldn't keep running away or hoping that faeries and kelpies would somehow fix her life for her.

She took hold of Murdoch's hand; he tightened his fingers around hers.

"Yes, take me home if you will, Mr Buchanan."

CHAPTER SEVENTEEN

Lachlan

I can solve this. I can murder my stepfamily without my full powers. I can definitely do this.

Lachlan repeated these thoughts over and over in his head until there was nothing else left inside of him. Before his curse this would have meant ignoring his feelings for Ailith and pretending he wasn't mourning his mother's death.

Now it meant acting as if what he'd done to Clara wasn't reprehensible at all. The worst part of it was that, a week ago, he wouldn't have thought twice about the morality of enchanting a human in their sleep. It wasn't something a faerie *should* have to think about. Humans were humans, and Lachlan the Seelie Prince.

But Clara was different and he knew it.

He hated that he knew it.

Forget her, you fool. She cannot help you. She never could.

Lachlan did not know where he was going, just as he did not know what he was doing. He pelted through the forest, which grew darker and more ominous around him the deeper into its centre he went. For a moment Lachlan entertained the idea of creeping back into the central faerie realm to find a member of the Court willing to help him. Ailith, even. But something told Lachlan that both Innis and Fergus would be keeping a keen eye out for him, and that he would find no help from those otherwise most willing to grant it.

No; Lachlan was on his own.

"If only that wizard were still around," he muttered, taking a rest beneath the rotting remains of a fallen pine tree. *He might not be able to lift my curse but his magic may well be capable of dealing a fatal blow to my damned false family.* But Lachlan did not have access to his full powers, so he could not locate the man nor his charming companion. Either he picked up their scent and tracked it down to where they were or he did not find them at all. *It might be a fool's errand. I might waste too much precious time seeking them out. Fergus' coronation is a mere week away.*

Lachlan, frustrated, collapsed into a pile of blackened leaves. He rolled around in them, willing them to scratch an itch they could never reach. For what other choice did he have but to at least try and seek out the wizard? There were no other viable options left in front of Lachlan to explore.

"The girl," Lachlan said, getting back up to his feet and shaking dirt and leaves from his fur, "track the girl's scent. She was more pronounced."

He headed off in the general direction that he had first met Julian and his golden-haired partner, hoping that he could pick up a trail from the clearing where they had been looking for a faerie turned into a fox.

Well, they found one, Lachlan thought as he picked up his pace through the dense, prickly undergrowth of the forest. *I wonder how many of us there are, hiding amongst the foxes who are foxes and the foxes who were once humans. Clearly we are not as rare as I had once believed.*

And then Lachlan heard a noise that froze him to the spot in an instant. An animal crying out, clearly in dreadful pain. To hear an animal vocalise that it was hurt meant it was likely close to death and therefore no longer cared about being found by something that might eat it.

"I am hungry, I suppose," Lachlan decided aloud, swinging to his right and darting towards the source of the noise. He could not tell what kind of animal had screamed; it sounded unlike a deer or a rabbit or a pheasant. But regardless of what it was, if it was dying it would be in no position to defend itself from Lachlan and his sharp, insistent teeth.

When the animal voiced its anguish again Lachlan knew he was almost upon it. The sound was harsh and tragic in his pointed ears; he fought the urge to cringe away from it. He slowed to a soft, careful crawl when he spied the hollowed-out remains of a gnarled tree trunk from which Lachlan could hear his prey breathing, fitful and desperate. He sniffed the air; it smelled of blood and encroaching death and –

"A faerie," he gasped, leaping the final few bounds to the hollow tree to see who was lying there.

It was a fox.

The poor creature was lying on its side, struggling to breathe. Its fur was greying round the muzzle, with a tail gone limp and lifeless. Its eyes were filmy and milky-white, and crusted round the edges. It had been shot in the stomach, though going by the festering of the wound the bullet had been fired days and days ago. Lachlan wrinkled his nose at the smell of it. Every one of his fox instincts told him to run away; it was his faerie instincts that kept him rooted to the spot.

"Who are you?" he asked, taking another step or two towards the damned animal. "You are not – you are not what you seem."

The fox merely stared at him with blind, unseeing eyes. It yelped helplessly, kicking out a leg as if to warn Lachlan away. He wondered if he had mistaken the scent of a faerie, for he could no longer smell it. But then, as if the wind had changed direction, his nose picked it up once more.

"A creature of no consequence," the fox croaked out with a surprisingly melodic, masculine voice, though his mouth seemed to struggle to form the words as if he had forgotten how to speak. "A fool, even."

"But not a human. A faerie."

He nodded. "Once. But I made a mistake, and now I am a fox. In a few minutes I will be a dead one."

Lachlan bent low to nudge his nose against the fox's muzzle. "How long have you been a fox?"

"F-four years," he coughed. Lachlan backed away, for there was blood in the fox's spittle. "Four years, and with every month I have been less a faerie and more a fox. But I thought...I thought I had more time. I should have had more time."

131

Lachlan's heart beat painfully fast. "What do you mean, you *should* have had more time?"

The fox twisted its head to point at the wound in its stomach for a moment before burying its nose back into the dirt. "Shot," he struggled to say. "Injuries to this cursed form take more and more of yourself away. And this one...I knew I would lose myself after this. But the wound is fatal, and I am glad of it."

"There must – there must be something that can be done!" Lachlan cried, feeling bile rise in his throat as he watched the dying creature in dismay. "There *must* be something! Who cursed you?"

"I...dare not say."

Lachlan stood up as tall as he could make himself. He stared down hard upon the faerie-fox. "You are Seelie, yes?"

The animal just barely managed to nod his assent.

"Then as your crown prince and should-be king, I demand that you tell me who cursed you."

The fox's sightless, rheumy eyes grew wide. He lifted his nose towards Lachlan, sniffing at the air until he gasped. "You truly are Lachlan, the golden prince. How did you come to be this way?"

"I suspect it was the same way as you. So tell me: who did this?"

Silence. Lachlan could hear the gentle hooting of a wood pigeon upon the wind. Then the other fox shifted in the dirt and raised its head once more. "It was Innis, the Unseelie King's brother. He – I opposed his marriage to Queen Evanna. I did not trust him, nor his intentions. I do not mean to imply that our good queen did not know what she was doing in marrying him!" the fox quickly added on, to the detriment of his laboured breathing. He coughed and spluttered until his greying muzzle was stained crimson.

Lachlan licked the fox's ear. "It is alright. Speak freely."

When the fox recovered from his coughing attack he continued his explanation, though his voice was far less substantial than it had been before. "He cursed me. Innis saw that I would not stay silent on the matter. He misliked the idea that I might vocalise my opposition far more publicly at their wedding, so he cursed me."

Four years ago, Lachlan thought, feeling as if something had finally clicked into place in his head. *My mother got married four years ago. I should have worked this out the moment Julian told me of the fox he met.*

"A wizard came upon you, after you'd been cursed," Lachlan told the fox, who almost seemed to smile.

"He did. A good human, and a skilled one. But even he could do nothing for me."

"I met him a sennight ago," Lachlan said. "He was looking for you. I think he wanted to see how you were doing, though since he could do nothing to help me I doubt he'd have been able to help you now, either."

"It would have been...good to see him. But I would not want him to see me like this."

The fox whined; Lachlan lay down beside him, for he did not know what else to do. Neither of them spoke for a while, until Lachlan began to wonder if the faerie beside him had lost himself entirely.

But then he spoke once more. "My prince...you must not - please do not let Innis and his kind take your mother's crown. I fear it will be the end of all the Seelie."

Lachlan barked. "I will do everything I can to ensure that never happens. Everything. You can be sure of that."

Everything including making a deal with a kelpie, he realised. *I should not have left Clara. I should have given her idea a final try. She said the kelpie planned to help; even if it meant to fool her I could still outsmart it and steal its bridle.*

Lachlan's heart twisted at the thought. He should have gone into the loch as soon as Clara disappeared beneath the surface. He should never have left her alone in the first place. It was because of *him* that she'd almost died.

He would not make the same mistake again.

"What is your name, faerie?" Lachlan asked, turning to look at his doomed compatriot when he did not answer. In the dim twilight he could have been sleeping, but that, of course, was not the case.

The fox was dead.

Lachlan cried out in fright, jumping back as if he had been struck by lightning. For before his very eyes lay his own fate if he did not undo the curse Fergus had cast. With a final whine for the dead faerie, Lachlan turned and crashed through the rapidly-darkening forest, barely aware of the trees and ferns and birds and deer all around him as he made his way back to the shore of Loch Lomond. He *was* aware of anything that might hurt him, however, and avoided every thorn and sharp stone protruding from the ground as if his life depended on it, for it did.

It was not difficult to track Clara down; Lachlan knew her scent by heart now. But as he drew closer and closer to the fire burning down to coals outside her tent he realised he could smell something else. *Someone* else.

Clara was not alone.

CHAPTER EIGHTEEN

Sorcha

"Won't you ride upon Galileo with me, Miss Darrow?"

"Won't you give the poor creature a break and walk on your own two feet, instead?"

Sorcha didn't expect Murdoch to actually get off his horse - much less in response to such an obvious jibe - but he did. He tucked Galileo's reins beneath the saddle and patted the animal's flank gently to let him know he could wander free for a while. Galileo subsequently trotted on far ahead, pausing to chew on several mouthfuls of grass until both Murdoch and Sorcha caught up with him once more.

"Are you happy now?" Murdoch asked as they walked along the stony shore. "Walking on my own two -"

The rest of his sentence was lost to a yell as the man tripped and just barely avoided crashing to the ground. Sorcha barked out a laugh before she could stop herself.

"Have you perhaps grown too accustomed to carriages and horses from your time in London, Mr Buchanan?" she teased. "Clearly you need to spend more time using your own legs."

Murdoch ran both of his hands through his dark, curly hair whilst he regained his composure. He threw Sorcha a sly smile that she didn't entirely understand. "Clearly indeed," he said, before striding on ahead so quickly that Sorcha had to jog to try and keep up.

"Now you are being unfair!"

"You were the one who insisted I walk," he called out over his shoulder, the words accompanied by a radiant, wicked grin that could easily have rivalled Lachlan's.

Do not think about him. He is gone.

"Why are you in such a rush?" Sorcha asked when she finally reached Murdoch's side.

He raised an eyebrow at Sorcha as though the answer was obvious. "We need to find somewhere to stay the night, of course. There should be a small settlement less than a mile away, if I remember your father's maps correctly."

Sorcha looked out across the loch; the sun was low on the horizon, reflecting off the water with a dazzling brightness that she could have watched, entranced, for the rest of her life. "I would rather camp," she uttered, thinking of the kelpie. "I do not want to stay with other people right now."

When she looked at Murdoch his expression was coloured by incredulity; Sorcha fully expected him to put his foot down and march her to the closest hamlet regardless of her wishes. It was therefore to her surprise when he said, "I suppose there's no harm in camping. The weather is fair and you are clearly rather adept at it. Do you have a location in mind?"

Sorcha blinked several times before answering. "Are you...serious?"

"Only if you are. Would you like me to collect some firewood whilst you pitch the tent wherever it is you'd like to put it?"

Sorcha nodded numbly in response, wrapping her hand around Galileo's reins to pull him along with her until they found a promising stretch of grass. It was closer to the forest than it was the loch, though Sorcha could still see the water, so she was satisfied with the placement for her tent.

As the sun bled out across the horizon she began to sing the first poem that came to her head as she pitched the tent and, then, rummaged through Galileo's saddle bag for a brush to smooth out his hair. The horse whinnied and pawed at the ground in satisfaction when Sorcha began to gently brush down his face and neck, singing softly in his ear all the while.

"O can ye sew cushions,

And can ye sew sheets,

And can ye sing ballalloo when the bairn greets?

And hee and haw birdie

And hee and haw lamb

And hee and haw, birdie, my bonnie wee lamb.

And hush a -"

"I love that song."

The rest of the poem was lost to the air. Sorcha

paused in her brushing of Galileo to turn around. Murdoch had returned from the forest, arms laden with fallen branches; going by his relaxed stance and the slight smile on his face he had been listening to Sorcha for some time.

She laughed self-consciously. "It is a poem, not a song. The melody I made up last summer, when my aunt came to visit with my crying cousin." Sorcha continued brushing Galileo, reaching his flank before continuing to recount the memory. "I'd carry him – my baby cousin – to the shore and sing the lullaby until he finally quietened, and then he would sleep all night. My aunt called it a gift from God himself."

Murdoch chuckled at the notion, though he cocked his head to one side and regarded Sorcha with curious eyes. "Why does the tune sound so familiar, if you constructed it yourself?"

She shrugged. "Perhaps you happened to be visiting Loch Lomond at the time and came across me singing. It is possible; I often do not realise other people are around when I am lost in a song. Such as precisely one minute ago, for example."

Murdoch stood on the spot and thought about this for a while, then dropped the branches in his arms to the grass in order to begin constructing a fire.

"It is good that I brought extra supplies with me considering how little food you have, Miss Darrow," he murmured some time later, when the fire was crackling merrily beneath a pot of bubbling rabbit stew. "Tell me, what were you going to do when you ran out of food and money?"

Sorcha sat a respectable distance away from Murdoch before replying, "I do not know. I hadn't thought that far ahead. To be honest I hadn't thought things through at all."

A large part of me assumed I'd be living in the Seelie Court – whether I willed it or not – once Lachlan got his body back. Sorcha shivered at the thought. She had been so dreadfully careless, putting her life into the hands of a wily faerie.

"Come sit closer to the fire, Miss Darrow," Murdoch said, clearly mistaking her shiver for a sign that she was cold. Sorcha supposed she *was* cold, and she certainly did not wish to tell Murdoch what had truly caused the shiver, so she somewhat timidly inched closer to the fire – and to him.

He would think me mad if he learned the primary reason for why I ran away from home, she thought, tucking her hair behind her ear and her knees to her chest. *Never mind the fact I almost died yesterday. It feels like it was years ago.*

"What is on your mind?" Murdoch asked softly. He ladled out a portion of stew into a bowl for Sorcha; she took it with a nod and a grateful word of thanks. The steaming bowl warmed her hands and chased the chill of her near-death encounter away until it felt like a distant nightmare.

"I do not know," Sorcha replied, for in truth she couldn't pinpoint exactly what *was* on it. There was too much rattling inside her skull to isolate one single, tangible answer for Murdoch, so instead of elaborating Sorcha held the bowl of stew to her lips and took an experimental sip.

Her eyes grew bright; she stared, impressed, at Murdoch. "This is wonderful, Mr Buchanan!"

He seemed pleased by the compliment. "I enjoyed cooking with the servants down in London, especially because my father worked such long hours," he explained, twisting and turning the ladle within the pot on the fire as he did so. "He was always craving good, Scottish fare, especially when he'd been eating out most nights at his club with clients. I knew I wasn't as good a cook as my mother – she loved the kitchen so much that she'd always refused to have anyone else cook when we lived up here – but it made my father happy nonetheless that I tried to recreate her favourite recipes."

"You miss him."

Murdoch stared into the fire with an unreadable expression. Sorcha was caught between the desire to touch his arm reassuringly and back away from the glassiness of his eyes.

"One has to lose those they love, eventually," he said, more to the fire than to Sorcha. "It is an irrefutable, immutable truth. Loneliness is something you get used to, until you no longer recognise it as something that needs fixing. You simply *are* lonely, and that is that."

"That...is unbelievably sad, Mr Buchanan," Sorcha told him, the words so quiet they were almost lost entirely to the cracking of the firewood as it burned to ashes. "That is no way to live your life."

"Sometimes it is the only way, Miss Darrow. Now come, we should retire for the night. If we start up early in the morning we should reach Darach by evening. I shall change clothes outside the tent to give you some privacy as you change yours."

Sorcha was torn between following Murdoch's request to get into the tent and insisting she stay by the fire, but something told her that Murdoch would not let

her out of his sight for long either way. And she was tired
- painfully so - which ultimately made up her mind.
With a final glance at the dancing flames
Sorcha retreated into the tent, quickly stripping off the
layers of clothing she'd been wearing and changing into
her father's shirt. She crawled beneath her favourite
woollen blanket and huddled into the corner of the tent
- as far away as she could get from Murdoch's huge frame
when he came in to lie down behind her.

There was an awkward beat of silence. Two.

Then Murdoch snaked an arm around Sorcha's
waist, causing her to yelp in fright. He pulled her
towards him as if she weighed nothing at all.

"Did you really think I'd let you lie so far away, Miss
Darrow?" he murmured into her ear. Sorcha tried to
shift her position so that she wasn't so close to the man,
but her struggle was pointless.

Murdoch was too strong.

"What do you imagine I can do two feet away from
you, Mr Buchanan?" she breathed, trying once more to
wriggle away from his arm to no avail.

He snickered. "Why, run away in the dead of night,
of course. You have done it before, after all, when I was
wide awake and watching your bedroom door. I have no
doubt you could easily do it again. I'm taking no
chances."

Sorcha twisted her neck around to look at Murdoch;
the dim light from the dying fire outside turned his eyes
to smouldering coals. She gulped. "I will not run away,
I swear it."

He merely tightened his grip. "Even if you mean it, I
will not let go."

She frowned. "And why not?"

Murdoch's answer was silence, though his lips twisted into the faintest hint of a smile. Resigned, frustrated and more than a little intimidated, Sorcha turned back around and closed her eyes, determined to get to sleep as quickly as possible. She had grown used to the sound of Lachlan-the-fox breathing by her head every night; having a human breathing behind her would be no different.

Except that it was, and Sorcha was achingly aware of it. Even an hour laden with fruitless attempts at sleeping later she knew that Murdoch was no more unconscious than she was. The tension in his body against hers told Sorcha he had no intention whatsoever of sleeping until he was quite certain that Sorcha herself was definitely no longer awake.

Her skin began to tingle as she thought of Murdoch, dark eyes alert and watching her. She squirmed as if she were a snake trying to shirk off its skin in an attempt to chase the uneasy feeling away.

Murdoch brought his mouth down to her ear. "I'd stop moving if I were you, Sorcha."

Sorcha bit her lip – both in response to Murdoch's solitary use of her given name and the tone in which he'd uttered it. It left no room for alternate interpretations of his current mood.

This is dangerous, Sorcha thought, a red-hot flush crawling up her skin when she found herself once more shifting against Murdoch despite his warning.

With gentle fingers, Murdoch swept Sorcha's hair away from her shoulder and kissed her neck. She sighed in response, though she hadn't meant to.

She did not know what she was *meant* to do – or want – at all.

"Are you still frightened of me?" Murdoch asked. "I cannot tell you how much I'd rather you were not." His voice was rough and low and excited, which ultimately sent a shiver of fear running down Sorcha's spine. But she was eager to feel it, and to hear more of Murdoch's enticing voice whispering in her ear. There was a pure, unbridled desire within it that held no promises of eternal imprisonment in a faerie realm. It spoke of *now,* and no consequences, and no thinking at all.

It was seductive. It was terrifying.

Murdoch's hand roamed from Sorcha's waist to her thigh, and his fingertips slid beneath the hem of her father's shirt. She did not stop him.

Am I doing this because of Lachlan? Sorcha thought, though her body was yelling at her to ignore the faerie and focus on the man who was leaving a trail of hungry kisses down her neck. *Because of what he did to me? Or because he did not trust that I could help him, and he left? Am I really so childish and reactionary?*

But in thinking about Lachlan a wave of familiar, unnatural heaviness invaded Sorcha's brain. Her eyelids fluttered. Her limbs grew slack. Her breathing slowed.

Murdoch noticed her change of state immediately. He sat up and gently pushed Sorcha onto her back. "Sorcha – Miss Darrow? What is wrong?"

But Sorcha could not answer him; she had been dragged into unconsciousness.

She did not know if she was relieved to escape the man, and what she had been about to do with him, or not.

CHAPTER NINETEEN

Lachlan

"Clara, I am sorry I had to put you to sleep once more –"

"What are you doing here, Lachlan?"

Clara's stare cut through Lachlan like a knife. It was obvious she was not happy to see him. He took a step towards her, almost crying with relief at having his own feet back. "Clara –"

"What do you want?"

She wasn't in the mood for any of Lachlan's usual charming, enchanting words, that much was clear. He couldn't blame her.

He lowered his head. "I am sorry, Clara Darrow. I am sorrier than I have ever been before. It is not a feeling I am used to experiencing."

A pause. "...and what, exactly, are you sorry *for*?"

"For leaving," Lachlan said, risking another step towards Clara when she did not back away. She cast her gaze up from his feet all the way to his eyes, searching for a sign that Lachlan was somehow lying. "I was angry that you'd almost died for me," he continued. "You, a human, die for *me*? For trying to help me in a situation where I could not help myself? It's pathetic."

Clara quirked an eyebrow. "Either your apology has a mind of its own or you do not sincerely wish to give it."

"I do!" Lachlan insisted. He closed the distance between them and enveloped Clara's hands in his own, squeezing them slightly too hard in his desperation for her to understand him.

Her expression grew uncertain at the gesture. "Lachlan –"

"I should never have let you go into the loch alone. You even *asked* me to join you. You asked me, and I arrogantly declined. The least I could have done to save my own skin was to get it wet in the process."

"And...is that all you're sorry for?" Clara asked, keeping her eyes on their hands as she entwined her fingers with Lachlan's. He didn't dare smile at the whispering of her skin against his, though he wanted to.

"Of course not. Of course not, Clara. What I did to you...even if I was angry and hurt and worried I should never have done what I did to you. I should never have enchanted you."

"Even though, from the very beginning, that's what you've intended to do once you have your body back?"

"That's...that's different," Lachlan muttered, averting his eyes from Clara's. He found that he could not stand to see her blue and green irises up close, so full of light and life that he had, barely a day ago, snuffed out.

"And what is that supposed to mean, Lachlan? How is it different?"

"Because one was supposed to teach you a lesson, and the other – the other..." He sighed, breaking away from Clara in order to run a hand through the unbraided side of his hair. He glanced at her; Clara was watching him with an understandably confused expression on her face, but then she frowned and crossed her arms over her chest.

"How is enchanting me forever different from what you did in my dream last night?" she asked again.

Lachlan almost laughed, for to him it was obvious. "Because I *want* you to live in the Seelie Court – with me," he said. Clara's cheeks turned pink at his admission, so Lachlan eagerly admitted to more. "I want you to live there and sing there and love the forest and adore me whilst I adore you. And I want you to be happy. Clara, a life with my kind would make you far happier than the life set out before you by your parents. You are too special for the realm of ordinary men. It –"

"You could have simply *asked* me, Lachlan."

He paused. "I did, did I not? When –"

"You asked if I would consider giving you my full name if I ended up being forced to marry Mr Buchanan," Clara corrected. "That is *not* the same as asking me if I would, of my own volition, live in the faerie realm."

Oh.

And then, to his and Clara's surprise, Lachlan *did* burst out laughing. It was a peal of genuine, good-for-his-soul laughter, so infectious that eventually Clara joined in, too. "I guess it's not in my nature to do such a human thing as to ask you to do something willingly."

"You'd ask if you knew you could trick me into staying forever, with no opportunity to ever leave," Clara replied, still giggling softly.

He shrugged. "What can I say? I am a faerie. You cannot hold me to your mortal standards."

"And you cannot hold me to yours."

"Well met, Clara."

"So what do we do now?"

Lachlan sat down, for the first time taking in his surroundings as Clara knelt beside him. Her dream was dyed the colours of a burning coal; Lachlan reckoned she must have been thinking of the smouldering fire outside her tent.

"We find the kelpie," he said. He slid his hand over Clara's, a smile creeping across his lips when she once more interlaced her fingers with his. He turned his head to look at her. "But no spontaneous diving into the loch. We plan this properly."

Clara nodded. "Properly. Which means...?"

"That we need to make it show itself. We cannot deal with it as an inconsequential shape in the water."

"He," Clara corrected. Her eyes glazed over slightly. "It's a he. The kelpie, I mean."

"Should I be jealous of this kelpie, Clara?"

She rested her head on Lachlan's shoulder. "Perhaps. He does lord over the loch, my most beloved place, after all."

"I thought you loved the forest and the loch equally?"

She snickered. "I do. But you and the forest are already here, beside me. And you are jealous. A human girl could not ask for more...however dangerous a jealous faerie might be."

Clara's words were playful as if she did not take them seriously – as if she did not take Lachlan's *feelings* seriously. He guessed he could not blame her. But her assumption was not wrong; a jealous faerie was dangerous indeed.

Lachlan curled a finger beneath Clara's chin and raised her lips to his. "If I asked you now," he whispered against them, "would you say yes?"

Clara stilled. Her beautiful eyes were steady and sure. "I could not live with you the way you want me to."

"But you would consider it, on your own terms? You would?"

She smiled mischievously. Lachlan wanted nothing more than to kiss it away and make it his. "That's something to discuss once you have your body back for good, do you not think?"

"I –"

It was Lachlan's turn to freeze. For in that moment there was something off about Clara's dream. Something *familiarly* off. Lachlan could sense a darkness – a heaviness – that told him they were no longer alone.

Clara bit her lip, concerned at the change in him. "Lachlan, what is it?"

"You cannot feel it," he said, eyes wide as he watched her. It was obvious she did not know what was going on. "You cannot –"

Get out of here.

Lachlan got to his feet and looked around wildly, though he could see nothing that had not been there before. But the heaviness he could feel got even more oppressive until Lachlan could hardly stand.

Leave her alone. She is not yours.

Clara stood up and tried to touch Lachlan's arm. He shrugged her off. "Lachlan," she asked again, "what is it?"

"We –"

And then, as if he had never been anywhere else in the first place, Lachlan found himself back inside his fox body, curled up in a ball behind Clara's tent. He was being prodded with a stick.

"Get away from here, fox," urged a voice Lachlan did not recognise. He scrambled to his feet, backing away from the stick before it could hit him again. When he looked up he saw that the voice belonged to the man who had been travelling with Clara, enveloped in shadow and smoke from the remains of the fire.

"Leave before I make you wish you had," he said. Though his voice was hushed Lachlan felt as if he had shouted. "I won't have vermin near my future wife."

So this is Mr Murdoch Buchanan.

Lachlan wanted to open his mouth and tell the man that Clara did not want him. That *he* should be the one to leave. But Lachlan didn't, because right now the stranger could easily kill him. And he was a fox; he was not supposed to speak. So Lachlan did the only thing he could.

He ran.

But he would not go far, and tomorrow he would

contact Clara again.

It's time for her to stage another escape, he thought, grinning wickedly at the idea of Mr Buchanan discovering his betrothed had, once more, ran from him.

For a faerie. For Lachlan.

CHAPTER TWENTY

Sorcha

Sorcha and Murdoch were but three miles from Darach and the sun was low. Sorcha had been sat upon Galileo all afternoon – having finally given into Murdoch's insistence that she should, at least for a while, ride on the horse. Given that her muscles ached from a solid sennight of non-stop walking Sorcha was eager for the respite it gave her feet.

Murdoch was not riding with her, choosing instead to walk by Galileo's side, the horse's reins looped twice around his left hand. She wondered if he was keeping his distance because of what had transpired in the tent the night before.

He had not once asked why Sorcha had fallen unconscious.

He must be suspicious, she thought. *He found me asleep on my bedroom floor nine days ago, too. He must know that something isn't right.*

But, even so, Murdoch remained resolutely quiet on

the matter, which only served to unsettle Sorcha further. She did not let it show on her face, of course, for ultimately she had much bigger problems to deal with than what Murdoch thought of her fainting habits.

He may well be thinking that I need to see a doctor and that is all. An understandable belief, given what happened.

Sorcha's face flushed as she recalled exactly what *happened* before Lachlan had driven her to sleep. She stole a glance at Murdoch only to realise that he was staring at her. She recoiled from him, forgetting that she was on Galileo, and was only saved from falling heavily onto her back by the man's iron grip on her arm.

"Just what are you thinking, Miss Darrow?!" he exclaimed, a frown shadowing his black eyes. "You need to be careful when riding such a large horse. Have you gone mad?"

"Perhaps..." she muttered, rubbing away the marks his fingers had left on her arm as her face grew ever more crimson out of sheer embarrassment. Sorcha was a more than serviceable rider; to have slipped from a horse at her age was folly. *It shouldn't matter if Murdoch thinks me an idiot. It shouldn't. After all, I need to break away from him to help Lachlan as soon as I can. And then...*

She sighed. After having spent the past two days with him Sorcha had to admit that Murdoch Buchanan was, as her father had told her, a decent man. He was honest, well-spoken and good company. His conversation was interesting. He was more that easy to look at. And when he'd snaked a hand around Sorcha's waist, whispered in her ear and kissed her neck –

"Truly, Miss Darrow, what *are* you thinking about?"

Murdoch asked insistently. Sorcha looked away, desperately trying to calm her red and flustered appearance.

"You said you wish to preserve the area as it is," she said, voice too quick and high-pitched to convince Murdoch that she'd truthfully been mulling over such a thing, "but you are still an investor. What would you intend to do after we – *if* we – married?"

Murdoch was silent for a while, clearly deep in thought. The quiet stretched out long enough for Sorcha to regain her composure once more; by the time the man was ready to respond she found that she could look at him again.

"I suppose you are right," Murdoch said, smiling up at Sorcha. "Certainly the company I work for would expect me to get *something* out of the land."

"So you would not resign and simply...live up here?"

He laughed incredulously. "Miss Darrow, I may be wealthy but I'm not *that* wealthy. Even if I sold my father's property in London I would not have enough saved up to allow us to live a comfortable life over the next few decades without any additional income – especially when I'd have to cover the deficit for the farmers your father has been paying up to now."

It was Sorcha's turn to be silent. She had not truly thought about what it meant to protect the people who lived on her father's land. What it cost to do so, in more than money. William Darrow was tired and sick; though he loved every one of his tenants dearly they were literally taking years off his life.

"Papa never speaks to me about the financial pressure he's under," Sorcha mumbled, feeling ashamed, "even though he taught me how to do the books and how to collect the rent and made me memorise the names of each and every farmer in the area. But he avoids talking to me about anything that causes him trouble. I wish he would."

"Then perhaps you could start by not running away, to prove you are responsible and trustworthy."

Sorcha cringed at the remark but, when she caught Murdoch's eye, it became apparent he had not meant it unkindly. "You mean well," he said, "but you do not truly understand the consequences of your actions yet, nor how the world truly works. Perhaps that is your father's fault for shielding you from so much."

"I –"

"I am not criticising him," Murdoch interrupted. He scratched Galileo's neck; the horse whinnied happily. "Your father is a great man. I respect him deeply. But there are things you must learn, Miss Darrow, whether you wish to or not."

Sorcha didn't know what to say. Murdoch was right, and it brought her right back to reality after her dream the night before. Though her memory of it was hazy towards the end – Lachlan had disappeared rather abruptly – Sorcha had been left in no doubt that the faerie sincerely wished for her to leave behind her human life altogether to live with him.

Could I really do that? she wondered. *If Lachlan agreed to allow me to stay human, and to come and go as I please, could I throw away my responsibilities in order to live within the Seelie Court?*

Sorcha's gaze fell upon Murdoch once more. He ran a hand across his jaw, where several days' worth of dark stubble covered his skin. *He would not look so bad if he chose not to shave it off,* Sorcha decided. *Though it would itch like my father's beard does against my face when he kisses me.* She shook her head to chase the ridiculous thought away, horrified, before her cheeks were set on fire once more.

"To answer your original question, though," Murdoch said, cutting through Sorcha's entirely impure thoughts with an almost knowing smile upon his face, "I do have some ideas."

"Oh?"

"I was considering encouraging tourism around the loch – don't look at me like that, Sorcha."

How easily Murdoch slipped into using her first name, as he had done the evening before. Sorcha could not say she disliked it.

"What kind of tourism are you proposing, then?" she asked.

"Boating. Ferry rides. Controlled tours that mean large groups of tourists are never left alone to cause any harm to the countryside – accidental or otherwise. The loch is large and beautiful; there is plenty of space to indulge tourists upon it without disrupting local life."

Sorcha frowned, thinking of the kelpie. "And you... you do not worry for the tourists?"

"And why would I *worry* for them?"

"They might become distracted," she said, more to herself than to Murdoch. "They might get dragged beneath the surface of the loch. They might –"

Murdoch's laugh cut across Sorcha's concerns. "Are you referring to the kelpie? The one in your book?"

She nodded, though his laugh made Sorcha feel altogether rather silly for voicing her worries.

"I must profess to having lived in London far too long to believe such fairy stories," Murdoch said. He watched the sun burning low in the sky, a thoughtful expression on his face. "As a child things were different. Whenever I swam in the loch I'd imagine a black horse standing on the very surface of the water, encouraging me to get further and further from the shore until I was too tired to swim back. But that's all it was: my imagination. Such things as kelpies are not real."

Sorcha was silent, for she knew perfectly well that Murdoch was wrong. But she could not blame him for not believing in the kelpie – he truly had spent too long away from home, surrounded by those who would laugh at him in much the same way he'd laughed at Sorcha for thinking such things as faeries and water horses were real.

The two of them did not speak for a while, the quiet stretching out around them like the long shadows caused by the setting sun. Not too far in front of them a small part of the loch diverted into the forest, narrowing as if it were a burn. Sorcha knew it expanded again to form a pool not too far off the path through the trees. A small waterfall crashed into it; she used to disappear there on adventures with her childhood friends, daring one another to leap from the top of the waterfall into the dark, glassy water below.

And then Sorcha had an idea.

Lachlan said we need to make the kelpie show itself. That we need to get it away from the depths of the loch. So wouldn't an offshoot of it nestled in the forest be the perfect location to try and make him appear? The pool is barely twice my height deep.

"There is – there is somewhere I'd like to go before we head back to my parents, Mr Buchanan," Sorcha said, breaking the silence between them. "It's –"

"Are you referring to the waterfall pool?" he asked, leading Galileo down a path that crossed through the forest. "I must confess I was considering visiting it, too. My parents and I used to go on long walks simply to see it. I imagine it is beautiful at twilight."

Sorcha found herself smiling at the man in response. *Perhaps Murdoch is not such a lost cause. He might not believe in faeries anymore but his love for the land upon which he grew up is as genuine as my own.*

Murdoch lit a lantern to help guide them through the darkening forest. The trees glimmered around the edges with the last vestiges of the sun, as if they were lined with liquid gold. The air was filled with the songs of larks and wrens and warblers alike – a sign they were preparing to retire for the evening.

"Perhaps we should camp here for the night," Murdoch suggested when they were forced to stray from the forest path in order to follow the water. "It would be dangerous footing for Galileo to travel through the forest when it is truly dark."

Sorcha could hardly believe her luck, for now she would not have to beg Murdoch to delay travelling home for a final evening. She nodded enthusiastically. "I would like that very much."

A soft breeze rippled through the autumn-yellow ash and hazel trees that circled the clearing when they finally reached it, bringing with it the echoes of tawny owls hunting out of sight. Sorcha leapt down from Galileo, brushing down her dress and inhaling deeply to soak in the achingly familiar smells of ferns and moss and, though it was very faint, wild garlic.

Murdoch tied Galileo's reins to a hazel tree and joined Sorcha by the edge of the impossibly reflective pool, just as the sun set for good. Its dying rays turned the waterfall to liquid fire for but a second, and transformed the damp slate and granite surrounding the water's edge to glittering quartz.

In that one, dazzling moment of sunlight, Sorcha found herself watching Murdoch's face instead of the spectacle in front of her, looking for a sign. A sign that, deep inside his soul, he knew such places were full to the brim with magic. A sign that his faithlessness in things he could not see was a lie.

Instead all Sorcha witnessed was a now familiar, unknowable expression upon Murdoch's face, his dark eyes seemingly impervious to the lustrous sight before him. Sorcha was stricken with an overwhelming desire to take a step away from the man in fear...or a step forwards, instead.

That Sorcha did not know what she would do thrilled and unsettled her to no end.

CHAPTER TWENTY-ONE

Lachlan

There was something about Mr Buchanan – Murdoch – that Lachlan misliked a great deal. Perhaps it was because he was to be married to Clara, or that his predominantly London accent grated on Lachlan's ears, or that he'd prodded Lachlan with a stick until he'd been forced to run off.

Perhaps it was because Clara did not seem to hate the man at all.

Lachlan had watched the pair of them all day from a safe distance, taking note of the way Murdoch's eyes never strayed from Clara for very long. He saw the hunger in his gaze that Clara had professed to being scared of; Lachlan could not blame her. Murdoch was doubtlessly intimidating, so why did Clara continue to steal glances of her so-called betrothed behind locks of hair with cheeks rosy as apples?

She does not truly like him, Lachlan told himself over and over again as the sun crossed the sky and dipped low on the horizon. *For every lingering glance she just as equally flinches away from him. Mister Buchanan is a mystery to her.*

He didn't like that a mere human was more mysterious to Clara than the Prince of Faeries. Imprisoned as he was in his damned fox body Lachlan felt entirely inferior to the dark-haired man.

And now that man had entered the forest. *Lachlan's* forest. He hated it with every fibre of his being. *Just what is Clara thinking, going into the forest?* Lachlan wondered, frustrated and confused. *You are supposed to be on the look-out for the kelpie, or heading home so that I can steal you away through your bedroom window once everyone else is asleep.*

But then Lachlan heard the rush of water and realised exactly what Clara was thinking. "Clever girl," he murmured, thoroughly impressed by her idea as he followed the sound. The small waterfall pool Clara had stopped by connected an uphill burn to the loch, and was a perfect location to force the kelpie to show itself. Lachlan had no doubt that it would appear.

It wanted Clara, after all.

Lachlan was sure it did, otherwise it would have eaten her the moment she answered its call. Lachlan still couldn't bring himself to think of the kelpie as a 'he', despite Clara's previous insistence. It was hard enough dealing with Murdoch and Lachlan's own disgusting sense of jealousy towards the man; he did not need another male to contend with.

He watched as Clara finished pitching her tent far enough away from the pool to avoid getting splashed by the waterfall. Murdoch hung several lanterns around the clearing, casting a warm, flickering glow over everything.

Lachlan kept low to the ground, hiding in the shadows to avoid being seen; he did not want Murdoch to spot him and chase him away. But Lachlan knew he could not risk putting Clara to sleep, either, especially not after the way her dream had been interrupted the night before.

He had to find a way to talk to Clara as a fox.

And then he heard Clara say, "There are apple trees very close by, if I remember correctly. I might search for them whilst you tend to the fire, Mr Buchanan." Lachlan could not have thought of a more perfect reason for Clara to wander off on her own. From his hiding place he grinned at her with all of his sharp, gleaming teeth.

Murdoch stared long and hard at Clara as if he was sure she was up to something, then slowly nodded. "Do not stray too far, and do not take too long."

Clara flashed him a smile before picking up one of the lanterns and heading west through the forest. Lachlan followed on silent feet, waiting until she stopped and raised the lantern into the boughs of a tree to check for apples to make himself known.

"Clara," he hissed, darting forward to snake between her ankles and brush his tail against her legs. She bent her head to watch him with wide eyes, surprised but clearly delighted.

"I had hoped you were nearby," she said. When Lachlan jumped up onto his hind paws Clara lowered herself to the ground, putting down her lantern before scooping Lachlan into her arms. She squeezed him tightly, burying her nose into his fur. "I missed my fox prince."

A noise of disgust left Lachlan's throat. "Do not call

me that. It's insulting." Clara responded by kissing his head and running her fingers through his ruff. Lachlan thoroughly enjoyed the attention, and it left him feeling decidedly superior to Murdoch Buchanan. Clara had no qualms or fears about touching *him* the way she did her betrothed. She never flinched away from his touch, regardless of whether Lachlan was a fox or truly himself.

"But foxes are clever, cunning and handsome," Clara said, countering his protest with a small smile. "Are you saying it is insulting for me to associate such traits with you, Lachlan?"

"Very funny. I'm assuming you came through here for the pool."

Clara nodded. She tickled Lachlan's ears until he licked her chin. "You said we needed the kelpie to physically appear in front of us, so I figured this was the best way to do that."

"I agree. But what about your future husband? He is here, too."

Clara said nothing. She stroked Lachlan absent-mindedly for a while, which he revelled in. Then she sighed. "For better or worse Mr Buchanan will be witness to what happens. There is nothing that can be done."

Lachlan nipped her earlobe. "We could wait until tomorrow. You could allow the man to return you to your parents' house and then travel back here with me in the dead of night."

"But we are already here, Lachlan," Clara protested. Her eyes were bright with infectious excitement. "And you do not know how much time you have. Better tonight than to delay."

Clara's words brought Lachlan starkly back to earth. He *was* running out of time, and with every day he left himself open to the possibility that he might be shot or trapped or otherwise injured, and then he'd lose himself forever.

He nodded. "You must make sure your Mr Buchanan does not interfere, then. Can you do that?"

She laughed. "I doubt he'd come swimming with me. You didn't, after all."

"I would have, had I not been a fox."

"Is that so?" Clara raised an eyebrow as if she did not believe Lachlan, though the fact that he'd said it meant it had to be true. Then she shook her head, laughing softly as she placed Lachlan down upon the forest floor and stood back up. She brushed stray strands of fur from her dress; in the lantern light they burned gold and orange and mahogany against the dark greens and blacks of the undergrowth. "I had best head back before Mr Buchanan grows suspicious."

"And what of the apples you promised him?"

She smirked. "The apples around here fell weeks ago. Mister Buchanan would know this, if he hadn't spent so many years in London."

Lachlan couldn't help but chuckle. *If it wasn't for the fact I dislike Murdoch I'd almost feel sorry for the man,* he thought, after Clara gave his ears a final stroke and rushed back towards the pool. Lachlan followed behind her at a much slower pace, hiding in a nook between two moss-covered rocks once he was close enough to the water's edge to keep a constant eye on Clara. Spray from the waterfall occasionally pattered against his head, but he didn't care.

"I think I was too late for the apples," he heard Clara inform Murdoch, who was cutting garlic and onions into a pot sitting over a merrily crackling fire. "Which is a shame. Apples from around here are delicious."

"A shame indeed," the man said. "Come by the fire and sit with me whilst I cook, Miss Darrow. It will be cold soon."

Clara looked at him strangely, then; Lachlan could not work out why. Then she gestured towards the pool with a flick of her wrist. "I thought I might...go for a swim, first. Care to join me?"

Murdoch laughed in disbelief. "You wish to swim? Now? The sun has gone down already!"

When Clara smiled at him it was devilish and enticing. Lachlan wondered if Clara knew how the man had been looking at her all day and was manipulating his feelings to her advantage, or whether she was simply like this all the time. *Both are as dangerous as each other, I suppose. She acts more like a faerie than a human.*

"I love swimming in the dark," she said, slyly unfastening her dress and allowing it fall to her feet. When she bent down to remove her stockings Lachlan was torn between watching Clara and watching Murdoch's reaction. He seemed stunned by her brazen attitude, though he did precisely nothing to stop Clara from slipping out of her chemise and letting it whisper past her skin to the ground.

Clara ran a hand through her hair, pulling it away from her face and shoulders to flow down her back. *She must know what she is doing,* Lachlan decided, unabashedly staring at the impossibly lovely, naked human before him. *She must.* A delighted shiver ran down Clara's spine when she dipped her toes in the –

presumably freezing – water. And then, with a final glance over her shoulder at Murdoch, she abandoned all caution and dived straight into the pool.

Jealousy stirred inside Lachlan when he looked at Murdoch. The man's eyes never left the pool as he waited for Clara to resurface, expression intent and dangerous to behold. His hands shook slightly at his side. Lachlan grew certain that if the kelpie did not appear tonight then the man would likely take Clara's bold actions as permission to lay his hands on her, and she could not possibly hope to fight him off.

He is bigger than me, Lachlan realised, then choked back a bitter laugh. Most anything was bigger than he was right now. But, at least, in his real form, Lachlan would have had his magic to fight the man. It would be no contest; Murdoch Buchanan would fall to the ground before he could touch a single hair on Clara's head.

But Lachlan wasn't himself. He was a fox.

He never thought he'd hope for a dangerous, deadly kelpie to show up in front of him; for the creature to try and take away a human he so badly wanted in front of Lachlan's very eyes. But it was better than watching Murdoch ravish Clara all night when Lachlan could do nothing about it, despite the obvious, deadly risks the kelpie posed.

Well, he supposed, as the surface of the pool settled back into a dark mirror above Clara's head, *there's a first time for everything.*

CHAPTER TWENTY-TWO

Sorcha

Knowing that both Murdoch Buchanan, her potential future husband, and Lachlan, the Prince of the Seelie Court, were watching Sorcha as she stripped off her clothes and slid beneath the cool, glassy surface of the forest pool sent a not-entirely-uncomfortable shiver down her spine.

The air was electric with tension. It was thrilling. It was dangerous.

There is something dreadfully wrong with me. I should not relish such an atmosphere.

But Sorcha did whether she wanted to admit it or not. She was playing a risky, potentially deadly game with her own life as bait and, instead of fleeing in fear, she was embracing the gamble. After all, if Lachlan was to be believed it wasn't just him and Murdoch who wanted her for something.

The moment her toes touched the water's edge Sorcha felt the kelpie's presence. She should have been scared, considering he'd almost drowned her before. She *was* scared. Terrified. But some instinct bigger than herself pulled Sorcha into the pool, diving straight into the centre of the freezing water to meet her fate.

Sorcha knew the water was barely twice her height deep; in the darkness of night it felt deeper. She could barely see a thing – the moon was yet to creep over the clearing to provide any light with which Sorcha could get her bearings. She swam down until she touched the bottom of the pool, feeling smooth granite beneath her fingertips as she edged over to the pressure of the waterfall. When she felt it hit her head Sorcha swam further still until she was behind it, then rose to the surface for air.

From her hiding place she could see the diffuse shape of Murdoch through the waterfall; he was walking towards the pool. Dread filled Sorcha's stomach, though it was mixed with excitement. *He cannot come in. Not when the kelpie is...somewhere. It is too dangerous.* Sorcha realised that perhaps Lachlan had been right to suggest waiting until Sorcha was alone once more to face the kelpie. If a giant, monstrous water horse showed up she had no idea what Murdoch might try to do.

But part of her wanted him to see it. Sorcha wanted him to know such things existed.

Lachlan himself was nowhere to be seen, though Sorcha assumed he was hiding close enough to the pool to jump in when he was needed. *And what exactly will he do?* she wondered. *And what will I do? When the kelpie appears do I simply continue our conversation where we left it last time? Or do I ask him why he let me get so close to death? Do I –*

Sorcha's thoughts were ripped from her head as the

168

current dragged her back beneath the surface of the pool and through the waterfall. But there hadn't *been* a current in the pool before; it had been still. Above Sorcha's head the water's surface remained calm, so completely at odds with the turbulence around her that she knew, instinctively, that it was the kelpie keeping her down.

She swung her head around wildly. "Where are you?" she called out. "I want to – I want to see you!"

Something even darker than the black water pinned Sorcha to the bottom of the pool. "Is that so?" the low, melodic voice of the kelpie said. "Or is it your fox friend who wishes to see me?"

Just like before, Sorcha caught a flash of silver and the glint of the kelpie's eyes for the smallest of moments before it dissipated once more. She reached out a hand through the darkness, desperate to cling to something. "We both want to see you!" she insisted, bubbles streaming from her mouth. "You said last time that you could help Lachlan. Won't you help him?"

"And what of you?" the kelpie replied. "Why do *you* wish to see me?"

"Because I –"

Something blocked her mouth, snaking around her teeth and tongue and lips to prevent her from speaking. Sorcha jerked away in panic, though the kelpie followed her.

"Stop wasting your air," he insisted. "Inside the water I can hear your thoughts. I told you that before."

This feels strange, Sorcha thought. Her eyes kept track of the ebb and flow of black-on-black in front of her, trying to catch a single defining detail of the creature keeping her locked in place. *How are you substantial enough to hold me down but not be seen?*

He laughed. "The loch is my domain. I control it. Now answer my question."

Sorcha was growing dizzy. She looked past the darkness of the kelpie to catch the glimmer of the pool's surface. Lachlan would be growing concerned. *And Murdoch? What will he think?*

"You are worried for both of them," the kelpie said. "Are you not worried for yourself?"

I should be, Sorcha admitted, *but I am not. I do not know why.*

"It is the same reason you wish to see me."

And then she *did* see him. The long line of an impossibly large horse's head, outlined in the silver of its intricate bridle. Flaring nostrils. Sleek, shining, ink-black hair. The flow of his mane in the water, entangled with weeds and shells and tiny, ghost-white bones.

And his eyes, darker than anything Sorcha had ever seen, and deeper than the loch.

Sorcha brushed a hand against the kelpie's face. He closed his eyes, long lashes fluttering for a moment before opening them once more. "You would never hurt me," she said, ignoring the kelpie's previous warning about using up her air. "You would never, because I have always wanted to meet you. That was all I wanted."

He nudged his nose against her face, reminding Sorcha of when Galileo had done the very same thing to her. "I will help you," he said. "But first you must do something for me."

170

Anything, she thought, knowing it to be true. *I'll do anything.*

"Then you must sleep, Sorcha Margaret Darrow."

Sorcha saw just a hint of the kelpie's teeth. They were wicked and sharp – not at all like a horse's. But Sorcha was feeling too euphoric to think them sinister. Too enthralled.

Too enchanted.

Without another thought Sorcha fell asleep, drifting into a dream just as heady and dark as the water around her had been. There was someone waiting for her, though their silhouette was indistinct. When Sorcha blinked focus into her eyes she took in his golden skin and pointed ears and lustrous, bronze hair.

"Lachlan," she cried, surprised, as he closed the distance between them.

His sun-coloured eyes were shining; his lips curled into a disbelieving smile. "You did it, Clara," he said. "You saved me."

"I did?" she wondered aloud. "I –"

Lachlan cut off her sentence with his mouth upon hers. "No more talking," he murmured, biting her lip the way he'd done the very first time he'd kissed her. "No more talking." He tangled his hands through Sorcha's hair, kissing her ever more insistently as she slid his shirt from his shoulders with fingers turned clumsy with desperate longing.

Sorcha was lost to Lachlan the moment their bodies fell to the floor.

CHAPTER TWENTY-THREE

Lachlan

When Clara hadn't resurfaced two minutes after diving into the pool Lachlan was seconds away from jumping in himself. He'd have done so sooner if the presence of Murdoch Buchanan hadn't given him pause; the man moved from his cooking fire over to the water's edge a few moments after Clara entered the water, taking off his boots to dangle his feet in the pool, and then –

Nothing. Murdoch had done nothing. He'd stared into the depths of the water, which in truth wasn't very deep at all, and had done absolutely nothing when Clara did not break back through the surface.

Lachlan felt the presence of the kelpie – that cold, horrific shiver down his spine that kept him frozen to the spot – shortly after Clara disappeared into the pool. Now it was stronger than ever. It was somewhere. *Somewhere.* But Lachlan could not see it; the water was too dark for him to make out any shifting, insubstantial shapes.

The monster was supposed to show its true form. It was supposed to appear before Clara to take her away. Was that not what it wanted? Was I wrong?

But then, when Lachlan moved a single paw forwards to slide into the water and find out what exactly was going on, Murdoch removed his coat and leapt in. He wasn't gone for long; the pool barely had time to settle above his head before he resurfaced with Clara in tow. She was unconscious, eyes closed and head lolling against the man's shoulder.

The presence of the kelpie did not disappear.

Every hair on Lachlan's body stood on end. *Just what is happening?* Lachlan thought, terribly concerned as he watched the man named Murdoch deftly climb out of the pool and gently place Clara down near the tent. Her skin was moon-white and glistening in the flickering glow of the fire; too ethereal to possibly be human. But Clara *was* human, and that was why she was so fragile. So easily threatened and subdued.

Murdoch slid Clara's sodden hair away from her face. He loomed over her, pressing his body against her own as if to protect her from the forest and all the nightmares it might contain. He stroked her cheek, a fond smile playing across his lips. The expression was so stark in contrast to what was actually going on that Lachlan found it deeply sinister. *What is he doing to Clara?* he wondered, tail twitching as Murdoch closed his eyes and lowered his forehead to touch Clara's.

When he kissed her Lachlan let out a hiss before he could stop himself. The man froze for but a moment, entire frame turned rigid, before he relaxed once more and returned his attention to Clara as if he had not heard anything awry.

Lachlan paced around in his hiding spot, infuriatingly confused. *He knows he is not alone. Something isn't adding up. Why is he doing this when Clara is unconscious?*

But then Murdoch's hands roved across Clara's breasts and waist and hips, and Lachlan forgot all about the fact he was currently a fox who had no chance of overpowering the man. He bolted forwards, stopping mere feet away him.

"Get away from Clara," he barked, hoping that Murdoch would be sufficiently shocked by the existence of a talking fox that he would back away from Clara immediately.

He did not. Instead, Murdoch continued his slow and assured exploration of Clara's body, though his lips curled into a wicked grin against hers. Lachlan bristled, forcing himself to take another step forward. "I mean it," he said. "Get away from –"

"What did you call Sorcha?" Murdoch asked softly, breaking away from Clara's lips for just long enough to respond. "Clara? How clever of her."

Sorcha?

But Lachlan refused to be rattled by the man's confusing response, for he realised in that moment that he did not, in fact, have to overpower Murdoch Buchanan.

All he had to do was put him to sleep.

But even as Lachlan thought of him with all his might, Murdoch laughed. "You are pathetic to even try such a trick, faerie. I suggest you don't come any closer; you can do nothing against me."

Lachlan moved closer nonetheless. "What are you?

You are not human."

"I could have rowan berries in my pocket. It is easy to block your kind from a human's sleep if one knows how to do it."

"And yet I do not believe you possess them. What do you want with Clara?"

Slowly, Murdoch moved away from the unconscious woman and retrieved his coat. He placed it over her just as gently as he'd stroked her cheek whilst Lachlan, desperate to keep him away from her, finally reached Clara's side. He caught sight of her face for just a moment; a disturbingly contented expression was upon it. Her lips were swollen and parted invitingly, and though the rest of her skin was ghostly pale her cheeks were flushed and hot.

She has been enchanted. She is dreaming. She –

Quick as lightning, Murdoch pulled out a dagger from his coat, taking advantage of Lachlan's temporary distraction to thrust it straight into his stomach.

"You know, for a fox, you aren't very clever," he said, twisting the blade until Lachlan screamed. He swayed dangerously on the spot until, finally, the man removed the dagger and allowed Lachlan to collapse to the forest floor. "You should have known not to get so close. I even warned you not to."

The last thing he saw before his eyes lost the ability to focus was Murdoch's very being twisting and turning into something else. Someone else. *No,* Lachlan thought, as he uselessly tried to fight off unconsciousness brought about by the intense pain in his stomach. *It can't be.*

But it was. For before Lachlan stood a perfect,

sneering imitation of himself, still shimmering around the edges, with a silver chain adorning his neck. It reflected the moonlight like a thousand tiny mirrors.

"Sleep peacefully, prince," the kelpie said, "for with an injury like that you will soon be naught but a fox."

By the time his doppelganger finished speaking Lachlan could no longer keep his eyes open. His muscles and then his brain grew heavy, smothering his blind panic for himself – and for Clara – until there was nothing left but darkness.

CHAPTER TWENTY-FOUR

Sorcha

"...to get up. Clara? Clara, you have been asleep for hours and hours!"

Sorcha's vision was hazy as she slowly blinked her way back into consciousness. Sunlight filtered down through the trees above them, informing her that it was almost noon. Sorcha had indeed slept for a long, long time.

Why did I sleep so heavily? I swam in the pool and –

Sorcha bolted upright so quickly that her head began to spin, but when she raised a hand to her forehead another hand beat her there. A golden hand.

Lachlan.

"Am I dreaming?!" Sorcha exclaimed, a wide smile growing across her face as she took in the appearance of the Prince of Faeries sitting beside her in the tent, not as a fox but very much as himself.

He matched her grin. "If this is a dream would you wish to wake from it?"

She shook her head, then noticed something shining around Lachlan's neck. An impossibly delicate, beautiful silver chain, just as stark against the faerie's golden skin as his mother's earring had been. Sorcha instinctively reached out a hand; Lachlan closed the distance between them until she could grasp it. She rubbed the metal between her fingertips, startled by the icy-cold surface of the tiny links that it was constructed from.

"Courtesy of the kelpie," Lachlan said. He tucked a lock of Sorcha's hair behind her ear, cocking his head to one side to look at her with curious, golden eyes. "What did you do to convince him to help us? I must admit I didn't believe it would be so easy."

"I...I do not know," Sorcha admitted. She frowned, trying hard to remember the night before. But then memories of her dream came rushing back and she recoiled from Lachlan, blushing furiously. "We –"

He chuckled at her response. "We did. You are not embarrassed, are you? We have so very nearly lain together in your dreams before, after all."

Sorcha's cheeks only grew ever more crimson. She crawled out of the tent and stumbled to her feet, realising in the process that someone had dressed her. "Did you –"

Lachlan chuckled as he exited behind her. "A gentleman cannot allow a young lady to sleep naked in a forest."

"And yet you left me to sleep naked by the loch-side three days ago."

"That was then. I'm a changed faerie."

Sorcha rolled her eyes, though she supposed Lachlan *had* changed since she first met him, even if only a little. She glanced at the kelpie's silver chain once more. "Were there...did the kelpie set conditions for your use of his bridle?"

"Yes," Lachlan said. "That much was expected. It must be returned after I've broken my stepfamily's curse, of course. He said you would know when he wanted it back; I'm assuming he'll contact you somehow."

"You're calling the kelpie a 'he' now. You didn't before."

Lachlan stilled for a moment then shrugged. "I suppose the least I can do after he helped us is to show the creature some basic courtesy." He picked up a fallen branch from a nearby hazel tree, using it to sweep away the ashes from the fire Murdoch had started the night before.

Murdoch.

Sorcha dashed around wildly to look for a sign of the man or his horse. But there was nothing left of him, not even his belongings.

"If you are looking for your betrothed," Lachlan called from behind her, "he saw me transform from a fox to a faerie. I told him to go. He did not want to leave you, but I assured him you would be safe."

"And he...believed you?"

"I cannot lie, can I?"

"He does not believe in faeries. He would not believe that."

Lachlan could only laugh. It was like a bell, chasing

179

away Sorcha's doubts and fears with every ringing note. "I think that, after seeing a beast materialise from water and a fox turn into a faerie, the man would believe anything."

Sorcha said nothing. She felt distinctly sorry for Murdoch; at the very least she had wanted to explain everything to his face. If he returned to her parents' house then perhaps she still could.

But first Sorcha had to help Lachlan.

"So...what now?" she asked, before turning to the tent to begin deconstructing it. Lachlan put a hand over hers; Sorcha's heart leapt at his touch. *He said it would be different to feel him in real life. If this is how I react to him merely touching my hand then how on earth will I handle anything else?*

"Leave the tent," Lachlan said, smiling wickedly at Sorcha's painfully flustered expression. "Leave everything. You will not need anything where we are going."

"So we're –"

"Going to the faerie realm, yes. I think it only fair that you get to witness the destruction of my stepfamily after everything you've done to help me, Clara."

She nodded, not trusting her voice to reply. Sorcha's heart was throbbing for an entirely different reason now – could she truly watch Lachlan murder his stepfather and stepbrother? *They are at fault,* she reminded herself. *They usurped his crown. They cursed him. They made him flee.*

"...yes," Sorcha finally said, entwining her fingers with Lachlan's despite the inevitable burning in her cheeks it caused. "Let us free you from your curse.

Though, I must profess, I was growing rather fond of you as a fox."

Lachlan kissed her hand, molten eyes locked on hers. "Something tells me I can make you far fonder of the real me."

"I very much look forward to it," Sorcha laughed softly, lips twisting into a smile that belied how sickeningly nervous she was. "But first..."

He grinned vindictively. "Yes: but first. First I have some Unseelie blood to spill."

CHAPTER TWENTY-FIVE

Lachlan

When Lachlan began to stir he felt inclined to fall straight back to sleep again. But then a stabbing pain in his stomach woke him with a start, and he yowled.

The kelpie. The kelpie. The kelpie was pretending to be Clara's betrothed, and now he is pretending to be me.

Lachlan didn't know what to do. He was in so much pain that he could barely move. But he *had* to; he had to reach the central faerie realm and foil the kelpie's nefarious plan before it was too late. Yet that thought gave Lachlan pause. "What *is* his plan?" he panted through gritted teeth. "Just what is he hoping to achieve by being me?"

It took everything Lachlan had inside him to struggle to his feet only to collapse to the ground once more. The pain from his stomach was blinding. *How can I move like this? How can I do anything at all?* He twisted his head around to look at the wound Murdoch – the kelpie – had inflicted. It wasn't enough to kill Lachlan if he kept it clean; it had been meant purely to slow him down.

"He said...he said I will soon be only a fox," Lachlan cried. "He wishes for me to suffer."

But if the kelpie wanted him to suffer then what did that mean for the rest of the Court? He had known Lachlan was a faerie – did he know exactly *which* faerie?

"Clara," he muttered. "He must have learned who I was from Clara. Which means..."

The kelpie knew everything he needed to know. He knew about Innis and Fergus, and of their plot to take over the throne. He knew they had tried to get rid of Lachlan. *But to what end is this information valuable to a creature of the loch? What does Murdoch want pretending to be me?*

It was hard not to think of the kelpie as 'Murdoch', though Lachlan knew it was a guise. But the kelpie had clearly been using the man's form for a few days, at the very least. He wondered when Murdoch Buchanan had ceased being himself.

Did Clara ever meet the real man? Did the kelpie drown him in the loch whilst he searched for her? Or had Murdoch been the monster from the beginning?

Lachlan's very bones turned to ice merely thinking about the kelpie inside Clara's house. "She told me he terrified her," he whispered, "and he did. He did. He was not a man. Not since she met him. I have to get up."

As a faerie Lachlan rarely spoke to himself out loud; as a fox he started doing so to ensure he was still 'himself'. Now, with the aching wound in his stomach, he needed to keep talking all the more, though words were difficult for him to wrap his sharp teeth and lolling tongue around. They sat thick in his throat. Foreign. Uncomfortable.

I am losing my speech.

It was this realisation that forced Lachlan back onto his feet, though he shook and whined and trembled as he did so. But he stayed up; though it took every ounce of concentration and strength of will Lachlan remained upright. He took an experimental step forwards and, though he flinched at how painful it was, Lachlan pushed through and took another. Another. Before he knew it Lachlan had made his way back to the waterfall pool where Clara's tent lay, unsurprisingly, abandoned.

He sniffed the canvas, revelling in her scent. She would be with the kelpie, Lachlan knew. After what he'd witnessed the night before he was sure the creature would not let Clara out of his sight.

He laughed at her name, Lachlan recalled. *He said she was clever. It was a false name all along.*

Her name is Sorcha.

Lachlan was deeply saddened by the knowledge that the kelpie had known Clara's real name when he had not. For he'd been able to enchant her, that much of which Lachlan was certain. For all he knew she was *still* enchanted, being forced to follow the kelpie against her will.

No, he thought. *Clara believes the kelpie is me. She is following the Prince of Faeries.*

That made Lachlan feel even worse.

Turning from the tent, Lachlan forced his feet to exit the clearing and begin the long, winding journey to the centre of the forest and the faerie realm. His stepfamily would be too threatened by the appearance of 'Lachlan' to realise that the real faerie prince was sneaking back in, still under the guise of a fox. He could get help. He *had* to get help – before it was too late for him to ask for it.

It took hours and hours for Lachlan to even reach the halfway point to the edge of the faerie realm. The pain in his stomach was excruciating; at this rate he wondered how he would ever make it. But then he picked up the scent of a faerie, and Lachlan stopped in his tracks. He sniffed the air to make sure he had not imagined the smell. It was coming from his right, towards the fringe of the forest where Lachlan had first met Clara.

On instinct he swung around and followed his nose, tail twitching in nervous excitement as the smell of the faerie grew stronger and stronger. *Someone,* Lachlan thought, darting through the trees as fast as he could physically bear to. *Anyone. Just one creature willing to –*

Lachlan froze. A tall, pale faerie waltzed through the twilit forest right in front of Lachlan's eyes, dressed in a sweeping, gauzy dress of periwinkle blue. Her ice-blonde hair flowed long and lustrous over her shoulders, never tangling or falling out of place. Her sapphire eyes were deeply, familiarly sad.

Ailith. It is Ailith.

If Lachlan had been in his original body he would have sobbed in relief; of all the faeries to run into he found the one who would help him no matter what. Without thinking he ran towards her, then yowled at the resultant stab of pain that clawed at his insides.

Ailith turned towards the noise, a frown shadowing her lovely eyes. When she spotted Lachlan she gasped.

"That is some wound, poor fox."

Lachlan opened his mouth to speak. But the words wouldn't come out; they stuck in his throat until he swallowed them back. He yipped and barked instead whilst every hair on his body stood on end.

"I shall leave you to get some rest," Ailith said soothingly. She backed away from Lachlan's display of aggression and fear, for she did not know he was angry and scared of himself, not her. But try as he might Lachlan could not force his body to follow the faerie; it resolutely did not want to.

No, no, no, no, he cried. *This can't be happening* now, *of all times.*

With a final sympathetic glance at him Ailith rushed off, walking too quickly for Lachlan to possibly keep up. He collapsed to the forest floor, exhausted beyond belief.

I have failed. I am going to be a fox for the rest of my life, and then I will die.

It was only then that Lachlan fully understood what the old faerie-fox had said before he'd passed away. His bullet wound was going to turn him into a fox forever, but it would kill him first. He was glad of it, for it meant he was still himself when he died.

Because of the cruelty of the kelpie Lachlan would not be granted that same small, blessed mercy.

He would die a fox, and nobody – not even Clara – would ever know.

CHAPTER TWENTY-SIX

Sorcha

Lachlan took hours leading Sorcha to the faerie realm. The sun had almost set by the time they drew close to the border, though Sorcha was glad of the longer journey; after everything that had happened thus far her nerves were decidedly frayed. Now they'd crossed over into the Seelie Court Sorcha's insides were roiling and leaping like Loch Lomond during a bad storm.

She sensed they'd entered the faerie realm before she saw any physical evidence of the change of location, for at first the realm itself looked no different from the forest surrounding it. Coniferous trees grew dark and close together, filling the air with the sweet smell of pine and preventing Sorcha from seeing much else of her surroundings but murky-coloured, prickly branches.

But then the trees began to spread apart once more and they changed from pine to ash and oak and hazel. The very ground upon which Sorcha walked seemed to glitter and glow; when she looked down her eyes picked out tiny fragments of semi-precious gemstones of every colour imaginable compounded into the earth. Quartz. Tourmaline. Jade. Amethyst. Lapis Lazuli.

Lanterns made of warped, clouded glass swung from every branch Sorcha locked eyes on, lighting up the gemstones to form a haphazard path through the forest. "Wow," she mouthed, at a loss for anything else to say. Part of her did not want to venture further into the faerie realm, for it unsettled her greatly, but for Lachlan's sake Sorcha resolutely took tentative step after tentative step down the path.

The eerie, swirling flames from the lanterns surrounding them made her skin so pale that Sorcha appeared almost a ghost. In contrast Lachlan's golden skin seemed more pronounced – luminous and rich and exotic. The glowing gemstone path filled his eyes with endless colours so beautiful that Sorcha could hardly bear to look at him.

Lachlan weaved his fingers through Sorcha's and squeezed her hand. "Do not be intimidated. This place is designed to make otherworldly creatures look as strange and alluring as possible to mortal eyes. Seelies are vain to a fault."

She couldn't help but snicker at Lachlan's easy admission of his kind's flaws. And it *did* make her feel better, though Sorcha still felt decidedly insubstantial in the torn and muddied dress she'd worn for three days straight and with her wild, tangled hair tumbling over her shoulders. She was reasonably certain there may have even been a twig or two stuck in it. But then Lachlan led her around a corner and Sorcha forgot all about her appearance.

" *Wow*," she said again, for in front of Sorcha was the strangest building she had ever seen. The walls were curved and expansive, with a burnished gold finish that shone in the last rays of the sun. The ceiling melted perfectly into them without a seam or crack in sight. The entire building twisted and turned through the trees like a snake instead of stone – a feat impossible for mere mortal architecture. Though it was only one floor high Sorcha had the sneaking suspicion that the building likely continued underground.

Directly in front of them was an intricately carved, massive set of oak doors, which stood ajar. She turned to Lachlan, mouth agape. "Is this the pal-"

"Prince Lachlan?"

Sorcha started at the sound of the voice. It was ragged and hoarse – not at all like Lachlan's – and when she located the source of the sound she gasped. The Seelie creature who had spoken was all scales and talons and a short, sharp beak, though they stood upright like a human and wore the garb of a soldier.

Lachlan nodded his head at them. "In the flesh, as it were. Tell me; where are Innis and my beloved stepbrother, Fergus?"

The Seelie hesitated; their beady eyes seemed nervous beyond reckoning. "They said you – we thought you were gone for good, my prince."

"A lie to be sure," Lachlan said, laughing at his comment, since of course faeries could not lie. "So where are they?"

"They're finalising the hunting grounds for the day after the coronation and should be back soon," the guard said. "Would you like to rest in your chambers whilst you wait?"

Lachlan nodded. "If you could lead the way. I must

admit to being wary of navigating the tunnels alone when my stepfamily are nowhere to be seen. Please arrange for someone to bring more appropriate clothing along for my lovely companion."

The birdlike creature did not comment on Lachlan's ominous first sentence, instead sparing Sorcha a glance for the first time. They recoiled at the sight of her, eyes wide with shock. "A human!"

"A human indeed," Lachlan said. "Now lead the way to my chambers, if you will."

Sorcha remained silent as they entered through the oak doors into the palace. The internal walls seemed to glow from within, lighting the labyrinthine corridors in impossibly soft, golden tones. There were tears in her eyes before Sorcha knew it; the place was achingly beautiful. Beside her Lachlan was equally as silent, his expression uncharacteristically serious.

He never let go of Sorcha's hand.

"I will have someone bring clothes for the lady immediately," their Seelie guide announced when they arrived in front of a heavy wooden door just as ornately carved as the palace entryway. They bowed deeply. "And I shall see to food and drink being brought along, too."

The creature walked off without waiting for a word of thanks from Lachlan or Sorcha, leaving them to push open the door into the prince's chamber. Sorcha's pulse accelerated until she was acutely aware of her blood flowing through her neck and wrists and temples.

Inside, Lachlan's bedroom was lushly furnished. The largest mirror Sorcha had ever seen took up almost the entirety of one wall, its frame gilded in bronze and carved into endless Celtic knots. A thick, forest green rug sat upon the polished hardwood floor in front of a gaping fireplace, with a mantelpiece which was similarly carved like the mirror. Gauzy, pale gold curtains hung from a four poster bed. They rippled faintly as if there was a breeze in the room, though the air was still.

Beside the bed was an ebony table with a silver jug upon it. Lachlan let go of Sorcha's hand, closed the door behind them and wandered over to look inside the vessel, but it was empty. "What I wouldn't give for some wine," he sighed, throwing open the curtains around the bed before collapsing onto its silken covers. He smiled at Sorcha. "Come join me."

The request would have been outrageous coming from anybody else. But from a lazily grinning faerie prince in his half-undone, fine white shirt it seemed normal. Natural. Sorcha walked over to stand in front of him, brazenly beginning to unfasten her dress as she did so. Lachlan watched her do so like a hawk anticipating its next meal, filling Sorcha with a red-hot desire all her own. Her breath caught in her throat. And then –

The heavy door behind her was thrown open. "Lachlan?!" cried a voice coloured with obvious disbelief. "How –"

Sorcha turned just as Lachlan sat up on the bed. His eyes narrowed at the figure by the door, but then he smiled entirely humourlessly. "Well, if it isn't my dear stepbrother."

The Unseelie was tall, broad-shouldered and as silver-skinned as Lachlan was gold. His pointed ears were longer and narrower than his stepbrother's, and they were adorned with a multitude of small, hooped earrings. Both his eyes and hair were murky, midnight blue, which shone oddly in the flickering light of

Lachlan's bedroom.

Fergus' mouth hung agape revealing gleaming, pointed teeth. As with the Seelie guard before he did not seem to notice Sorcha. His gaze was locked solely on Lachlan. "You cannot – you should not be here."

"And yet I am. Is there a problem with that?"

"Lachlan?"

Behind Fergus another two figures appeared. One was male, and was paler and taller than Fergus. His irises were turquoise in colour, which suggested to Sorcha that he must be Lachlan's half-Unseelie stepfather, Innis. But it was the other faerie she took most notice of, with the long, ice-blonde hair, angelic white dress and wide, blue eyes, for she was the one who had spoken.

Sorcha knew that the heartbreakingly beautiful faerie could only be Ailith. On her left ear was the silver cuff Lachlan had been wearing the first time Sorcha met him – the one Fergus had stolen from him as proof that Lachlan had left the palace, and Ailith, forever. Sorcha didn't have it in her to be jealous of the faerie, even when Ailith's eyes filled with tears and she rushed past Sorcha to cling to Lachlan.

"They said you were gone!" she cried. "That you had left! How could you leave without speaking a single word to me first? How could you?"

Lachlan's face was blank as he reciprocated Ailith's embrace. "It does not matter. I am back now."

"We were certain you were gone for good," Innis said, inclining his head politely towards Lachlan. "I will admit I believed you to be."

When Lachlan extricated himself from Ailith to stand upright Sorcha had to admit that it certainly looked as if Ailith's love for him was genuine, despite Lachlan's previous assertions that she might never have felt for him what he felt for her. The faerie could not tear her eyes away from him. "We must celebrate your return tomorrow night," she said, a bright smile on her face.

Innis nodded. "Of course. The realm will rejoice to know that Lachlan has returned to us." His tone was mild and reasonable; if Sorcha hadn't known any better then she would not have believed Innis had anything to do with the plot to dispatch of his late wife's son. It was his *own* son who struggled to maintain his composure, making it obvious that something was awry, though when Innis fired him a warning glance the enraged faerie closed his mouth and remained silent.

What is this? Sorcha wondered, casting her gaze over first Innis, then Fergus, then Ailith and Lachlan. *Are they not going to discuss what actually happened? Surely Lachlan would want Ailith to know what her future husband did to her old love?*

But nobody said a thing. The conversation moved onto planning the following evening's celebration, leaving Sorcha feeling decidedly isolated and left out. This was not a place in which she belonged. But just as she began to shift away from the group Lachlan reached out a hand for hers, a gentle smile playing across his lips. Sorcha took it, simply because she did not know what else to do. She wished the top of her dress was not halfway unfastened, though she could do nothing about the state of her clothing now.

It was only then that the other faeries seemed to realise that Sorcha was there at all. "Lachlan, who is your human companion?" Innis asked, eyeing her curiously.

Lachlan grinned and pulled Sorcha close. "Why,

this is the human who helped my find my way back home. I very much intend for her to stay by my side in the long years to come." Lachlan kissed her hand, golden eyes full of such genuine affection that Sorcha's heart rate rapidly increased in earnest, despite their current audience. "My dear family," he announced, "this is Sorcha Darrow."

Just as quickly as Sorcha's heart had quickened it froze between beats, stuck on that one word that had not once fallen from the faerie's lips before now. A cold sweat began to form along her spine.

I never told Lachlan my real name.

CHAPTER TWENTY-SEVEN

Lachlan

"Julian, are you sure this is –"

"I was sure I could sense one of the Fair Folk, Evie, and there he was. This must be the faerie."

"Will he be alright?"

"Do not worry. He's –"

Lachlan coughed and spluttered, scrabbling to his feet when he realised he had fallen unconscious once more. It was daylight, though the sun was hitting Lachlan oddly. When his eyes finally focused he realised he was standing on a blanket-covered bench inside a stable. A dirt-streaked window was responsible for the diffuse light entering the room.

The wizard and his golden-haired partner stood in front of Lachlan, both wearing frowns of concern. "Faerie?" Julian wondered aloud. "It *is* you, isn't it?"

Lachlan nodded, not trusting his voice – fearful that it was gone forever. But then he became aware of something. Or, rather, the absence of something.

The pain in his stomach was gone.

"What did you do?!" he exclaimed, barking in excitement when he realised he could talk once more. Lachlan turned on the spot, inspecting the location where Murdoch had stabbed him. The fur was no longer matted with blood; all traces of the wound had disappeared.

"I healed you," Julian said. He scratched his chin as he cast a critical gaze over Lachlan. "My healing abilities are serviceable, so you should be fine, but I would still recommend you spending a day or two off your -"

"I do not have a day or two!" Lachlan cut in, all his urgency from the previous day returning in one fell swoop. Now that he was healed and could run and talk once more he had to head to the Seelie Court as soon as possible. This time he could not fail.

Julian's companion - whom the wizard had referred to as Evie when Lachlan was stirring from his sleep - stroked Lachlan's head and tickled his ears. "You must eat something, at least. I don't imagine you've eaten since you were attacked. Who did this to you, anyway? Does it have something to do with what you told us before? The change in 'management'?"

"...somewhat," Lachlan replied, licking the woman's hand in appreciation when she placed a bowl of chicken in front of him. His jaws snapped at the meat hungrily; now that his stomach had healed it had the capacity to recognise that it was painfully empty. He glanced up at the pair of humans. "A kelpie is posing as me right now and has made its way to the Seelie Court."

Julian's eyes widened. "A *kelpie?* That is dangerous

indeed."

Evie frowned at him. "What is a kelpie?"

"A water horse. It draws people to the loch in which it lives and drowns them, consuming their flesh and blood when they can no longer escape. They can change their shape at will using their silver bridle."

"But that is horrific!"

Lachlan stared at Julian, thoroughly impressed. "You know a lot for a foreign wizard."

"I enjoy learning about all kinds of magic," the man replied, as if his far-reaching knowledge was nothing of consequence. "So what is it that you need to do? How do you vanquish a kelpie?"

"I shall work that out when I reach the faerie realm."

"That doesn't sound like much of a plan," Evie admitted. "What can you do as a fox?"

Lachlan finished off the chicken before he replied. He twitched his tail, impatient to be off now that he was healed and full. "The Court will be distracted by the false me. I can use said distraction to find someone who can help to break my curse."

"You know how to?"

He grinned at the beautiful, golden-haired woman, thinking of how it would feel to see Fergus' lifeless body laying on the ground. "Indeed I do. Now, if you may be so kind: where exactly are we?"

"Darach," Julian replied. "MacPherson farm."

Unbidden, Lachlan thought of Clara's tale from back in the tent – of a red-haired boy stealing away her first kiss when they were children. *I need to save her,* he realised. *I must save her from the kelpie and then save myself. I am the reason she became embroiled in all of this in the first place.*

Without another word Lachlan leapt off the table and headed for the open stable door. He paused when he reached it, nose twitching. It had rained in the night; he hoped the forest floor would not be too slippery. The last thing Lachlan needed was to fall in the mud and break a leg. *How fragile I am when I am not a faerie.*

"Wait!"

Lachlan turned; Julian held out a hand as if to stop him. "What is it?"

"You owe me a favour for saving you," the wizard said, smiling slightly. "I just thought it prudent to ensure you acknowledged this."

Lachlan chuckled. "If I live through this then, indeed, the future King of the Seelie Court will owe you a favour. Thank you, human."

The sound of Evie crying out in wonder at the revelation that Lachlan was royalty kept a smile plastered on his face all the way back to the forest. Lachlan decidedly did not look at Loch Lomond, though it was mere feet away on his left. It would cause him to think about the kelpie, after all, and Lachlan did not want to think about the creature until he was in a position to get rid of it.

Lachlan glanced up at the sky and realised it was already late afternoon. *By the time I reach the faerie realm it will be past twilight. Everybody will be awake and celebrating 'my' return, no doubt. The more distracted they are the better.*

He reached the dark, forbidding pine trees that grew on the barrier between the mortal and faerie world much faster than he could possibly have reached them the day before. Lachlan barely dared to breathe as he passed beneath their boughs; every hair on his body stood on end at the subtle change in atmosphere. The birdsong filling the air lowered in pitch and intensity. Even the soft breeze felt altered.

Out of the corner of his eye Lachlan spotted a flash of brilliant white – a lithe, well-muscled stag, complete with impressive sixteen-pronged antlers. It stared at him as if it knew exactly who Lachlan was and was unafraid. Then, in the space of a blink, the stag was gone, silent as a ghost upon the wind.

Does it know it is to be hunted the day after the coronation ceremony? Lachlan wondered. He decided that, if he miraculously managed to get both his body and his throne back, he would call off the hunt. He'd spent long enough as a fox to understand the fear of being hunted in one's very home.

Lachlan crept through the realm, reaching the curved walls of the palace just as a group of drunk, revelrous faeries passed by the front entrance, taking turns to swig from a wine skin as they went. But they did not go through the intricately-carved wooden front doors; they carried on walking through the trees.

The celebrations are outdoors, then, Lachlan decided, stalking the group as closely as he dared until they reached the wide, moonlit clearing where most Seelie festivities took place. The clearing was encircled by a shallow, winter-cold burn, which bubbled merrily over innumerable fragments of amethyst and obsidian. Lanterns and torches burning with orange and blue and green flames were strung from tree branches and tall, wooden posts, casting the clearing in strange, swirling colour.

Everywhere there was dancing and eating and music. All manner of Seelie creatures were thoroughly absorbed in the celebration, though it could not have begun more than half an hour ago. Some were clothed in fine, expensively-woven garments adorned with gold buttons and glass droplets and every gemstone one could imagine. Others were stark naked, their skin taking on the colour of the flames burning all around them.

The sight should have filled Lachlan with a sense of relief; it was a familiar, beloved scene, after all. Instead his hackles were raised and his heart beat painfully fast, for there upon the centre plinth sat his silvered stepfather, Innis, and his stepbrother, Fergus. Ailith was sitting beside the treacherous Unseelie that was her future husband, one hand on his shoulder, though her crystalline, haunting eyes were on someone else entirely.

Lachlan. Or, rather, the kelpie. He stood there, contented and relaxed as if he had always belonged within the faerie realm. One hand rested on the pommel of a narrow sword hanging lazily from his waist. His right arm was slung around Clara.

Clara.

Lachlan had never seen her so beautiful. Someone had woven her unruly hair around her head and decorated it with bluebells, magicked back into season for this sole purpose. A translucent, sea-green dress fell to her bare feet in large swathes of weightless material, though it was cinched in at her waist and was held up by delicate straps made of silver chains. Despite the outrageousness of the dress – by human standards – Clara seemed decidedly unperturbed by the revealing outfit, though Lachlan could not say he was surprised. She'd swum naked in front of him on more than one occasion, after all.

And in front of Murdoch, Lachlan added on as he watched the kelpie parade about in Lachlan's best finery. The turquoise tailcoat he'd chosen to wear complemented both his borrowed golden skin and Clara's entire ensemble so achingly perfectly that jealousy clawed its way through Lachlan's throat. But he pushed it away for now; he had to.

And then he noticed the distance Clara had put between herself and the kelpie. It was subtle, but it was there. Only Lachlan could have noticed it, though, for after the many hours he'd spent curled against Clara's chest as a fox there was no requirement for distance between the two of them at all. Which meant –

"She knows," Lachlan whispered, winding his way through the packed clearing to get a closer view of the plinth. "She knows something is awry."

"I am so happy you are all here today to celebrate my return!" the Lachlan that was not Lachlan called out suddenly, so unnaturally loudly that the real Lachlan flinched where he stood. A claw-footed faerie trampled on his tail; he bit back a yowl before stalking behind a tree for his own safety. Everyone hushed to listen to their prince, immediately enraptured.

Innis was smiling good-naturedly from his high-backed, wooden chair, for he was well-practised at hiding his emotions. Fergus, on the other hand, could barely suppress a scowl at the figure of Lachlan. His entire body seemed to be shaking, though Ailith ran her hand up and down his arm as if to calm him.

The false Lachlan continued, a wide grin plastered to his face, "I am sure you are all wondering where I disappeared off to. My loving stepfamily told you that I ran away in my grief over my mother's death. I am here

201

to tell you that isn't true. Not at all."

The clearing erupted into mutterings of confusion, but then Lachlan raised a hand and they grew silent once more. "I was betrayed, you see. Usurped. It pains me even now to say it, for I struggle to believe it."

"Who would dare usurp the prince?" someone wondered aloud, not far from the real Lachlan.

"There was nobody else vying for the throne before good Queen Evanna's death, was there?" said another.

The kelpie slid his arm away from Clara's waist, bringing her hand up to his lips to kiss it before leaving her to walk across the plinth. She took half a step after him, face coloured with concern, then seemed to think better of doing so. *Get away from there,* Lachlan thought at her, wishing more than ever that he could simply knock Clara unconscious on the spot and warn her about what was going on.

And then, without another word, the false Lachlan unsheathed his sword and drove it straight through Innis' heart, all the while grinning with ferocious pleasure. The Unseelie faerie stared at him, mouth open wide in shock, though Lachlan could see from his expression that he'd expected such a thing to happen. For how could he not, the moment 'Lachlan' returned to reclaim his throne?

It was Fergus who was genuinely surprised. Fergus, in his superiority and arrogance, who clearly believed that Lachlan would never return. When the kelpie removed his sword from Innis' crumpled, lifeless body Lachlan saw that, through the blood that was staining the metal, the sword was black.

Iron. Of course. The kelpie knew what he was

doing. But why is he helping *me? Does he truly mean to live as me for the rest of his days?*

But Lachlan knew what the kelpie did not. He was not a wounded, nameless fox, which the wretched creature had intended him to be by now. Once Fergus was dealt with Lachlan would return to his original body, and then he could destroy the kelpie with his own two hands.

Fergus leapt to his feet to face his false stepbrother, ire dripping from every pore of his silvery body. The kelpie seemed unperturbed; he took his time wiping the blood of Fergus' father upon the dead faerie's shirt. Ailith tried to pull her betrothed away, though Fergus shrugged her off.

"Tell me you did not betray Lachlan!" she demanded, voice full of tears and disbelief. "Tell me you did not –"

"You know I cannot tell you that," Fergus said, sparing Ailith half a glance before turning back and –

The kelpie swung its sword and took the Unseelie's head clean off. There had been no warning. No indication or tic that the sword was directed at Fergus' head. The kelpie had moved too quickly – so quickly, in fact, that Lachlan barely knew what had happened until the act was complete. The headless body collapsed first to its knees then onto its side. Ailith looked on, pale, glassy-eyed and horrified.

Clara could not look at the dead faerie at all; she turned away and buried her head in her hands. Lachlan thought for a moment that she might be sick.

The crowd screamed and cried, though many of the reactions were the result of vicious, riotous joy. Their prince was exacting his clearly well-deserved revenge, after all, and he was not the only faerie in the court who had mistrusted their Unseelie brethren. But as Lachlan stared at the kelpie kicking Fergus' grotesque, bloody head off the plinth and into the crowd something inside him grew cold.

For the one who had cursed him was dead, and he was still a fox.

CHAPTER TWENTY-EIGHT

Sorcha

Sorcha couldn't look at the bleeding, twisted bodies of the Unseelie faeries lain to waste at Lachlan's hands. *No, not Lachlan's,* she realised, frozen by the thought. *He is someone else. Something else.* For she was certain Lachlan had never known her real name. But there was another who had – someone who had read her thoughts and whose silver chain the false Lachlan was wearing around his neck, hidden by a high-collared shirt.

The kelpie.

"You..." Sorcha began, the word barely audible over the noise of the crowd. She stared at the Lachlan who was not Lachlan, though he was too busy riling up his audience to realise she was talking to him. She caught Ailith's eye but the faerie didn't seem to see her. She had fallen to her knees in a pool of Fergus' blood, staining her beautiful dress a dark, painful red.

Sorcha did not know why she did what she did next, nor how she found the strength to do it. She rushed across the plinth – ignoring the lifeless body of Lachlan's stepfather as he sagged from his chair to the floor, ignoring the sickening churning of her stomach – and grabbed Ailith's arm. One warning glare from Sorcha was all Ailith needed to wordlessly follow her through the crowd; by the time they reached the edge of the clearing the two of them were running full-pelt away from the bloody revelry.

"What just happened?!" Ailith cried between shallow, staggered breaths. "Why did he kill them?" Tears ran down her cheeks, glittering in the moonlight as if they were made from crystal. *She is beautiful even when she is heartbroken,* Sorcha thought. *No wonder Lachlan loves her so.*

"They deserved it," Sorcha gasped. "They turned Lachlan into a fox." Her stomach was in blinding pain from running so fast and so far, though she dared not stop. Something heavy and dreadful inside her told Sorcha that she could not let the kelpie find her. She fired a glance at Ailith who was, in turn, staring at Sorcha in disbelief.

"But that – on the plinth. That was not Lachlan. I know it in my very soul."

Sorcha nodded. "That was a kelpie."

Ailith jolted to a halt, her grip surprisingly strong on Sorcha's arm as she forced her to stop alongside her. The faerie's eyes were wide and horrified. "A *kelpie?*"

"From Loch Lomond," Sorcha replied. She looked at the ground, kicking at a fallen pile of leaves and pine needles as she did so. She was uncomfortable discussing the past fortnight of her life with a relative stranger – with the one Lachlan loved, no less. But she had to, so she did. "Lachlan and I, we...we sought it out. We needed

206

his help."

"How could a kelpie have helped –"

"His bridle would have given me my body back and thus allowed me to drive a sword through my stepfather, and stepbrother, and break the curse they put on me."

Sorcha thought her heart would stop. She gulped, fearing having to turn and face 'Lachlan'. But when she inched around she was met not with the kelpie.

It was the real Lachlan.

He was still a fox.

"Lachlan!" Sorcha cried, delighted, bending down to scoop him up into her arms. She held him tight. "Where have you been? What happened to you?"

He nipped Sorcha's ear. "The kelpie enchanted you and put you to sleep," he explained, "then he drove a dagger through my stomach. When I awoke the two of you were gone, and I tried desperately to find some help before my wound turned me into a fox for good."

Ailith dropped to her knees, ashen-faced. "You – I saw you yesterday. I saw you, and I walked away."

Lachlan slid out from Sorcha's grasp to sit in front of Ailith. He rested his front paws on her knees, though her dress was soaked through with dark, sticky blood. When she lowered her head Lachlan touched the tip of his twitching nose to hers. Ailith closed her eyes and let out a sob.

"You believed me a fox," Lachlan reassured her. He licked her cheek. "When I found you I *was* one, because of my injury. If it wasn't for Julian then I –"

"Julian?"

"A foreign wizard," he explained, glancing back at

Sorcha as he spoke. "I met him in the forest a sennight ago. He was searching for another faerie who had been turned into a fox four years ago."

Sorcha frowned. "That wouldn't have anything to do with your stepbrother cursing *you*, would it?"

"It was Innis who cursed the unfortunate creature. The faerie in question vocally protested the bloody Unseelie's marriage to my mother. Innis silenced him in the cruellest way imaginable. Clearly the son takes after the father."

Ailith let out a garbled cry. "Why did they do this, Lachlan? Why did they curse you? What were they hoping to achieve?"

"A question for another time," Sorcha cut in, realising in that very moment that there was a far more pressing matter to discuss. She brushed her fingers against Lachlan's tail. "Why are you still a fox, Lachlan? With Fergus' death your curse should have been lifted."

Even as a fox Lachlan looked obviously troubled. "I do not know. I don't understand what's going on. It makes no sense."

The three of them sat upon the forest floor in silence, both Sorcha and Ailith staring at the conundrum that was Lachlan, the fox prince. A cool, heady breeze passed through the trees, billowing Sorcha's insubstantial dress around her and causing Ailith's earring to chime like a bell.

No, not Ailith's earring, Sorcha realised, a flash of inspiration and certainty crossing through her brain in response to the sound. *Lachlan's.*

Without a warning to either of her companions Sorcha darted out her hand and wrenched the silver cuff from Ailith's ear, causing her to yelp in pain and surprise. Sorcha had no time to apologise; she held the beautiful, innocuous piece of jewellery up to the moonlight, looking for some kind of sign that it was more than it seemed. The tiny chains and minuscule sapphires that adorned it blew gently in the breeze, threatening to enchant Sorcha then and there by virtue of simply existing.

Then she threw it to the ground and unceremoniously smashed it over and over again with a rock, much to the shock and dismay of Ailith.

"What are you doing?! That was –"

"Cursed," Sorcha bit out, lips curling in bitter satisfaction as the chains were shorn from the earring and the beaten silver cuff began to warp beneath the weight of the rock. "We need to destroy it."

"Clara – Sorcha – you're a genius," Lachlan muttered. He stood up and turned to Ailith. "Ailith, it will take more than a rock to dismantle it. Could you do the honours?"

The faerie regarded him somewhat doubtfully but picked up the earring nonetheless when Sorcha obediently stopped trying to smash it into pieces. Ailith curled her hand around it, squeezing it tightly as if her body contained the strength to pulverise metal. Her pupils contracted and expanded, and she breathed in deeply through her nose, and when she opened her hand a few moments later the earring had been reduced to a tiny pile of glittering dust.

Sorcha gasped. "You are so strong!"

Ailith laughed softly. "Not strong in the physical sense. That was magic."

"And excellently done, as usual," Lachlan said. He leaned forward to blow the dust away, startling both Sorcha and Ailith in the process, for he was no longer a fox.

The curse had been broken, and neither of them had thought to watch Lachlan as they broke it.

He grinned at Sorcha, all perfect, white teeth and golden cheeks. "I can't believe I hadn't realised the earring held the curse. You are so clever."

"If I was clever I'd have thought of it *before* I dived into the loch and – oh. *Oh.*"

"What is it?" Lachlan asked when Sorcha did not elaborate. She stood up and walked over to a hazel tree, rubbing her fingertips across the bark as she lost herself to a deeply troubling thought. Ailith and Lachlan both stood up and followed her; Lachlan took Sorcha's hands in his own, a frown of concern colouring his expression. "What is wrong?"

"I was told that Mr Buchanan left after 'you' turned back into a faerie and made him go," she said, very, very quietly. "He had not wanted to leave me, but you convinced him otherwise. But it was not you that Murdoch was speaking to; it was the kelpie." Sorcha was shaking; she couldn't help it. She stared at Lachlan, hoping against hope that he could assuage her fears. "Lachlan, do you know what really happened to him? If he is dead because of me I couldn't –"

"Sorcha," Lachlan interrupted. His face was so grave Sorcha could hardly bear to keep her eyes on his, so she broke away from his touch as if he had burned her.

"No," she uttered. "He can't be dead. He can't –"

"Murdoch Buchanan *is* the kelpie."

CHAPTER TWENTY-NINE

Lachlan

"Cla–Sorcha," Lachlan began, "say something. Anything."

Sorcha's real name felt odd upon Lachlan's tongue as if it didn't belong there. But, in truth, it was the name she had given *him* that did not belong. Lachlan had to remember that. It had been a line of defence against him; given what the kelpie had done with her real name Lachlan fully understood why Sorcha had been so cautious.

"You are lying," Sorcha whispered. She ran her hands up and down her arms as if she was freezing. Considering how thin and wispy the material of her dress was she may well have been. With every gust of wind that blew through the trees a bluebell fell from her woven hair, which was itself beginning to come undone. It gave Sorcha the appearance of a girl whose enchantment had come to a stark and shocking end, which was not far from the truth at all.

"You know I cannot lie," Lachlan said, not unkindly. "Sorcha, Murdoch is the kelpie. He was masquerading as the man for as long as you knew him. I am so deeply sorry."

"Miss Sorcha, you – you knew the kelpie *personally?*" Ailith asked, incredulous. "How in the world..."

"He had taken on the form of the man she was engaged to marry," Lachlan explained, keeping his voice soft for Sorcha's benefit. She was staring at her bare feet; they were filthy from having fled so quickly through the forest. "He knew her full name."

Ailith's mouth formed an *o* of understanding. She turned a sympathetic eye to Sorcha. "This must be very hard for you to wrap your head around, Miss Sorcha. You –"

"I am fine," Sorcha cut in, clearly not fine at all. She looked at Lachlan. "We have to stop him. How?"

"Surely all we have to do is expose him as the imposter that he is," Ailith thought aloud.

But Lachlan shook his head. "And then what? We have no idea what it is that the kelpie actually wants. So long as he has the power to take on the form of anyone he pleases then he will be free to trick anyone and everyone time and time again."

"Then we take his bridle." Both Lachlan and Ailith stared at Sorcha. She smiled grimly. "We take the silver chain from his neck and keep it from him until the end of time. If he cannot change shape they'll have no choice but to return to Loch Lomond."

"But how do we take the bridle from him?" Ailith asked. Lachlan scratched his chin as he pondered a solution but it was Sorcha who, once more, provided the answer.

"I will do it," she said, gazing past Lachlan in the direction of the palace. Her mismatched eyes seemed made of glass – emotionless and empty. He knew it was a front, so he closed the gap between them once more and encircled Sorcha in his arms.

"I will not have you do this," Lachlan murmured into her hair, breathing in the smell of bluebells and the faintest hint of lilac as he did so. He crushed her against his chest. "You can't face him alone. You can't."

"I can and I shall. I have to." Sorcha softly pushed Lachlan away to look up at him; her lips were set in a miserable, determined line. "I can take the chain from him when he's sleeping. It is our best option."

"The coronation ceremony is tomorrow," Lachlan countered. "We could do it then, when we have an audience to witness what happens. We would have support against the kelpie."

Sorcha nodded. "If I fail then we can do that. But as it stands my plan is safer...for everyone. Which means I must go now."

"You – no," Lachlan insisted. He squeezed Sorcha's forearms a little too tightly until she winced. "I don't want you to be alone with –"

"Lachlan, let her go," Ailith cut in, reaching forward and forcibly loosening his grip on Sorcha. "She is right. Let her do what needs to be done."

Sorcha inclined her head politely towards Ailith before shaking Lachlan off. "You will know if I have failed if you don't see me before the sun is up," she said, before turning to run back towards the palace like a pale green, bare-footed ghost. Lachlan strode a few steps after her; a delicate hand on his wrist stopped him from getting very far.

"She will be fine," Ailith reassured him. "I trust her."

"You do? You do not know her at all."

"Yes, but you do, and she has done right by you so far. How could I *not* trust her?"

Lachlan sighed heavily and crumpled against a tree, sliding down to the forest floor to languish in amongst fallen pine needles and yellowed ash leaves. He almost wished he were a fox so that he could roll about in them. "This is madness, Ailith," he muttered. "Utter madness. Is this what being king will be like each and every day?"

Ailith gracefully folded her knees beneath her to kneel by Lachlan. "Why did Innis and Fergus try to remove you from the throne?" she asked, voice barely a whisper. The stench of Fergus' blood on her dress was so overwhelming that Lachlan had to fight the urge to recoil away from her.

He cocked his head to one side, frowning as he scratched his ear where his earring used to be. "They deemed me unfit to rule," he explained. "They were certain Fergus himself would do a far better job in my stead, with you by his side. To be honest I haven't yet discounted the idea that this was all a ploy to overthrow the Seelie Court."

"That...would be a serious problem, indeed," Ailith replied. She wiped away her remaining, unshed tears and sat up a little straighter. "There haven't been any problems between our races for decades, Lachlan. What

214

makes you think this is a direct attack on us?"

"Because they are Unseelie, and we are not."

"That isn't a good enough reason, Lachlan! Innis loved your mother!"

"That may be so," Lachlan acknowledged. "I do not deny that he did, but that does not mean my theory isn't correct, either. But at least now I know why Fergus fought so hard for your hand."

Ailith hesitated. "And why is that?"

"Because everyone loves you. You would make a great queen. I would know, given the fact I wished to marry you myself."

"Lachlan –"

"Why did you agree to marry him, Ailith?" he interrupted, forcing Ailith to maintain eye contact with a sharp stare she had no power to turn away from. "I do not believe you loved him. So why did you break my heart to be with him?"

She was silent for a minute; to Lachlan it felt as if it stretched on for forever. But just as he was about to repeat his question Ailith sighed and shook her head. "Because your mother told me I could not be with you. She had foreseen who I would be with in the end – and it wasn't you. She did not want me to marry you only to break your heart when I inevitably left you for another in the future."

"And you *listened* to her?" Lachlan asked, incredulous. "You followed a premonition instead of the way you felt? Ailith, you know that Seelie visions have been wrong before! There are so many ways to interpret them. There –"

"You would have had me disobey a direct order from my queen?"

"That still does not explain why you agreed to marry *Fergus*," Lachlan countered, quietly furious. "How could you do that to me?"

"Fergus was good to me," Ailith said, eyes bright and shining with a fresh batch of tears. "I thought I could be happy with him, and I could at least be a sister to you. I –"

"I never wanted you to be my sister!"

In a rush of fumbled footsteps and ragged breaths Lachlan tore himself away from her, no longer able to sit beside the faerie who had broken his heart. But Ailith followed, clinging to his sleeve to force him to stop.

"Lachlan, I'm sorry," she said. He did not look at her. "You know I love you dearly. I believed I was doing what was best for the both of us. If I was wrong then so be it; I'm mature enough to admit it."

"He was the one who cursed me," he muttered. "Fergus, I mean. He laughed in my face, sneering that he was much better suited to the throne than I was, and doomed me to die as a fox. His father agreed that I wasn't ready to be king, too. And it wasn't a lie, for he could not have said it if it was." He glanced at Ailith; her expression was endlessly sad. "What do you think? Do you think I would make a useless king?"

"I think that, as long as you're open to listening to those who want the best for the realm – and for you – you will make a fine king, Lachlan."

"So if I asked you to rule by my side, you would agree?"

Ailith hesitated for a moment. "You want me to be

queen? After everything that's happened?"

"*Especially* after everything that's happened. Fergus had one thing completely right," Lachlan said, finally turning to face her. "You would make a wonderful queen. You are rational and fair, and you would ensure I do not destroy our relationship with the Unseelie on the basis of a grudge. The Court loves you. And I love you, though in what way I can no longer be sure."

Ailith cast her gaze over her shoulder towards the palace. "Is your change of heart related to Miss Sorcha?"

Lachlan said nothing, which spoke far louder than any words he might have uttered. Ailith smiled when she caught the hint of a blush spreading across his cheeks.

"I never thought I would see the day. Lachlan, Prince of Faeries, enchanted by a mortal girl."

"That's because she *is* enchanting. You should hear her sing, Ailith."

She took his hand. "Then I hope that, one day, I will. But for now I must keep you hidden and trust that Miss Sorcha will be successful tonight."

Lachlan shuddered. For everyone's sake he hoped she would be able to strip the kelpie of his silver chain and be done with it sooner rather than later. But he could not stand the thought of Sorcha being alone with the monster.

He knows her name. He could enchant her again.

Abruptly Lachlan did an about-turn and headed towards the palace. "Whatever are you doing, Lachlan?!" Ailith cried out in shock. "You will be seen!"

"I won't and you know it," he replied, grinning. "I am an expert at sneaking about, or have you forgotten? I cannot leave Sorcha without any protection. I shall keep watch from the shadows."

Ailith couldn't help but laugh into her hand at his certainty. "You truly are a fox."

If it meant he could keep Sorcha safe then Lachlan was happy to agree with her.

CHAPTER THIRTY

Sorcha

The golden palace corridors cast Sorcha's skin in a warm, ephemeral glow as she crept along to Lachlan's chambers. Given how many twists and turns there were she was surprised she remembered the way, but by resolutely following her instincts Sorcha found herself outside the heavy wooden door of his room before she knew it.

Let the kelpie still be at the revel, she begged. *Let me have some time alone to collect my thoughts.* For Sorcha had no idea how she was supposed to act as if she didn't know who the false Lachlan really was, and she was still reeling from the revelation that the kelpie had been posing as Murdoch Buchanan all along. If Lachlan was to be believed then Sorcha had never known the real Murdoch at all.

A shiver ran down her spine as she recalled all the time she'd spent alone with the kelpie, thinking him her potential future husband. *What would have happened if I never ran off to look for him with Lachlan? Would*

the kelpie have continued to pretend to be Murdoch?
For what reason? What could a kelpie hope to gain by
marrying a human?

Sorcha had never been so conflicted and confused
in all her life. But she couldn't stand there by the door,
shaking and shivering and over-thinking everything to
death, when she had a job to do. No matter what
happened Sorcha had to steal the kelpie's bridle away.
She *had* to. There was too much riding on her being
successful to fail now.

And so, inhaling deeply, Sorcha turned a carved,
bronze doorknob and eased her way into Lachlan's
chambers. The door closed behind her on well-oiled
hinges, barely making a sound as it clicked back into
place. Sorcha surveyed her surroundings; the room was
dark save for a fire burning merrily in the hearth casting
long shadows across the floor. For a moment Sorcha was
certain she was alone, so she let out her breath in one
large gust of air.

"I was looking for you."

Sorcha jumped in fright, for Lachlan's voice echoed
all around the room. But then she realised that it
originated from the four poster bed; the gauzy curtains
had been pulled shut, effectively obscuring the kelpie
posing as Lachlan from view. But now that Sorcha was
looking at the bed she could just barely make out a
shape shifting behind the airy fabric.

She gulped. "I...was not prepared for what I saw
today," she said, hating that her voice trembled. "I must
confess to having run from it."

A golden hand pulled back one of the curtains. The
false Lachlan swung his legs around to sit on the edge of
the bed, eyes locked on Sorcha's every move. His hair

was wavy and unbraided down his back as if he had only just brushed it through, and he had removed much of his bloodied clothing from earlier to leave only a pair of doe-skin breeches and the silver chain around his neck preserving his modesty. Sorcha found herself staring at him with increasingly rosy cheeks even though she knew it was not truly Lachlan.

When I lay with him in my dream, Sorcha realised with dismay, *it was not Lachlan, either. It was a fantasy woven by the kelpie. Does that mean –*

"I know you aren't Lachlan," Sorcha said before she could stop herself. But there was no way she could continue to lie, not when the faerie's eyes held an intensity Sorcha knew belonged in Murdoch's impossibly dark ones.

The kelpie did not respond for a second. Two. Sorcha hardly dared to breathe. And then, when she thought that her heart might burst through her chest from anticipation and fear, the kelpie dropped his faerie prince guise and returned to the form of Murdoch Buchanan.

"How did you know?" he asked, in a voice that Sorcha had been certain she would never hear again.

"My name," she whispered. "You used my real name yesterday. Lachlan never knew it."

The kelpie burst out laughing; Sorcha bristled away from it. "A foolish slip-up on my part. But it was so hard to keep calling you Clara, Miss Darrow. Come, sit with me."

"I –"

"If I was going to harm you I'd have done it by now. You must know that, given how many opportunities I had to do so over the past fortnight."

Sorcha hesitated for a moment. Then, on unsteady legs, she stumbled over to the bed and sat by the kelpie without once looking at him. When he brushed his hand against her hair and pulled out a bluebell Sorcha struggled not to flinch.

"Your hair is coming undone," he murmured, leaning in close to twist a lock of it back into place. "You looked so beautiful today. I could hardly take my eyes off you."

"What – what is it that you want from me, kelpie?" Sorcha stammered. She kept her eyes forward, still too fearful to look at him as he continued to fix her hair with gentle fingers. All she could think about was how those same fingers had so easily wrapped themselves around the hilt of a blackened, iron sword and driven it through the heart of a faerie.

And decapitated another.

The kelpie stroked the back of his hand along Sorcha's jaw. "You can call me Murdoch, if you want to. Or Mr Buchanan, if you prefer the formality. I've grown rather fond of the name."

Sorcha twisted around to face him, her desire to gather answers finally overcoming her fear of the creature. "You killed him. You *killed* him. When did you –"

"You never met the man," Murdoch explained. "Your father met him twice. On his third visit – before arriving at the Darrow household – Mr Buchanan took Galileo for a stroll along the loch shore. Suffice to say he never returned from his walk." He chuckled darkly. "He was an ambitious man, Sorcha. A good man, once, but

London changed him. And a Lothario if ever there was one. You would have quite rightfully run from him."

"But *why* did you pretend to be him?" she asked insistently. "What possible reason could you have to do such a thing? You did not know about Lachlan and his curse until I told you about it in the loch four days ago. So why did you do it?"

Murdoch stared at Sorcha as if she had lost her mind. He shook his head in disbelief. "I saw an opportunity to protect the loch and I took it. By taking on Mr Buchanan's appearance I could control any external influences trying to change the area. I'll admit, when I dragged him beneath the water and consumed his body and soul I had not expected him to be so useful."

He smiled at Sorcha, his dark eyes warm and happy for once. "And to think that he was to marry *you,* Sorcha. You, whom I had heard on countless occasions singing to the ducks and regaling the swans about your day cleaning up after bouts of particularly untidy tourists. I saw the way you watched the loch ebb and flow for hours, doing naught but thinking. Of course I wanted to meet you. Murdoch Buchanan was the perfect vessel through which to do so."

Sorcha was overwhelmed by Murdoch's explanation. It had not been what she expected in the slightest. *But what was I expecting, anyway? After all my previous encounters with the kelpie, in both the loch and as Murdoch, I'd have been lying to myself if I thought he meant me harm. But this means...*

Her face burned red-hot, so Sorcha turned away from Murdoch to hide the flush of her cheeks. But then, to her surprise, he dragged her down to lie upon the pillows with a hand on her shoulder, turning her back around to meet his eyes in the process.

"I do not need to be in the loch to read your thoughts with a face like this, Sorcha," Murdoch said, smiling softly. There was a glint in his eyes that Sorcha had seen on numerous, dangerous occasions – a glint that constantly had her torn between running away screaming and leaning in closer to surrender to it.

Murdoch ran the pad of his thumb over Sorcha's lips, smile widening into a grin when she gasped. "What are you doing?" she asked in a whisper. Sorcha became all too aware, in that moment, of how translucent her soft green dress was, and how easily Murdoch could slip its delicate, silvered chain straps off her shoulders.

The chain, she remembered with a start, eyes locking on the flashing metal around Murdoch's neck. It looked different on him than it had done on 'Lachlan'. It was like it belonged there – silver on moon-white skin instead of clashing with gold – though in truth the man's body was no more the kelpie's than Lachlan's had been.

Murdoch frowned when he noticed where Sorcha had diverted her attention. "What are *you* doing?" he asked. "Why are you looking at my bridle like that?"

Though Sorcha was flustered and Murdoch much too close, she steadied her heart and urged herself to ask the most important question of all. "Why are you pretending to be Lachlan? What do you hope to gain from it all? And where is – where is he?"

Sorcha added her final question when she realised that Murdoch did not know that she'd already seen Lachlan, and broken his curse, and that it would be strange for her not to ask after him.

Murdoch grimaced. "Do not think of him, Sorcha. He wished to enchant you into doing his bidding from the very moment he met you. He –"

"I already knew that," she cut in, "and yet you did the same thing. You enchanted me into thinking I was with him. You are no better than he is."

"I...deserve that," Murdoch relented, though every muscle in his body had grown tense. "But I had to do it. I could not pass up an opportunity to infiltrate the Seelie Court."

"But *why?*"

"...you will see. Tomorrow. I do not wish to talk about faeries and their vile, parasitic ways right now."

"So where is –"

"Gone," he spat. "A fox for good. I could have killed him, but I didn't. I knew you would never forgive me if I did."

"And you thought I would be willing to forgive you for dooming him to lose himself, instead?"

Murdoch sighed. He stroked Sorcha's cheek somewhat absent-mindedly. "You had hardly known him for any time at all, Sorcha. I have known you your entire life. You will get over this."

She stilled beneath his fingers, struggling to comprehend such an idea as the kelpie having known of her existence for twenty years. She wondered how immeasurably old he was, but could not bring herself to ask him.

And then Murdoch rolled onto his back and closed his eyes. "Won't you sing for me?" he asked, the question so quiet it was barely audible. "The way you always did before, when you could not see me listening from the loch."

Sorcha found herself watching Murdoch for a long, drawn-out minute without responding. She took note of the planes of his pale, angular face; his black hair curling around his ears and falling across his forehead; his broad shoulders and well-defined chest; the way he drew in his stomach when he breathed.

"Keep looking at me like that at your own risk, Sorcha," Murdoch murmured without opening his eyes. She sat up immediately, mortified. She hated how painful the throbbing of her heart was against her ribcage, and how her mind had gone racing back to the night when Murdoch had held her close and kissed her neck.

"O thou pale orb that silent shines," Sorcha began, desperate to rid herself of any and all dangerous thoughts and desires. Her voice was quavery and insubstantial at first, so she coughed to clear her throat before continuing.

"While care-untroubled mortals sleep!

Thou seest a wretch who inly pines.

And wanders here to wail and weep!

With woe I nightly vigils keep,

Beneath thy wan, unwarming beam;

And mourn, in lamentation deep,

How life and love are all a dream!"

Sorcha sang and sang her way through the long, impossibly relevant poem, watching the smallest of smiles curl Murdoch's lips as his breathing grew ever more relaxed. She had never witnessed him so calm and free before. The feeling of singing to him was achingly nostalgic, as if she truly was sitting upon the loch-side watching the sun set across the water.

When she reached the final verse of her song Sorcha realised that she was sad it was coming to an end; it felt like no time had passed at all. She had hoped the seconds would somehow stretch out into eternity.

"Oh! scenes in strong remembrance set!

Scenes, never, never to return!

Scenes, if in stupor I forget,

Again I feel, again I burn!

From ev'ry joy and pleasure torn,

Life's weary vale I'll wander thro';

And hopeless, comfortless, I'll mourn

A faithless woman's broken vow!"

The silence that followed Sorcha's final note was tense and tragic. She realised she was waiting for a reaction from Murdoch. A smile, perhaps. For him to open his eyes and stare into her very soul. Part of her wanted Murdoch to reach out a hand and grab her – to pull Sorcha beneath him and crush his mouth to hers with desperate, intense longing.

But Murdoch had fallen asleep.

CHAPTER THIRTY-ONE

Lachlan

She sang for him. The kelpie. Why did she sing for him?

Lachlan reached the door to his chambers just after Sorcha herself entered the room. He hadn't been able to stand the idea of leaving her alone with the kelpie – not after witnessing the way the creature had looked at her through Murdoch Buchanan's eyes. Now his suspicions were confirmed.

I was right to believe he wanted her from the very beginning. And now I know why. The damn thing is in love with her.

He never thought he'd see the day a kelpie fell prey to such emotions.

The final straw was when Sorcha's melodic, haunting voice began to filter through the door. Lachlan was beyond jealous; he hated feeling this way. He was supposed to be above such emotions. Beyond it. But when the silence stretched out for far longer than he expected once Sorcha finished her song Lachlan began to grow suspicious. *Just what is going on?*

He was seconds away from cracking open the door to see what was going on when Sorcha herself opened it, a thin sliver of firelight creeping through to filter across the corridor. Her blue-and-green eyes caught sight of Lachlan immediately.

Her expression was carefully constructed into an impossibly neutral mask. "I thought you might be here."

"Do you have the chain?" he whispered, as Sorcha squeezed through the gap in the door and closed it silently behind her. She shook her head. "He has only just fallen asleep. I will do it in a few hours when he is in a deeper slumber."

"Clara –"

"I will do it, I swear," she cut in, not commenting on Lachlan slipping back into using her false name. "But for now I need to...cool off. I need to get out of here."

He grinned despite the perilous situation they were in and his ugly, unbecoming jealousy. "I know just the place, if you do not mind the company."

Sorcha knocked her hand against his in lieu of a spoken response, so Lachlan entwined their fingers and rushed her noiselessly through the palace and down a flight of steps hewn from the very bedrock itself.

"Where is everyone?" Sorcha asked in hushed tones as they descended further and further underground. The air became colder, biting at the tips of Lachlan's ears and nose.

He squeezed her hand. "Celebrating outside. They'll be at it until the early hours of the morning."

"But the coronation ceremony is tomorrow evening!"

"One day you will stop basing a faerie's lifestyle on your boring, human sensibilities," Lachlan chuckled. When they reached a blackened iron door he glanced at her. "Most of our kind aren't strong enough to get past an iron door. But, then again, most of my kind aren't princes."

Sorcha's eyes brightened in interest as she watched Lachlan blow on his hands then hold them out in front of him, inches from the door. He muttered a string of unintelligible words under his breath until the hinges creaked and the door swung open.

He swept a hand forward and gave Sorcha a mocking bow. "After you, my lady."

Her lips quirked into the hint of a smile as she walked past him into the glimmering darkness of the room. It was only then that Lachlan realised Sorcha's hair had been tidied; a fresh wave of possessive jealousy washed over him as he imagined the kelpie's hands all over her.

Did he choose that dress for her? Did he do anything to her last night when she believed that he was me? Did he –

"Lachlan?"

Sorcha was staring at him standing there in the doorway. He shook his head. "It is nothing. Keep walking."

"I cannot see."

"Your eyes will adjust," Lachlan assured her as he closed the door behind them and led Sorcha further into the room. Pinpoints of glowing, glittering light punctuated the darkness, the result of phosphorescent mushrooms growing from the floor and ceiling surrounded by all manner of gemstones. The gentle sounds of a burn flowing over porous rock could be heard echoing all around.

Lachlan wound Sorcha across the floor with practised eyes, for it was littered with recessed pits full of silken cushions and blankets. If he had truly been the one leading up the revel outside then many beautiful, lustful Seelie would have ended up in here with him in due time.

But there was only Sorcha, and she was all Lachlan wanted. Needed.

Sorcha's mismatched eyes were like gemstones themselves as they adjusted to the low light. "What is this place, Lachlan?" she asked very quietly. "What – *ah*!"

For Lachlan wrapped his arms around Sorcha's waist, picking her up and bodily tossing the two of them into the largest pit, landing on top of innumerable gold-fringed pillows. His lips founds hers before Sorcha had an opportunity to collect her thoughts, though once she worked out what was going on she eagerly reciprocated.

Sorcha slid Lachlan's shirt from his shoulders just as his fingers made quick work of the silvered chains that held up her dress. He was desperate to remove all traces of the garment; to have every inch of Sorcha's skin belonging to him and him alone.

"When the kelpie enchanted you," he asked in an undertone, breaking away from Sorcha's mouth in order to rove his eyes up and down her body. The ethereal light in the room stained her skin first blue, then green, then sunset orange and ruby red. "What did you dream of?"

Sorcha regarded him from beneath her eyelashes; even in the darkness he noticed the blush that crossed her cheeks. She glanced away. "You," she whispered. "Of course I dreamed of you."

Desire coiled up inside Lachlan like a snake, tense and ready to strike. He kicked off his breeches and rolled Sorcha on top of him, who gasped in shock and delight. He pressed his fingertips into the curve of her thighs and let out a low, longing moan.

"It is different in real life," he said. "I told you that before. Everything is better."

Sorcha bent her head low to brush her lips against Lachlan's. "Is that simply because it is real, or is there another reason?"

"I've never thought about it all that much before," he admitted. He ran a hand through Sorcha's hair, unravelling all the beautiful handiwork the kelpie had used to keep it up. Bluebells scattered all around them; Sorcha shook her head until her hair fell wild and wavy around her shoulders. "But this is you," Lachlan continued. "This is the real you, and this is the real me. I want nothing more than to experience this night with you outside of your dreams."

Sorcha smiled. She bit Lachlan's lip the way he'd done to her the first time they kissed.

"I've been waiting for that since the very moment I met you."

CHAPTER THIRTY-TWO

Sorcha

For the second time that night Sorcha crept back into Lachlan's chambers. Murdoch lay sleeping on the bed, partially obscured by the translucent curtains. The fire was low in the hearth, so Sorcha sat on the rug beside it and stared into the smouldering coals. She was sure that, if she touched them, her skin would be just as hot as they were.

I can't believe I truly lay with Lachlan.

Sorcha hadn't wanted to leave the dark, glittering cave to return to Murdoch's side. To reality. Though the last few hours with Lachlan hadn't been the product of a dream they still very much felt like one compared to what Sorcha must now do.

She ran her fingers through her hair, finding a stray bluebell that had not yet fallen out, then padded over to an oak-and-gold wardrobe to choose something else to wear. Sorcha felt filthy in her green dress, though she knew the fabric itself was almost as clean as it had been when she'd first put it on. But it was Sorcha herself that felt dirty. Wrong. Murdoch had chosen the dress for her, and she'd let Lachlan remove it.

She wished her heart would stop beating so fast.

All I need to do is unclasp the chain from Murdoch's neck. Once I do that I am done. Lachlan and the Seelie Court will be free from any danger.

And the kelpie would be forced to retreat into Loch Lomond, never to be seen by Sorcha again. It hurt her to think of such a thing, but what else could she do? Murdoch could not be left to continue masquerading as the Prince – and, from tomorrow, King – of Faeries. If they did not take his bridle from him then there would be no way to control Murdoch whatsoever.

That didn't make Sorcha feel any better.

She ended up settling for a large, billowing shirt from the wardrobe, which was clearly Lachlan's. Sorcha removed her dress, remembering Lachlan doing the same in a flurry of fingers and kisses mere hours earlier. When it whispered to the floor she slid on Lachlan's shirt over her head, which fell to just above her knees. The sheer size of it reminded her of her father's shirt.

Sorcha's heart constricted painfully in her chest. *I hope he is alright,* she thought, realising in that moment how much she missed her parents. *I hope I will see them soon.*

Whether she did or not was entirely up to what Sorcha did next.

When she reached the bed Sorcha wanted nothing more than to run away. Instead she forced herself to sit by Murdoch's side, watching as he slept so peacefully that she almost cried. *Why are you doing this?* Sorcha thought at him. She held out a shaking hand towards the delicate silver chain around his neck, shining like diamonds in the light from the dying fire. *Why did you have to pretend to be Lachlan? Why did you doom him to be a fox? Just what, exactly, are you planning?*

All Sorcha had to do was yank the chain away from Murdoch. Once it was removed he would revert to his original form and Sorcha could flee. Murdoch would have no choice but to return to the loch from whence he came or his very being would unravel.

Sorcha's part of the job was so easy. So simple.

She couldn't do it.

Sorcha traced the line of Murdoch's collarbone with her fingertips, never quite touching the chain. Her heart fluttered in her chest as her brain desperately tried to work out an alternative plan. Something. Anything. A solution that didn't involve ruining the kelpie's life.

Murdoch's eyes flashed open.

He darted a hand out and grabbed Sorcha's wrist, squeezing it painfully as he pulled it away from his neck. She cried out in shock and tried to claw his hand away, but Murdoch wouldn't budge.

"Was this your plan all along?" he asked, tone as dark and dangerous as his eyes. "Lull me into a false sense of security and –"

"No! No, I –"

"Are you sure? Because that is what you're doing, is it not?"

"But I haven't – I didn't –"

"And why not? What is staying your hand?"

Sorcha wavered. She did not know what to say. She

looked at Murdoch's fingers crushing her wrist until, eventually, he let her go. She held her arm to her chest and rubbed where he had held it, wincing at the pain. "Why are you doing this?" she asked. "You said I would find out tomorrow. I need to know now."

Murdoch sat up, a scowl warping his handsome features. "You should understand already, Sorcha. They are as bad as your own kind."

"What do you mean?"

"They are taking over the lochs!" he exclaimed. "With every year more and more of them creep along the shore, deciding that they like the water and can trick more humans from within it. Already the moors are overrun with Unseelie and many of the lakes and shorelines in England, too. And that's not to mention the selkies they entrap with forced, binding promises simply because they can. It sickens me."

Sorcha hesitated. "You said Unseelie. What about –"

"They are all the same, in the end! Seelie, Unseelie, I do not care." Murdoch clucked his tongue in disgust. "Your precious Lachlan and his brethren scorn and hate Loch Lomond and its creatures. They fear it, because they cannot control it. You do not think they would take it over if given the opportunity? Of course they would! Call what I am doing a pre-emptive strike."

"And what is it that you're doing, exactly?"

Murdoch's eyes glittered with vicious delight. "Why, I am inciting a war."

"You..." Sorcha was speechless. Murdoch's vendetta against the Fair Folk was more than a simple whim. It had been bubbling under the surface for longer than she could possibly know, and Murdoch had been biding his time until an opportune moment arose.

Sorcha – silly, mortal Sorcha Margaret Darrow – had accidentally provided him with one.

"You want the Seelie and Unseelie to fight each other until they both perish," she murmured, certain. "That has been your plan all along."

Murdoch nodded. He ran his hands through his hair to push it out of his face, exhaling deeply as he collapsed against the pillows. He glanced at Sorcha out of the corner of his eye. "So you see, Sorcha, I am not truly the villain here. You have merely become caught in the crossfire on an ongoing, centuries-long feud. It is not your fault, so do not feel responsible for the fate of your fox."

Sorcha looked at her hands, knowing that what she was about to say was going to be shot down immediately. "Why can't you all try to compromise, instead? Can't you talk it out?"

"To what end?" Murdoch snarled, back on-edge once more. "Tell me, *Miss Darrow,* would you be willing to compromise with the slew of city folk who wish to sully your beloved land? Who want nothing more than to buy you out and force every farmer, child and lowly maiden to move away? Would you?"

"I –"

"Would you?"

"Of course not!" Sorcha wailed. She did not care that there were tears streaming down her face as she locked eyes with Murdoch. "I could never do that! But this –"

"Do not dare say this is different. It is the same. You

wish to protect your land, and so do I. Out of everyone, I *know* you can understand me. I am not wrong here."

Sorcha averted her eyes, at a loss for what else she could say. When she tried to stand up from the bed Murdoch pulled her back down. "Let me go!" she protested, kicking at the kelpie for all the good it would do. "How dare – let me go!" But Murdoch held her tightly against his chest no matter what she did, as if he was about to stroke her hair and kiss all her troubles away.

"I cannot do that," he murmured, genuinely apologetic despite the way his hands clung to her every curve. "You know I can't. Just stay by my side, Sorcha. Don't make this harder than it already is."

Sorcha couldn't stop crying. She had failed Lachlan, and Ailith, and their entire realm. Murdoch was right, of course; she was not responsible for them. She did not owe them anything. What happened tomorrow was beyond Sorcha's control and scope of understanding. She was only human, after all.

And yet.

"I will stay," she sobbed, before swallowing away the rest of her tears. She stopped struggling against Murdoch's tightly-muscled arms, growing limp against him.

He sighed in relief. With a smile he relaxed his hold on her. "Good," he said. "Good. You are a clever girl, Sorcha. I –"

"But you will leave me alone," she interrupted, extricating herself from his grip to roll over to the other side of the bed. "You will not touch me."

Murdoch's only response was silence. He didn't

have to say anything; Sorcha could sense his sadness, anger and longing upon the very air between them.

She wondered if he could sense hers.

CHAPTER THIRTY-THREE

Lachlan

"Are you sure about this, Lachlan?"

"No, but what other choice do we have? I do not believe any of us are strong enough to defeat a kelpie on our own."

"But if we waited –"

Lachlan threw Ailith a scathing look. "The swearing-in ceremony is today. *Now.* If the kelpie is crowned king then it does not matter if the Seelie believed him to be me when it happens. The magic in the ceremony is binding; you know this, Ailith. It has to be now."

Lachlan was wearing a heavy burgundy cloak to hide his appearance from the growing crowd. Soon he would reveal his true identity, but not yet. He had to pick the right moment. He had to know that Sorcha was safe and unharmed. He had to know that he could wrangle the kelpie's silver bridle away.

For there was no doubt that, for whatever reason, Sorcha had failed in stealing it.

Did the creature catch her in the middle of the night ripping it from his throat? Did he hurt her? He better not have hurt her. Or was Sorcha simply...unable to do it?

Lachlan did not want to dwell on what that meant.

"I am worried for Miss Sorcha," Ailith murmured, as if reading Lachlan's mind. She squeezed his hand. "She is just a human, Lachlan. She should never have been brought here – not when there is so much unrest."

Lachlan snorted. "It was not as if I brought her here! It was the –"

"You allowed her to become involved in breaking your curse," she said, disconcertingly mildly. "You should never have done that."

"I could not seek help from the Court – not when Innis and Fergus were still alive and keeping watch for me. I had to stop them before the coronation ceremony, which meant I had a fortnight to get my body back. *Fourteen days,* Ailith, with no Seelie help. What would you have had me do?"

"I..."

"Precisely. Now let us get closer. Everyone expects you to be up on the plinth, anyway."

"I do not wish to be so close to the kelpie," Ailith muttered, averting her eyes. "The beast is strong. He has to be, to have held Loch Lomond as his domain for half a millennium."

Lachlan kept his eyes on the plinth as they weaved through the clamouring, excited crowd. No traces of blood remained upon the elaborately carved wooden throne which Innis had been sitting on the day before, nor upon the floor where Fergus' head had rolled.

It was as if they'd never existed at all.

"Lachlan, you are scaring me."

He looked at Ailith, realising in the process that his mouth had curled into a savage, snarling grin. "How do you know the same kelpie has resided in the loch for five hundred years?" he asked, redirecting the subject and schooling his expression in the process.

"Are you...did you listen to none of your mother's lessons as you grew up? Or any of your teachers'?"

Lachlan could only laugh. "Why would I have done, when I could rely on your far superior memory to recall such facts for me?"

Ailith said nothing; the look she gave Lachlan spoke volumes. But they had treated each other like this for the best part of a hundred years – it was the way they worked and lived and loved each other. Lachlan doubted either of them would change any time soon.

He was about to comment on the promise of rain in the twilight sky above them when the noise of the crowd hushed in one sweeping moment, only to erupt into cheers almost immediately afterwards. Lachlan and Ailith focused all of their attention onto the plinth once more; the regally dressed figure of the false Lachlan swept into the centre, bowing gracefully to the crowd as their shouting grew louder.

"He may well be better at riling up the Court than you ever were," Ailith mused in an undertone.

Lachlan rolled his eyes. "I'd crave attention, too, if I lived at the bottom of a loch for five hundred years."

And then he spotted Sorcha as she joined the kelpie on the plinth, and Lachlan's blood ran cold. For there was no doubt from the look on her pale, troubled face that something had gone dreadfully wrong the night before. He hated to see her so obviously upset after their stolen hours together.

She should be flushed and breathless and clinging to me, not a morose, crying slave to a water horse. But at least she has not been harmed.

Even thinking such a thing reminded Lachlan of the fact that the kelpie loved Sorcha; if he'd ever doubted it then the way he looked at her now, in front of everyone – with Lachlan's own eyes, no less – was all he needed to confirm his fears. Bitterly he wondered if Sorcha had not technically *failed* to steal the creature's silver chain but instead had chosen not to.

But Lachlan shook his head at such a notion. *After what we did last night I do not think she has feelings for the kelpie the way she might have done when he was Murdoch. I should have faith in her.*

"How kind of you all to be so enthusiastic after the revel last night!" the Lachlan who was not Lachlan announced, in the unnaturally loud voice he had used before he'd slaughtered Innis and Fergus. "To have your support after everything that has happened means everything to me. Queen Evanna would have loved to see you like this."

The crowd went wild, for how could they not? The kelpie knew how to manipulate them as if they were mere simple-minded humans. Lachlan cringed to witness it.

The kelpie paced back and forth. "I have a confession to make. Yesterday I was not forthcoming about my dearly departed stepfamily's plot to overthrow me. I feel I owe you a full explanation."

Lachlan froze along with the rest of the tense, excited crowd. For here would be the answers that had evaded him ever since the kelpie took his skin. Sorcha was looking anywhere but at the kelpie; she bit her lip and scanned the crowd with desperate eyes. Looking for Lachlan.

She could not see him.

We need a distraction to get her out of here, he realised. *If Sorcha is up there when we tackle the kelpie then she could get hurt.*

When he caught Ailith's eye Lachlan saw that she had reached the same conclusion and was thinking hard about a solution. But then the false Lachlan continued his speech, so the two of them temporarily redirected their attention back him.

"I had been made to believe that my suspicions towards my Unseelie stepfamily were unfounded," the kelpie said. He stopped pacing to stand in front of the faerie throne. "I was told to be tolerant. My mother loved her new husband, after all. And he loved her, too. But that was not enough to assuage my fears, and I was correct to cling to them!"

All around Lachlan the crowd was beginning to grasp what the kelpie was insinuating. It unsettled Lachlan to no end, for everything the creature was saying were his own beliefs. *Just what is he planning?*

"And so, my good, dear Seelie Court, though it pains me to be right in such a situation I have no choice but to tell you the truth: my disappearance was a direct attack from the Unseelie king himself. He would have us under his thumb, to rule and manipulate as he sees fit. This cannot stand. I will not let it stand!"

Oh, no.

Though Lachlan had hated his stepfamily and their Unseelie blood, and had not discounted the notion that their attempt to usurp the throne was indeed part of a much bigger plan, now that he was listening to somebody else say as much with his own voice Lachlan realised what a horrific mistake it would have been for him to blame the Unseelie for what happened to him.

The kelpie was starting a war, which Lachlan knew his own Court could not hope to win.

"And nor should you!"

Lachlan stared at Ailith, for it was she who had shouted. Everyone looked at her; she squeezed Lachlan's hand before sweeping up onto the plinth to join the kelpie. The creature was looking at her, suspicion clear as day on his face. Lachlan held back a grin.

He does not know Ailith. He does not love her the way Lachlan, the Prince of Faeries, should. This is the distraction we need.

Ailith smiled angelically for the kelpie, enveloping his hands with her own. She turned to the enraptured crowd. "I, too, was duped by the bloody traitor Fergus and his father. I had been ordered to end my relationship with Lachlan, though I loved him so."

Everywhere there was outrage. Lachlan used the opportunity to close the gap between him and the plinth, readying himself to spring upon it and attack the kelpie. It was then that Sorcha, finally, spotted him, and her face paled. Lachlan frowned; he had thought Sorcha would be relieved to see him.

The kelpie seemed at a loss for what to do in the

face of Ailith's physical proximity. "We were all duped," he said. "We –"

"And I love you still!" Ailith cried, before embracing the false Lachlan, running a hand across his face and kissing him.

Now is your chance, Ailith, Lachlan thought. *Grab the chain and I'll grab Sorcha.*

The crowd was going wild at the kiss, eyes blind to the glassiness of their prince's expression. But their delight turned to shock when 'Lachlan' wrenched Ailith away and tossed her to the floor, a look of unbridled disgust upon his face.

"You –"

"How dare you lay a hand on her," Lachlan raged, throwing away his cloak as he jumped up onto the plinth. All around were gasps and exclamations of shock, and then –

Silence.

The kelpie stared at Lachlan in wide-eyed disbelief. "You should be a fox."

"And you should be in the loch, where you belong, yet here you are. So let Sorcha go and leave this place."

Lachlan watched as the kelpie dropped his disguise, returning to Murdoch Buchanan's appearance. The very air seemed to crackle around him; he ignored Lachlan to stare at Sorcha with fathomless, empty eyes.

"No."

CHAPTER THIRTY-FOUR

Sorcha

For one excruciatingly long moment nothing but silence surrounded Sorcha. She did not know who to look at: Lachlan, whose face was coloured with anger and concern at the way Murdoch had tossed Ailith to the floor; Ailith, who looked grimly satisfied that she had shown the crowd who the Lachlan preparing to take the crown actually was; the crowd, who did not yet truly understand what was going on, or Murdoch.

Murdoch, who had dropped his disguise and was staring right at Sorcha as if nobody else existed.

"No," he said, and though his voice was quiet it carried across the entire clearing. "You cannot have her. And you cannot have your kingdom, either."

The air around Murdoch seemed almost liquid. It ebbed and flowed around him, distorting the trees and flowers and sky. And the strange effect was spreading; when it reached the crowd the faeries in the front line froze in place, jaws gone slack as their eyes lost all life.

Wordlessly they pushed through the throng to reach the burn which encircled the clearing. They knelt in front of it. Nobody spoke.

Then they dunked their heads into the deepest part of the water and everyone screamed.

"Somebody pull them out of the burn!" Ailith cried, getting to her feet as she spoke. "They are drowning!"

But more and more Seelies joined them in their suicidal enchantment instead, until the water was brimming with thrashing, oxygen-starved bodies. Lachlan took a step towards Murdoch, face contorted with fury, but the kelpie held a hand out to stop him.

"Come any closer and I'll drown your beloved Ailith next," he warned. "How dare you pursue Miss Darrow when you had her, fox. How *dare* you."

Lachlan could only shake his head in disbelief. "Your problem is with me, not my people. Stop what you are doing!"

"Are you truly so arrogant as to assume this is all because of a grudge against *you*?" Murdoch laughed; it was an ugly, twisted sound. "Seelie, Unseelie – you are all the same. Self-centred, vain, arrogant creatures who covet anything they do not have, and scheme and bribe and blackmail until they possess it!"

"A war will destroy us all!"

"Exactly."

Lachlan's chest was heaving as he swung his head around, taking in the sight of the kelpie's ongoing massacre. "You will not get away with this," he said, but Murdoch merely snorted at the useless exclamation.

"Anyone who was here today to witness this will *die*

today. They will die, and I will blame it on the Unseelie, and I shall remain as you – as king – until you are all destroyed."

Sorcha had to do something. She knew it, so why was she standing there merely watching as dozens upon dozens of faeries slowly drowned themselves? Ailith was rushing around trying desperately to pull those closest to her out of the burn alongside a handful of Seelie Court guards who were still unaffected by the kelpie's strange, murderous powers. Sorcha was likewise unaffected; she could help them.

But when she moved forward to do so it was Lachlan, not Murdoch, who rushed towards her and pulled her away. His golden eyes bored into her own. "Get out of here, you fool!" he demanded. "Run away whilst you still can. *Please.*"

"Sorcha will not leave me," Murdoch called over, certain. He smiled at her, so agonisingly innocent in his surety that she would do as he said that Sorcha had to dig her nails into her palms to keep herself from crying. For even after she had told him not to touch her in the dead of night – to leave her alone to shake and shiver herself to sleep – the kelpie clearly had no doubt that he could make things right between them once today was over.

But he couldn't. Sorcha could not allow him to murder hundreds of members of the Seelie Court in front of her very eyes.

"Stand aside, Lachlan," she said in an undertone. His eyes widened when he saw her expression, but then, slowly, he nodded in understanding and let Sorcha past him. She walked towards the kelpie, careful to keep her face calm and collected. When she reached the dark-haired man she saw his eyes were wild and blood-thirsty; Sorcha knew nothing she said to him would make him stop.

Except, perhaps, one very specific, lone word.

"Murdoch," she murmured, stroking the kelpie's cheek with the tips of her fingers. His face lost some of its madness for just a moment, and all around them the sound of a hundred faeries breaking through water to claw and gasp at air filled Sorcha's ears.

Murdoch's lips curled into just the hint of a smile. "You have never used his first name before. Not to me. I rather like it, Sorcha. I –"

Her hand moved to his neck and snapped his silver chain.

"You should have kept me enchanted until you were crowned king," Sorcha said through tears, for in front of her it was clear the kelpie's heart was breaking. "Why didn't you simply keep me enchanted? Why allow me to be myself?"

Murdoch swallowed. It was his own form that was shimmering now, not the air. He closed his eyes for a moment. "I sent Galileo back to your parents' house, Miss Darrow. He is fond of you. Please look after him for me."

"You did not answer me!" Sorcha yelled, reaching up on her tiptoes to run a hand through Murdoch's hair to try and force his face down to her level. "If your plan was so important to you then why –"

"You already know why." Murdoch's voice was so quiet nobody but Sorcha could hear his confession. "I think everybody knows, even your fox. I am sorry I did not meet you in person sooner. Before him. Perhaps I should have remained your Mr Buchanan and never come to this wicked place at all."

"Mur–"

When Murdoch finally bent his head towards hers Sorcha thought he was going to kiss her. But then the lines of his body warped and disappeared and, in the space of three wretched seconds, he became the kelpie once more.

The huge, monstrous stallion reared onto his hind legs and screamed, his dark eyes tragically sad and betrayed. Sorcha could only watch him, clinging uselessly to the broken silver chain, as he leapt from the plinth in a flurry of shattered wood and crying, panicked faeries rolling out of his way.

"Return from whence you came, kelpie!" Lachlan yelled above all the deathly commotion. The creature turned to face him, baring his unnaturally sharp teeth in response. But he could not attack; his powers had been stripped from him along with his bridle. "Fall into the deepest, darkest depths of the loch and do not let any of my kind see you again, for if we do then know that your bridle will be melted down to nothing."

Sorcha wanted the kelpie to look at her just as badly as she dearly hoped he wouldn't. But he turned tail and fled through the forest without doing so, leaving Sorcha looking at the chain in her hands, instead. It had returned to its original form, allowing her to see – for the first time – the intricate links and loops and lengths of metal and blackened leather that constructed it.

"You did it, Sorcha. You truly did it."

Sorcha did not hear Lachlan at first; it was only when he picked her up and spun her around that her brain understood what he had said. She forced a smile upon her face for the obviously delighted faerie. "I said I would, did I not?"

Lachlan seemed barely aware of the pandemonium all around him when he kissed Sorcha. She wrapped her arms around his neck, clinging to him as if his presence might somehow keep her grounded.

"Miss Sorcha?"

Lachlan turned Sorcha around with him to face Ailith, who curtsied to them both. She was drenched from her efforts to save her people; behind them Sorcha couldn't help but notice the dozen or so twisted bodies of faeries lying in the burn who would never move again.

A chill ran down her spine.

"We owe you a debt of gratitude," the beautiful faerie said. "You must stay and live as one of us so we can repay you."

Lachlan's eyes lit up at the suggestion. He placed Sorcha back on her feet, took a step back from her and dropped down into a low, sweeping bow. "It would be our privilege and honour to have one as brave as you within our number."

But Sorcha shook her head. She had never wanted immortality, nor to live within the Seelie Court for the rest of her life. The way she felt for Lachlan was not enough to change that. She knew that he knew that, despite what he was currently asking. "You know I do not want that, Lachlan - Ailith - though it is beyond generous," she said, smiling sadly. "You may believe me a fool for refusing such an offer, but I..."

"I understand," Lachlan replied, though his expression was glum and disheartened. "Perhaps, in time, I might convince you otherwise."

"Perhaps," she said, for there was no harm in allowing the faerie a small shred of hope. "Perhaps one day, if my parents ever try to force me to marry a Londoner again."

It was a joke, but Lachlan did not laugh. He held out a hand towards Sorcha. "The bridle," he said. "We will protect it."

"*No!*"

Sorcha hadn't meant to react so viscerally. She clutched Murdoch's bridle protectively to her chest, though the hurt in both Lachlan and Ailith's eyes was plain to see. She sighed. "No," she said again, gentler this time. "I wish to keep it. I was the one who took it; it is mine."

Lachlan said nothing. Sorcha knew that, by his kind's own laws, he could not take the bridle from her. It *was* Sorcha's. He ran a hand through his hair and averted his eyes, clearly at a loss for what to say or do. Eventually he asked, "You are returning home now, aren't you? You really will not stay?"

"My father is sick," Sorcha explained, making her way off the plinth and towards the long pathway home as she did so. Part of her instinctively knew that if she stayed within the faerie realm for a final night then she may not leave at all. "I must go home. I cannot delay any further; it is high time I acted like the adult I am and faced my responsibilities head-on."

He chuckled. "I would prefer that you didn't. But I can see you again? When will I see you again?"

Sorcha turned to look at Lachlan over her shoulder, flashing him a grin that was clearly too infectious for him not to reciprocate, though they both knew her smile was tinged with a sadness Sorcha might never recover from.

"You know where I like to sing."

EPILØGUE

Sorcha

September rolled into October before Sorcha was truly aware of it and, with it, she turned twenty years old.

She never imagined she'd be forbidden to leave the Darrow grounds at *twenty years old.*

Sorcha supposed she couldn't blame her parents for keeping her locked up. She'd run away, after all. When she'd returned without Murdoch Buchanan only to discover that Galileo was indeed tied up in her father's stable Sorcha had to come up with a plausible excuse for why the man had disappeared, but his horse had not.

Even now, weeks later, she was sure her parents did not believe that Murdoch simply returned to London on urgent business, leaving behind his beloved stallion because Sorcha had grown fond of it. But – perhaps because they hoped it meant their daughter may still marry the man – neither her mother nor father questioned her lie. And Sorcha *was* fond of Galileo. Her parents only allowed her to leave the house at all because of him; to care for him.

Sorcha would ride him down to the loch shore simply to stare at the grey, wintry water. It almost looked to be made of steel. She hadn't dared touch the loch, fearing that the kelpie would sense her presence and drag her down into the depths to join him.

Sorcha was equally terrified that he *wouldn't.*

That the kelpie would ignore her, and Sorcha would never see or feel him again in the water, constricted the muscles of her heart until she could hardly breathe. Sorcha always fled back to the Darrow house on Galileo the moment she felt this way. She didn't *want* to feel this way, but neither did she wish to forget about the kelpie.

Because she'd been locked inside the house Sorcha had not been to her favourite spot to sing even once. She was therefore yet to see Lachlan; he hadn't even crept into her dreams.

He must be busy, she reasoned late one night, tossing and turning restlessly as sleep – not for the first time – evaded her. *He is king now, after all. I am not important.*

Thinking as much caused Sorcha's heart to tighten just as it did when dwelling on the kelpie. It wasn't that she revelled in being special or important to either of them – it was that they'd grown very much important to *her.* And she missed Lachan greatly. Sorcha wanted nothing more than to see him, for she did not want their short, tumultuous time together to become a faded memory as years passed by, and she grew older, and he did not. She wanted more. She wasn't done; her relationship with the faerie felt as if it had barely started.

Just as Sorcha closed her eyes and decided that she

should genuinely try and get some sleep she heard a rapping on her window. She stilled, listening patiently as the wooden frame was pried open from the outside. A horrifically bitter gust of wind whistled into her room; she ducked her head beneath the covers and tightened them around her.

But Sorcha was not worried about who the intruder was, for there was only one person who would do such a thing in the middle of the night, and she had only just been thinking of said person.

Or, rather, faerie.

"You have not been in your usual place, Clara."

Sorcha smiled at the sound of the familiar voice, though she did not open her eyes. "You won't call me by my real name, King Lachlan of the Seelie Court?"

"I decided I like Clara too much to abandon it. It is the name you gave me to use, so it is mine. Where have you been over the past few weeks?"

"Under house arrest. I was sorry to miss your coronation."

When Sorcha heard the window shut she finally turned over to face it, then lowered the covers from her head and opened her eyes. Lachlan was perched on the sill, a lopsided grin twisting his lips. The moonlight shone behind him. It illuminated his hair and skin alike with brilliant white-gold; a wicked glint set his molten eyes on fire.

"I almost came to steal you away for it, you know," he said before climbing down onto her bed. Sorcha moved over to make room for him, so Lachlan eagerly slid beneath the covers and propped his head up on his hand to stare at her.

Sorcha was glad for the darkness in her room to hide the blush that spread across her cheeks. "Why didn't you come for me, then?"

"If you'd wanted to go to the coronation you would have made it known. I thought the best thing I could do was wait for you to appear in the forest, looking for me."

"Considering your presence in my bed at present I somehow doubt that."

Lachlan held a hand over his mouth to cover a snicker. Sorcha was glad for it; her father would likely have a heart attack if he opened the door to find a faerie in his daughter's room.

"I grew impatient, admittedly," Lachlan said. "Do you wish for me to go?"

Sorcha shook her head. She glanced out of the window just as a blast of wind buffeted against the pane – the mere sound of it screamed *cold* and *unpleasant* at her. She raised herself up on her elbows, tilting her head towards Lachlan's. "It sounds awful out there."

"It *is* awful. My journey here was rather rough."

"You must be weary. Would you care to spend the night here, King of Faeries?"

Lachlan whispered a hand along Sorcha's thigh, smiling with his brilliantly white teeth at her resultant intake of breath. He leaned his head forward and bit her lip. "I shall gladly take you up on such a generous offer, Clara."

Sorcha had always hated the anglicisation of her name. Now she adored it. *Only when he says it,* she thought, slinging her arms around Lachlan's neck to pull him on top of her. *Only for him. Nobody else.*

In the morning Sorcha could worry about her parents, and taking over her father's responsibilities, and what was going to happen when more English investors showed up vying to buy their land. She could continue to stare at the loch and mull over the kelpie, and wonder if it might simply be better to run off to the Seelie Court and live with the faeries forever.

But, at least for now, Sorcha did not have to dwell over the unknowable concept of forever. Lachlan was with her, and they wanted each other, and 'now' only lasted a night.

Everything else could wait until tomorrow.

LØRD ØF HØRSES

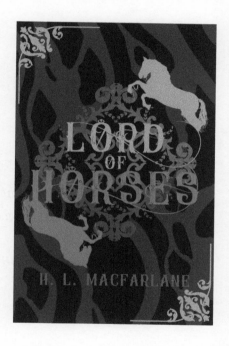

THE KELPIE

Folk alone in lonely lanes
Gladly take the horse's reins,
Innocence the creature feigns
Then takes the rider down
To the loch-side so remote;
The rider who the Kelpie caught
Is murdered now without a thought;
In icy loch they drown.
The Kelpie (N. Baker; 2010)

CHAPTER ONE

Murdoch

Murdoch loved the water more than anything, and he adored the loch he lived in most of all.

Spending two years banished to the bottom of it by the golden faerie king and his ice-blue queen changed his perspective on things.

In truth Murdoch wasn't even Murdoch. He'd taken the unfortunate Mister Buchanan's name, as well as his face and memories, when he'd dragged the man down into the loch and consumed his body and soul. But Murdoch didn't have the guise of the human anymore; without his bridle he could not change his form at all.

He liked the man's name, though, so even now he kept it.

For months Murdoch glowered and mulled and rued his fate at the very bottom of Loch Lomond. There was nothing else he could do, after all. If he dared show up at the surface and was spied by a damned faerie then his bridle would be destroyed, and Murdoch would have no chance of ever recovering his full powers again.

He'd had no intention of risking his very existence by leaving the depths of the loch. He truly hadn't. That was, until Murdoch heard something that changed his priorities entirely.

For there were plans to fill in the shallow, southern shores of his home, funded by the very company Murdoch Buchanan himself had worked for, before the kelpie had devoured him. He had to do something to stop the plan. If he didn't then he would not be the only one who suffered.

He desperately needed to talk to Sorcha Darrow.

It hadn't been easy, finding a way through which he could reach her. Murdoch could not come galloping out of the loch in his true form to find her; he would be far too conspicuous, and if a wary local attacked him with silver then he would die.

Murdoch had hoped Sorcha would come into the loch to swim. That way, without raising any suspicion, he could talk to her. But the first summer after his banishment she did not so much as dip her toes in the water, and the second she seemed to avoid even coming down to the shore.

I have ruined things with her, Murdoch despaired on more than one occasion. *I should have told her that I would love to speak to her again. She must be so afraid.*

And so, with no easy way to tell Sorcha about what was going on, Murdoch had to find another way to allow him to walk upon land unnoticed. Luckily for him, the very creatures infesting the loch that had caused Murdoch to try and destroy the faerie realms and, in turn, landed him in his current, powerless state, were the answer to his problems.

The Unseelie.

Murdoch hunted, ensnared and consumed every dark, sly, creeping faerie that had sought to make Loch Lomond their new home. With every drop of blood spilled he learned more and more of how their magic worked until, when autumn was truly turning into winter, Murdoch discovered where an Unseelie creature strong enough to help him resided – in his own home.

"Why should I help a kelpie?" the ill-begotten ghoul asked when Murdoch found it. Its murky, midnight-coloured hair swirled around its face like dead weeds, and its silvered skin shone akin to fish scales in the water. When it grinned Murdoch saw a set of sharp, broken teeth that had clearly been used to rend through flesh and bone.

"You like my home," Murdoch countered. "You revel in lost souls, just as I do. If you help me then I will not kill you where you stand, and you will be free to live out your days here with no further danger from me."

The creature laughed an ugly, garbled laugh. "You water folk can lie. I know you can. So how can I trust this deal you are suggesting?"

Murdoch solidified his ghostly, insubstantial form until he could tear open his flesh upon his own teeth, which were even sharper than the Unseelie's. His blood darkened the water; the faerie's odd, metallic eyes gleamed at the sight of it.

"A blood pact will ensure we both keep our sides of the bargain," Murdoch said. "Is that enough to gain your trust?"

"Then what is it that you want?" the Unseelie asked, lapping up Murdoch's blood with a forked tongue as it spoke.

"I wish to take on the form of a human. There is someone I need to see."

"That is some tough magic. Where is your bridle?"

Murdoch pawed at the sandy loch floor in frustration. "Currently indisposed. Will you help me or not?"

The creature stared at him, unblinking, for a long time. Eventually it said, "Twelve hours. That is all I can give you, so that is all you will have."

"Deal," Murdoch replied, heartbeat quickening in earnest. With this he would finally be able to talk to Sorcha, though convincing her to take back his bridle from her Seelie prince would be no easy task. Twelve hours really was no time at all.

Twelve hours would have to be enough.

The creature grinned. With a sharp nail it cut open the palm of its hand, smearing the silver-blue blood that spilled from its wound across Murdoch's forehead. "The moment you surface you will be transformed," it warned, "so do not break through the loch until you are where you need to be."

Wordlessly, Murdoch dissolved into the loch and used underwater currents to help speed up his journey to its southern shores, where the hamlet of Darach – and Sorcha Darrow's house – was. *I will have to appear as Murdoch Buchanan,* he realised as he neared the shore. *She will not recognise anyone else, and her parents would not let anyone they do not know into their house.*

The thought of Sorcha's parents gave Murdoch

266

pause. He hadn't considered how to handle them upon reaching the Darrow household. Ultimately deciding that he would cross that bridge when he came to it, Murdoch closed his eyes as he reached the upper layer of the loch, broke through the surface and –

Inhaled the ice-cold night air deeply into a pair of unfamiliar, human lungs. He swam the last fifty feet to the shore, wobbling unsteadily on legs that had not been used to walk for a long, long time. A gigantic shiver wracked Murdoch's body.

"It is f-freezing," he muttered, running his hands up and down his arms as he got his bearings. A strong gust of wind blew a load of wet, bitter snow into his face; Murdoch sneezed and cowered from the next lot before it could sting his eyes again.

I need clothes, Murdoch realised as he staggered across the sand. *I cannot show up to the Darrow house completely naked.*

But it quickly became apparent that Murdoch had no other choice. The weather was so brutal not a single clothes line was hanging up outside, and the MacPherson farm's barn and outbuildings were firmly locked and bolted against the wind.

"How do I explain all this to Sorcha?" Murdoch screamed into the wind, beyond frustrated that such a simple, stupid problem as needing *clothes* was wasting so much of his precious time. He stomped and slid through mud and slush until he spied her house, mind drawing a complete blank for the words to tell her what exactly was going on.

Just go up to the front door and knock, Murdoch thought. *There is no other way around it. Be thankful you have this opportunity at all. Do not waste it.*

When Murdoch finally crept along the gravelled pathway to the Darrow house he noticed that their carriage was missing, and that Sorcha's parents' room – as well as her father's study – was dark. Not daring to believe that he had managed to stumble across Sorcha when she was completely alone, Murdoch ran a hand through his dark, sodden hair and breathed deeply through his nose.

This is it, he told himself as he held a fist up to the front door. *She hasn't seen you in two years. She probably believes she'd never see you again – probably doesn't want to see you again.*

For the sake of both their homes Murdoch had to ignore the stinging in his heart at the thought of Sorcha trying to push him away. And so, with an overwhelming sense of fear washing over him, Murdoch knocked on the door...just as it was flung open.

Sorcha stood in the doorway, bucket of water in her hands. It came crashing and clattering to the floor as soon as she saw Murdoch, dripping wet and naked, standing a mere foot away from her.

He risked a smile, though his frozen muscles protested strongly against it.

"Miss Darrow," he said, inclining his head politely. "It has been too long."

CHAPTER TWO

Lachlan

"...Lachlan. Lachlan? *Lachlan!*"

"...what is it?"

Lachlan's gaze slid lazily over to Ailith. He had been dozing on the throne, he knew, but he did not care. The day had been long and dark and dreary, and all he wanted was a jug of wine and his bed.

And a song.

Ailith tutted, delicately crossing her legs on the ornate throne that had been built for her when she had become Lachlan's queen. "If you do not wish to discuss this now it can wait until the morrow," she said, "but it cannot be delayed any longer than that. Things are tense enough with the Unseelie as it is without you ignoring Eirian's emissaries."

"Then let said emissaries wait until tomorrow," Lachan drawled. "Given what the Unseelie king's brethren tried to do to me they can bloody wait another day."

His ice-blonde queen sighed patiently. "If he was going to wage war to avenge his brother and nephew he'd have made that clear already."

"Would he? The Unseelie are known for their deceptiveness, even to us. He might be waiting."

"For what?"

"...I do not know," Lachlan admitted, turning from Ailith in the process.

Life had been hard-going for Lachlan during the past two years. As if being cursed to live as a fox by his stepfather and stepbrother hadn't been enough for him to deal with, the fallout from a *kelpie* having posed as the Golden Prince of Faeries to assassinate both traitorous Unseelies had left Lachlan with utter pandemonium within his realm to calm and control. The creature had drowned fifteen members of the Seelie Court in its rampage, all to incite a war between the two faerie factions.

And steal Sorcha Darrow in the process.

It was Lachlan's turn to sigh. He hadn't seen Sorcha for two months, his work as king having taken up too much of his time to visit her. And Sorcha was working hard herself – her father's health had deteriorated so much that both he and her mother had moved to Glasgow to be closer to a respectable doctor. That left Sorcha to take up her father's business: looking after the land that surrounded Loch Lomond and the people that lived upon it.

For the hundredth time, Lachlan wished Sorcha had accepted his offer to live with him in the Seelie Court. He missed her dearly, and felt uneasy about how close she was to the loch. Lachlan may have cast the kelpie back from whence it came – and promised to destroy its bridle should it dare resurface again – but that didn't mean Lachlan trusted his threat would be enough to keep the creature away from Sorcha.

It loved her, after all.

"You are thinking of Miss Sorcha, aren't you?" Ailith asked, a knowing smile on her face.

Lachlan rolled his eyes. "Don't give me that look."

"I never thought I would see the day that you were so interested in a human, Lachlan," she laughed. "And for two years, no less! I must admit, I thought you would have lost interest in her by now. I am glad that you have proved me wrong."

"Why, because it means you get to watch me suffer?"

She slapped his arm gently. "You are so over-dramatic."

"I know. You love it."

"Is there really no way Miss Sorcha can be convinced to live as one of us?" Ailith wondered aloud for both herself and Lachlan. "Surely things are different for her now. A lot can change for a human in two years."

"She has more responsibilities now, certainly," he complained. "Though that only seems to make her want to remain exactly the way she is even more. Damn mortal sensibilities."

Neither of them said anything for a minute or two, their silence punctuated only by the arrival of a servant proffering them a bronze tray with two goblets of wine upon it. Both Lachlan and Ailith happily took one each.

After a long draught of the heady, crimson liquid,

Lachlan slumped even deeper into his throne. "Winter is boring," he moaned. "Hardly anyone comes into the forest. No humans lurking and searching, wishing to make a deal with a faerie, or seeking a revel, or searching for a whisper of a soul already lost to us."

Ailith squeezed his hand. "It has always been this way in the weeks leading to the winter solstice."

"Yes, but before I was king I could come and go as I please, seeking out mischief wherever I went. Now I must stay here...ruling. How did my mother ever manage it? It is suffocating."

"Maybe so, but you are good at it," Ailith reassured. "You are proving those wrong who believed that you were not ready."

"Too bad the lead perpetrators are too *dead* to see that they were wrong," Lachlan muttered darkly.

Ailith said nothing. She did not like to talk about Queen Evanna's second husband, the half-Unseelie Innis, nor of the faerie's son, Fergus. She had been engaged to marry Fergus, after all, though she had not agreed to the union out of love. But she clearly had some feelings that remained for her tempestuous husband-to-be, even after discovering he had been the one who cursed Lachlan.

Just as Sorcha still has feelings for the kelpie, though she would never admit to it.

For it did not matter that Sorcha delighted in seeing Lachlan whenever they managed to snatch a few hours of time together, nor that all they thought of was each other during those hours. Sorcha was alone with the loch right outside her door, and Lachlan had seen the way she looked out across it when she thought nobody was watching.

It tore Lachlan apart with jealousy.

"Speaking of the solstice," Ailith said, magicking a thick, silvery card out of thin air to spin it between her hands, "you still haven't responded to Eirian's invitation to the winter revel. You know you must go."

Lachlan made a face. "What is wrong with us having our own one? Why must he hold dominion over all things dark and frozen?"

"Because you get to hold the revel during the summer solstice, and it is only fair." Ailith threw the invitation at Lachlan, who caught it without looking at it. Sighing heavily, he pressed his thumbprint against the card and closed his eyes. When he opened them again the invitation was gone.

He made a face at Ailith. "There. It is done. Are you happy n-"

"King Lachlan," a frantic-looking, red-faced Seelie with the ears and antlers of a young buck announced as it skittered across the throne room, startling Lachlan out of his bad mood. Both he and Ailith perked up at the intrusion.

"What is it?" she asked.

The creature shifted on the spot uncomfortably. Lachlan's heart rate sped up; something told him he would not like what he was about to hear.

"You said you wished to be informed the moment the - the moment the kelpie emerged from the loch," they stammered. "I saw a man swimming out of the water down on the southern shore, and it looked -"

"A *man*?"

The buck nodded.

"Then it could not be the kelpie," Ailith said, smiling warmly for the trembling Seelie. "But thank you for your information –"

"No, it looked like – I was there when the kelpie tried to d-drown us all," they insisted. "This man looked just like the guise the monster took two years ago."

Lachlan's face darkened. "The southern shore of the loch, you say? Did you see where the man was headed?"

The creature looked too terrified to reply. Lachlan knew that he cut an intimidating figure, particularly now that his magical powers increased with every day he sat upon the Seelie throne. Even draped across said throne in a half-undone shirt, breeches and no shoes he had the capacity to incite fear in those he faced.

He was not in the mood to dull his presence for the sake of a quivering faun.

"Where was he headed?" Lachlan asked again, voice full of warning. "You must tell me."

The creature gulped.

"Miss Darrow's house."

Lachlan stared at Ailith, who stared right back at him. In her haunting blue eyes Lachlan could see his own face, golden and livid and full of a fear he would never admit to.

Am I stronger than the kelpie now? Can I end his life where I could not before?

"Time to pay Sorcha a visit," Lachlan said, a vicious, vulpine snarl curling his lips.

There was only one way to find out.

CHAPTER THREE

Sorcha

Sorcha couldn't believe her eyes. She simply couldn't. For there was no way Murdoch Buchanan was standing on the threshold of her house, his dark hair dripping glacial water down his ghostly-pale, naked skin.

Very, very naked skin, Sorcha thought, forcing her eyes back up the man's face as soon as she realised they had wandered downward.

"Can I come in?" Murdoch asked. Sorcha became aware of the fact that he'd already asked the question twice already, and all she'd done was stare blankly at him. He was shivering and shaking; clearly he had been wandering around outside for a while.

Sorcha numbly waved Murdoch inside, forcing the heavy wooden door shut behind him to keep out the howling storm threatening to blow snow down the hallway. She stumbled along to the parlour room – where she had been sitting by the fire to read a book – and yanked open a chest of drawers to pull out a large, tartan blanket.

She flung it at Murdoch.

"You – what is this?" Sorcha asked, so quietly she could barely hear herself over the crackling of the fire. She didn't dare to look at him. "Are you...are you –"

"The kelpie, yes," Murdoch coughed. He wrapped the blanket around himself, waiting until Sorcha indicated for him to sit by the fire with a panicky jolt of her head to fall to the carpeted floor. "We both know the real Murdoch is dead."

Sorcha was torn between collapsing onto the armchair by the hearth and pacing back and forth in distress. In the end she perched upon the very edge of the chair, back stock straight as she stared down at the shivering figure of Murdoch Buchanan wrapped in a blanket.

His hair has grown longer, Sorcha thought when she noticed the way it almost reached his shoulders. *How could that be possible? The kelpie is merely borrowing the man's form to – to –*

"How are you human?" she demanded, finally vocalising the first question she should have asked the very moment she saw Murdoch standing outside her door.

The kelpie's impossibly dark eyes bored into her own. There were deep-set shadows beneath them; along with the hollowness of his cheeks Murdoch looked altogether haunted. *Or dead, which the man himself has long-since been.*

Sorcha pushed the disturbing thought away.

"I made a deal with an Unseelie ghoul," he explained, though his voice was so cracked Sorcha barely understood him. With a swish of her dress she got to her feet, waving for Murdoch to stay exactly where he was in the process.

"I'll get you some water," she said, "and food. You look half-starved."

The smallest of smiles quirked his lips. "That will happen, when all you eat for months and months are the lowest of the fae."

Sorcha did not respond. She did not know how.

She took her time in the kitchen, browsing through the pantry to locate cheese, oatcakes and some salted ham her parents had brought back from Glasgow a few days prior. Alongside these Sorcha filled a cup with water that had been boiled over the fire an hour ago; it was pleasantly warm to the touch. She added a dash of honey to it to help ease Murdoch's throat.

Lastly Sorcha threw a few cubes of tablet that she had made the evening before for lack of anything better to do. It still didn't have the texture her mother's tablet had, but she was getting better and better at making the sugary confection with every new attempt.

And then, because it would not do to stall any further, Sorcha placed everything onto a wooden tray and brought it back through to the parlour room. Murdoch was staring at the fire as he warmed his hands against it, though when he heard Sorcha's footsteps he turned to smile at her.

He does not look angry with me, she thought. *Even after what I did to him. How could that be?*

Sorcha placed the tray of food down on the floor in front of Murdoch before sitting opposite him. "I apologise," she said, "I didn't have any leftovers from dinner, so cold meat and cheese will have to do."

But Murdoch shook his head at Sorcha's apology. "I did not expect you to feed me, Miss Darrow. This is far more than I deserve." He picked up the cup of honeyed water, sighing contentedly when the liquid passed his lips.

"...you said you made a deal with an Unseelie," Sorcha ventured, curiosity finally overcoming her need to be a gracious host. The kelpie was hardly her usual kind of house guest, after all. "Are you – does that mean you can change your form again?"

Murdoch gulped down a mouthful of cheese before replying. He glanced at the ornately carved, oak-wood clock hanging on the wall. "I have another ten hours in this skin, or thereabouts. When my time is up I will return back to the way I was before."

"Then why...what are you doing here? What do you need?"

"Miss Darrow..." Murdoch held her gaze for a long moment then cast his eyes downward. "I need my bridle back. But it is not to do anything nefarious, I swear. I need to go to London."

London?

Of all the answers the kelpie could have given, this was the last one Sorcha had expected. She slid from the armchair to kneel in front of Murdoch. "What is in London?" she asked. "Just what is wrong?"

"Grey and MacKinnon – the company Murdoch Buchanan still officially works for – have grown impatient with his extended stay up here, Miss Darrow."

A pause. It did not take Sorcha long to work out what Murdoch meant. "...they want to do something with the land around the loch again, don't they?" she said. "How have you been holding them off for so long in the first place? You were – I mean, you aren't actually *Mr Buchanan*."

Murdoch laughed humourlessly. "No, I am not, but considering I planned to use this appearance to ensure no harm was wrought on my home, I had certain countermeasures put in place before I went searching for my runaway bride two years ago."

Sorcha blushed before she could stop herself. She looked away. "What kind of countermeasures?" she mumbled, twisting her hands in her lap as she did so.

"Everyone in London believes that you and Mr Buchanan have spent the last two years enjoying an extended engagement. It has held the company off until now, but I'm afraid the time I managed to borrow has been spent. Miss Darrow, they intend to fill in the shallowest southern shores of the loch to make room for official hunting and holiday lodges."

"They *what*?!"

Gone was Sorcha's previous wariness of Murdoch; with a furious expression on her face she pushed away the tray of food that separated them and leaned towards him, hands balanced on Murdoch's knees to keep her from falling over. He seemed entirely surprised by her sudden closeness, though Sorcha did not have it in her to care right now.

"I own the land around here!" she shouted at him. "My father signed it over to me last year so they could not bully him into handing it over! They cannot walk onto *my land* and –"

Murdoch cupped Sorcha's face between his hands,

silencing her tirade prematurely. There was a softness in his eyes that Sorcha had dreamed about more often than she dared to admit, not least because the kelpie had looked at her with the same exact expression transforming his features before she had ripped his bridle away from him.

And broken his heart.

"Miss Darrow," he said, an agonisingly fond smile upon his lips, "I plan to stop them, rest assured. But for that, I need to beg of you a favour." He inhaled deeply through his nose. "Is there any way I can convince you to ask your golden faerie for my bridle back?"

Sorcha froze. Murdoch seemed to take this as a *no,* for the smile fell from his face and he made to drop his hands. But Sorcha raised her own to keep them there, instead, and in doing so lost her balance. When she began to fall towards Murdoch's chest his grip tightened on her face to keep her upright.

"There is no need for me to do such a thing," Sorcha said, laughing giddily. Her heart was beating so hard and fast it felt as if it would burst from her chest; she had not felt this alive in months.

Murdoch frowned, confused by both Sorcha's answer and their new-found proximity. "...what do you mean, Miss Darrow?" he asked, very quietly.

She grinned. "Lachlan does not have your bridle. I do; it is mine."

It took a few moments for the truth of what Sorcha had said to sink in for Murdoch. His frown deepened, and then disappeared, and he ran a hand through Sorcha's hair to bring her even closer to him.

Sorcha hardly dared to breathe. The air between her

and the kelpie was dark and electric – an achingly familiar, dangerously seductive atmosphere that Sorcha had been sure she'd never feel wash over her again.

She leaned into his touch just a little more.

"You would let me have it?" Murdoch asked, voice low and melodic and full of hope.

Of course Sorcha was going to let him have it. She had never wanted to take it from him in the first place.

Her lips parted. "Ye–"

"Absolutely not."

Murdoch and Sorcha's eyes widened in unison. They turned their heads to face the door. For there stood Lachlan, as thunderous and wild as the storm currently battering the Darrow household.

A growl leapt from his lips. "Get away from Clara or so help you, kelpie, I shall destroy you where you stand."

CHAPTER FOUR

Murdoch

"Do I have to repeat myself, you bloody horse?" Lachlan fired at Murdoch. "Get away from her – *now.*"

But Murdoch did not move. How could he? Sorcha Darrow was in his arms. She was in his arms, and she had his bridle, and she wanted to give it back to him. Her passion to protect her home – *their home* – had ignited her mismatched eyes like fire.

He would never willingly let that go.

But then Sorcha shifted away from him, and the spell was broken.

"Lachlan," she said, standing up to greet him with a wary smile on her face, "once you have heard what is going on you will understand why I wish to give him his bridle back."

"That *monster* was told not to resurface!" the faerie snarled, ire dripping from every syllable he spoke. He glared at Murdoch. "But you just had to see her, didn't you? You couldn't leave her well enough alone. And you have the gall to demand she help you? Why would you ever think that –"

Sorcha slapped him.

"If you do not *listen*, Lachlan," she warned, "then I will give Murdoch back his bridle without so much as including you in the conversation. Are we clear?"

Murdoch did not think he could love Sorcha Darrow more than he already did, but he was blissfully, painfully wrong. Watching a human have the power to physically harm a faerie with no repercussions was immensely satisfying, especially when said faerie was the Seelie king.

Lachlan was positively stunned by both Sorcha's slap and her threat. Clearly he did not know what to say, torn between incandescent rage and disbelief as he was.

"Miss Sorcha, it is good to see you...despite the circumstances," came a soft, feminine voice from the doorway. Murdoch stood up, wrapping the tartan blanket Sorcha had given him a little tighter around his body in the process. For there was Ailith, the beautiful faerie who had become Lachlan's queen after he ascended the throne.

The one who loved Lachlan with all her heart, yet had decided to break his anyway. The one who was responsible for Lachlan seeking to enchant Sorcha into being his until the end of time.

Sorcha rushed over to embrace the female faerie, who happily reciprocated the gesture. She kissed Sorcha's brow, then pulled away from her to give Murdoch a once-over. "You do not look well, kelpie," she said. "How is it that you appear before us as the late Mr Buchanan once more?"

Murdoch took a moment to inhale the heady woodsmoke emitted from the fireplace before he spoke; the smell helped to ground him. For he did *not* feel well, not at all. Clearly the Unseelie ghoul's magic did not agree with him in the slightest.

"I made a deal with a darker fae," he explained for Ailith's benefit, and Lachlan's. "I have another ten or so hours left before their magic wears off."

Lachlan barked at the explanation, sounding entirely like the fox he had once been. "An Unseelie was foolish enough to help the creature that killed its own kin?"

"Given that they were skulking in Loch Lomond I somehow doubt they care much for their brethren," Murdoch countered. "Or they do not wish to be found by said kin." That was how most fae – Seelie and Unseelie alike – ended up hiding underwater, after all.

"And what was *so important* that you had to make a deal with their kind in order to show up at Clara's door?"

"Why don't you sit down, Lachlan, and he can tell you," Sorcha cut in, gesturing for both Lachlan and Ailith to sit upon the armchairs by the parlour room's bay window, which overlooked the loch. Once upon a time Murdoch had sat there with Sorcha to have their first real conversation, and he had teased and scared her.

It felt like forever ago.

It was Ailith who sat down first, giving Lachlan a pointed look until he, too, collapsed onto the chair beside her with a scowl on his face.

"Fine," the faerie muttered. "Explain away, kelpie, whilst I am in the mood to listen."

And so Murdoch told the King and Queen of the

Seelie Court all about Grey and MacKinnon, and the looming threat the company posed to the Darrow land. Sorcha fussed around them, pouring drams of pale amber whisky and topping up Murdoch's cup of honeyed water.

When Murdoch's explanation came to an end nobody spoke for a few minutes. Clearly Lachlan and Ailith were mulling over what he had told them, though with every passing second Sorcha grew more and more restless. She sat on her armchair, then stoked the fire, then wandered over to a chest of drawers to rearrange the contents. Murdoch was tempted to pull her down to sit on the floor beside him; it took everything in him to resist doing so.

Eventually, Lachlan turned his golden eyes on Murdoch and said, "There is no way I am allowing you to travel *anywhere* with your full powers unsupervised."

"He won't be unsupervised," Sorcha said. Everyone stared at her as she finished refolding a blanket that did not need refolding.

"What do you mean, Miss Darrow?" Murdoch asked, just as curious as Lachlan and Ailith were.

She straightened her back and cleared her throat. "I'm going with you, of course."

"Absolutely not!"

"But it makes sense, Lachlan," Sorcha countered, silencing the faerie with a single glance. She twisted her hair over one shoulder with her fidgeting, restless hands. She was nervous, that much was apparent, but Sorcha also had a determined expression on her face which told Murdoch she had resolutely made up her mind.

"I am meant to be engaged to Mr Buchanan," she

said. "Grey and MacKinnon believe he has spent the last two years up here living with me. It would be better for me to travel down to London with Murdoch to meet the man's associates. That way I can keep track of what is actually going on...as well as ensuring the kelpie does not get up to no good."

Lachlan looked as if he desperately wished to complain. Murdoch himself was torn between protesting Sorcha's suggestion and gleefully accepting it. For there was no doubt Mr Buchanan's associates had few qualms with stooping low and using questionable methods to acquire things they wanted, going by the man's memories. It would be dangerous to put Sorcha in front of them. But on the other hand...

I would get to spend time with her by myself, with no fox-cursed faeries getting in our way.

When Lachlan stood up Ailith followed suit. He took her hand and raised it to his lips, then let it go in order to face Sorcha. "We need to talk, Clara," he said, temper clearly barely contained. He fired another glare at Murdoch. "In private."

She nodded, sparing Murdoch a glance before following Lachlan out of the parlour room. Murdoch and Ailith sat in awkward, agonised silence punctuated only by the snap and crackle of the fire and the roaring storm unsettling Loch Lomond outside the curtained window.

"So you wed him," Murdoch murmured, simply to break the unbearable tension. He kept his eyes on the fox-orange flames blackening the stone hearth. "You really did love him; that was not a lie."

"You know my kind cannot lie," Ailith said. "I have always loved Lachlan."

"If that is the case then why do you appear unperturbed by his feelings for Miss Darrow?"

She let out an impassioned sigh. "There is so much you do not understand, kelpie. Your solitary life has left you woefully ignorant."

Murdoch bristled at Ailith's comment, though her tone had not been patronising – she had simply spoken something which she believed to be the truth.

He scowled at her. "And what does that mean, exactly?"

"It means that the Seelie are not constrained by such restrictive notions as monogamy. It is possible for us to love more than one soul at a time, and deeply. You rarely hear of faeries slaughtering one another in jealous rages; this is why."

"That may work well for you," Murdoch countered, "but Miss Darrow is human. She –"

"Has been more than happy with her and Lachlan's arrangement up to now," the faerie interrupted, "though it is clear from your face that you do not wish to acknowledge that."

Murdoch had no reply.

"Although," Ailith added on, voice very soft. She pulled aside the curtain to stare into the dark, unruly night with almost vacant eyes. "I do believe Lachlan would throw me aside if Sorcha asked him to. If Sorcha accepted his offer."

"If she...what has he offered her?"

Ailith's laugh was like a winter burn bubbling over stone – the kind of sound that enchanted mortal men and otherwordly creatures alike. "Oh, kelpie," she said,

"Lachlan has offered her the world, and will continue to do so until the end of time."

Murdoch did not want to work out what that meant.

CHAPTER FIVE

Lachlan

It was freezing outside the Darrow house. Wet, stinging snow buffeted Lachlan and Sorcha; she wrapped her father's old coat a little tighter around herself.

"Did we really have to talk *out here,* Lachlan?" Sorcha complained, disapproval clear as day on her scrunched-up face. "The weather is horrible."

He pointed towards the parlour room window. "I do not want that damn horse listening to us as we speak, Clara."

"Do you have to talk about him like that? Lachlan, he came to me for *help.* He does not mean any –"

"If you say *harm,* Clara –"

"But all he wants to do is use **Mr Buchanan's** identity to stop our home from being destroyed!" Sorcha cut in, furious. "We all knew this was coming, and do not deny it. The entire reason my father betrothed me to Murdoch was to prevent this! If we sit around and do nothing then the man's colleagues – Grey and

MacKinnon and whoever else – will take everything away! They will come for my land and the loch and before you know it, Lachlan, they will come for the forest. So do not say we cannot help the kelpie."

Lachlan was taken aback; he had not seen a fire in Sorcha's eyes like this for months and months. For her to have *shouted* at him about the matter meant she truly had been worried about it for a long time. *She never talked to me about her concerns for the land. Why would she not confide in me?*

But the answer was right there, in front of him: she assumed Lachlan would not do what she had known in her heart had to be done over the past two years.

The kelpie needed its bridle back.

Lachlan punched the stone wall of Sorcha's house, then immediately regretted it. He hated demonstrating such physical acts of violence and frustration in front of *anyone,* let alone Sorcha. And now his hand throbbed.

He gritted his teeth against what he had to say next. "Fine," he muttered, without looking at Sorcha. "Fine. But there will be conditions, you hear me? You cannot simply –"

Lachlan's words were cut off by Sorcha flinging her arms around him. She was already cold and wet from the snow, but he did not care; he returned the embrace eagerly, lifting her off her feet in the process.

"Thank you," Sorcha said, voice sincere and affectionate. "Thank you, Lachlan. I knew you would not be foolish on this matter." When he finally placed her back on the ground she smiled and tucked a lock of flyaway hair behind an ear. "Now, can we *please* go back inside? I cannot feel my fingers."

He let out an exaggerated sigh. "If we must."

"We must."

It was with begrudging reluctance that Lachlan trudged back through to the parlour room, Sorcha not far behind him once she had removed her boots and her father's coat. She rushed over to the fire, crying out in happiness when the heat from the flames began to warm her hands up.

Murdoch watched her with such fondness that Lachlan almost picked up William Darrow's nearby silver letter opener and drove it through the kelpie's heart. But he resisted, though Ailith's keen eyes caught the subconscious flick of his wrist towards the potentially deadly weapon.

"Going by the look on your face," she said, "you have decided to relent to the kelpie's request."

"It seems we have no other choice, if we mean to protect our home," Lachlan replied, though it pained him to admit it.

Murdoch turned his gaze from Sorcha to Lachlan, eyes sharp with suspicion. "There are conditions, I am assuming?"

"Of course there are, you murderous, water-dwelling –"

"*Lachlan.*"

Both Sorcha and Ailith had spoken his name in identical warning tones. They glanced at each other, smiling softly; this was not the first time both of them had felt the need to chastise him in this manner. *You find a paramour and your queen becomes her best friend. Though it's only one more reason for Sorcha to join the Seelie Court.*

Murdoch watched the minute interaction between the two women with an expression that suggested he had come to the same conclusion as Lachlan had – that despite her growing responsibilities as an adult, Sorcha had been given more and more reasons to abandon her human life altogether over the past two years. Once she secured the Darrow land for good that would only be another point in the faerie realm's favour. Eventually, Lachlan hoped, she would give in and accept his offer to live in the Seelie Court – forever, if he had his way.

He relished that the kelpie clearly did not like that idea one bit.

Murdoch's voice was tightly controlled as he asked, "So what are the conditions?"

"Clara – Sorcha – will go with you to London, as Murdoch Buchanan's bride-to-be," Lachlan said, detesting the idea with every fibre of his being. "She will have complete control over your bridle. Where is it, Clara?"

Wordlessly she vacated the parlour room to retrieve it. Lachlan wondered where she kept it, for he had forced himself never to ask. If he knew then he would be tempted to destroy it, laws of ownership be damned. Instead, Lachlan contented himself with glaring at the kelpie, who bristled beneath the blanket Sorcha had given him to dry off. He looked frustratingly pitiable – the kind of pitiable that Sorcha would take it upon herself to address.

It was how she had come to help Lachlan break his fox curse, after all.

When Sorcha returned she had the kelpie's intricate silver bridle clutched protectively to her chest. Murdoch's entire being seemed to brighten simply by being in the same room as it.

Lachlan held out a hand. With noticeable hesitance Sorcha allowed him to touch the bridle; he did not wish to dwell upon that hesitance. "If you are ever further than a mile from Sorcha outside of London's borders," he began, "or if you try to take her anywhere she does not wish to go, you will lose your human form and all your powers. Take it or leave it, kelpie."

"I will take it, of course," Murdoch said. His jaw clenched as Lachlan wove his words into the bridle. Out of the corner of his eye Lachlan spied Ailith, poised and ready to defend him if Murdoch decided to use his temporary defencelessness to strike him down.

When Lachlan was done he let go of the bridle as if it had burned him, though in truth it was because he could not bear to touch it. It brought back too many memories of drowned faeries, and blood drenching the Seelie coronation plinth, and the kelpie telling him that he would not let Sorcha go.

"It is done," he muttered. Sorcha laid the bridle down on her armchair by the fire before returning to Lachlan's side to thank him. Clearly she intended to give it to Murdoch privately, which was an idea Lachlan did not relish. The two of them would be alone for days and potentially weeks on end, from the second Lachlan and Ailith walked out of the Darrow house until the moment Sorcha and Murdoch returned from London.

Lachlan did not want to leave without letting the kelpie know exactly what Sorcha was to him. "Do not make me regret helping you more than I already have," he warned the beast. "And..."

He wrapped an arm around Sorcha's waist and pulled her against him, hungrily kissing her as if it were the last time he might ever get to do so. For one awful moment she flinched, and Lachlan thought she might push him away, but then the tension melted and Sorcha allowed the kiss to happen.

Lachlan wanted to push it further. He wanted to, but he resisted.

He had a feeling Sorcha would tell him to stop, and Lachlan did not want to hear her say as much.

"Be careful, Clara," he whispered against her lips, for nobody to hear but her. Sorcha nodded the smallest of nods in return. When he finally broke away from her he turned to face Murdoch, a ferocious grin plastered to his face.

Murdoch looked positively murderous, which had of course been Lachlan's desired outcome. "...touch a single hair on Clara's head, kelpie," he said, voice eerily sing-song as he threatened Murdoch, "and I will ensure you lose *your* head in return."

He and Ailith spirited themselves out of Sorcha Darrow's house before the creature could respond.

CHAPTER SIX

Sorcha

It was three hours past midnight and Sorcha could not sleep.

The storm from earlier in the evening had finally abated, leaving the night soft and eerily quiet. Sorcha pulled back the curtain from her window and watched the clouds blow away, leaving the sky crisp and perfectly clear. Stars shone brightly upon the ink-black canvas; she thought there was something sad about them. Lonely. Heartbreakingly beautiful.

She wanted to be beneath them.

Without another thought Sorcha pulled on her boots and rushed out of her bedroom, forcing herself not to look at the guest bedroom door as she passed it. After Lachlan and Ailith left earlier that evening Murdoch had quickly admitted to being exhausted and excused himself for the night. Sorcha hadn't wanted him to, of course, but in truth Murdoch had looked so terrible she didn't feel like she had the right to stand between him and a soft bed. But one thing had confused Sorcha.

Murdoch hadn't put on his bridle.

She had taken it from the parlour room and laid it upon the floor outside the guest bedroom, in the hopes that Murdoch would open the door and find it during the night. However, it was currently exactly where Sorcha had left it, which caused her to frown in concern. *He has three hours of Unseelie magic left to use,* she thought, throwing on her father's old coat before easing open the front door and creeping outside. *I will have to awaken him soon. That is, if he is actually asleep.*

Given the last time Murdoch had slept in the Darrow guest bedroom, Sorcha doubted it very much.

"I wonder if he will follow me outside," she murmured, the words escaping her lips as puffs of icy breath upon the night air. It was even colder now than it had been when Lachlan dragged Sorcha outside to speak to her in private.

Too cold for snow. Too cold for noise.

Sorcha crunched over frozen grass towards the Darrow stable; since she was outside she reasoned she should check on Galileo. She was worried his water had iced over, and that the blankets she had thrown over him would not keep him warm enough against the bitter winter cold.

When she was halfway across the garden Sorcha paused to look up at the night sky. It seemed fathomless to her eyes, holding secrets that she would never be privy to. Knowledge of people and places and planets well beyond the scope of her understanding. It made her feel distinctly alone.

Perhaps it is not the stars that are lonely, then, Sorcha thought somewhat wistfully, letting out a heavy sigh before continuing on to Galileo's stable. She knew she'd been teetering on the edge of unhappiness ever since her parents had moved to Glasgow. It had been the right choice for them – and Sorcha was grateful that her father trusted her enough with the family business that he could leave her to work alone – but Sorcha missed them greatly.

"If only there were more unattached people my age around here," Sorcha grumbled for only the stars to hear, "but even Gregor MacPherson is now married with a babe on the way. There is only me left."

Sorcha flinched when the iron lock of Galileo's stable bit at her skin. It had not been this cold in Darach for years; Sorcha only vaguely remembered one winter as bitter as this from her youth. The snow had arrived early that year, and Old Man MacPherson and the other farmers had suffered a loss to their crop yields due to the frost. It had been a hard time for everyone, so Sorcha's father hadn't taken any rent from the residents on his land that winter.

One of many reasons why we have little and less money now, Sorcha thought, *though I would have done the same thing in my father's position.*

It was to her relief that Galileo's water trough was safe from the sub-zero temperatures; the fabric Sorcha had padded the metal and wooden barrel with had done a more than a serviceable job at keeping the water from freezing over. Galileo pawed at the straw floor of his stall as he watched her approach him, whinnying softly in response to Sorcha stroking a hand down along his nose.

"Are you warm enough, my love?" she cooed at the

stallion, rubbing her face against his when Galileo leaned in against her. His brown eyes shone in the darkness between slow, long-lashed blinks. "If I could have you inside the house with me I would, you know. You are my closest friend."

"That is both heartwarming and unbearably sad, Miss Darrow."

Sorcha's breath caught in her throat. "I had a feeling you were not asleep," she said, not daring to turn around. "Though I was going to awaken you soon if you were. You need to put on your bridle."

"I was merely relishing my final few hours in a human form that did not rely upon a silver chain," Murdoch said. Sorcha glanced over her shoulder; the kelpie was leaning against the door frame, body outlined in pale, luminous silver from the almost-full moon behind him. Along with the billowy white shirt he was wearing, the shadows beneath his eyes and the gauntness of his cheeks he appeared almost a ghost.

"You should not delay putting your bridle back on for such a reason. You really do not look well, Mist-Murdoch," Sorcha said, correcting her knee-jerk reaction to fall back on formalities.

Murdoch chuckled. "You can call me by whichever name you prefer, though I'd rather you didn't follow in your faerie's footsteps and call me *horse*."

"He is not *my* faerie," she protested, turning back to tickle Galileo's neck when he *harrumphed* at being ignored.

"It certainly seemed as if he considered you his," Murdoch countered. He walked towards Sorcha and Galileo, footsteps echoing all around the stable as he did so. When he held out a hand the stallion nibbled his fingers. "Hello, Galileo. It has been a while."

Sorcha frowned at the man who was not a man. "If Galileo was Mr Buchanan's horse then why does he like you? Surely he must know that you are not –"

"He knows," Murdoch cut in, voice quiet. He smoothed his hand along Galileo's neck; Sorcha watched him do so with rapt eyes. "He knows that I am not the master he had. But I am his friend, and he mine. That I ate Murdoch Buchanan is ultimately of no consequence to Galileo. It is simply my nature to consume humans, as it is his nature to feast upon grass."

When Murdoch's hand grazed against Sorcha's she did not pull away, though his touch was icy and his words sent a chill running down her spine. Her stomach was full of nerves at the prospect of acting as a dead man's wife-to-be, too, which only served to further discomfort her. It had been easy to stand up and tell Lachlan that she would gladly travel down to London to help the kelpie save her home.

Doing it was another thing entirely.

She sighed. "Murdoch –"

"Won't you take a walk with me, Sorcha?" he asked. She turned to see a knowing look upon his face, as if he had correctly surmised what was troubling her. He inclined his head politely. "If you are not too cold, that is."

Wordlessly Sorcha accepted, giving Galileo one final pat before exiting and locking the stable behind them. It should have come as no surprise that Murdoch wound his way across the Darrow garden towards the loch, though Sorcha did not complain. It was where she had planned to go herself, after all.

"You are concerned about London," Murdoch said after a while. He was shivering slightly; the shirt and breeches Sorcha had found for him from her father's wardrobe were hardly enough to keep out the winter air.

She made a face. "You should have put on a coat."

"And you are deflecting."

"We should head back and get –"

Murdoch reached out and squeezed Sorcha's wrist. Her cheeks began to burn at his touch, though she passed it off as a reaction to the cold. "I will be fine," he said. "I am not human, and this vessel the Unseelie gave me is near spent, anyway. Once I put on my bridle I will be in good health once more."

Sorcha did not like the idea of Murdoch's current form dying before her very eyes at all, though it was clear the kelpie did not care, so eventually she let go of her concern. "Yes," she sighed, taking several long strides towards Loch Lomond across slippery, ice-encrusted grass. "I am worried about London. Are you not, Murdoch?"

His ears pricked at Sorcha's use of the name. When they reached the shore along the water's edge he kicked at the sand, sending it flying several feet in front of him. "Of course I am," he admitted. "It is not often I find myself venturing out of Scotland – not least to live as a human in the busiest city in Britain."

"Do you...do you know what we need to do when we get there?"

Murdoch nodded. He pointed to his temple. "Mister Buchanan's memories are invaluable. I should have no problem acting as the man himself whilst we are in London."

Sorcha's stomach lurched once more. She knelt by the loch, holding a shaking hand a mere inch above its surface. She had not touched it in two years, for fear of what she would – or wouldn't – find in the water upon making contact. But now the kelpie was beside her, carelessly skimming stones across the very loch that was his home.

Why am I so nervous? Sorcha worried. *I was not so bad back in my house earlier this evening. What has changed?* She stole a glance at Murdoch through her wild, tangled hair. He was kneeling beside her now, and had stuck his hand into the freezing water without a moment's hesitation. His eyes were dark and vacant, like a mirror in a shadowy corridor.

Perhaps it was because of the frost, or the moonlight, or the proximity of the loch, or the Unseelie's magic, but even under the guise of a human Sorcha did not think the kelpie *looked* human. Not at all.

How did I ever think he was simply a man?

"You truly do have an unfortunate habit of staring, Miss Darrow," Murdoch said without tearing his eyes away from the loch. "I thought your parents raised you to have better manners than this."

Sorcha bristled, then stood up with her hands curled into fists at her side. "I –"

"I jest," Murdoch laughed, thoroughly amused. He removed his hand from the loch and dried it upon his breeches. "I forgot how easy it is to burrow under your skin, Sorcha."

When Sorcha's insides twisted this time it was not

entirely uncomfortable. She scratched behind her ear and looked away. "That is not very kind of you, you know," she mumbled, but Murdoch merely laughed again.

"Says the woman who once fled out of her bedroom window to avoid having to speak to me when I had not done anything wrong."

"You ate the man you were masquerading as!"

"I suppose I did. Should we head back inside?"

Sorcha nodded, thinking as they headed back towards her house that it should not have been so easy for her to talk about a man's horrific death as if it were merely a piece of casual, passing conversation. But the kelpie had been correct back in the stable – it was in his nature to devour humans. Sorcha could not blame him for eating Mr Buchanan, no more than she could blame the men who hunted deer in the forest for venison.

The two of them walked in companionable silence across the garden, the only sound the soft lapping of the loch upon the shore, when Murdoch slipped on the icy grass with a yell of surprise, and grabbed onto Sorcha's arm before he could stop himself.

"Careful!" she exclaimed, heart hammering in her chest as she just barely kept herself upright. Murdoch had fallen down on one knee, so Sorcha held out a hand to help him back up. A smile crossed her lips before she could stop herself. "Perhaps you should spend more time on your own two feet," she said, thinking back to the first time she had said such a thing to the kelpie before she knew he was anything but a man.

Murdoch's dark, fathomless eyes were perfect reflections of the starry night sky as he looked up at

Sorcha; she almost gasped at the sight of it. His fingers tightened around her hand, and he slowly got back up on his feet. "Perhaps I should," he agreed, "though if my balance got better then I would not have the pleasure of you saving me, Miss Darrow."

He is dangerous, Sorcha thought, stricken by the memory of being held by the kelpie in her tent two years ago. *He was dangerous then and he is even more dangerous now.*

She did not have it in her to be scared of that danger anymore.

"Come," Sorcha mumbled, tearing her hand away from Murdoch's before her mind raced even further down memory lane. "You should get back inside and put on your bridle. You look like death."

"I feel like it, too."

Sorcha chuckled softly. "And that just won't do. We need to be in the best of health for travelling down to London. The journey will take us days."

"...it may not be as long as you think."

She cocked her head to one side, regarding Murdoch suspiciously as he closed the front door behind them and made for the guest bedroom. He picked up his bridle from the floor when he reached it, an unreadable expression on his face that hid everything he was thinking about.

"What do you mean by that?" she asked, continuing down the corridor until she reached her own bedroom door. Something told her that she should give the kelpie his privacy when putting on his bridle, though Sorcha did not know why. She was hardly an expert on magical creature etiquette, after all.

But Murdoch did not answer her question. He merely smirked.

"Good night, Sorcha Darrow," he said, closing the guest bedroom door before Sorcha had an opportunity to press him further on the matter.

When she lay back in bed it came as absolutely no surprise that her mind was racing far too wildly to fall asleep. *Morning cannot come quickly enough,* Sorcha thought, staring at her door as if she could see right through it to Murdoch's bedroom.

With a sigh she rolled over and forced herself to close her eyes. "What a strange day this has been," she whispered, simply to acknowledge that the events of the day had indeed happened.

Sorcha knew in her heart that the following days were only going to get stranger.

CHAPTER SEVEN

Sorcha

By the time Sorcha had washed, dressed, combed her hair and laced on her boots Murdoch was already out in the stable preparing Galileo for the long ride to London. But when she spied him walking the stallion towards Old Man MacPherson's farm Sorcha grew confused and concerned.

Just what is going on? she wondered, trying her best to settle her nerves by preparing breakfast for herself and Murdoch. Sorcha still had to pack for the trip but in truth she had no idea what to bring. She certainly had no clothes that were expensive enough to wear surrounded by the upper classes of London gentry. *Murdoch will know what to pack,* she reassured herself. *Or, at least, Mister Buchanan will.*

It was getting very confusing for Sorcha, constantly thinking of the kelpie and the man as different people. Perhaps she was better combining the two for the sake of her act as his bride-to-be...as well as her sanity.

"Something smells wonderful," Murdoch called out when he returned to the house fifteen minutes later. He breathed in deeply through his nose, smiling broadly for Sorcha when she turned from the cooking fire to say good morning.

"There's little point in leaving any sausages or eggs in the house when we do not know when we'll be back," she said, emptying the overfull contents of a large cast iron pan onto two plates. She frowned at Murdoch. "Why did you take Galileo over to the MacPherson farm?"

He avoided her gaze, evading answering the question by spearing a sausage off his plate and consuming the entire thing whole. With a sigh of impatience Sorcha dug into her own breakfast. *I suppose I'll find out exactly how we're travelling in due time,* she thought, inspecting Murdoch with careful eyes as he devoured every morsel of food on his plate.

Murdoch looked a thousand times better than he had done the night before. Gone were the shadows beneath his eyes, the skull-like hollowness of his cheeks, the hunched posture of someone trying hard not to vomit, and the sickly pallor of his skin. He had returned to being just as handsome, broad-shouldered and strong as Sorcha remembered the man being two years ago, even in her father's ill-fitting clothes. Around Murdoch's neck the delicate silver chain of his bridle was just barely visible beneath the collar of his borrowed shirt.

But one thing remained changed from two years ago.

"Why is your hair longer than it was when I met you?" Sorcha asked, curiosity getting the better of her as she took both of their empty plates over to the wash basin. "Surely Mr Buchanan's form does not need to age."

Murdoch ran a hand through his loose, shoulder-length curls and shrugged. "It is a reflection of how much time has passed for me. Of how things have changed."

"So *you* altered it? Deliberately?"

He nodded. "Do you mislike it, Sorcha?"

"No," she replied a little too quickly, taken entirely by surprise by the kelpie wanting her opinion on the matter. She blushed. "No," Sorcha said again, slowly this time. "I like it. Though it may get meddlesome as we travel down to London through all this bad weather we've been having. Heaven knows I wish I could simply chop off all of my –"

"Do not even dare suggesting cutting off your hair," Murdoch warned. "It is beautiful."

She scoffed, then blew an errant lock of hair out of her face. "It is always a mess," Sorcha complained. "I'm no good at making it look nice the way my mother does. I wonder how I'll ever manage to pass myself off as a *lady* in London. I don't even know what to pack! And –"

"Ah, so that was what you were fussing over for so long in your bedroom," Murdoch said, understanding dawning on his face as he smiled. He stood up from the kitchen table, waving for Sorcha to join him in the hallway. When he removed her father's old coat from a hook on the wall and passed it over to her she hesitated before putting it on.

"You do not need to pack anything," he said. "We can buy everything we need in London." He fished through a small bureau that sat beneath the hallway mirror until he found a length of thin rope. Murdoch grinned at it. "Perfect," he murmured, scraping back his hair from his face before using the rope to tie it back. Sorcha had to admit she liked the look of him with his hair this way, though she resisted saying as much out loud.

She used her reflection in the mirror to braid back her own unruly hair, spinning it into a knot at the base of her neck before asking, "Are we really not taking Galileo to London?"

Murdoch caught hold of Sorcha's gaze in the mirror. His shoulders straightened, and he coughed softly. "There are...far faster ways to travel than by road, especially when the weather is so disagreeable." He turned towards the front door and unlocked it, letting a burst of bitter air through that stung Sorcha's cheeks. His eyes narrowed against the brightness of the frost covering the Darrow garden. "The sooner we set out, the sooner we will arrive at our destination."

Sorcha made to follow Murdoch to the door, but a glint in the mirror gave her pause. She peered at it, believing it to be the sun shining through and hitting the glass before realising that said sun was obscured by thick, white clouds. The glimmer remained even when she looked at the mirror from a different angle, cocking her head so far to the side that her ear brushed against her shoulder.

Murdoch laughed at her from the porch. "What on earth are you doing, Sorcha?"

"Nothing," she murmured softly. When Sorcha focused on the mirror again the glint was gone. She blinked a few times, confused, then decided she was clearly very tired and was therefore seeing things. *It will be a long time before I reach a bed,* Sorcha thought, glancing wistfully at her bedroom door. *But it is my own fault I could not sleep.*

When Murdoch led Sorcha through the dull, freezing morning towards Loch Lomond she grew ever more uncertain. "Just what are we doing here?" she demanded, when Murdoch stopped precisely where the water lapped against the shore.

He rolled his left shoulder until it cracked, staring out across the loch instead of answering Sorcha's question. Then he tugged the silver chain of his bridle an inch or two away from his neck so she could see it clearly, glittering like diamonds in the winter air. Sorcha held out a hand towards it before she could stop herself.

"You now hold dominion over my powers, Miss Darrow," Murdoch said, tone careful and serious. "I have not been in this position before. I never thought I would be able to bear it. But if the person in control of me is *you,* then..." He smiled. "I think I can handle it. And since you are now connected to the bridle..."

Sorcha was just barely beginning to grasp at what Murdoch was insinuating when his form began to ripple and warp. She had seen him transform into his true self only once, in the memory of a nightmare in the middle of the Seelie Court. Now, in the broad light of day outside her house, the way the very lines of his body dissolved and changed in front of Sorcha's eyes seemed more a hallucination than anything real, just like the glimmer in the hallway mirror.

Between the space of one blink and the next Murdoch Buchanan was gone, replaced with an enormous, hulking, pitch-black horse. Tiny bones and strands of murky green weed were knotted into the kelpie's long, flowing mane, and when he opened his mouth two rows of sharp, deadly teeth were revealed. The chain around his neck had become a silver and blackened leather bridle once more.

When Murdoch-the-kelpie spoke he startled Sorcha so badly she tripped. "Get on," he said, bending low on his front legs for her to climb onto his back.

"I can't – Murdoch, how do we get from here to London like this?" she asked, at a loss for anything else to say. She was transfixed by the form of the enormous creature kneeling before her.

His tail twitched. "Through the water, of course."

"But I can't breathe under water! And Loch Lomond is not in any way connected to –"

"Just get on, and you will see," Murdoch said. He laughed at the look on Sorcha's face, though it sounded distinctly inhuman. She crept towards him on unsteady legs, holding an outstretched hand an inch or two away from his neck before stopping.

Sorcha knew she was trembling. "I am afraid," she admitted, for there was no use in lying to the kelpie. He turned his head and knocked against Sorcha's cheek with his nose; the air he huffed out was warm and reassuring on her skin.

Murdoch kept one large, impossibly dark eye on Sorcha's face. "To be afraid of the unknown is natural," he said. "But I will not let any harm come to you. You will be safe. I swear it."

Her hand was still trembling when Sorcha ran it through the kelpie's mane, but she ignored it. Taking a deep breath she hitched herself onto the creature's back, swinging a leg over and wobbling unsteadily as Murdoch lifted himself onto all four of his gargantuan hooves.

Now that he was standing at his full height Sorcha realised just how much taller he was than a real horse.

I am riding a giant, she thought. *An otherworldly, incomprehensible giant.*

"Do not let me fall," she said, smoothing her hands against the glossy hair of Murdoch's neck before entwining her fingers through his mane for dear life.

Murdoch chuckled his inhuman chuckle once more, then took a few steps into the loch. "I won't," he replied, and then – against all logic or sense – dove straight into the loch and dissolved into the water, taking Sorcha with him.

Sorcha had always thought that if she found herself riding a kelpie it would be to her doom. That was what all the stories warned people about, after all.

She never imagined she would use such a creature to travel down to London.

CHAPTER EIGHT

Murdoch

Murdoch had never felt so free. Despite the fact a human had complete control over his powers, and that same human was currently riding on his back, he felt ecstatic. Wild. Invincible.

If he'd ever doubted whether he still had feelings for Sorcha Darrow after two years banished to the bottom of Loch Lomond, he most certainly didn't now. Everything that had happened over the span of the last twenty-four hours was enough to tell him that he was still hopelessly, painfully in love with her.

Particularly the way she clung to his ghostly, ever-changing form as he barrelled down to London through every body of water he could find.

I am not scared, I am not scared, I am not –

"I can hear you, remember."

Sorcha flinched against Murdoch's back, and he laughed. "I told you not to be frightened," he said, as they left Loch Lomond behind to pass through the Firth of Clyde. Murdoch planned to follow the Firth into the Irish Sea, then head back inland via the River Mersey. Then it was a case of hopping from river to river, lake to lake, and stream to stream until they reached London.

Murdoch had not travelled in such a way over a distance as long as this for at least three human generations. After spending two long years imprisoned in his own home he found the space around him incredibly liberating. And he was getting to show Sorcha Darrow how exactly he could move from place to place so quickly, too, thus teaching her more about him.

He never wanted the journey to end.

Though Murdoch was melting into each body of water he passed through, making use of currents to travel as quickly as possible, he was still keenly aware of Sorcha's arms wrapped around his neck and her thighs squeezing against his back. Her face was buried in his mane; whenever he made a sharp turn she cried out a mouthful of bubbles and buried herself even deeper into his hair.

How can I breathe? she thought at him. *How am I alive? How are we travelling so fast?*

"Because you can wield my bridle," Murdoch said, veering out of the way of a large shoal of cod when they appeared on his left. "It is difficult to explain. But so long as you are touching me you will not drown."

Sorcha's mind was silent of all but the barest thought for a long time after that, but eventually her grip began to loosen just a little and Murdoch felt her relax. *Can you always move this fast?* she asked him.

He nodded. "Only if I merge with the water, though. To keep a solid form I must move far more slowly."

Do other kelpies not mind when you swim through their homes?

"We are only passing through, so it is acceptable. If I were to linger and challenge them then they would not be so hospitable."

Sorcha mulled over this for a few moments; Murdoch thoroughly enjoyed listening into her thought process. He came to quickly realise that, for every question she vocalised, another dozen or so went unsaid. Murdoch had always thought Sorcha spoke her mind without consequence – just as she acted without consequence – but now he wasn't so sure.

There was so much he did not know about the woman currently wondering how on earth the two of them were going to avoid suspicion upon arriving in London, dripping wet and without any luggage.

"Murdoch Buchanan's townhouse lies close to the Thames," he explained for Sorcha's benefit. "It will be dark when we arrive, so it is unlikely anybody will see us appear from the water. It is but a minute or two's walk to the front door."

Sorcha lifted her head from Murdoch's neck as if she meant to speak out loud. *Won't the house be locked?* she asked. *And in disrepair? Mister Buchanan has not been back for two years.*

"The house has been kept in good condition by his housekeeper, Mrs Ferguson," Murdoch replied. He flinched at the drop in water temperature when they moved into the Irish Sea from the Firth of Clyde. "I have kept in contact with her all this time."

How?

"There is a selkie who lives in London who has

314

been writing letters on Murdoch's behalf and passing them over to her," he said. "Last night I sent word to the selkie to inform Mrs Ferguson of our imminent arrival, so the house should be ready for us by the time we reach it."

How did you send word down? Sorcha asked. *You never –*

"Remember when I dipped my hand in the loch? I called for a messenger to pass along my orders to another messenger in the Firth of Clyde, and so on and so forth."

...oh.

Murdoch felt a pang of sympathy for Sorcha. He was springing a lot of information on her at once in his excitement and eagerness for her to understand how the life of a kelpie worked. How *his* life worked. It was not fair of him to do so.

"You do not need to think about these things so much if you cannot wrap your head around them just now," Murdoch said after a moment of silence. "The magic of kelpies is –"

"I have spent two years as a friend to the Seelie Court," Sorcha said aloud, the words escaping her mouth as a riot of bubbles. "I might not understand magic the way I would if I possessed it, but it does not trouble me. I simply wish..." Her sentence trailed off to nothing.

"Sorcha?"

She sighed. *I wish I had known all of this about you before now.*

Murdoch's heart stung; his entire body rippled beneath Sorcha's. "I would have told you," he said, very quietly, "had you touched the loch even once over the last two years."

I thought you might drag me down to die for how I betrayed you, Sorcha admitted. *Or worse, ignore me.*

"You believe me ignoring you is worse than killing you?"

Yes.

"You are so strange."

Says the kelpie to the human.

Neither of them spoke to each other for a while after that, Sorcha's mind growing distant as she fell prey to drowsiness and Murdoch concentrating on hopping from river to lake and stream until he finally caught the murky scent of the Thames. By the time he crashed through the dark surface of the river to land upon the paved street beside it Sorcha had almost fallen asleep; Murdoch's change back to a human abruptly brought her back to consciousness.

"We are – we are here?" she spluttered, coughing and shivering as she did so. She stared at Murdoch with wide eyes. "The water did not feel so cold when we were in it, but the air is freezing!"

Murdoch smiled sympathetically, wrapping an arm around Sorcha's shoulders before leading her on shaking legs along the abandoned promenade in the direction of Mr Buchanan's townhouse. It was bizarre, to know exactly where he was going based on someone else's memories masquerading as his own, though it was not the first time Murdoch had taken on the guise of a man he had consumed. It was merely the longest time he had done so, and the most serious.

By the time he reached a grand, handsomely-carved

front door Murdoch had to admit he was nervous. But he couldn't be nervous – not when Sorcha was relying on him to know what he was doing. *Just be Murdoch Buchanan,* he thought. *You did it before. You can do it again.*

But that meant not being himself, and Murdoch did not like that at all. It had been hard enough to blend the man's personality with his own back when he had first introduced himself to Sorcha Darrow; even harder when he had travelled around the loch with her. Now Murdoch would have to ensure none of his own self slipped through the cracks whilst he was in London, for if Grey and MacKinnon or any of Mr Buchanan's other associates suspected something was awry then his and Sorcha's attempts to save their home would be ruined.

Feeling in a distinctly worse mood than he had been but a moment ago, Murdoch rang the bell that hung over the door and waited patiently for the sound of someone scurrying down the stairs to wrench it open. They were greeted by Mrs Ferguson, Mr Buchanan's housekeeper: a woman of slight stature, middling age and greying hair, whose blue eyes widened when she took in Murdoch and Sorcha's appearance.

"Mister Buchanan!" she exclaimed, ushering the two of them inside before closing the door behind them. "What ever happened to you? And you must be Miss Darrow! You are frozen half to death!"

Sorcha smiled somewhat rigidly, as if her face was truly made of ice. "It is a pleasure to meet you, Mrs Ferguson."

"We were caught in a bit of a flurry just outside the city," Murdoch lied in lieu of having to explain how exactly the two of them were soaked through. "I will admit that we certainly feel frozen half to death. Is the fire going in my bedroom?"

The servant nodded, following them up the stairs until they reached the main hallway of a house that was both familiar and alien to Murdoch's eyes. "The bath is ready," she said, "and I have prepared a platter of food in your room should you be hungry."

"Thank you, Mrs Ferguson," Murdoch replied, touching Sorcha gently on the shoulder to direct her towards Mr Buchanan's bedroom. "Miss Darrow and I are both exhausted, so that will be all for the evening. We shall talk in the morning."

Without another word the housekeeper retreated into what Murdoch knew was the kitchen. Sorcha began staring unabashedly at everything she saw, but Murdoch put an end to her gawking by gently pushing her into his bedroom.

"You take the bath," he said, shoulders slumping with relief the moment the heat from the fire Mrs Ferguson had lit in the hearth tickled his skin.

Sorcha shook her head. "I am...too tired," she yawned, stripping off her soaked and frozen clothing without so much as an ounce of modesty; Murdoch watched her in stunned silence for a long moment before turning from her in a panic. "I wish merely to heat up by the fire and crawl into bed. Don't you, Murdoch? Murdoch?"

"...ah, yes, I agree," he mumbled, pulling off his own clothes and throwing on the first voluminous shirt he could find in the wardrobe as quickly as he could. He filtered through the clothes inside until he located another, then flung it at Sorcha without looking at her. "This will have to do until tomorrow."

318

She laughed softly. "It will do after tomorrow, too. You know I am not fussy with my clothes."

Murdoch risked a glance behind him and was relieved to find that Sorcha had put on the shirt. It fell to the mid-point of her thighs and was so wide around the shoulder that it threatened to slip off her frame entirely, causing Murdoch to remember the one night in Sorcha's tent when he had slept with her curled against his chest.

An ache of longing twisted somewhere beneath his stomach.

But Murdoch could not act on his impulses; not when he was supposed to be someone else. For Sorcha was not *his* wife-to-be, and the entire engagement was a charade in the first place. No, Murdoch had to keep a respectful distance, at least whilst the two of them were in London.

He wished he had asked Mrs Ferguson to prepare the guest bedroom but Murdoch, in his excitement and distinct lack of human sense and sensibility, hadn't wanted to part from Sorcha for even a moment whilst they stayed together.

How he regretted that decision now.

Sorcha perched herself delicately on the bed, wincing as she ran her fingers through her hair to detangle it. She raised an eyebrow at Murdoch. "Are you going to stand by the fire all night, or are you coming to bed?" she asked, clearly oblivious to the thoughts currently tormenting Murdoch at that very moment.

He closed the distance between them and crept beneath the covers, careful to avoid looking at Sorcha as she collapsed against the pillow beside him with a contented cry. "Good night, Miss Darrow," Murdoch said, turning his back on her before he could do anything he might later regret.

"...good night, *Mister Buchanan*," Sorcha replied, the amused tone to her voice only stinging Murdoch further as she settled herself down to sleep. Despite everything that had happened since he had shown up at her door – the electric current between them, the fact Sorcha had not let anyone take his bridle away from her, the ease with which they had spoken to each other – Murdoch knew he had to be careful. He could not be himself right now.

He had to be Mr Buchanan.

And yet, regardless of the circumstances, sharing a room with Sorcha Darrow and not being able to touch her was a torment even worse for Murdoch than losing his powers to the Seelie King.

CHAPTER NINE

Lachlan

Lachlan's eyes were wide open, though he knew the sun was already as high in the sky as it would go. He should have been fast asleep. He *should* have, but thoughts of Sorcha in London with the kelpie were haunting him. They had been gone for but two days. Two.

Lachlan had no idea how he was supposed to cope with her being alone with the creature for weeks.

"Sleep, Lachlan," Ailith murmured without opening her eyes, rolling over to place a placating hand on his bare chest. But Lachlan slid away from it, creeping out of bed and tossing on a deep green, spider-silk robe that fell in large swathes of fabric to the floor. Though he was loathe to leave the warmth the dying embers in the massive hearth provided, Lachlan could stand to stay still even less.

And so, bracing himself against the chill of the palace corridors, Lachlan eased the large, carved doors of his chambers open on silent hinges. He spared a final glance at the sleeping figure of his queen, whose pale hair was perfectly dishevelled across several pillows and glimmered in the low light of the room like white gold. He smiled at her, then carefully closed the doors behind him and stalked aimlessly away.

Ailith would say I was over-reacting if I told her how I felt, Lachlan thought. *She would tell me that Sorcha can handle herself. That she has full control over the kelpie's powers. Perhaps I am over-reacting. But I cannot help it, all things considered.*

The sconces along the smooth, curved walls of the palace were barely lit with flickering flames, and all windows were covered from the dull noonday sun; most everyone was asleep save for a sparse scattering of guards. They bowed their heads respectfully when then realised their king was passing them by. Even in darkness the corridors shone faintly gold, illuminating Lachlan's skin as if from within.

He remembered the first time he had stolen away through the palace with Sorcha in tow. She had lulled the kelpie to sleep in Lachlan's bedroom – had sung him a song in a voice so soft and gentle Lachlan had almost bowled down the door to interrupt it. Even now, two years later, he hated that Sorcha had sung for anyone but him.

She might sing for the kelpie again, Lachlan's brain chimed in unhelpfully. He bit at his lip and shook his long hair out of his face, beyond irritated. Lachlan wished it was acceptable for him to travel down to London himself to keep watch over her, but he knew it was impossible. Until the winter solstice revel he could not justify leaving the Seelie Court – not even for Sorcha.

Lachlan found himself outside the heavy iron door that protected his favourite place in the entire palace from lesser fae. The power of the metal thrummed in the air, stinging Lachlan's hands even though he was not quite touching it, but with a singular thought the door swung open and granted him entrance.

The room was dark, as usual, but Lachan's keen eyes quickly adjusted until he could pick out every phosphorescent mushroom, coloured gemstone and pit of pillows and blankets that punctuated the floor. A shallow burn snaked its way across the ages-worn stone, bubbling into the room from some hidden, underground spring and leaving via an invisible crack in a wall into the forest.

Lachlan watched his reflection in the crystalline water for a few moments, distressed to see a scowl curling his lips back from his teeth. He quickly wiped it from his face. It was a remnant of his time as a fox, he knew – something that the kelpie had made even worse by stabbing Lachlan whilst he had been cursed. Sometimes Lachlan woke up unable to speak, or found himself longing to leap into a pile of fallen leaves to rub his non-existent fur across them. He craved raw pheasant and rabbit on occasion, too, which wouldn't have been so odd if he didn't also desire to catch the birds with his own jaws.

If the foreign wizard Julian hadn't healed Lachlan's stab wound he would still be a fox. All these tics served as reminders of how close he had been to losing himself forever.

"Clara," he murmured at his reflection, before breaking the surface with his hand in order to splash the bracing water of the burn over his face. He wished dearly to see her; to braid her hair and slip her dress from her shoulders and whisper promises of forever into her ear. He wanted all the things he currently could not have.

If only I could reach her dreams, Lachlan thought longingly, collapsing into the pit of pillows where they had first lain together in real life. If he closed his eyes Lachlan could almost imagine the smell of Sorcha from that heady, dangerous night. Bluebells and lilac. Dirt beneath her fingernails and sweat on her skin. The hint of the loch, ever-present in her hair.

"I want her," he moaned, grasping onto a red-and-gold cushion as if it were Sorcha herself. And then Lachlan had an idea. His powers had grown since he'd first ascended the throne of the Seelie king. Just because he'd never tried to enter a mortal's dreams from as far away as London before did not mean he *couldn't* do it.

A small smile curled his lips at the thought. If he could do it – if he could reach Sorcha across hundreds and hundreds of miles – then it would not matter that Lachlan could not currently leave the faerie realm.

He couldn't wait to see the look on her face when she realised that she was not imagining Lachlan inside her head, just like the first time he had invaded the girl's dreams. Sorcha would be happy about it. More than happy, Lachlan knew. They had a relationship that nobody else understood, least of all the kelpie.

"She is mine, horse," Lachlan said, the promise of seeing Sorcha finally lulling him into a slow, contented sleep.

CHAPTER TEN

Murdoch

It was simultaneously awkward, pleasing and incredibly frustrating for Murdoch to wake up with Sorcha beside him for the third morning in a row. Awkward, because they were still somewhat surprised to see the other upon first waking up. Pleasing, because Murdoch could think of nothing better than watching Sorcha struggle between curling back beneath the covers to sleep for longer and deciding to stay awake. Incredibly frustrating, because there was nothing worse than resisting the urge to touch Sorcha when she, still half-asleep, rolled right into Murdoch's arms and slid her bare legs between his own.

It was a delicious torture.

They had spent their first full day in London largely unconscious, so exhausted from the previous twenty-four hours that their bodies demanded an exorbitant amount of rest to make up for it.

On the second day, Murdoch arranged a messenger

to send word to Grey and MacKinnon that Mr Buchanan had returned to London and wished to meet as soon as was possible, as well as organised the man's personal office and finances. Sorcha had contented herself with exploring the house, talking to Mrs Ferguson and memorising maps of London.

If she noticed the distance Murdoch had put between them she did not make it apparent.

On the third morning the two of them were woken by Mrs Ferguson, informing Murdoch that Grey and MacKinnon wished for him to come to their office that very day. Sorcha complained profusely when Murdoch rose from bed and ripped open the curtains, shining morning sunshine through the window straight onto her face. It was a beautiful day, for which Murdoch was grateful; he did not have it in him to put up with sleet and snow.

"Am I coming with you?" Sorcha grumbled, huddled beneath the covers with an expression that very much implied she did not wish to move from the bed ever again.

Murdoch shook his head, then pulled a white shirt over his hair. "No; I imagine the company will invite you to some kind of luncheon or dinner party once I have spoken to them," he said. He stumbled slightly as he pulled on a pair of deep, wine-coloured trousers that he'd taken a fancy to from Mr Buchanan's wardrobe. "Though, with any luck, we can convince them to leave Loch Lomond alone and head back home before we have to do much socialising."

"I would not mind socialising."

He raised an eyebrow in Sorcha's direction. *"I am scared of strangers. Particularly those from London. A* fiery, opinionated lass once told me that."

Sorcha rolled onto her back, tilting her head to watch Murdoch upside-down. She snickered. "You have a good memory. But I am here to be Mr Buchanan's wife-to-be, am I not? And I have never been to London before. It would be a waste not to look around and be a tourist. Heaven knows I've had to deal with my fair share of them back home; it's about time I get to be one myself!"

"I suppose that is fair." Murdoch considered her answer as he slipped on a tailcoat that matched his trousers and a pair of knee-high, black leather boots. A tall, round hat hung innocuously from a hook by a full-length mirror; Murdoch put it on and fussed around with his curly locks of hair.

Sorcha let out a low whistle. "Those clothes look absurdly good on you, Murdoch," she said. Through the reflection in the mirror he noticed a flush had spread across her cheeks; it spelled trouble for his heart rate.

He coughed softly, picking up a soft pair of white, doe-skin gloves and a black overcoat as he made his way to the door. "It appears our Mr Buchanan has excellent taste," he murmured. He turned to face the bed. "Speaking of clothes, Mrs Ferguson is going to accompany you shopping today, if you are up to it."

"I suppose I could be convinced to leave this bed," Sorcha drawled, a lazy grin spreading across her face as she stretched her arms across a silken, brocade coverlet. Her shirt was no longer covering her legs at all; Murdoch had to remind himself to stop openly staring at her in such a state of undress.

She is making my life impossible.

Murdoch coughed once more. "I...should be off, then," he said, thrusting open the bedroom door and darting out of the house before Sorcha or even Mrs Ferguson had an opportunity to say goodbye.

*

"Well if it isn't our long, lost Mr Buchanan!"

Murdoch plastered a genial smile to his face as he greeted a room full of people he largely recognised. The oldest gentleman in the room, Howard Grey, was portly, grey-haired and nearly sixty years old. He grinned as he shook Murdoch's hand. His business partner, Gregory MacKinnon, was a few years younger and several pounds lighter than him, with hair that was still black as pitch. His smile was a little tight as he took his turn in shaking Murdoch's hand.

There were three other men whom Murdoch recognised sitting at the large, polished mahogany table which took up much of the room: the board's treasurer, James Campbell; their secretary, William Wright, and a junior partner to the firm, Francis Smith. But there was one final person Murdoch had not met before sitting at the table, who was perhaps around thirty years old. Going by his similar appearance to Gregory MacKinnon, Murdoch could only assume the man was his son.

"Mister Buchanan, this is my son Donald," Gregory said, confirming Murdoch's assumption as he sat down beside him.

"Don," his son corrected, rolling his eyes at the older man. "Calling me Mr MacKinnon would be confusing with my father around, and I rather dislike *Donald.* It sounds like a farmer's name."

Murdoch could say nothing to the contrary, for he

328

had known several farmers called Donald over the past few centuries. He had even eaten a few of them.

"It is a pleasure to meet you," Murdoch said politely. When Howard handed him a crystalline glass full of whisky Murdoch had no choice but to accept it, though it was barely noon – going by Mr Buchanan's memories the man never turned down a drink. The fact that they'd chosen *whisky* to drink was clearly a jibe made at Murdoch's expense because he'd lived in Scotland for the past two years; all of his previous memories pointed to the board members of Grey and MacKinnon favouring port.

"We brought him in to take over most of your duties in your absence," Gregory said, indicating towards Don, "though Norman over at the bank was not happy to lose him."

Ah, that explains why he is tense with me, Murdoch realised. *He does not want his son to give up his position within the business. Well, once I've dealt with the matter of Sorcha's land then he can have it.*

"So, Murdoch," Howard said, forgoing formalities now that everyone was sitting down and sipping upon amber whisky, "how goes it up in Scotland? Must have been something wonderful there to keep you from London for so long. Or some*one*, rather."

Murdoch did not have to fake his reaction to the man's question. The top of his ears began to burn merely thinking of Sorcha, and an abashed smile flashed across his face before he could contain it. Howard laughed at his response.

"She is that lovely? Why, we must meet the lass if she is fair enough to entrap our dear Murdoch Buchanan."

"Miss Darrow has travelled down with me to London," Murdoch said, straightening his back as he spoke. It was time to get down to business. "She has never been out of Scotland before, and was curious to meet the people I work with."

Gregory clapped his hands together. "Then so she shall! Although – and permit me for being intrusive – why have you not married Miss Darrow yet? We expected you to own the land long before now, Mr Buchanan."

"She wished to take things slowly. Considering the other option was to run back to London, thoroughly rejected, I had no choice but to oblige her request."

"A careful woman," Gregory observed. "Which is no surprise, considering how resistant her father was to anyone buying the land when it was in his name." He narrowed his eyes at Murdoch. "Does she have any idea what you plan to do with the land once it is signed over to you?"

"Considering I am unsure about what exactly the plans *are,* no," Murdoch admitted. He threw back the rest of the whisky in his glass and turned to Howard. He wasn't as sly as Gregory; he was more likely to get the truth out of him. "I have heard rumour of your intention to fill in the shallowest shores along the southern bank of Loch Lomond," he said. "Is this true?"

Howard shrugged. "We were growing impatient with your extended, love-struck stay with your betrothed, Murdoch. The Darrows do not own every stretch of the southern shore. If we turn those areas into holiday and hunting accommodation then we can work around the Darrow land until, eventually, the lass will have us on all sides forcing her to sell. It is not the first time we have used such a tactic."

"No," Murdoch said, working hard to keep his voice level, "but it is the first time you have done it behind the back of one of your own."

"Well now that you're here we won't have to resort to such disreputable tactics," Howard said, patting Murdoch amiably on the back. "Have you considered marrying Miss Darrow whilst in London? We are hosting a winter ball on the twenty-first. It would make everything far easier if she signed all of the property paperwork down here."

Murdoch hesitated. "The twenty-first is almost three weeks away," he said. "I did not intend to –"

"Surely you do not plan to move up to Scotland permanently, Mr Buchanan?" Don interrupted, incredulous. He waved towards the window. "Have you not missed London? Surely your wife-to-be will learn to love the city after spending three weeks in it!"

The entire board nodded in agreement. It was becoming quickly apparent that Murdoch was not going to be able to voice his opinion that the Darrow land should be left well alone during this particular meeting, which meant he needed more time. He suppressed a sigh and smiled.

"Of course. You are right. Miss Darrow will enjoy her time here, I'm sure. As to wedding her in three weeks...well, better to leave that up to her, I think."

"Don't be ridiculous," Gregory said. "You've given the girl far more leeway than you should have ever given her. It's time you put your foot down on the matter, Mr Buchanan, and lock her down."

Keep your temper in check, Murdoch thought,

taking care to breathe deeply and evenly. He did not like the way Gregory MacKinnon spoke of Sorcha, nor the way everyone else agreed with him. He wished for her to meet them even less than he had before, though Murdoch knew he had no choice in the matter. They would find a way to meet Sorcha regardless of what he wanted, so it was better for it to be on his own terms.

"Speaking of locking Miss Darrow down," Murdoch said, hating the sentence even as he said it, "I must find her before she spends all of my money. London fashion is expensive, after all."

"See, she will fall for London before you know it, and then she will be happy that you grant her land over to us to oversee," Don exclaimed, a smug smile on his face. Clearly he thought himself far cleverer than he actually was, and would probably credit himself with the success of the entire land deal when it was complete.

Which it never will be, Murdoch swore, saying his goodbyes before exiting the meeting room and storming down the corridor. *To think they were going to strong-arm Sorcha into giving up the land. They had already given up on their expectation that Mr Buchanan would hand it over. I must be careful, and so must Sorcha.*

"I hate this place," Murdoch grumbled, for nobody to hear but himself. "I wish we could go home." But until said home was safe Murdoch knew he was stuck in London, with its detestable people, busy streets and filthy air.

That only made him hate it even more.

CHAPTER ELEVEN

Sorcha

"I never thought shopping would be so *exhausting!*" Sorcha complained to Mrs Ferguson, who had accompanied her on her excursion to buy clothes more appropriate for London.

They had visited no fewer than ten shops and had purchased items from eight of them: high-necked, long-sleeved day dresses; low-cut, gathered-sleeve evening gowns; richly-coloured silk scarves and shawls; delicate slipper-like shoes that Sorcha would never have worn back home, and bonnets, gloves and bags in an array of different finishes and sizes.

A long, woollen riding coat was the final purchase of the morning, since it was popular in the city to wear riding attire when one was not actually riding a horse. Sorcha found this especially baffling. She felt entirely insubstantial in her borrowed coat and cotton dress – which had both been Mrs Ferguson's once upon a time – now that she knew what she was supposed to be wearing, though in truth she felt far more comfortable in the servant's clothing than she perhaps ever would in the garments Murdoch Buchanan's money had bought.

But on the other hand, Sorcha thought, glancing critically at her reflection, *perhaps Murdoch will pay more attention to me if I put in some effort with my appearance.* For it was clear to Sorcha that the kelpie was keeping his distance from her, and she had no idea why. It did not seem to matter that she undressed in front of him, and told him that he looked good, and tried to sneak into his arms whilst they were in bed. Nothing seemed to sway him.

Has spending time with me away from his home caused Murdoch to realise I am not who he thought I was? Sorcha wondered, smoothing back errant strands of hair self-consciously as she continued down Oxford Street with Mrs Ferguson. *I had been sure he still felt something for me when we reunited. Was I...wrong?*

"It is a good thing your clothes will be ready by next week," Mrs Ferguson said, pulling Sorcha out of her negative thoughts. "I do not think I could carry much more than these hats and shoes!" She struggled with a pile of boxes in her arms, having staunchly refused Sorcha's multiple offers to help her with them.

Sorcha looked up at the sky; it was a beautiful day, and only a little past noon. She was not yet hungry, and she didn't feel like going back to Murdoch's house to while away the rest of the day indoors. She glanced at Mrs Ferguson. "You can return to Mr Buchanan's abode, Mrs Ferguson," she said. "I wish to explore the city for a while."

But the servant shook her head. "I cannot leave you on your own, Miss Darrow. You do not know your way around!"

"I have memorised Mr Buchanan's maps of London," Sorcha insisted. "And you have all those heavy boxes. I will be quite content on my own, I swear."

The woman eyed her suspiciously. Sorcha could tell what she was thinking – that a lowly country girl was sure to lose herself in the sprawling streets of Britain's largest city. But that was half of the appeal for Sorcha. She *wanted* an adventure, to see things that she had not seen before. And, after two years of bearing witness to the wonders of the Seelie Court, it was high time Sorcha gave the marvels of human ingenuity and architecture a chance.

Eventually Mrs Ferguson relented with a heavy sigh. "Do not stray far," she warned. "Stay close to Oxford Street where you can. If you ever get lost, enter a shop and ask for directions – do *not* approach anybody on the street, especially if they appear uncouth or –"

"I understand," Sorcha laughed, tightening her borrowed jacket against her chest when a bitter breeze blew past her. "I have visited Glasgow before; this is not my first time in a city."

Mrs Ferguson did not seem reassured by this, though she protested no further. With a final goodbye she turned from Sorcha to head back to Murdoch's house, leaving her alone for the first time in four days.

I do not know where the time has gone, Sorcha thought as she took a right turn and began traipsing down a pretty cobblestone street. *It feels as if it has been stolen from me.* When she passed a bakery she stared at the cakes and pastries in the window, though she did not wish to eat one. A towering bowl of sugar plums glittered in the noonday sun, distinctly reminding Sorcha of the gemstones that lined the path to the Seelie Court.

A flash of light crossed the glass, and Sorcha frowned. "Definitely not the sun," she murmured, resisting the urge to touch the window out of sheer curiosity. This wasn't the first window she had caught glimmering and glinting in a way it shouldn't have been. *Perhaps the grime and smoke in the air affects the way light hits glass,* she thought, though Sorcha wasn't so sure. She had caught a similarly odd show of light in the mirror of her own home before leaving for London, after all.

"I cannot dismiss these as sleep-deprived hallucinations," she said, turning from the window with an uncomfortable, hollow pit in her stomach. Sorcha began to whistle softly in an effort to calm her nerves as she wound further away from Oxford Street without really knowing where she was going. But as she passed more shop windows and glass lanterns and mirrored surfaces she became certain that there was something wrong with what was being reflected back at her. There were odd, unexplained lights...

And eerie, fleeting shadows.

"I am imagining it," Sorcha said, louder than was strictly necessary. A passing gentleman looked at her strangely, so she scurried off the street to another, and then another and another, until Sorcha was all alone on a street with no windows at all. That should have reassured her, but it only set Sorcha's nerves further on edge. She had clearly come upon an *uncouth* area, as Mrs Ferguson would have put it, and she had no idea how to get back to where she started.

So much for memorising Murdoch's maps, Sorcha mused, heart racing with every turn she took onto new,

336

even further abandoned streets. Fog was beginning to roll across the cobblestones, which made Sorcha think that perhaps she was close to the Thames. *If I can get to the river I can find my way back to Murdoch's house. I can do this.*

But as Sorcha walked on and on she realised she was getting ever further from anything she could hope to use as a landmark to help her find the river. She was turned entirely on her head, and with the sun at a noonday position Sorcha was finding it difficult to tell north from south.

"And now I cannot see it at all," she complained, shivering when a blanket of cloud appeared as if from nowhere to obscure most of the sky in the space of ten minutes. It only caused the fog to grow thicker across the street, until Sorcha was almost convinced it was entirely solid matter.

Sing for us, girlie.

She froze.

"Is someone there?" Sorcha asked, hating the way her voice trembled as she spoke. She hitched up the skirt of her dress a few inches from the ground, ready to flee at any given moment. But there was nobody there, and when Sorcha turned onto the next street not a soul was there, either.

Just one song, pretty lass, another voice insisted. *One song for your love.*

"L-leave me alone," Sorcha stuttered, flinching when she caught a shadow out of the corner of her eye that appeared to be moving. Her footsteps grew quicker and more insistent, though the fog absorbed the sound the soles of her shoes made against the cobblestones.

Everything was oppressively, dangerously silent.

A song, a third voice asked. *One and we shall leave you. A verse.*

Sorcha took a deep breath. She did not know what was going on, but she'd had enough experience in the faerie realm to know that what was currently happening was decidedly not the work of a human. *"L-lost is my quiet forever,"* she began, voice uneven and frightened as she sang the first song that popped into her head. She desperately searched around for an escape.

There was none.

All around her the fog and shadows began to shift, as if they were restless and excited. Sorcha knew she had to be careful, but now that she had begun singing she found that the next words in the verse left her tongue before she could stop them.

"Lost is life's happiest part;

Lost all my tender endeavours,

To touch an insensible heart."

Sorcha fled down a narrow alleyway, regretting the decision the moment she realised she could easily become boxed into it. A shadow flitted across her vision, then another and another.

"But tho' my despair is past – leave me alone!" Sorcha screamed, beyond terrified, when a hand appeared from nowhere to yank her out of the alleyway by her wrist. Freezing, bitter tears were streaming down her face, obscuring her vision. "Let me go!" she cried. "Please, let me go."

But the stranger did not release her. He was wrapped up against the cold from head to toe, though a few strands of silvered hair poked out between his woollen cap and scarf. Wordlessly he pulled on Sorcha's arm with a strength that belied the aged colour of his hair; Sorcha had no choice but to follow him.

He wove his way down street after street, waving away shadows and odd reflections in a discomfitingly spritely manner whenever they presented themselves before him. Within ten minutes Sorcha found herself back on Oxford Street, several shops away from where she had started her dangerous adventure.

"I – thank you," she mouthed, but no sound came out. Her chest ached from the force of her heart battering against her ribcage; she barely dared to breathe.

The strange old man – who was perhaps not so old at all – merely inclined his head politely and promptly disappeared down an alleyway, leaving Sorcha all alone once more. But the shadows were gone. The glimmers of light had disappeared.

The danger had passed...for now.

"Lachlan," Sorcha cried miserably before she could stop herself. "Lachlan, help me."

CHAPTER TWELVE

Murdoch

There was only one word to describe Sorcha's behaviour over the past two days: listless.

When she returned from her shopping trip and retired straight to bed Murdoch had been suspicious, especially since she spoke not a single word to either him or Mrs Ferguson when they checked up on her. Mrs Ferguson had informed him that Sorcha insisted upon exploring the city on her own, which he had bristled at, but the servant also said that Sorcha had been gone for under two hours – barely any time at all to walk around London before heading back to Murdoch's house.

Sorcha had remained quiet and morose since then, fidgeting constantly and finding herself distracted by seemingly nothing at all whilst in the middle of reading a book, or brushing her hair, or eating a meal.

She had barely touched her food at all.

And now they were sitting at the dining table in silence, and Murdoch did not know what to say. In truth

Sorcha's new-found awkwardness had been a blessing in disguise, for it made it easier for him to keep his distance.

He fiddled with a heavy, ivory card between his hands; both of them had been invited to a company luncheon at the weekend, and Murdoch was concerned that Sorcha would not fare well at the event in her current condition. He hid a heavy sigh by gulping down a large measure of red wine.

"What is it?" Sorcha asked, voice so quiet Murdoch barely heard her. She was staring at the card he was holding, a slight frown creasing her brow. "You have been looking at that all evening."

Murdoch handed it over to her. "Grey and MacKinnon have invited us to join the company for a luncheon on Saturday. I was not sure if you would like to go."

"Of course I'm going!" Sorcha insisted, more lively than she had been in two days. "I *have* to go, otherwise I will not be able to get the measure of these men who wish to take our home away."

"You must be careful around them, Sorcha," Murdoch replied, taking another sip of wine as he did so. "They will not treat you the same way the people of Darach do."

She rolled her eyes. "Of course I know that. My mother would kill me if I wasn't on my best behaviour down here."

"I wasn't aware you could *be* on your best behaviour."

The hint of a smile curled Sorcha's lips, and Murdoch began to relax. Whatever had been burdening her seemed finally to be passing, for which he was grateful. "You will be able to wear your new clothes," he said, eager to keep up their new-found line of pleasant conversation. "And Mrs Ferguson can help with your hair, so you do not need to worry over it."

"Was that a not-so-subtle attempt at telling me my hair is a mess?" Sorcha asked, running her fingers through her admittedly disastrously tangled locks until she hit a snag and winced.

He laughed. "You and I both know I do not care how you present yourself; it is merely others that do."

"You don't?"

"Of course not," Murdoch said, confused by the question. *When have I ever given Sorcha reason to think that I am superficial? And she is beautiful, anyway, particularly when her hair is wild around her face.* He thought of the faerie revel, when he had slain Lachlan's step family. Sorcha's hair had been braided through with bluebells, so delicate that they whispered to the floor whenever Murdoch had touched her.

He pushed the memory away.

There was a strange look on Sorcha's face, as if she was unsure if Murdoch was lying to her or not about her appearance being unimportant to him. But then she shook her head, picked up her fork and began to eat, much to Murdoch's immense relief.

When they were finished eating the two of them retired to the drawing room, sitting in front of a merrily blazing hearth to read and relax. Sorcha was scanning through reams of music she had found by the piano Mr Buchanan's father used to play, though the instrument was in desperate need of tuning from two years of disuse.

She hummed softly as her fingers trailed across notes and bars and verses, occasionally vocalising entire phrases when she came upon ones she particularly liked.

"I have missed your singing," Murdoch said after a while, closing the heavy book on English law that he was reading with a thump. Sorcha looked up at him from where she lay sprawled across the carpet, dark hair flickering and glowing like burnished copper wire in the light of the flames. Her cheeks were flushed, and they only grew redder in response to Murdoch's comment.

"I did not dare sing by the loch, after what happened," she admitted, turning her mismatched eyes to the fire. "I only sang for Lachlan – and Galileo, of course. I hope he is all right on the MacPherson farm."

A surge of jealousy wracked through Murdoch's body. He did not want to know that Sorcha continued to sing for the Seelie king, but in his heart he'd always known she would. It was how Lachlan had met her, after all, something which Murdoch had gleaned from Sorcha's thoughts the first time he'd spoken to her in the water of Loch Lomond.

She had been singing to me a long time before he met her, Murdoch thought glumly. *Yet it is the faerie who has become indispensable in Sorcha's life.*

He scratched his chin, where a fine layer of stubble was beginning to grow. Murdoch wanted to shave, but he didn't have the energy to. There was an unbearable, itching dryness creeping through his veins and threatening to desiccate his very being. He knew he needed to swim; to be part of a body of water and feel himself again.

Right now, in the middle of winter and posing as Murdoch Buchanan, that was impossible.

"What has been on your mind the last couple of days, Sorcha?" he asked before he could stop himself. Her eyes had grown glassy as they stared into the fire. She almost looked transfixed, but when she realised Murdoch had asked her a question she blinked life back into her eyes.

"I...may have been followed when I was walking about alone," she said, very slowly. She did not meet Murdoch's gaze, as if she were afraid of his reaction.

His hand curled into a taut fist in his lap before he could stop himself. "Followed?" he echoed back. "Did you see who it was?"

Sorcha shook her head. "No, I don't know who it was, but I was lost and –"

"You cannot act so reckless down here!" Murdoch exclaimed, dropping from his chair to kneel in front of her. Sorcha pushed herself up into a sitting position, running a hand through her hair to push it out of her face as she did so.

She bit her lip. "I was all right in the end," she said, a little uncertainly. "An old man helped me back to Oxford Street and –"

Murdoch grabbed onto her arms before he could stop himself. He was angry at Sorcha, and scared for her. He shook her slightly. "You must be more careful, Sorcha!" he insisted. "London is a dangerous city. You could get hurt!"

"Do you think I don't know that?" she demanded, growing angry herself. "I am not a child, Murdoch. I know what I did was foolish. Why do you think I hadn't told you about it yet?"

A moment of silence passed. Two. Three.

Murdoch let out a long, low breath through gritted teeth. His shoulders slumped. "I apologise," he said. "Really, I am sorry. I do not mean to be so short with you."

"It is my own fault," Sorcha admitted, holding Murdoch's gaze as she shifted closer to him. "London is doing strange things to me. I feel so out of sorts."

He barked out a laugh. "You have just described precisely how I feel, too."

Sorcha glanced downward at Murdoch's hands, still gripping her forearms. Her dress had slipped from one shoulder, the material just barely covering her breasts as she shifted her sitting position. A heat that had entirely nothing to do with his proximity to the fire burned through Murdoch, and his grip tightened.

I must let her go, he thought, though his eyes were trained on Sorcha's lower lip as she ran the tip of her tongue across it. She leaned a little closer towards him.

"Murdoch," she began, voice low and lilting and full of something Murdoch thought might be agonisingly close to desire, "what are we –"

He pushed her away. "I should prepare some documents for my meeting tomorrow," he muttered, standing up without looking at Sorcha. But out of the corner of his eye Murdoch saw a look of humiliation creep across her face, which hadn't been his intention at all. *I did not mean to hurt her,* he worried, *but I am not myself right now.* "Sorcha –" Murdoch said, but he cut her off with a wave of her hand.

"I am tired," she bit out, dragging herself to her feet and fleeing the drawing room without waiting for a response. Murdoch stood frozen to the spot for a

345

moment, torn by indecision, before finally bounding out after her.

"Sorcha," he said again, "I did not mean to offend you. It's just – Sorcha?"

When Murdoch reached his bedroom he found Sorcha half-draped across the bed, thoroughly unconscious. His eye twitched, and his hand curled into a fist once more. Frustrated, he kicked at a chest of drawers and cursed loudly, before very carefully placing Sorcha on the bed properly and wrapping her beneath the covers. The hint of a smile was on her lips; gone was all her anger at Murdoch.

He was beyond jealous, for there was only one creature who could have done this to Sorcha, and he could do nothing to rouse her.

Murdoch had no choice but to wait for Lachlan to allow Sorcha to wake from her enchanted sleep.

CHAPTER THIRTEEN

Lachlan

"Lachlan! I knew it had to be you. I have not fallen asleep so abruptly in a long time."

The flood of relief that washed over Lachlan upon seeing Sorcha was overwhelming. And she was *happy* to see him. Delighted and relieved, going by the way she bounded into his arms and melted against his chest.

The kelpie has not turned her on me yet, he thought, viciously pleased. *And he never will.*

He extended their embrace for longer than was strictly necessary, simply because he did not want to let go. Sorcha made no indication she wanted to let go, either, but eventually the pair of them acknowledged that clinging to each other was hardly the easiest way to talk to one another. So Lachlan released her, but not before he kissed her forehead softly.

"I hope I did not catch you at a bad time," Lachlan said, smiling at the sheer vision that was the human in front of him. Sorcha's hair was in such familiar disarray it made his heart ache. "It is hard to keep track of the hour when it is dark for so much of the day."

For a moment Lachlan almost thought that Sorcha blushed, but then she scowled and fell backwards into the soft, vague darkness of her dream. "Not a bad time," she told him. "Ideal timing, in fact."

Lachlan collapsed beside her, an intrigued eyebrow raised. "How so? Have you grown tired of your horse husband yet?"

Sorcha snorted at the comment, which in turn caused Lachlan to laugh. Already he could feel his very soul relaxing by her proximity. *Indulging in easy, non-judgemental conversation that has absolutely nothing to do with ruling a kingdom certainly helps lift my mood, too.*

"I think he may be tired of me, in all honesty," Sorcha murmured in answer to his question.

"I do not believe that for a moment."

"Well he's putting on an excellent show of it, then," she huffed, blowing stray strands of hair out of her face in the process. She glanced at Lachlan, her blue and green eyes pale mirrors against the darkness of her dream. "It is as if Murdoch can barely stand to have me near."

Oh.

Lachlan worked out what that meant immediately. He didn't know how to feel about it – that the kelpie was keeping Sorcha at arm's length because he didn't want to push his feelings onto her. *I didn't realise he had a single ounce of maturity beneath all his possessiveness. I suppose you don't live to be five hundred without learning how to hold your feelings in check. He is more of a foe for Sorcha's heart than I gave him credit for.*

"Lachlan?"

He smiled at her reassuringly, reaching out to stroke Sorcha's hand with his own. "I am here, do not worry."

Her eyes narrowed. "But *how* are you here? I am hundreds of miles away! Do not tell me you've travelled all the way down and –"

"Oh, for the love of the forest, no," he chuckled. "Ailith would kill me if she realised I'd gone gallivanting down to London before the solstice revel."

"So how...?"

"My powers have grown since I became king," Lachlan explained. He flexed and unflexed a golden hand above his head, allowing his very being to glow from within for Sorcha's benefit. She reached up to touch his palm; sparks flew from where her fingertips grazed his skin.

She gasped at the marvel of it all. "Does that mean you put me to sleep and invaded my dreams all the way from the Seelie Court?" she asked, eyes shining with interest.

Lachlan flashed her a grin. "I did not expect it to work – I have been trying for several days with no success – though I am sincerely glad that it did. So tell me, Clara: how goes things down in London? Have you and the horse made much progress getting Grey and MacKinnon to back down?"

"Not exactly," she admitted. "Murdoch is doing his best to convince them to leave the land alone – I swear he is – but they will not budge. They look at Loch Lomond and the Darrow land and see a goldmine."

Lachlan did not like the sound of that. "These men could be dangerous," he said. "Please tell me you are being careful – that the kelpie is keeping you out of harm's reach." *It is the very least the monster could do, after all.*

"In truth I have not met them yet, though the company is hosting a luncheon this weekend that I am expected to attend."

"You are not nervous, are you?" Lachlan laughed incredulously at the slight frown creasing Sorcha's brow. He rolled onto his front and propped himself up on his elbows, then flicked his thumb and forefinger against her frown until Sorcha, too, was laughing. "Come on, Clara," he continued. "You live in the company of faeries and kelpies. You have witnessed beheadings and drownings and curses and you are nervous of mere *humans?*"

"Strangers," Sorcha muttered, averting her eyes. "They are strangers. I do not do well with strangers, especially ones from London meaning to convince me into handing over everything I am trying to protect."

"I was a stranger, once. So was your kelpie."

Sorcha shifted onto her side to face Lachlan. "You are strange, but you were never a stranger. The forest and loch are both as familiar to me as my parents are." But beneath the lovely smile she had painted on her face Lachlan could tell that Sorcha's entire body was tense, as if ready to bolt at any given second.

He edged closer to her. "But there are other strangers, aren't they? Do not lie to me; I can see it on your face. What is wrong, Sorcha?"

Sorcha's eyes widened at Lachlan's use of her real name, for he only used it when he was truly serious. She bit her lip, which was trembling slightly. "There is something...different about London," she eventually said. "I do not know how to explain it. Reflections and shadows all feel wrong, somehow. Like they're keeping something from me and taunting me at the same time."

Lachlan pinned Sorcha beneath him before he truly knew what he was doing, catching her wrists in his hands and squeezing them tightly. "Do not go near them!" he barked, feeling a panic rise in his throat that he had not felt since he was a fox. "The moment something feels wrong, *run*. Do not walk anywhere in London without the kelpie."

"You – Lachlan – what is wrong? What exactly are the shadows?" Sorcha's chest was heaving in fright; clearly she had not expected such a visceral reaction from him.

"It could well be the Unseelie," Lachlan said. His grip on her wrists tightened even further. "Sorcha, I am being serious here. *Do not take this lightly.* If you think something is in your head then it isn't. It never is with them. They are the worst kinds of faeries to become involved with – you won't just lose your time or your memories or your tears to them. Do not give them anything, for you will lose everything and more."

Slowly, very slowly, Sorcha nodded. "I will be careful, I swear it," she told him. "I will not run off on my own."

Relieved that Sorcha had truly understood the gravity of his warning, Lachlan let go of her wrists and collapsed on top of her. He nuzzled his face against her neck. "You did not break my step family's curse only for me to lose you to the damn Unseelie," he muttered. "I will not have it. You are not theirs to take."

Sorcha ran a hand over the back of Lachlan's hair. The gesture was soothing enough that he found himself moulding his body to Sorcha's, sliding a leg between hers to lessen the pressure of his weight on her chest. They lay like that, content not to move, and listened to each other do naught but breathe for a long, long time.

"I am nobody's to take," Sorcha eventually whispered. "I only belong to me."

Lachlan grazed his lips across Sorcha's jawline. "That is the biggest problem of all."

"You do not truly mean that."

"I do. I cannot lie, as well you know."

Sorcha did not reply to Lachlan's easy admission of possessiveness. *Perhaps the kelpie is not so dissimilar to me,* he reasoned. *I thought I could accept Sorcha being mortal and living a human life, but I can't. It isn't enough. It never will be.*

For Sorcha's continued trust and affection of him, it had to be.

"Will you stay with me tonight?" she asked, when Lachlan finally rolled off her to rest her head against his chest.

He placed a gentle kiss upon her brow. "I would stay with you forever, if you would only let me."

CHAPTER FOURTEEN

Murdoch

Murdoch watched as Sorcha struggled to fasten the buttons running up the back of her bodice by herself. He wanted to help, but was terrified of touching her.

The image of her sleeping, enchanted face was burned into his retinas. Whenever Murdoch thought about Lachlan spending the night with Sorcha inside her dreams he found he could barely control his temper. Watching Sorcha get dressed did not help matters at all.

They were late for Grey and MacKinnon's luncheon, but Murdoch didn't have it in him to be concerned. There was no way he was going to be able to talk to them about giving up the Darrow land whilst they were feasting and drinking and socialising, anyway; all Murdoch could do was introduce them to Sorcha and hope that they were as enamoured with her as he was.

Not that I want that, either, he grumbled, a shiver running down his spine at the thought of any of the board members eyeing up Sorcha. *But if she charms*

*them then they may be inclined to give up on their
Loch Lomond plans.*

He laughed humourlessly. Something like that was
never going to happen.

Sorcha cast a curious glance his way, which was the
closest Murdoch had gotten to holding eye contact with
her for three days. "What is so funny?" she asked.

"Nothing. Do you need some help?"

She shook her head, the apples of her cheeks
turning pink as she twisted her arms behind her back to
finish fastening the buttons. Sorcha's periwinkle dress
was cut low across her breastbone and cinched in high
up on her waist, with delicate, floral embroidery
decorating the bodice and matching, elbow-length gloves
to complete the look. Her hair was twisted elegantly at
the nape of her neck, with a few artfully curled tendrils
left hanging to frame her face. A darker blue, silken
shawl was hanging over the mirror, obscuring her
reflection from view.

"You look beautiful," Murdoch said when Sorcha
turned to face him. It was painfully true; her delicate,
sloping shoulders and pale skin perfectly balanced the
wintry-coloured ensemble.

Sorcha ignored the compliment, grabbing the shawl
before moving past Murdoch towards the door. "Come
on," she mumbled, "we are late enough as it is."

He grabbed Sorcha's wrist before he could stop
himself. She glared at him until Murdoch let her go.
"We cannot act like this in front of my – in front of Mr
Buchanan's colleagues," he insisted, though that was not
what Murdoch wanted to say at all. *How can it be so
difficult to tell her that I'm sorry? That I'm deathly*

jealous of Lachlan stealing into her dreams, and that the last thing I wanted to do was push her away into his arms?

But Murdoch did not say these things.

Sorcha stared at him with hard, searching eyes for a moment or two, then bowed her head and sighed. "I know," she said. "I know. Our home depends on it."

When she offered him a small smile Murdoch eagerly returned it. But despite their mutual agreement that they could not act so cold to each other, neither of them spoke a word during the carriage ride over to Howard Grey's ostentatiously large townhouse in the middle of Mayfair. Every time Murdoch came close to asking Sorcha about Lachlan he fidgeted with his sleeve, instead, or fiddled with the silver pocket-watch Mr Buchanan's father had once gifted his son.

Sorcha was equally restless, looking out the window of the carriage every two or three minutes only to dart her eyes away from the glass as if she had seen something monstrous or disturbing outside. Once or twice she opened her mouth to speak but, just as with Murdoch, she thought better of it before any words were formed.

It was with great relief that their carriage rolled up to Mr Grey's house having made good time; they were but ten minutes late. Murdoch exited the carriage first, crunching across the gravelled driveway to help Sorcha down from her side of it. She took hold of his hand without so much as a flinch, an angelic smile plastered to her face.

"Thank you, Mr Buchanan," she said without an ounce of animosity. She linked her arm with Murdoch's, knocking the top of her head affectionately against his shoulder before allowing him to lead her through a set of tall, heavy brass doors.

A servant led them up a flight of stairs heavily decorated with grand, ostentatious portraits of the men of the house of Grey. Sorcha stared at each of them with a glint of mischief in her eyes.

Murdoch squeezed her hand softly and whispered into her ear, "Just what are you thinking, Miss Darrow?"

"That you are far more handsome than any of these portraits, Mr Buchanan."

He snickered softly at the comment. "I wouldn't say that to Howard Grey's face. You might break his poor heart!"

"Oh, the horror! I would never dare do such a thing," Sorcha murmured back, holding a hand over her mouth to stifle a wicked laugh as the two of them were brought into a very large, high-ceilinged, extravagantly decorated dining room. But there was no table sitting in the centre of the room; instead, trestle tables covered in pristine, white cloths were set against the walls and were laden with all manner of bite-size morsels, with several servants on-hand to pile plates high with food and pour drinks.

There were around thirty people filtering around the room, with two more appearing from a door at the opposite end that led to another part of the house. At Murdoch's side Sorcha gulped almost imperceptibly and closed her eyes for a moment, steeling herself for the onslaught of strangers.

Murdoch felt a stab of sympathy for his fake wife-to-be; for all Sorcha's insistence that she would be fine, it was clear that she truly did not like strangers. *How I must have scared her when first we met simply by being a man rather than a creature from the deep,* he thought, feeling somewhat guilty about having originally enjoyed her fear. Murdoch resolved himself to put Sorcha at ease in any way he could.

"Would you like a drink, Miss Da–"

"Murdoch, you're late!" Howard called over the noise of the room, cutting through the crowd with the speed of a man half his age. Going by his ruddy cheeks Murdoch could only assume the man was already halfway drunk.

"My deepest apologies," he said, bowing his head.

"It is my fault," Sorcha chimed in, smiling a brilliant smile for the older man before curtsying. She turned her smile on Murdoch before saying, "It is all my fault that we are late. I simply couldn't decide what to wear!"

Howard beamed at her, reaching for Sorcha's hand with both of his own. "You can only be Miss Darrow, the charming lass who stole our Mister Buchanan away from us!" he exclaimed. "It is a pleasure to finally meet you."

"All things considered, the pleasure is mine, Mister...?"

"Howard Grey," Murdoch cut in, remembering his own manners. "Howard, this is indeed Sorcha Darrow. Miss Darrow, this is the co-founder of Grey and MacKinnon, Howard Grey."

"I should have known someone of such distinction was the man who owned this house," Sorcha told Howard, before thanking a servant who proffered her a glass of champagne. She looked at the contents of the glass curiously – Murdoch could only assume she had never been given the opportunity to drink such a

357

beverage before.

Neither have I, technically, he thought, taking a glass for himself and cautiously taking a sip. The sweet alcohol fizzed and bubbled on his tongue, a bizarre sensation Murdoch was unsure whether he enjoyed or not.

Howard laughed heartily at Sorcha's remark, approval plain as day on his face. "I like you, Miss Darrow, though if you continue to ply me with such compliments then I may be inclined to steal you away for myself!"

And so it was that Murdoch watched as Sorcha charmed her way around each and every one of the board members of Grey and MacKinnon, discussing atlases with James Campbell and ships with William Wright, then moving on to discuss the works of Robert Burns with an attentive Donald MacKinnon. Murdoch resisted the urge to step in and whisk Sorcha away, for the entire purpose of bringing her to the luncheon was for her to meet everyone.

But still, I do not like it.

"Jealousy is unseemly, Mr Buchanan." Murdoch flinched; Don's father had sidled up beside him, a sly smile on his face. He inclined his head towards Sorcha. "I can certainly see why you were loathe to return to London, though I must profess I believed that no woman could tie *you* down. And a lowly country girl, no less! I am truly surprised. Though she is certainly holding her own this afternoon. Her mother must have worked hard to give her a respectable upbringing."

Murdoch struggled to maintain a neutral demeanour. "The Darrows are fine people," he said. "They have been nothing but welcoming to me. And Miss Darrow –"

"Has clearly put you firmly under her spell," Gregory laughed, though his eyes were sharp and serious. "Just remember, Mr Buchanan, that you are marrying the girl for a reason. Do not allow yourself to be swept away."

The man walked away once he had voiced his opinion, leaving Murdoch to watch Sorcha with a heavy cloud hanging above him. *The more time I spend as Mr Buchanan the more I despise him,* he thought glumly, tilting the rest of his champagne down his throat. *London turned him into a womanising, parasitic businessman. I am glad I ate him.*

But it only served to further conflict Murdoch over the matter of his feelings for Sorcha. He could not stand the person he was pretending to be; to touch her using the skin he was borrowing was unthinkable. Murdoch could scarcely believe he had once thought the vessel a suitable one for him to possess.

"I would never have met her the way I did without him," Murdoch whispered, so quietly even he struggled to hear the words. He wondered if Sorcha would still accept him if he took on another face; another voice; another body. *Or is her attraction to me predicated on me looking like this?*

Murdoch did not want to consider that at all, but by the time he worked that out it was too late – it was all he could think about. When he caught his moody reflection in his empty champagne glass he scowled.

"I hate you."

CHAPTER FIFTEEN

Sorcha

Sorcha hadn't experienced such deafening silence since she'd returned from her stint as a runaway and had to bear the brunt of her parents' abject disappointment in her. Murdoch wasn't the only one responsible for it, of course; Sorcha was equally to blame for the arctic atmosphere between the two of them.

After they'd successfully acted as a happy couple at Howard Grey's luncheon Sorcha had thought that, perhaps, she and Murdoch would be able to bridge the gap that had formed between them. Instead it had only grown wider.

Why did he push me away? Sorcha thought sullenly, aimlessly pushing around the chicken on her plate with no intention whatsoever of eating it. She was alone; Murdoch had locked himself in his office, working through another book of English law to try and find some decree or case that could help him force his work colleagues to back off from procuring the Darrow land. Murdoch was staying quiet on his progress, which only caused Sorcha to believe that he was trying to protect her from something.

"Or simply wishes to keep me out of it," she grumbled, stabbing a potato so violently that it broke into pieces. *It is as if he wants nothing to do with me. Just what is going on?* Sorcha was sure she hadn't imagined the way Murdoch looked at her when they sat by the fire and she confessed to having been followed. And when they'd pretended to be happily engaged at the work luncheon she'd thought his affection for her was genuine.

Now Sorcha was considering that it truly was all an act. Or that, at least, whatever feelings the kelpie once held for her were long gone.

She sighed heavily. It certainly didn't help that Murdoch was tetchy and irritable most of the time, and that aside from heading out for work meetings he did not get out of the house at all. Sorcha herself was sticking to Lachlan's advice not to go anywhere without Murdoch in tow and had subsequently not left the house for days, either, which didn't serve to improve her mood.

But Murdoch was much worse.

There must be something seriously wrong, Sorcha thought, picking up her mostly uneaten dinner and carrying it through to the kitchen. Mrs Ferguson was nowhere to be found, which suggested she was eating her own dinner elsewhere, so Sorcha tended to her dishes and washed whatever was left by the basin, too. A large tub of water was hanging over a fire; Sorcha stood and stared at it boiling for a few minutes simply because she had nothing else to do.

And then it hit her.

"Water!" Sorcha cried, feeling stupid for not having realised it earlier. Murdoch was a kelpie, and he had said himself it had been a long, long time since he'd ventured away from his home. The last time he'd lived as Murdoch Buchanan he had been by the loch at all times, and shifted back and forth into his original form.

London had so far been cold, grey and, above all, bone dry. Sorcha's hair had suffered from the harsh conditions, which meant she could only imagine how Murdoch's entire being was faring.

"Oh, my, Miss Darrow, let me wash those!" Mrs Ferguson exclaimed, horrified to enter the kitchen and discover that she had largely finished the dishes. "You should be spending time with Mr Buchanan, not acting as his servant."

"Mrs Ferguson," Sorcha said, ignoring the woman's protests. "Would you be able to fill the tub in the main bathroom? The really large one?"

"It will take at least two hours for it to heat up properly," Mrs Ferguson said, "would it not be better to use the smaller tub in Mr Buchanan's private bathroom?"

"It doesn't need to be very hot," Sorcha countered. She pointed at the water boiling over the fire. "And if you put some of that in the bath then it will take even less time to do so. You can retire for the evening when it is run."

The servant nodded. "As you wish, Miss Darrow. I will prepare the bath immediately."

Sorcha paced the drawing room impatiently as Mrs Ferguson got to work, half-heartedly reading an encyclopaedia entry on Egyptian hieroglyphs before putting the tome down to stare through the darkened window at the empty street below. It felt like hours passed before Mrs Ferguson knocked on the door to inform Sorcha that the bath was ready. She thanked the woman, sent her to her own quarters, then took a deep breath.

Here goes nothing, she thought, hesitating with her fist against the door of Murdoch's study. *If he turns me away then there is nothing I can do...except use the bath myself.*

She knocked upon the door. No response. She knocked again.

"Murdoch?" she called through the wood. "Murdoch, do you –"

"What is it, Sorcha?" Murdoch asked, swinging open the door as he spoke. Sorcha took a step back from him in surprise. She swept her gaze over his dishevelled, exhausted appearance.

"Your hair is more of a mess than mine usually is," she said, smiling despite the fact neither of them had spoken in days.

Murdoch ran a hand over his face. "I don't see much point in tidying it when I do not intend to leave the house nor entertain guests tonight," he said. "Was there something you needed, Sorcha?"

She shifted on the spot. *How on earth do I tell a kelpie I think he's dehydrated?* Eventually she reached out, grabbed Murdoch's wrist and pulled on it. "Just follow me," she said, knowing that if Murdoch did not want to move then no amount of hauling and dragging would enable Sorcha to shift his towering frame. But Murdoch, blessedly, obliged, wordlessly following

Sorcha until she stopped inside the main bathroom.

The metal tub inside was so large Sorcha reckoned she could have fit Galileo inside of it. It was filled two-thirds of the way with lightly steaming, cloudy water; clearly Mrs Ferguson had poured in some mineral salts. She pointed towards it for lack of anything else to do.

"Get in," she ordered, without looking at Murdoch.

He didn't respond for a moment, then let out a long, low laugh that filled Sorcha's heart with joy. She glanced at him; Murdoch was scratching the dark shadow of stubble that covered his chin, a small smile on his face. He shook his head in disbelief. "How did you know?" he asked.

"You've been...temperamental," Sorcha replied. "Can I assume from the look on your face that this was the right thing to do?"

"I think it may well be."

They stood there in awkward silence, both staring at the bathtub for a while until eventually Murdoch turned to Sorcha and asked, "Are you going to leave so I can get in?"

"Oh!" she cried, feeling her cheeks begin to heat up out of sheer embarrassment. "Yes, of course! Enjoy your soak!" Sorcha knew she was speaking far too quickly and far too loudly, but clearly Murdoch found the entire situation rather amusing. His dark eyes had a shine to them that Sorcha had not seen in days.

Sorcha pulled the door mostly closed behind her, fleeing down the corridor towards Murdoch's bedroom feeling entirely like an idiot. *What was I expecting to happen?* she thought, feeling disappointed nonetheless. *That he would ask me to join him? That he would take me in his arms and...I don't know.*

Once Sorcha reached the bedroom she stripped out of her day clothes and let her hair down. She collapsed onto a chair in front of Murdoch's full-length mirror and ran a soft brush through it, watching her reflection as she worked through every tangled section until it shone like burnished copper. Sorcha had avoided mirrors for days, but looking at herself now she saw that her cheeks were a little gaunt.

I should have eaten dinner, she mused, leaning over to grab the shirt she'd been wearing to bed from where she'd abandoned it on the floor that morning and tossing it on. Murdoch had encouraged her to wear the floor-length night dress that she'd bought with Mrs Ferguson the week before, but Sorcha had insisted on continuing to use his shirt regardless. She felt far more comfortable in the thigh-length fabric.

It reminded her of curling up in a tent on the shores of Loch Lomond, dreaming of foxes and kelpies and curses.

I wish I could speak to Lachlan again, Sorcha thought longingly. *I should have told him about how I sang a song for those voices.* But Sorcha did not know if her incomplete song had technically counted as having given those that had followed her what they wanted. *'Do not give them anything, for you will lose everything.' That was what Lachlan said. So did I give them anything? Is that why I can still see –*

Sorcha stopped mid-thought. In the mirror all of the long shadows in the bedroom seemed to be stretching and shifting, but when Sorcha turned to look behind her all was still and solid. Slowly, very slowly, she stood up and backed away until she could no longer see the mirror's surface. But when she passed a shiny metal decanter by the bed an impossibly fast shadow crossed its surface, followed by a flash of light.

And laughter.

In her haste to leave the bedroom Sorcha tripped over her own feet, narrowly avoiding falling flat on her face by clinging to the door. Taking a moment to catch her breath, Sorcha barely made it past the hallway mirror before she saw the shadows had followed her. They ebbed and flowed like water, with glimmering edges of silver and blue and, occasionally, white-hot gold.

"What do you *want?*" she asked some point past her pale reflection, stepping right up to the ornately-framed mirror until she was close enough that her breath fogged up the glass. She raised her trembling hands and splayed her fingertips a mere inch from the surface. *Do not touch the glass,* Sorcha thought, somehow certain that if she did then no good would come of it.

But she did not step away, and the shadows crept closer.

A song, a song, a voice called, the sound echoing all around her.

Just one song, cried another.

The rush of blood in Sorcha's ears was deafening – almost loud enough to drown out the voices, but not quite. She opened her mouth, then closed it, chewing on her lip in her desperate attempt to keep herself from singing.

Sorcha shook her head at her reflection, stumbling away from the mirror on unbalanced feet that desperately wanted her to move forwards, not back. She did not stop moving, knowing that she had to find a way to block out the voices before it was too late.

It was in this precise manner that Sorcha crashed through the bathroom door, slipped on the ceramic tiles and fell straight into the lap of a wide-eyed kelpie in the shape of Murdoch Buchanan.

CHAPTER SIXTEEN

Lachlan

Lachlan was growing worrisomely accustomed to being awake during daylight, though as the winter solstice was fast approaching there were very few such hours to actually be concerned about.

"That colour suits you, Lachlan," Ailith said from her position curled up by the fire, strumming her fingers across a handheld harp and filling the room with the delicate notes of a nameless melody.

Lachlan fussed with the large jade stone attached to his cravat until it was nestled in the hollow of his throat. He had spent the last few hours trying to decide what to wear to the winter solstice revel and, though he had gone through most every colour he could think of, Lachlan kept returning to greens and turquoises and seafoams.

Sorcha's colours.

He was wearing a pair of scandalously tight, jewel-green trousers attached over his frothy white shirt with similarly-coloured braces, which were embroidered with a delicate pattern of golden oak leaves. A pine-needle-coloured tailcoat so dark it was almost black was thrown over the back of a chair, and several pairs of boots and shoes were scattered across the floor.

Lachlan scowled. "It is no use," he complained, collapsing onto his bed in an incredibly exaggerated manner. He blew an errant strand of long, bronze-coloured hair out of his face. "It does not matter what I wear; there will be nobody at the revel I wish to impress."

With a chuckle Ailith stopped playing her harp and unfolded herself from the floor, gliding over to bend down and kiss Lachlan softly upon his lips. He reciprocated for a moment, and then another, but just when he thought Ailith might take things further she straightened up and sat beside him.

"You are thinking of Miss Sorcha," she said, a frustratingly knowing edge to her voice. "It is a good thing I have to stay here to watch the Court whilst you attend the revel, otherwise I might be deeply upset that you do not wish to impress me."

Lachlan rolled his eyes at the jibe. "Go attend to Eirian in my stead, then," he said, half-serious.

But Ailith merely shook her head and nudged Lachlan's shoulder. "What would it look like, for the King of the Seelie Court to deign not to show up to the winter solstice celebrations? You must go, Lachlan, and you know it."

"It would be a whole lot more bearable if Clara were with me," he mumbled, stretching his hands up above his head, interlacing his fingers and pushing against them until his knuckles cracked.

Ailith winced at the noise but did not comment on it. Wordlessly she pulled a sapphire-encrusted comb from her sleeve and began running it through Lachlan's hair, fanning it out on the bed like a golden halo. She stroked it gently. "Your hair is getting very long again."

"And?"

"And perhaps it is time for a change," she suggested. "Perhaps it is time for you to have the courage to actually do the things you need to do."

Lachlan swung up into a sitting position. He narrowed his eyes at her. "What is that supposed to imply?"

"Oh, Lachlan, just *ask Miss Sorcha to the revel.*"

"Just...how?"

"I know you managed to sneak into her dreams a sennight ago," Ailith said, tone disarmingly casual as she ran her comb through her hair.

Lachlan leaned forward and propped his chin up on his hands. "How did you know about that?" he mumbled, thoroughly discomfited that he'd been caught out.

But Ailith merely laughed. "It was as if a weight had been lifted from your shoulders the next day. You would have walked on air if it were possible. So put her to sleep once more and ask her to the revel."

"I cannot do that?"

"And why not?"

"Because I have tried to ease Clara into sleep more than once since then, and it has not worked."

Ailith considered this for a moment. "If you managed it once, you should be able to do it again," she said, choosing her words carefully. "Which implies that something else is blocking you from reaching her."

"I think it may be Clara herself," Lachlan admitted. "It does not seem like she is sleeping well, for whenever it feels as if I may have finally hooked her into unconsciousness she shakes it off."

"That's impressive, for a mortal."

"It is only because she is so far away," he said, throwing his head back to stare blindly up at the ceiling of his four poster bed. Gilded, gossamer fabric shone in the firelight as if it was made of liquid. "If she were close by I could put her to sleep no matter her mental state."

When Ailith squeezed his arm Lachlan did not shrug her off. "Why don't you head to London first, then, and invite Miss Sorcha to the revel face-to-face? I'm sure she would love a surprise like that. It would only add an extra day to your journey."

"I – are you serious, Ailith?"

"Very."

"I am the Seelie king," Lachlan said, gesturing at himself as he spoke. "I cannot simply gallivant off to London on a whim just to ask a mortal to –"

"It is precisely *because* you are the Seelie king that you can do whatever you want, you fool," Ailith scolded. "You have been a responsible ruler these past two years; nobody would criticise you for acting selfishly this one time. On the contrary, perhaps it would be better for you to indulge in more of your old pastimes to connect with the lower fae."

Ailith grinned a grin full of perfect, gleaming teeth at the suggestion that Lachlan was not acting nearly hedonistic enough to be a faerie king. But she was right,

Lachlan knew. After the debacle with the kelpie – after nearly losing his very being to the body of a fox at the hands of Fergus and his father – Lachlan had become an agonisingly careful creature.

It was time for that to change.

"You are right, of course," he said, a smile curling his lips to match Ailith's. "You are always right."

"That is what I am here for."

Lachlan ran a hand through her pale, perfect hair and brought Ailith's lips to his own. He just barely planted a kiss upon them. "I will bring Sorcha back with me to live in the Seelie Court, just wait and see," he murmured, his voice shaking from barely-contained excitement.

"Does that mean you're wearing the jade outfit to the revel, then?"

"Absolutely."

Ailith's nose wrinkled in amusement. "Oh, thank the forest you've decided. Now we can finally retire to bed."

For the first time in a long time Lachlan slept a sound, uninterrupted sleep, the promise of whisking Sorcha into his arms once more dancing through his dreams in a tantalising, never-ending loop.

CHAPTER SEVENTEEN

Murdoch

"Sorcha, just what are you – Sorcha?"

Murdoch didn't know what to do. One moment he was relaxing in the bath, allowing himself to quite literally dissolve in the water as his mood lifted drastically, and the next...

Sorcha had come crashing through the door and fallen straight into the tub. Going by the look on her face it hadn't been deliberate; she was pale and surprised. *And frightened,* Murdoch realised, going by how much her pupils had contracted. But the very first moment she'd fallen into the bath Sorcha had been wearing a decidedly different look on her face.

She'd almost appeared charmed.

"Sorcha?" Murdoch ventured again. When he tried to help steady her Sorcha merely collapsed with her back against his chest, shaking slightly as she looked up at him through her eyelashes.

"I'm – I saw things," she whispered. "Heard things."

Murdoch held a hand to her forehead; she was deathly cold, so he wrapped his arms around her to pull her even closer to him.

"What kind of things?" he asked. "Where did you see them?"

Sorcha didn't respond at first. She dropped her head back down to stare at the steaming, frothy bathwater swirling all around them. "...the mirrors," she finally admitted. "In the mirrors, and in the water jug, and in the windows, and in every shadowy corner I see them."

It was Murdoch's turn to feel his very core turn to ice. "The Unseelie," he said through gritted teeth. "You are seeing the Unseelie, Sorcha."

"I...thought it might be them," she said. She fidgeted with the collar of her sodden bed-shirt; Murdoch imagined it wasn't particularly comfortable to wear in a bath. Sorcha glanced back up at him. "Lachlan warned me about them when I told him about being followed through the streets."

Murdoch stiffened. He tightened his grip around Sorcha's waist. "You never mentioned anything supernatural about your being followed to me," he bit out tersely. "Why did you tell Lachlan, when he is hundreds of miles away?"

"I do not know."

She trusts him more than me, Murdoch realised. *Down here, in an unfamiliar place dealing with unfamiliar people, she trusts her faerie more than me. And I have made it worse for her by staying distant. What can I do now to be the one she will rely on?*

Sorcha turned her head to stare at the doorway, growing pale once more. "They keep following me.

They beg me for songs. I don't know what their intentions are. What am I to do, Murdoch?"

"Well you can stay in the bath with me, for one," he said, an idea finally blooming in his mind.

She frowned. "And what will – how does that help me?"

Murdoch released his iron grip of her waist in order to trail his fingertips through the water; Sorcha followed the patterns they made with her eyes. "So long as there is no competition for a particular body of water," he explained, "a kelpie automatically claims dominion over it. The Unseelie cannot touch you in here."

When the water began to darken and swirl around them Sorcha gasped. "What are you doing? she asked, lifting a leg out of the water to see if the blackness had stained her skin. She carefully lowered it back in when she saw that it hadn't.

Murdoch let out a low chuckle. "I'm stretching myself out, so to speak. This was how I talked to you back in the waterfall pool, when I had to pretend to be Murdoch Buchanan whilst also meeting you as *me.*" He solidified a tendril of his very being and wrapped it around Sorcha's ankle, only to have it dissipate the moment she reached out a hand to try and touch it. "I sat by the water's edge and dipped my feet in it," Murdoch continued, "then toyed with you until you were almost out of breath."

Sorcha's eyes darted from one point in the bath to another, then another and another, never quite fast enough to catch sight of the next dark, twisting shape Murdoch hardened into being around her. "You enjoy toying with me," she murmured.

It wasn't a question.

Sorcha twisted her neck around until she could see Murdoch's expression. He let an amused smile cross his lips. "What do you expect me to say?" he asked. "Of course I enjoy it. Most all *otherwordly beings* like teasing humans. You are such easy targets."

"...you have hardly acted like this since you came to ask for your bridle back."

"That is because I have not had the means to act like this until now," Murdoch replied, indicating pointedly towards the water. "I can't make full use of my powers unless I'm in or near water."

Sorcha let out a bark of surprised laughter, though she held a hand over her mouth to try and cover the sound. "That is so obvious. I feel stupid for not realising that was the answer."

"I thought that was why you ran me the bath?" Murdoch asked, eyebrow raised. "Because you worked out I needed some time in water?"

"That was...p-part of the reason," she stammered, "but I thought it was more akin to being dehydrated than to you being cut off from your powers." A blush spread up Sorcha's neck, ears and cheeks, causing a stir somewhere below Murdoch's stomach, and he remembered that all that lay between himself and Sorcha's skin was her shirt. Feeling bold, and fuelled by lingering jealousy at her continued closeness to Lachlan and the insistent longing he'd held for her for years, Murdoch slid a hand beneath the hem of the garment to run his fingers against Sorcha's waist.

"For what other reason did you run me the bath then, Sorcha?" he murmured into her ear, thoroughly enjoying the resultant hitch in her breath at his question. "Were you hoping for something?"

"It d-doesn't matter," she stammered, trying to look away only to find Murdoch's other hand winding through her hair to keep her head in place. Murdoch allowed more of his body beneath the water to slide and dissolve and solidify again all around her until the artery in Sorcha's neck was throbbing painfully against his lips.

After two weeks of keeping his careful distance, Murdoch found every ounce of his resolve now evaporating as if it had never existed. He swept his hand further up Sorcha's body, delighting in the feeling of her squirming against him in response.

But not protesting. Not fighting to get away.

Murdoch grazed his lips along Sorcha's neck to the point where her jaw met her ear. "Do you want me to stop, Sorcha?" he breathed against her skin. "Do you want me to stop, or do you enjoy being toyed with as much as I enjoy doing it?"

Sorcha closed her eyes for a moment, lashes fluttering against her cheekbones as she shook her head. "I would not have run the bath if I wanted you to stop doing this," she said. "But..."

"But?"

Her gaze lingered on Murdoch's face. There was no mistaking the desire in her eyes; Murdoch felt a fool for ever believing it was truly gone.

Sorcha gulped. "Will you ever kiss me?" she whispered. "Or is torturing me all you want to do?"

"And what about you, Miss Darrow?" Murdoch bodily turned Sorcha around in his lap so that she was facing him. *For I have kissed you already,* he thought, *but you were enchanted. Why won't you kiss me first?*

Slowly but surely he worked his way through the buttons of her shirt until he reached her navel. Sorcha's breathing grew ever more uneven the lower his hands went. Murdoch watched her intently. "Will *you* ever kiss *me?*" he asked.

Sorcha blinked. She bit her lip. She breathed in through her nose. And then –

The two of them closed the gap between them simultaneously, Sorcha's hands crawling up Murdoch's neck to twist through his hair whilst he wrapped his arms around her waist to pull her closer, closer, closer. When their mouths found each other Murdoch leaned back to slide lower into the bath, pulling Sorcha with him. All around them the steaming water grew wild and turbulent, splashing over the edge of the tub to spill down onto the floor.

It can soak and stain the hallway carpet for all I care, Murdoch thought, dragging his lips away from Sorcha's to run hungry kisses down her neck. He wondered how he could have resisted putting her hands on her for as long as he had; now Sorcha was against his skin – in *his* environment – Murdoch didn't see how he could ever let her go.

He wanted her so badly. Loved her so much it was painful. It didn't matter that he currently despised Murdoch Buchanan; he would do anything to use the man's form to show Sorcha just how much he longed for her.

When Sorcha's hand grazed against Murdoch's hipbone it was his turn to gulp down a breath. He repositioned her in his lap, half a second away from flipping their positions so he could tower over her, when

378

The sound of porcelain smashing filled the air. Sorcha flinched; she broke away from Murdoch immediately, sitting stock straight in his lap in order to listen for further disturbances. "What was that?" she asked, eyes glued to the dark corridor through the doorway.

Murdoch tightened his grip on her, not ready for the magic woven around the two of them to break. "Mrs Ferguson probably had an accident –"

"I sent her to her room almost an hour ago," Sorcha interrupted. She placed a hand on Murdoch's shoulder to keep her balance as she stood up and exited the bath, further drenching the tiled floor as she did so. Murdoch watched her leave the bathroom, torn between leaping out to drag Sorcha back in to finish what they'd only just started and going to investigate alongside her.

Eventually his concern and curiosity got the better of him, and Murdoch lifted himself out of the bath. *We can talk about what we want to happen next after seeing what caused the noise,* he decided, wrapping a towel around his hips before following Sorcha into the shadowy corridor.

A tall, delicate vase that sat on the table near the hallway mirror had fallen to the floor. Heather, thistles and roses were scattered across the carpet alongside dangerously sharp fragments of porcelain. Sorcha stood in a dark puddle of water, eyes focused on a small, perfectly square card that she'd picked up with trembling hands.

"Sorcha?" Murdoch worried aloud, closing the distance between them in three broad strides. "Sorcha, what do you have in your –"

"To the kelpie's bride," she said, voice taking on a sing-song lilt that disturbed Murdoch to no end, *"we suggest you choose your company a little more wisely in the days to come."*

Murdoch grabbed onto Sorcha's arm to turn her around. Her eyes were glassy. "Where did you get that note?" he asked. "Do you recognise the handwriting?"

She shook her head, glanced at the table and said, "It was there. On the table. By the...by the mirror."

The mirror.

Murdoch stared at the reflective surface, trying desperately to see something within it that shouldn't have been there. But there was nothing.

It was just a mirror.

CHAPTER EIGHTEEN

Sorcha

Sorcha's head drooped over her cup of tea. The steam from the beverage caught in her lashes, making her eyes even heavier than they already were. So she closed them for just a moment, jolting herself back to reality when she realised she was beginning to doze in public.

Several days had passed since she had been given the Unseelie warning and Sorcha had barely slept. For how could she? There could be no mistaking that the note was a threat.

But for whom, exactly? Sorcha wondered for the hundredth time. *Me or Murdoch or Lachlan? They called me the kelpie's bride, but did not specify that it was his company I should be wary about. It could well be Lachlan's, since he is the Seelie king. Or it could be somebody else's company entirely.*

She sighed heavily, fighting the insatiable urge to rest her head upon the table and block out the rest of the world. On Murdoch's orders, Mrs Ferguson had taken Sorcha to a coffee house near the Grey and MacKinnon offices in Mayfair whilst he attended a meeting.

"Miss Darrow, are you quite all right?" Mrs Ferguson asked, a frown of worry creasing her brow. She held a hand to Sorcha's forehead. "You seem to have a chill."

"I am just tired, Mrs Ferguson," Sorcha replied, which was at the very least a half-truth. She blew upon the surface of her tea. "Do you think Mr Buchanan will be much longer?"

"I imagine he should be here any moment. I must confess, I am most pleased that Mr Buchanan has finally settled down. His father would be very happy if he were around to see it."

Finally settled down? Sorcha wondered. *If his own housekeeper is saying such a thing then he truly must have been quite a Lothario. I always thought the kelpie was exaggerating when he told me that two years ago.*

But it did not matter how Murdoch Buchanan acted around women one way or the other. The man was dead, and the creature who had replaced him only had eyes for Sorcha.

Or at least I think that must be true, she mused, hating how conflicted she still felt over the subject. After their altercation in the bath Sorcha had thought that perhaps she and the kelpie would end up on more of an even keel with each other, and though Murdoch had not reverted to silence after the note from the Unseelie there was still something distinctly careful about the way he talked and acted around Sorcha in the days that followed.

He was never so conflicted two years ago. Even when

he was pretending to be someone else I never doubted his interest in me. What has him so distracted now? Does he mislike bearing a human form for so long?

It would not surprise Sorcha if she were to discover that this was the case, but it hurt her heart to believe such a thing. For if the kelpie could only stand to be human for a short duration of time then it would not matter if she sorted out how she felt for him; their relationship would be doomed from the beginning.

Even if I were immortal things would not change, Sorcha thought, taking a long draught of her quickly-cooling tea as she did so. *I would still be no more magical than I am now.*

Sorcha had been mulling over Lachlan's not-so-subtle wishes that she accept his offer to live in the Seelie Court amongst the faeries for a long time now. Though she loved her home, and wished to protect the land around the loch as had always been the Darrow tradition, Sorcha had to admit that the allure of a human life was waning.

My father is not long for this world, and my mother may not be far behind for all I know. When they are gone, who else ties me to this life?

But, even taking that into account, over the past two years Sorcha had still staunchly refused Lachlan's offer. For she *was* human, and this was her life. It felt as if she would be running away from her responsibilities if she left the human realm.

That was before she received the note from the Unseelie.

Now all Sorcha could think about was whether she would be safer becoming immortal and living under the protection of the Seelie Court. It seemed like her best course of action. But then...

Sorcha sighed once more. It was folly for her to think such a solution was her best option. She was human and forever was a long, long time. Even after her parents were gone she would have decades to live. Sorcha had to carve a life out for *herself,* instead of relying on Lachlan and Ailith and their otherworldly magic.

When she heard the bell above the coffee house door ring Sorcha glanced over at the entrance. A man and a woman dressed in long, vibrant-coloured cloaks headed to the counter, a paper-wrapped package held firmly in the woman's hands. Their hoods were pulled high over their heads so Sorcha could not see what they looked like, but as they spoke Sorcha realised they both had distinctly German accents.

"Not often we get foreigners here," Mrs Ferguson said, eyeing the couple curiously. "Their clothes are expensive, though. They must be important."

Whilst the woman dealt with the coffee house owner, giving the man hushed instructions that were clearly to do with the package in her hands, her companion wandered around the shop until he spotted Sorcha, locking his gaze on her as if he had been searching for her. She was startled into sitting stock straight, for his eyes were almost as golden as Lachlan's.

Amber, she realised. *Not gold. Is he a faerie?*

The man cocked his head to one side as he regarded Sorcha. She fidgeted with her tea cup, wondering what on earth to say to him when he finally broke the silence instead. "What strange eyes you have," he murmured, frowning slightly. Sorcha distinctly felt like he was staring right through her. She wanted to look away, but forced herself to match the man's stare.

"Not as strange as yours, perhaps," she said – a comment which was bold enough to elicit a gasp of shock from Mrs Ferguson. But Sorcha did not care if the servant thought her rude; if the man was at all offended then it was his own fault for talking to Sorcha first.

The stranger's frown grew deeper, though it seemed altogether more out of concern than offence. "Be careful so far from home," he warned Sorcha. "Be very careful." He retreated back to his companion's side just as Murdoch opened the door to the coffee house and strode right on past him; his unsettling eyes peered at the kelpie in disguise as if he were confused. "But...not of him," the man said, so quietly Sorcha almost missed it.

Murdoch glanced at the stranger, wariness and suspicion apparent on his face, before sitting down to join Sorcha and Mrs Ferguson. "Do you know him, Miss Darrow?" he asked, firing another look behind him as he spoke.

It took Sorcha a long moment before she shook her head. The amber-eyed man's words struck a chord with her, especially after the Unseelie warning. *Just who is he?* she wondered, curious and just a little bit frightened.

"You attract the most bizarre folk," Murdoch said, stealing a bite of Sorcha's untouched lemon cake much to the distress of a scandalised Mrs Ferguson. Sorcha held his gaze, fighting the urge to smile. For wasn't Murdoch the most bizarre creature of all that Sorcha had attracted?

"How did your meeting go?" she asked, quickly

changing the subject. "Have you made any headway?"

Murdoch's face darkened immediately. "They are most insistent that they want this land. We have been invited to a private art viewing by Mr MacKinnon this Saturday, and I have a feeling they will use the opportunity to attempt to corral you into signing it over to them directly."

Sorcha mulled this over for a minute. She did not much like the idea of being *corralled* into anything, but she could stand to stay trapped in Mr Buchanan's house for another few days even less.

"Let us go," she said, "and they will see just how foolish they are to think they can convince *me* to do something I do not wish to do."

Murdoch raised an eyebrow. "You wouldn't be thinking of escaping through a window, would you?"

"That depends – would you follow me?"

A knowing smile crossed his face. "You did say you would be difficult, two years ago. But I do recall telling you that I was willing to put the effort in, regardless."

"Is that a yes?" Sorcha asked, heart thumping so painfully in her chest that she thought it might stop. She wished she and Murdoch were alone and in private. But they were not, which meant so much could not be said.

Murdoch's black eyes glittered with the promise of something Sorcha was desperate to explore again. "I suppose it is," he said, before sweeping back onto his feet. "Now, come; it is time we went home."

Sorcha wished the kelpie meant Darach. Going by the look on his face, so did he.

CHAPTER NINETEEN

Murdoch

"Mister Buchanan, are you listening to me?"

"Probably not; he's too busy pretending not to stare at his betrothed."

Murdoch bit his tongue in surprise at having been caught out, for he was indeed not listening to the conversation his colleagues were having in favour of watching Sorcha. She was milling from painting to painting, taking note of the artist's name and the year the painting was completed before scanning each piece from top to bottom, searching for...something.

I want to ask her what she's thinking when she looks at each painting, Murdoch pined, curling his hands into fists at his side for but a moment before relaxing them again. Things had been incredibly tense ever since the Unseelie left their note of warning for Sorcha. Given that they had referred to her as 'the kelpie's bride' Murdoch could only run on the assumption that the dark fae were following her because of him.

Because he murdered the Unseelie king's brother and nephew.

That was never supposed to hurt Sorcha, he thought, glancing wistfully at her as she twirled her cream dress around her feet and headed to look at an ancient Egyptian vessel. Gregory MacKinnon's art collection was admittedly impressive but the wing of his estate which housed said collection was far too ostentatious for Murdoch's liking. There was a lot of gold, for one, which reminded Murdoch too much of Lachlan's palace for his comfort. *And too many reflective surfaces through which the Unseelie could reach out to Sorcha.*

"Mister Buchanan, you are seriously distracted."

"To be distracted by my betrothed seems like a blessing, given I shall be spending the rest of my life with her," Murdoch replied, altogether rather wry. It was difficult for him *not* to make a joke of anything pertaining to Mr Buchanan still being alive.

Gregory let out a decidedly cruel laugh; there was a sneer on his face that Murdoch did not like at all. "Given your behaviour in the past, I somehow doubt Miss Darrow will hold your attention for as long as you think she will. I doubt any woman would, no matter how charming."

Murdoch resisted responding. From combing through Mr Buchanan's memories he had come to discover just how free with his affections the man had been whilst living in London. He had ventured up to visit William Darrow with no intention whatsoever of staying true to Sorcha, though his glib charm and lingering fondness for the area that used to be his home had won her father over and concealed his ultimate goal for seeking her hand.

He was useful, in order to meet her, Murdoch thought. *And he was supposed to be useful now, but he has become such a burden to me.*

"Speaking of Miss Darrow," Howard Grey chimed in, a mischievous look creasing the lines around his eyes, "have you broached the subject of a winter wedding to her yet? The ball is just around the corner, Murdoch! You are running out of time to ask her."

"I do not think it fair to spring such a thing on her," Murdoch replied. "She has always wanted to get married by the loch-side." He scratched his chin and pretended to be thoughtful as he lied, for in truth Murdoch was fairly certain Sorcha did not wish to get married at all.

No marriage to a mere mortal could best a relationship with a faerie king, he thought, though Murdoch hated acknowledging Lachlan as one of Sorcha's suitors at all. But what Ailith had said to him still rang in his head – that the Seelie king had offered Sorcha the world. Murdoch wondered what *the world* entailed, for it wasn't as if Sorcha spoke to him about her thoughts on the faerie.

She was always guarded when it came to Lachlan.

"One wonders if you are delaying the proceedings deliberately," Gregory remarked, forcing Murdoch out of his own head once more. "If you truly love Miss Darrow then why do you seem so reluctant to marry her?"

Murdoch knew this was as good an opportunity as any to say that he did not wish to hand over the Darrow land to Grey and MacKinnon, and hope that their respect and friendship with Mr Buchanan would prevent them from using much more underhanded techniques to procure it. After a handful of meetings with the board he had found no way to convince them that their plan was a bad one, which left Murdoch with no choice but to go down the personal route.

He turned to the two men, making himself as tall and imposing as possible. "After having spent the last fortnight in London I must confess that the city has lost its charm for me," he began. From the looks on the faces of both Howard and Gregory they could already tell where this was going – and did not like it. Murdoch continued on anyway. "I have enjoyed my life back by Loch Lomond these past two years. I do not wish to see it end."

"There would be no need for that to change," Howard said. "From the money we make from Miss Darrow's land we will all be very, very wealthy men. You could retire early wherever you wanted!"

"I do not see how Miss Darrow would ever forgive me if I sold her home to investors the moment we wed. It is the one thing she and her family do not want, and I would be loathe to betray her like that."

"You –" Gregory spluttered, his pale face slowly turning scarlet. "I knew you were not right for this job! I should have sent my son and been done with it!"

Howard did not seem as visibly angry, though there was a tightness to his eyes that had not been there before. He wagged his glass of port at Murdoch. "Now, now, Murdoch," he said, as if he were scorning a child, "you cannot back out of this now. You were *paid* to do this, and handsomely. Do not turn away from a promising career with people who respect you over a lowly country girl!"

"The problem is that I do not respect *you*," Murdoch countered, seething with anger on Sorcha's behalf. "Anybody who would tear apart such a beautiful area of the country for money – upending the lives of hundreds of honest-working families in the process – deserves the respect of no-one. Good evening."

And with that Murdoch stormed away from his colleagues, knowing that he was bound to pay dearly for having spoken to them the way he had. *If they try to take the land by force I shall kill them all,* he thought, a shiver of wicked excitement tingling his spine. *I have spent too long as someone else. It is time I fight for my home as myself. For* our *home,* Murdoch added on, making a beeline for Sorcha.

He had wasted so much time hating the vessel he was in. Precious time. Time Murdoch should have been spending with the woman he loved.

Sorcha turned from the painting she was looking at as if she could tell Murdoch was making his way to her. A radiant smile lit up her face, and she tucked a stray lock of hair behind her ear. But just as she opened her mouth to greet him, a hand on Murdoch's arm tugged him away.

His eyes flashed a warning as he looked to see who had touched him, but it was merely a blonde-haired woman around Sorcha's age. "Mister Buchanan?" she said, a little unsure, and then, brightly, "Oh, it *is* you! It has been so long!"

"Oh my goodness, you have gotten even more handsome since last I saw you," another woman agreed when she joined the first. Murdoch cast a furtive glance at Sorcha, whose eyes narrowed at the scene in front of her. He did not like that at all. "How long has it been?" the woman continued. "Two, three years?"

Murdoch did not know what to say. He vaguely

recognised the two women from Mr Buchanan's memories – casual dalliances from the man's past. "Whilst it is wonderful to see the two of you," he said, forcing a smile to his face, "it is with regret I must inform you that I am on my way out. I was just about to fetch – Miss Darrow?"

He searched over the heads of the women, but Murdoch could not see Sorcha. He felt like pulling his hair out. *Just once I wish things could be easy between us,* he raged, walking away from the two women without so much as a goodbye. *Why must there always be faerie usurpers and fox curses and golden princes and greedy, filthy Londoners to contend with?*

"And your hedonistic, awful past," Murdoch glowered at his reflection when he passed a vase encased in glass. "This is your fault. Yours."

He did not want to admit that, had he been more open and honest with Sorcha from the beginning, Murdoch may well have avoided this situation entirely.

Being a human is terrible.

CHAPTER TWENTY

Sorcha

I guess Murdoch Buchanan really was the Lothario the kelpie warned me about.

Sorcha couldn't stand to watch it.

"This is so stupid," she muttered, snaking around all the well-dressed people who had come to bear witness to Gregory MacKinnon's new art collection in her attempt to escape the sight of Murdoch surrounded by pretty, English socialites. Mister MacKinnon had come to procure a few paintings that Sorcha was familiar with – works by Scottish artists whom her mother and father knew – and many of the guests stood idolising the bleak, Scottish landscapes captured on the canvas, describing them as *romantic* and *heartbreakingly beautiful.*

They do not get to think that if they do not live there, she grumbled, growing more and more frustrated with everyone around her. *You cannot appreciate the Scottish wilderness if you have not also suffered through its stormy autumns and tempestuous winters.*

Sorcha knew she couldn't exactly blame anyone for adoring the paintings, for they *were* beautiful. But there was a heavy, leaden pit within her, gnawing away at her nerves and leaving her feeling raw and exposed. Sorcha had thought attending the art exhibit would have allowed her and Murdoch to at least spend some time together as a couple, even if their engagement was false. She'd hoped it would encourage them to talk about how they actually felt for each other.

Instead, Murdoch had spent most of the evening embroiled with his colleagues and then surrounded by lovely-looking, fawning women. Sorcha did not think she had ever been jealous before – not even of Ailith, who was perfect in every way a creature could be perfect. But she was jealous now, and she hated it.

Why is it that the only one who does not get to spend time with Murdoch is me? I am the only one who truly knows him. All the people around me are chasing a ghost.

As she always did, Sorcha pushed the man's death to the back of her mind. There was nothing she could do about the fact the kelpie had devoured him and, considering how Mr Buchanan had intended to trick her into handing over the Darrow land, Sorcha had to admit that part of her was glad that he had died.

If that makes me a terrible person then so be it. Given the otherworldy nature of the folk I consider my friends, I have not been all that great at being human for a while.

Something about that made Sorcha feel wildly uncomfortable. Was she beginning to lose sight of who she was? Had she spent too long in London with a terrifying, powerful beast masquerading as a man for her

394

own good? For when the two of them had been in the bath – when the kelpie had been more like himself than he had been since Sorcha stole away his bridle – Murdoch *had* been terrifying. He'd been full of the same dark intensity that had caused Sorcha to run from him the very first night she met him.

But it was that darkness that kept drawing Sorcha to him, too. That made her want and desire him; that made her wish dearly to *know* him.

London, and the people within it, were preventing her from doing so.

"I want to go home," she wailed, so softly that she was sure nobody could hear her.

Somebody did.

"I had a feeling London was not to your tastes, lass," a man said from over on her left, his voice so light and airy that Sorcha thought for a moment she had imagined it. She turned to face him, taking a step back in surprise when she noticed there was something familiar about him.

The man was tall and lithe, dressed in a resplendent, elaborately-embroidered tailcoat the colour of deep, dark wine. He inclined his head politely at Sorcha, a spirited smile lighting up his fine features. Though he had long, silver hair kept tied away from his face, the man seemed to be no more than a year or two older than Murdoch Buchanan.

And then Sorcha realised why she thought he seemed familiar.

Silver hair.

"We have met before," she said carefully. "You helped me find my way when I was lost."

"Consider me a concerned third party looking out for your welfare," he said, grey eyes glittering as they swept from Sorcha's head to her feet. She blushed and looked away.

"I believed you to be an old man, truth be told," she admitted.

He laughed easily and ran a hand across his temple. "Because of my hair?"

Sorcha nodded. "Your face was covered, too, so I did not see it. But you are not so old."

"How generous of you to say so. Might you accompany me whilst I take a turn around this exhibit?" The man proffered an arm and Sorcha, before she knew what she was doing, took it. When he guided her down the corridor it almost felt as if they were gliding across the marble rather than walking. Sorcha had not felt such ease in moving since she had travelled down to London on the back of a kelpie.

Murdoch, Sorcha remembered, coming back to her senses in a moment of clarity. *Where is he?*

"It seems as if your companion is otherwise occupied," the silver-haired man said, glancing at Sorcha out of the corner of his eye. "The tall, dark, brooding gentleman who was surrounded by ladies, yes?"

Sorcha did not respond, though her silence was more than enough of an answer.

"Is he part of the reason you wish to leave London?" he ventured, taking two glasses of wine from a passing servant and handing one to Sorcha. She accepted the glass but did not drink from it, wary as she was, choosing instead to concentrate on looking at the paintings they passed as they walked.

"He is and he is not," she said, which was the truth. It was because of the kelpie that she wanted to go home; it was because of *Murdoch Buchanan* that she did not wish to stay in London.

"A perfectly evasive answer, Miss Darrow."

A terribly foreboding shiver ran down Sorcha's spine. She dared not look at the man as she asked, "How do you know my name?"

"If I could lie, I would say I learned it from your Mr Buchanan's colleagues. But he is no more a man than I am, Miss Darrow, and you need to be careful. Kelpies are dark, dangerous creatures, and this one in particular even more so. You did receive my note, did you not?"

He is Unseelie, Sorcha realised, so shocked she could barely process anything but this one, all-consuming fact. *He is Unseelie. He is –*

"Oh, I am not here to harm you," the faerie said, laughing his light, disarming laugh again. Sorcha risked a glance at him; he was staring at her with a highly curious expression painting his angular features. "I am merely here to pose a question to you. I was hoping you would be so kind as to answer it."

"I...I suppose it would depend on the question," Sorcha replied, very slowly. She hardly felt able to wrap her mouth around the words she said; they felt thick and foreign on her tongue.

The mysterious stranger came to a stop and took a long draught from his wine; when he pulled the glass away his lips were stained a purple just as deep as his tailcoat. It unsettled Sorcha greatly, especially when the faerie leaned towards her, boxing her in against the wall.

"Tell me," he began, "why do you continue to

decline the Seelie king's most generous offer of immortality?"

"What did you just say?"

Sorcha froze, for she had not asked the question.

It was Murdoch.

CHAPTER TWENTY-ONE

Murdoch

"You turned down *what?*"

Sorcha's eyes widened in shock as she turned her head to stare at Murdoch. A tall, silver-haired man was looming over her, dangerously close to her face, but in the space of a blink he disappeared.

A faerie. Which is why he knew about the offer of immortality.

Sorcha's head swung around wildly when she realised the person she'd been speaking to was gone. Her skin was pale, and the wine glass in her hand was shaking. "Murdoch, I never meant to keep it from –"

"*Why were you talking to an Unseelie?*" he demanded, too furious with the immediate issue at hand to focus on what the faerie himself had said. He stalked towards Sorcha, grabbed her sleeve and dragged her towards the nearest exit, not caring if anybody could see them. The two of them had to leave London *now,* before their situation grew worse than it already was.

"Murdoch, stop – stop pulling me along!" Sorcha cried out the moment they hit the bracing night air. She scrabbled at his hand, digging in her nails until he let her go. "I did not know he was Unseelie when he started talking to me!"

"And yet you followed him down an empty corridor and allowed him to corner you like a cat with a mouse. Have you listened to nothing either myself or Lachlan has warned you about? Have you?"

Sorcha glowered at him. She ran her hands up and down her arms, for in Murdoch's haste to leave Gregory MacKinnon's abode he had left their coats and scarves back inside. "There would have been no opportunity for me to be cornered if you hadn't been so *occupied,* Mister Buchanan."

Murdoch recoiled as if Sorcha had slapped him. "You know that was not me they were wishing to talk to," he said, hating the scathing look in her eyes before she turned her back on him. "Sorcha, you cannot blame me for –"

"I know I cannot blame you!" she cut in. Her hands curled into small, angry fists at her sides, entire back shivering from either fury or cold. Murdoch reasoned that it was likely both. "I cannot blame you for what Mr Buchanan was like in the past," Sorcha continued, "but that does not mean I like it, nor the way you – you –"

"Nor the way I *what*, Sorcha?"

"It does not matter," she sniffed.

Murdoch reached out a hand to touch her arm but Sorcha pulled away. "I will get our coats," he said, trying desperately to calm his temper even though he was still viciously angry. But he was not angry *with* Sorcha. He was, however, confused and hurt because of her. *She did not once tell me Lachlan offered her immortality,* Murdoch thought as he jogged back to the front door, where a servant was dutifully waiting with his and Sorcha's outerwear. He thanked the man, wasting no time in throwing on his coat before turning back the way he had come, and froze.

Sorcha had disappeared into the night.

"Do not do this now, Sorcha!" Murdoch called out, hating the way his voice shook as he shouted. It felt as if bile was rising in his throat; every time he turned away from Sorcha for even a moment she seemed to get into trouble.

Going by the appearance of the Unseelie tonight, she was running out of opportunities to escape said trouble unscathed.

"Sorcha," Murdoch said into the night, gentler this time as he crunched across gravel and reached the elaborately-designed, wrought-iron front gates of the MacKinnon estate. "Sorcha, please. You know this is dangerous. Let us return home and *talk*. We have not done nearly enough of that. Sorcha? Sorcha!"

His heart beat erratically in his chest when he realised the front gates had not been opened, which meant Sorcha hadn't left the dark, expansive grounds of the estate. *Just where have you gone, you fool?* Murdoch thought as he ran across a stretch of frost-covered grass, slipping more than once and just barely regaining his balance before he fell over each time. He searched around for something – anything.

And then he saw it: footprints.

Footprints that matched the slippers Sorcha had

been wearing, heading towards a glassy, largely frozen-over ornamental pond. It was a rather enormous body of water, more akin to a lake now that Murdoch was growing nearer to it, but all around its frosted edges Sorcha was nowhere to be seen.

"Where *are* you, Sorcha?!" Murdoch boomed, voice echoing all around. But then he noticed a fault in the ice upon the water, as if someone had come across a crack and fallen straight down.

Murdoch's heart stopped beating for one sick, terrible moment.

He dived into the lake without a second thought, reverting to his true form the moment the water's surface settled above him. Shards of ice filtered through the inky-black water; what little light Murdoch could make out with his keen eyes reflected off their sharp edges, turning them into silvered knives. He kicked at the long, tumbling weeds growing from the bottom of the lake the moment they touched him, all the while searching, searching, searching for anything even vaguely human-shaped.

"Sorcha," he whispered, the water carrying his voice to the farthest corners of the lake as if he had screamed. "Sorcha," he said again, "where are you?"

C-cold, came a faint, stuttering reply. Murdoch swung immediately to his right, dissolving into the water to hurtle through it as fast as he could. *Caught on something. C-can't breathe.*

"Just hold on!" he cried, growing desperate when he still could not locate Sorcha. "Call out again! Tell me where you are!"

Slipped, Sorcha thought. *So s-stupid. I am so stupid.*

"You are a fool, but you are not stupid," Murdoch replied. He had to keep Sorcha thinking – had to ensure her brain continued to function until he found and freed her. He scanned the bottom of the lake, fighting with the strangling weeds for a sight of a hand or a foot or the hem of a dress, and then –

A long, flowing tendril that was not a weed glinted in a stray sliver of moonlight, flashing deep copper against the murky water.

"Found you!" Murdoch roared, relief washing over him as he galloped through the lake to reach Sorcha. Several weeds had wound themselves around her legs; he tore at them with vicious, frantic teeth until Sorcha, finally, floated free.

Her eyes were closed, her face ghostly pale. Murdoch could tell Sorcha was no longer breathing.

"Don't you dare die!" he screamed, forcing Sorcha onto his back until her hands brushed against his bridle, filling her with the power to breathe and stay attached to Murdoch. *Don't you dare die like this. You cannot drown. It is impossible.*

But as Murdoch hurtled away from the lake and through the streets of London back to Mr Buchanan's house, his thoughts from before kept circling in his head. Perhaps Sorcha really *had* run out of opportunities to escape from danger – but not at the hands of the Unseelie. No, they may well have been the ones who were correct, after all. She should have chosen her company a little more wisely.

If she'd never dallied with a kelpie then Sorcha Darrow would not have found herself drowning in that lake.

CHAPTER TWENTY-TWO

Sorcha

All around Sorcha was cold, cold, cold, so bitter and biting that her skin felt like it was burning or had been stabbed with a million tiny needles. Her lungs gasped for air, but when she opened her mouth she was greeted with a torrent of ice water, instead. She could not move her legs; could not kick away from whatever was trapping her beneath the surface of the lake.

I am going to die, Sorcha thought, so deliriously oxygen-deprived that she did not notice the way the water around her solidified just before she closed her eyes. Then everything went black, and Sorcha knew she would never again wake up.

*

"...cha. Sorcha. Sorcha, please, you must wake up!"

A flicker of warmth went through her, growing stronger with every passing second. Eventually that heat was all Sorcha could feel, and the darkness around her abated a little.

She opened her eyes.

Murdoch was looming over her, unfocused at first until she blinked a few times. His face was pale and terrified and wretched; the whites of his eyes were red and bleary, as if he had been crying. Sorcha realised she was lying on the floor of his bedroom by the fire, and several blankets were wrapped around her body. Out of the corner of her eye Sorcha spotted her sodden clothes abandoned by the door.

I really did – I almost drowned. I almost died. All because I threw a childish tantrum.

Sorcha coughed and spluttered as she tried to sit up. Her chest was in agony; she clutched her hands to it and heaved.

Murdoch placed firm but gentle hands on her shoulders to push her back to the floor. "Don't get up," he soothed. "Just stay where you are for a while. You are frozen through."

Now that Sorcha was becoming aware of her own body she realised that Murdoch was right. Every inch of her skin prickled and stung with the cold, and the fire hurt equally as much as it thawed her out. "S-sorry," she apologised through chattering teeth. She could hardly stand to look at Murdoch, she felt so miserably guilty. "I'm s–"

"I know you are. I know you are, but I should have expected something like this to happen."

Sorcha frowned, and peered at Murdoch through the dim, crackling light of the fire. "What do you mean?"

"You are the girl who flees through windows into the dead of night," he laughed bitterly, leaning against the hearth and closing his eyes to the heat. Murdoch had stripped down to his shirt and breeches, which were both dripping wet. They steamed faintly as the fire dried them out. "I should have known it was only a matter of time before you ran from me again."

Sorcha gulped on a throat full of tears. "That wasn't – I didn't – I was *angry*, Murdoch, and I –"

"You almost *died,* Sorcha!" Murdoch bit out. She realised he *was* crying; a trail of moisture down his cheek glinted in the fire light. "You almost died, because of me. The Unseelie warned you about being in my company and they were *right.*"

With tremendous effort Sorcha forced herself into a sitting position. Her hair hung in cold, wet tendrils around her face, so she ran a shaking hand through it all to push it back. She edged out a foot to touch Murdoch's knee, desperately wanting him to open his eyes and look at her.

"You would never hurt me," Sorcha said, very softly. "You said so yourself. I have always trusted you, Murdoch."

"But it is my actions against others that are putting you in danger. I am a kelpie who has waged war against the faerie realm. You should never have been put in the middle of it."

Sorcha said nothing. She knew Murdoch was right, in some respects, but it had always been her choice to get involved with both the kelpie and the Seelie. If anyone was to blame for Sorcha being in danger then it was herself.

Especially tonight.

Neither of them spoke for a while, Sorcha staring at

Murdoch whilst he kept his eyes closed as they both warmed their frozen bodies by the fire. Eventually Sorcha stopped shaking, and her nerves stopped hurting, and the blankets wrapped around her grew uncomfortably hot.

She pulled them off until all but one silken cover remained.

"You will get cold again, Sorcha," Murdoch mumbled. She realised he was watching her beneath barely-open, heavy-hooded eyes; she blushed profusely.

"I am too hot now," she said. "The blankets were sticking to my skin. Your wet clothes most be uncomfortable, too."

Murdoch glanced down at his shirt, causing Sorcha's eyes to wander with his. The material was clinging to every plane of his body, as were his breeches. She looked away before her imagination could run rampant.

"I suppose you are right," he replied, pulling off his shirt with a wince when the wet material brushed past his face. Murdoch threw it into some dark corner of the room, then grabbed for one of Sorcha's abandoned blankets to cover him from the waist down so he could remove the rest of his clothes, too.

Sorcha giggled despite herself. "I never knew kelpies were so modest."

"I'd rather say that it is *your* immodesty that is strange here," he countered. "I have never known a human to have such blatant disregard for her own privacy. You stripped off all your clothes in front of me back when you swam in the waterfall pool, though you still believed me to be a man!"

"That was because I wanted to," Sorcha replied,

arching her back until she felt a satisfying pop in her upper spine.

"You wanted to?"

"Well, considering what had almost happened the night before in my tent –"

"So you wanted to continue on from where Lachlan had so rudely interrupted us?" Murdoch asked, dark eyes intent on Sorcha's. He leaned towards her just a little. "Because as I recall, you went to the waterfall pool to try and talk to the kelpie, not seduce a man."

"I...may have wanted both," Sorcha admitted, turning her gaze to the fire out of sheer embarrassment. Her body was still burning, though the source of the heat was entirely internal. "I did not understand it at the time, but once I discovered who you were – who Murdoch Buchanan was – it finally made sense to me."

"So it was not the man himself who you were attracted to?"

"Oh, lord no!" Sorcha cried out, putting her hands up in protest in front of her chest. She glanced at Murdoch; a somewhat confused look was plastered to his handsome face. "I mean," she corrected, "of course he is...good to look at. But I could never have been attracted to the real man. Tonight only further solidified that point."

"Tonight did?"

"You had no time for me at the exhibit," Sorcha explained. "It was all about work and being distracted by other women. I...could never put up with that. It was infuriating."

The smallest of smiles quirked Murdoch's lips. "You were *jealous,* Sorcha?"

"...yes."

And then, out of nowhere, Murdoch threw his head back and burst out laughing. It was hearty and genuine – a sound Sorcha had not heard in two years. She ached for it. "You are – you have nothing to be jealous of, Miss Darrow," he said, still laughing. "You know I only have eyes for you."

"So why have you been so distant these past three weeks?"

Sorcha moved forward on her knees, barely covering herself with the silk blanket as she closed the gap between herself and Murdoch. He watched her every move like a hawk, all humour lost from his face in an instant.

"Because I hate him," Murdoch replied, very quietly. "Mister Buchanan, that is. I cannot stand him. Down here, in London, it has been harder and harder for me to split myself from the man I look like. I did not want to be near you when I felt this way."

"I do not see him when I look at you." Sorcha moved even closer to Murdoch, until it was the easiest thing in the world to reach out a hand to stroke her fingers along the planes of his face. His eyes burned like coals as she traced a line across his cheekbones and down his jaw. "I have never seen him," she continued, "I have only seen you. How could you not know that?"

When Murdoch took hold of her hand and placed it over his heart Sorcha gasped in surprise. "Because I am so nervous I think I might be sick," he admitted, pressing her hand even further against his chest until all Sorcha could feel was an erratic, throbbing pulse from behind his ribs. "I have been like this ever since I knocked upon your door and begged for your help. I forced you to choose sides, two years ago, and you chose the faeries. You chose Lachlan. I thought –"

"I did not *choose* Lachlan over you," Sorcha scolded. "If it were as easy as that I would have stolen away your bridle the moment you fell asleep. But I couldn't. Even when we were up on the plinth and you were drowning everyone in sight I struggled to do what needed to be done. But the fight I was put in the middle of...it was bigger than me. I could not let anyone suffer if I could stop it, even if the last thing I wanted to do was betray you."

Murdoch's eyes widened. He slid a hand over Sorcha's. "You did not betray me. You –"

"I did. But it was the right thing to do, though it tortured me to think about it after you were banished to the loch. Murdoch...you have no idea how much I missed you, after you were gone."

A flash of desire crossed his face; in the mirror of the kelpie's dark, fathomless eyes Sorcha could see the same desire on her own face, too. His grip tightened on her hand. "Why did you refuse Lachlan's offer of immortality?"

Sorcha bit her lip. *How do I make an immortal being understand when I barely understand it myself?* She looked down at their entwined hands. "Because I am human," she said eventually, "and I would rather carve out a meaningful life of sixty years – a life where I feel everything – than live forever and grow numb to the world. I –"

Murdoch kissed her, very softly. "Then let's feel something," he murmured, the words dancing on Sorcha's lips. He snaked a tightly-muscled arm around her, easily flipping their positions so that Sorcha's back was to the wall with Murdoch pressed against her.

Sorcha slid a hand through his hair, still sodden and cold from the lake beneath her fingertips. She ran kisses down Murdoch's neck the way he'd done to her in the bath and, two years ago, in her tent, digging her teeth in when she reached his shoulder. Murdoch groaned at the sensation, and he pulled at Sorcha's thighs to wrap them around his waist.

"Was that a yes?" he asked, voice low and dark and full of longing against Sorcha's ear.

And there it was – the terrifying thrill Sorcha had been longing for from the very first moment she met the kelpie. An inexorable hook that pulled her towards him even as the creature's sheer power loomed all around, reminding Sorcha that he could – and did – kill without a second thought.

But not her. Never her.

"That was a yes," she said, tightening her arms around Murdoch's neck and crushing her lips to his. "It was always a yes."

CHAPTER TWENTY-THREE

Murdoch

The first time Murdoch witnessed Sorcha Margaret Darrow sleeping she had been three years old.

Her parents had taken her down to the shore in front of their house, letting their little girl play in the shallow end of the loch to her heart's content beneath the high-summer son. It had been very hot that year, even for July, so the family of three had lingered by the water's edge for much of the day.

Little Sorcha had played for hours and hours before tiring herself out. She sprawled out across the wet sand, fingers of her right hand just barely touching the loch, and sang along inexpertly to the melody her mother was whistling. Sorcha giggled when the water began swirling around her hand, moving in a way that seemed impossible. But she was three, and exhausted, so she did not think anything of it at the time.

Murdoch had made sure to check in on her every summer since then, delighted with how much time she spent in and around Loch Lomond. It was his home but it was hers, too, and it was clear that she adored it.

He would have done anything to protect her from harm.

And so it was that the kelpie of Loch Lomond had never imagined he would find himself lying in bed with that same mortal girl, now a full-fledged woman, in the form of a human himself. When Murdoch had first taken on Mr Buchanan's form he'd thought to take advantage of it simply to meet Sorcha – to talk with her in her house and perhaps gather more information on Grey and MacKinnon's plans for the Darrow land in the process.

It should not have surprised him that he merely fell for Sorcha even more. Murdoch knew it would not be possible to return to the loch without getting to spend more time with her. And the vessel he was using was going to *marry* her. It had seemed all too fortuitous.

But then Sorcha had fled out of her bedroom window, and dallied with a fox who was a faerie prince. Murdoch had thought things to be ruined between them before they had even started, but then Sorcha had sought out a kelpie.

She had sought out *him.*

And though so much had happened since then, and Sorcha had broken Murdoch's heart as easily as she'd snapped off his bridle, somehow the two of them were together now. They were together, and they were happy in each other's arms, and soon they would be home, too. Which meant there was just one, lingering problem.

Lachlan's offer of immortality.

"Mister Buchanan?" Mrs Ferguson called through

his bedroom door, knocking gently as she did so. "You have a letter from the office. It seems as if it may be urgent."

Murdoch stroked Sorcha's hair, revelling in the sound of her soft breathing and the rosy colouring of her cheeks. She was completely, wondrously at ease, a word that had not once described her in the three weeks since Murdoch had shown up at her door begging for his bridle back.

He slid out of bed, throwing on a robe before answering the door to receive the letter from Mrs Ferguson. The flicker of a smile crossed her face at her employer's unkempt appearance, though she quickly schooled her expression back to neutral.

"Would you like some breakfast?" she asked. "It is almost ten."

But Murdoch shook his head. "We are fine for now, Mrs Ferguson. In fact, take the day off if you like. We will be quite content on our own."

The woman wordlessly receded as Murdoch closed the door and ripped open the envelope in his hands. He recognised the handwriting as that of Gregory MacKinnon's; he wondered if it was an official notice of his termination from the company. Murdoch sat down upon his bed as softly as he could so as not to rouse Sorcha from her sleep, unfurling the letter with a sense of grim satisfaction.

Dear Mr Buchanan, it read;

We at Grey and MacKinnon sincerely apologise for the manner in which the Darrow land was discussed at my abode. I am sorry in particular for the way I personally acted. We understand now that the land is more important to your future family than we gave it credit for.

As a gesture of our continued friendship, please do consider still attending our winter ball with the charming Miss Darrow. It would be a shame to return to Scotland without showing her London at its very best.

Kindest regards,

Gregory MacKinnon

Murdoch frowned as he reread the letter. It had not contained the information he expected. For the most part he did not wish to attend the expensive party the company was hosting in two days; on the other hand, now that Grey and MacKinnon had apologised it would be considered impolite to refuse their invitation.

It would be better to return to Darach on good terms with them, Murdoch realised. *For the sake of Sorcha, the security of the people who live on the Darrow land and the loch itself.*

He put down the letter to lie back beside her; Sorcha turned in her sleep to face him, blowing the same strand of hair away from her face over and over again until Murdoch relented and tucked it behind her ear. His fingertips grazed against her cheek, then traced the curve of her upper lip.

You would not have to worry about such human problems as greedy investors and rent payments if you accepted Lachlan's offer, Sorcha.

Immortality did not seem so odd to Murdoch. He had lived for over five hundred years, after all. A human's life was frightfully short and insignificant by comparison. It would be a joy for Sorcha to accept immortality and live forever alongside him.

Except for the fact that Sorcha did not want to live forever. She wished to remain as she was.

Murdoch's heart sank. If Sorcha stayed human then, sooner or later, she would be gone from his life. A decade would pass, then another and another, and she would grow old. Eventually she would die.

He could not bear it.

"I want to be with you my whole life," he murmured into Sorcha's ear, though she was too far wrapped up in her dreams to hear him. "I cannot imagine my world without you."

And then clarity struck like a bolt of lightning.

If Sorcha would not accept immortality, then Murdoch simply had to accept the opposite on her behalf.

It was a terrifying thought. Murdoch had struggled to be human over the past three weeks, but that was because he remained a kelpie on the inside, bound by laws of power and water and nature itself. If he could give all of that up then he could enjoy a mortal life just as easily as Sorcha did.

Can I really do this? Murdoch thought. *It will not be easy to become a human. Only the most powerful of faeries can grant such a wish. Which means...*

He made a face for nobody to see.

It meant asking Lachlan for a favour.

But all it took was one look at Sorcha's face – at the smallest of smiles that curled her lips as she slept – to tell Murdoch that he could do it. For all of her mortal flaws, from her impulsive, reckless nature to her stubborn insistence that she fix all her problems on her own, Sorcha was the one Murdoch loved. The one he dreamed of being with. He was determined to make that dream a reality.

If that meant getting down on his knees to beg the Seelie king for help then so be it.

CHAPTER TWENTY-FØUR

Lachlan

Ever since Lachlan had decided to call off the hunt for the white stag the animal had become something of a friend to him. Even now, in the bitter cold of midwinter, the animal folded its legs beneath itself to sit beside Lachlan as he dozed beneath the empty boughs of an ancient oak tree. He loved oak more than any other kind of tree, for they reminded him of Sorcha; he had met her whilst standing upon the branches of one.

"I have not seen you in a while," he told the animal when it inched closer to him. Lachlan reached into his pocket and pulled out a handful of winter blackberries. The stag nosed at them curiously, eventually abandoning all caution and devouring them in one go. Lachlan smiled as the berries began to stain its muzzle a deep, dark purple, a colour akin to the blood of most water-dwelling monsters. He could almost imagine the stag possessing sharp, terrifying teeth within its jaws and using them to tear into the flesh of some unfortunate, supernatural creature.

Like a kelpie, Lachlan thought, his smile turning wicked as he imagined the beast's death.

But he could do nothing about the kelpie, nor the fact that Sorcha was alone with him down in London. *Not yet, at least. Tomorrow I will surprise Clara by whisking her off to the solstice revel.*

Lachlan couldn't wait.

The stag knocked its antlers against Lachlan's head, entangling several sharp points through his hair in the process. "Ow," he complained, carefully extricating his hair as the stag watched him with bright, almost amused eyes. *He is making fun of me,* Lachlan thought, *or he is trying to distract me.*

It took him nearly ten minutes to completely free his hair from the creature's antlers, after which he was left with a mess of knots around his head. On impulse Lachlan dug into the calf of his boot and pulled out a small dagger; the metal flashed in the pale winter sun and caused the stag to back away in fright.

"I guess you are wary of even your friends if they hold a blade," Lachlan murmured, before yanking a length of hair away from his head and cutting straight through it. He continued slicing away at his hair until the forest underbrush all around him was covered in it, glittering like threads of pure gold amongst moss and grass and acorns. By the time he was finished the stag had disappeared, only to be replaced by the almost ghostly figure of Ailith. The faerie was resplendent in a sheer, white gown that trailed behind her as she walked.

Ailith tutted in disapproval when she saw what Lachlan had done, then held out a hand for the dagger. "You were foolish to do this to yourself, Lachlan," she scolded, settling down behind him to fix what was presumably a mess of a hair cut. "You know I am much better than you at these things."

"And here you are, fixing it for me, so all is well that ends well."

"Are you nervous?"

Lachlan barked out a laugh. "Excuse me?"

"Are you nervous?" Ailith asked again, amusement plain as day in her voice as she methodically worked her way around Lachlan's hair with the dagger. "About heading down to London, I mean. One does not simply cut their hair on impulse like this unless they are trying to distract themselves."

He didn't reply. Of course Lachlan was nervous, for what if Sorcha declined his invitation to the solstice revel? She had no reason to, but even so...

I know she has feelings for the horse, he thought bitterly. *They were present two years ago, and they are still there now. There's a connection between the two of them that I do not understand.*

Lachlan wished he had met Sorcha even three days earlier than he had done. Just three days, with no interruption from the kelpie posing as Murdoch Buchanan, and perhaps Sorcha would have been his. *But then I would have ended up a fox, and she would have been stuck in the faerie realm at the mercy of my step family.*

"There, all done," Ailith said. She turned Lachlan around, working a spell upon the air in front of him until it hardened and turned into a mirror. "What do you think?"

Lachlan inspected his reflection with a critical eye. His hair was still long enough on top that it swept across his forehead and caught in his lashes, but the back and sides had been cropped into a layer of short, golden fuzz that felt pleasant against his skin when he ran his hands across it. Lachlan did not recall ever keeping his hair so short before.

He grinned. "I love it, Ailith. You have saved me."

"You will look particularly dashing for the revel, now," she said, stroking his hair away from his face as she did so. Her sapphire eyes were soft and lovely as she smiled. "Miss Sorcha will be so surprised. I'm sure you will have no problem bringing her back to the Seelie Court this time."

Lachlan chuckled. "I bloody well hope –"

"The Golden King."

Both Lachlan and Ailith turned to see who had spoken. A woman stood there, black hair long and thick and tangled down her back. She looked to be perhaps thirty, with a belly swollen with the final months of pregnancy. Her eyes were glassy; her expression manic. When Lachlan glanced at her feet he saw that she wore no shoes, and her feet were cut and bruised and blue from the cold. Clearly she had been walking for some time.

A human, he realised. *A human who has been enchanted. Who thought it clever to enchant a pregnant woman to walk through the woods in winter?*

"What is it, my fair lady?" he asked, taking off his thick, woollen cloak as he carefully approached the woman. He threw it over her shoulders, for she was shivering heavily, and motioned for her to sit down beneath the oak tree.

But the woman did not move. A wild smile that did

not meet her eyes stretched her mouth wide, and she recited: "*Never may my woes be relieved,*

Since pity is fled;

And tears and sighs and groans my weary days, my weary days

Of all joys have deprived."

A chill ran down Lachlan's spine. "Am I supposed to know what that means?" he pressed, frowning when he saw a flash of recognition cross Ailith's face.

"Miss Sorcha has sung this before," she said. "Once, when you were sleeping and the two of us could not, I shared a few cups of blackberry wine with her and she began to sing. It was unbearably sad. When I asked her who the song was for she said it was for the birds, but I did not think she was being truthful."

"A bird! A bird!" the woman called back, leaping from one foot to the other as if the ground beneath her toes was made of burning coals. "A singing bird in a silver cage. A silver cage to be locked forever and a day, if only she will sing."

"Sorcha," Lachlan whispered, not quite understanding the woman's riddles but knowing enough to be deathly afraid. He placed his hands on the woman's head, closed his eyes and said, "Sleep, and forget, and in the morning you will remember nothing of your enchantment or how you came to be here." The woman slumped against him, so Lachlan gently lowered her to the ground. He turned to Ailith. "Find her a bed to sleep in, and some clothes to wear, then work a location spell to find out where she came from."

"You wish to return her?" Ailith asked, a little unsure. "Surely it would be safer to have her live with us, Lachlan. She has clearly been enchanted for days!"

"She is pregnant!" Lachlan exclaimed, feeling sick that Ailith would even suggest keeping the woman in their realm, though it truly was the faerie way. "She must have a family! I will not break that family apart."

Lachlan knew it was Sorcha's doing that had him thinking this way; her love for her family was strong enough for her to have rebuffed his offer of immortality and a life in the Seelie Court time and time again. He no longer had the stomach to force anybody to leave the ones they adored unless it was their own choice.

Sorcha has affected my thinking more than I could have ever imagined. Two years ago I'd have never considered sending a human back from whence they came in a state of sanity.

Ailith nodded gravely. "You are heading down to London early, I am assuming?"

"Of course." He kissed her gently on her forehead. "I will change my clothes and be off. Look after our kingdom for me while I am gone."

"That is a given. Be careful, Lachlan."

"I shall be as careful as I can."

"That doesn't sound very careful at all."

Lachlan gave her a small smile. "Perhaps that is because I have never been careful. I will see you when I return."

And with that Lachlan fled back to the palace and to his chambers. He had no time to waste, but he knew he had to dress appropriately for the winter solstice revel. Something told Lachlan that his search for Sorcha would end up with him at it; after all, it was being hosted by the

Unseelie.

A singing bird in a silver cage, he thought. *Silver, like the Unseelie.*

Lachlan stared at his reflection, resplendent in all his green-and-gold finery, and hated himself. He might already be too late, and it was all his fault. "I should have stolen Sorcha away from London days and days ago," he snarled at his own face, then with a twirl of his pine-green cloak he was gone.

CHAPTER TWENTY-FIVE

Sorcha

The way Murdoch couldn't take his eyes off Sorcha caused a near-permanent blush across her cheeks. It had been that way for the last three days and now, dressed in a low-cut, feather-light, pale blue gown, his gaze was even more intense.

"Stop looking at me like that," Sorcha murmured, though she was smiling. She moved to tuck a lock of hair behind her ear but there was none; Mrs Ferguson had helped her pin her hair back with delicate silver chains and tiny, ornamental flowers.

"But you are so beautiful," Murdoch replied, squeezing Sorcha's hand with his own gloved one.

"So are you," Sorcha countered, which was the truth. He'd paired ebony, tight-fitting trousers with a high-collared white shirt and a silvery waistcoat intricately embroidered with a paisley pattern. Black, knee-high boots, a black velvet-lined tailcoat and a tall, round hat atop his curly hair completed the look.

"I had to look good enough to justify standing next to you," Murdoch said, only causing Sorcha's cheeks to flush ever more scarlet.

Their carriage was beginning to pull to a stop outside the location of the winter ball – a grand, stone-columned building that was lit up by lanterns atop ornate, iron poles. The lanterns reminded Sorcha of the Seelie revels she had attended in the past, though the flames in the faerie realm were all manner of colours rather than merely orange and yellow.

There were dozens of guests flooding into the hall when Murdoch and Sorcha finally stepped out of the carriage and onto the paved courtyard. He wrapped a royal blue, silken shawl around her shoulders before proffering his arm to her. She took it, smiling somewhat nervously up at him as they made their way into the building.

Murdoch noticed her discomfort. "What is wrong?" he asked, eyes widening when he spied the impressive, hulking evergreen trees that had been hauled in to line the walls all the way to the ballroom. A fiddle could be heard upon the air, as well as the sound of people's shoes dancing across the floor.

Sorcha's grip on his arm tightened. "I have not – this is the largest ball I have attended by far," she admitted. "There are so many people here. Are you sure it is a good idea to be here?"

"Oh, Sor – Miss Darrow," Murdoch said, only just remembering to correct himself now that they were in public, "I am sure we will have a grand time. And we have only to show our faces to Grey and MacKinnon to prove that we have made peace with them. Then we can leave, if that is what you truly wish. I simply do not want to risk the safety of our home over something so inconsequential as manners."

"I suppose not."

"And besides," he added, gently encouraging Sorcha inside the ballroom with a hand on her back, "we never got to dance at the faerie revel two years ago, did we? Now is our chance to make up for that."

"You were pretending to be Lachlan and had just murdered his stepfather and stepbrother," Sorcha pointed out, wrinkling her nose at the memory. "Something tells me I would not have been in the mood for dancing even if I *hadn't* run off in horror."

Murdoch snickered, pulling away from Sorcha in order to remove his hat and place it on a table. "Granted, that probably wasn't the best way to put you in the mood for courtship," he murmured, turning to face Sorcha as a ten-piece orchestra began playing a new song, "so let me make it up to you now."

He bowed deeply, though there was a mischievous smile upon Murdoch's face that was anything but polite. He held out a hand. "May I have this dance, Miss Darrow?"

"I guess I can oblige your request, Mr Buchanan," Sorcha replied, curtsying before accepting Murdoch's hand.

Whoever thought I'd be dancing at a ball in London with the kelpie of Loch Lomond? she thought as they began to move through the steps of the dance. Sorcha was hesitant at first, for she was not so familiar with them, but it became quickly apparent that Murdoch Buchanan's memories granted the kelpie an adeptness with dancing that eventually put Sorcha at ease.

"You are much better at this than you are at walking, you know," she teased, laughing softly when a scandalised look crossed Murdoch's face.

"Humans are so slow on their two legs," he complained. "You are such frail, clumsy creatures."

"And yet here you are, dancing as one of them."

"And dressed as one of them."

"And talking like one of them."

"Having fallen for one of them."

Sorcha's heart twisted in her chest. She had thought things would get easier for her after they gave in to their desire for one another. Instead, when Murdoch gazed at her with unabashed, honest fondness Sorcha found that she could hardly stand it.

He will live forever and I will not, she thought, working hard to stop herself from crying. *It is the same problem as with Lachlan. Nothing will change that. If I want to live as a human then I will be gone before the kelpie can even blink.*

Murdoch's hand tightened on Sorcha's, and he pulled her a little closer to him. His expression had grown very, very serious, which Sorcha did not like one bit. "Miss Darrow," he began, "there is something I need to -"

"I - think I need some air," Sorcha interrupted, breaking away from Murdoch before he could finish his sentence. "I will not be long, I promise. I just -"

She rushed off, not really knowing what else she could say as an excuse. *What could I have told him?* Sorcha despaired, exiting the ballroom and turning down a random corridor between two evergreen trees

428

without really looking where she was going. *That I care for him so deeply that I would do most anything for him? That I love him, but even that is not enough for me to be with him the way he wants me to? I saw the way he reacted to me declining Lachlan's offer of immortality. It shattered him.*

It was in that moment Sorcha realised just how much her refusal may well have shattered *Lachlan,* too. Since the faerie could not lie he had grown adept at concealing his emotions behind frivolity and pretty words, so much so that Sorcha had been able to pretend for the last two years that his desire to take Sorcha's mortality was still merely a whim. That his feelings for her would pass, and in no time at all he would forget about her.

In reality, Sorcha knew that had never been the case.

"I saw her go down there," a male voice Sorcha vaguely recognised muttered, causing her to hide behind a well-polished suit of armour to see who had spoken. A man with dark hair appeared at the entrance to the corridor, followed by an older man with equally dark hair.

That is Gregory MacKinnon and his son, Donald, Sorcha realised, inching further away from them as quietly as she was able.

The older man turned to the younger. "We will not get this opportunity again. Take her to the office whilst Buchanan is nowhere to be seen. Discreetly, Donald."

His son nodded before stalking down the corridor after Sorcha. She hardly dared to breathe as she flitted from shadow to shadow away from him, realising in the process that said shadows were twisting and warping and growing darker to help conceal her from the man. When Sorcha caught a glimmer in a mirror she realised what was happening.

The Unseelie, she thought, heart racing as Sorcha was forced to choose between which option posed a greater immediate risk to her. *If the Unseelie meant for me to die they would have killed me already, whereas I know these man cannot mean for anything good to happen to me,* she decided, glancing back over her shoulder at Donald MacKinnon as he continued purposefully towards her.

And then, just as Sorcha took another step down the corridor, a hand that had not been there before yanked her against the mirror, whilst another covered her mouth to stifle her cry of shock. Sorcha struggled for but a moment before growing rigid in sheer terror when she realised the hands were pulling her *through* the mirror, away from the hallway and the man who meant her harm.

"What is – let go of me!" Sorcha bit out the moment she had been completely pulled through the glassy surface, staring in shock as she watched Donald reach the very spot where she herself had only just been. It was like watching a moving painting; Sorcha reached out a hand to touch the mirror, only for it to be dragged away by the hand that had been on her mouth.

"I would not go back through there right now if I were you," a silky, familiar voice purred into her ear. "How about you attend a far more *exciting* party until you are no longer quite so hunted?"

Sorcha turned when the hands finally let her go. The silver-haired faerie who had inexorably been involved with her life from the moment she arrived in London stood there, no longer hiding under the glamour of a man.

His ears had grown long and pointed – longer than Lachlan's and the rest of the Seelie. His grey eyes had turned to liquid mercury, and his skin held a blue-silver tint Sorcha had only witnessed once before when she met Lachlan's stepbrother, Fergus.

He was dressed in midnight blue finery over a white, frothy shirt left unlaced to his navel; Sorcha's eyes trailed the deep V the material made of his skin before finding her way back to his face.

The faerie smiled a smile full of teeth filed to dangerously sharp points. "Won't you join our solstice revel, Miss Darrow, as the guest of the Unseelie king?"

Sorcha took a step back from him out of sheer disbelief. *Eirian. He is King Eirian.*

And though Sorcha wanted to say no – wished for nothing more than to crawl back through the mirror and scream for Murdoch to help her – as at the art exhibit when the faerie had asked her to walk around with him, Sorcha found she could do nothing but numbly accept the king's request.

CHAPTER TWENTY-SIX

Murdoch

Something is wrong.

Murdoch felt it in his very core, his mood flipping in an instant from deliriously happy to panic-stricken and painful.

Painful?

He clutched at his heart, bending double over his stomach. Murdoch's vision went hazy; he reached out a hand for the closest wall to stop himself from falling over.

"Sir?" a concerned gentleman said when he saw him. "Sir, are you quite all right?"

"Too much – too much brandy," Murdoch lied through gritted teeth. He could barely breathe. Barely talk. Barely stand.

Barely hold his shape.

Where is Sorcha?! Murdoch panicked, forcing himself back upright through sheer willpower alone. He stumbled around the ballroom, desperate to find her, but Sorcha was nowhere to be found. He exited down a long, gilded, empty corridor. "She can't have gone far," Murdoch panted, breaths coming shallow and ragged with every step he took. His lungs were closing in on him. "She can't have gone far, but somehow she is gone."

"How did you lose her, useless son of mine?" Murdoch heard a familiar voice mutter angrily from down a narrower, darker corridor to his left. Gregory MacKinnon stood there, fury contorting his features as he berated his son.

Don looked beyond perplexed. "Miss Darrow went down here alone, I swear it," he insisted. "It should have been simple to subdue her! But she...disappeared."

Disappeared? Disappeared where?

Then Murdoch noticed a large, silver-framed mirror hanging on the wall behind Don, and he realised with terrifying certainty what had happened to Sorcha.

No. Not the faerie realm. In travelling there – in being dragged there, Murdoch assumed – she had become separated from his bridle. But Sorcha was not *gone;* she was merely in a parallel, magically obscured world. Clearly the rules Lachlan had spelled onto Murdoch's bridle did not know how to deal with this, going by the pain he was in.

"You must *find her,*" Gregory fumed, eyes wide as he pointed down the corridor. "Before Buchanan –"

"Before I what?"

Both MacKinnons flinched. Slowly they turned to face Murdoch, who staggered towards them with barely-contained contempt. He was shaking all over, and he knew he was going to lose his human form at any given moment, but right now he did not care. These men had been looking for Sorcha and he needed to know *why*.

"Mister Buchanan," Gregory said, voice altogether too panicked to match the smile he quickly plastered onto his face. He wiped at his brow. "We merely wished to speak to Miss Darrow ourselves, to see if – to see if she might be convinced to sell her land to us after all. We had never posed the question to her directly before."

"I do not believe you," Murdoch spat, stalking forward another step or two. He resisted the urge to use the wall for support. "I heard you talk about *subduing* her. What were you planning to do to Miss Darrow?"

"N-nothing," Don stuttered, terrified. It was the terror on his face that told Murdoch he was already changing form, for the man was of a similar height and build to Mr Buchanan. If it came down to a fight the father and son in front of him may well have overpowered Murdoch.

If he were human.

"*What were you planning to do to Miss Darrow?*" Murdoch demanded once more, catching his gloved hands shimmering and shaking out of the corner of his eye. And then, between one moment and the next, Murdoch's line of sight grew much taller, and the corridor seemed altogether much smaller. Don swallowed back a cry; his father stumbled away from the monster that had appeared before him.

"What are you?" Gregory whispered, eyes so wide that Murdoch could see white all around his irises.

Murdoch's hooves scratched and screeched across

the floor as he dragged himself closer to the two men. *Something still isn't right,* he realised, for the lurching, twisting feeling in his stomach had not disappeared. But he could deal with that later; first he had to sort out Gregory and Donald MacKinnon.

When he bared his teeth and let out a low snarl the younger man slipped and fell to the floor, scrambling backwards until he reached his father. He fumbled through his pocket and brought out a bible, holding it out in front of him with a wildly trembling hand.

Murdoch merely laughed. "You think I am unholy? Your petty religion can do nothing to me. Where is Miss Darrow?"

"We do not know!" Gregory said, letting out a garbled cry when Murdoch reared onto his hind legs and crashed back down inches from his face. "I swear we don't!"

"I was following her but she disappeared!" Don chimed in, eyes never leaving Murdoch's mouthful of sickeningly sharp teeth. "All we were going to do was force her to sign over the Darrow land, I swear!"

"*Force her?*" Murdoch snarled. "You were going to force my bride to do something she expressly did not wish to do, and all behind my back? Was this the real reason you wanted us to attend the ball tonight even after what was said at your home?"

The silence from Gregory MacKinnon was deafening. Murdoch could not stand to look at him; he ground his hooves into the marble floor until it cracked beneath the man's feet. Gregory tried to back further away, but there was no more corridor left for him to do so.

He stared up at Murdoch's wild, inhuman face. "We did not know – how were we to know that you were not – not –"

"Human? It should not have mattered!" he screamed, incandescent with rage. "But now you will pay. One does not cross a kelpie and live to tell the tale."

"Please!" Don begged, kicking away from Murdoch as if he might somehow avoid him by escaping along the left side of the corridor; Murdoch swatted him against the wall as if he weighed nothing at all. A sickening crack filled the air as the man hit his head then slumped, motionless, to the floor.

Gregory stared at the slack body of his son with stark-white horror. Blood was beginning to pool beneath Don's head, filling Murdoch's nose with the intoxicating scent of death and destruction. His nostrils flared, and he bent low to pin Gregory MacKinnon beneath his hooves.

"D-do not kill me!" he begged. "We will leave your home well enough alone, I assure you! If you kill me then my colleagues will not know to abandon the project!"

"I should kill you *all.*"

"They did not know my son and I were planning to do this," Gregory insisted. "Please, Mr Buchanan –"

"*That is not who I am.*"

But even as Murdoch spoke he felt his form beginning to revert back to the man in question. He let out an involuntary cry, knocked Gregory unconscious, then shuffled backwards out of the corridor until he had enough space to turn himself around. His hooves

436

clacked against marble and tile and stone as he galloped through the hall, frantic to find an exit even as people screeched at the sight of him and desperately dodged out of the way.

By the time Murdoch reached the cold release of bitter winter air he had turned back into a man again, but not for long. For no sooner than he reached the line of carriages waiting to take party-goers home he transformed once more, so with a roar he turned in the direction of the nearest body of water and plunged straight into it.

Lachlan, Murdoch thought, almost blind with pain. *I must get to Lachlan. Only he can help me now.*

Murdoch had no idea how he was supposed to get all the way back to Loch Lomond when he kept changing form every five minutes, but he had to try. Sorcha's life depended on it. He only hoped he would not reach Lachlan too late to help her.

And so it was to Murdoch's great surprise and fortune when, barely out of London, he crashed straight into the Seelie king himself between jumps from one body of water to the next. The faerie's eyes widened in baffled disbelief as he watched Murdoch change from kelpie to man right in front of him, then back again and again and again, so uncontrollably fast that Murdoch could no longer see or breathe as he collapsed to the ground at Lachlan's feet.

If this kept on going for much longer Murdoch knew that he would die.

"Is that – what is going on with you?!" Lachlan demanded, though Murdoch could scarcely hear him. "Why do you keep changing? Where is Sorcha?" He crunched a foot against Murdoch's shoulder when he did not answer. "*Where is Sorcha?*" he asked again, fear colouring his tone this time instead of anger.

It took everything Murdoch had to find the strength to reply.

"Gone."

CHAPTER TWENTY-SEVEN

Lachlan

Lachlan had been slipping in and out of the faerie realm to travel to London as fast as possible, for given the infuriating riddle he'd been threatened with he knew he did not have much time to reach Sorcha.

So what was the kelpie of Loch Lomond doing out here, all alone, shape-shifting so quickly that it hurt Lachlan's eyes to watch him change form? He was supposed to be protecting Sorcha. But if she was nowhere to be seen, and Murdoch could not hold his shape, then –

"The Unseelie have taken her, haven't they?" Lachlan demanded, blood turning to ice as he slammed his foot against the kelpie's shoulder. He was a man now, but the bubbling of his skin told Lachlan that he would change again at any given moment. "How in the name of the bloody forest did you allow them to *take her*?!"

"Mirror," Murdoch gasped. The whites of his eyes

were red; dark, evil-looking blood was beginning to leak from them to stain his face. "A mirror. They took her through a..." But then the kelpie began to scream, and he reverted to his original form once more.

Lachlan couldn't stand the noise. He kicked at the beast, furious that he could not simply let Murdoch die. So many of his problems would be solved if he were gone, after all, but now he needed his help. Lachlan could not storm the Unseelie Court without back-up.

"Damn you to death, horse!" he screeched in response to the kelpie's cries, bending low to place his hands over the bridle that was currently the source of all the monster's pain. Forcing himself to concentrate through all his fear and panic and anger, Lachlan closed his eyes and slowly but surely unravelled the binding magic he had placed upon the item.

When he stood back up and opened his eyes the kelpie had returned to the form of Murdoch Buchanan once more, his bridle an innocuous silver chain hanging around his neck, barely visible over the high collar of his shirt. The man who was not a man retched and heaved upon the grass, tremors wracking through his body so violently that Lachlan thought Murdoch was in danger of breaking every bone in his body.

"Get yourself together," he spat. "We have no time to waste. How long has Sorcha been missing?"

Murdoch glared up at him, taking a deep, shuddering breath before forcing himself onto unsteady feet. Lachlan realised he was dressed up as if he had been at a formal dance, though he was drenched from head to toe.

"T-twenty minutes," Murdoch finally bit out. He wiped the back of a hand across his forehead, then smeared away the blood that had trickled down his cheeks. "Mister Buchanan's colleagues were attempting to corner her on her own, but she disappeared through a mirror."

"But why was she *alone*? I warned her not to be!"

Murdoch flinched at this, but then he scowled. "She was gone from my side for but five minutes, faerie. If that damn MacKinnon hadn't stalked her down a corridor then –"

"And that is your fault!" Lachlan countered. "I should never have allowed Sorcha to come down here with you. Every second since the two of you left I have regretted it."

"You could not have forbidden her from going. She would have gone anyway."

"Do you think I do not *know* that?" Lachlan stormed off for a few seconds, thinking that perhaps it was not worth saving the kelpie's life after all, but then he stopped. He pinched the bridge of his nose, a low growl forming in his throat that he struggled not to let loose. *I should have locked Sorcha up. I should have found out her full name and enchanted her to stay with me. She might have hated me but she would have been safe. And now the Unseelie have her.*

With a long, frustrated sigh, Lachlan muttered, "How does she do it?"

A pause. "Do what, exactly?"

"Get herself embroiled in inhuman schemes without having a single clue about them, of course!" Lachlan yelled, losing his temper once more. He looked at the kelpie over his shoulder, unabashedly baring his teeth in the process. "She knew nothing of the Unseelie and yet they followed her through the streets of London, taunting her."

"And snuck into my house through the mirrors to leave her a warning."

Lachlan stilled. He had not known about that. "... what did the warning say?" he asked, very, very quietly.

"*To the kelpie's bride,*" Murdoch recited, shaking himself of water in the process like a dog, "*we suggest you choose your company a little more wisely in the days to come.* I assumed they were warning her against interacting with me, since I murdered Innis and Fergus."

"As if I needed to be reminded of that," Lachlan growled. But then he considered the Unseelie threat without the cloud of resentment he held towards the kelpie hanging over him, and he frowned. "It may not be about you. It could be about me."

The troubled look on Murdoch's face confirmed Lachlan's suspicions. "Sorcha believed that might be the case, I think. She was concerned it was about us both."

They exchanged a wary, meaningful glance. They both knew what that meant: they could be walking right into a trap by going after Sorcha.

Knowing that changed nothing at all.

With an overwhelming sense of foreboding, Lachlan waved a hand in Murdoch's direction and watched as the man's clothes and hair and skin dried and tidied themselves in an instant.

"Why did you do that?" Murdoch demanded, closing the gap between them with a scandalised look on his face. "I do not need your –"

"You will stand out if you show up to the Unseelie

solstice revel looking like a drowned man," Lachlan cut in. He sidled a glance at the kelpie out of the corner of his eye. "Even though that is what you are."

"Charming."

"Have you stopped dying yet?"

"...almost."

"Then come," Lachlan said, walking towards a nearby grove of pine trees with both his hands held out in front of him. "We have a revel to interrupt, and a damsel to rescue."

"Do not let Sorcha hear you call her that."

Lachlan grinned a vicious grin. "No; I suppose you are right. But she is a damsel in need of rescue nonetheless, and we have a silver dragon going by the name of Eirian to slay."

CHAPTER TWENTY-EIGHT

Sorcha

There was absolutely no doubt that the revel King Eirian led Sorcha to was the work of the fae, though everything about the celebration seemed altogether darker and more sinister than those hosted by the Seelie Court.

It wasn't held outside, for a start. The massive, high-ceilinged hall Eirian pulled Sorcha into was opulent and glittering but it was clear that it was very, very old. Ancient, even. Chandeliers of burnished silver hung from the ceiling, and candlesticks of a similar metal sat atop long, gnarled tables overladen with food so colourful and exotic Sorcha thought for a moment that it could not possibly be real. Wax from the candles steadily melted down onto the tables as slow, molten rivers before solidifying into large clumps the colour of snow.

Thick, velvet curtains of deepest purple and midnight blue adorned the walls, draping down onto the floor where groups of fae lay upon the fabric and lost themselves in each other. In the corners of the hall were far more translucent, silvery curtains, gently billowing and floating all around as if caught upon the wind.

The light in the room seemed to flicker and change with every blink Sorcha took, imitating the glimmers she had noticed reflected at her back in the human world. There were dozens of mirrors around her now, too, haphazardly lining the walls in all shapes and sizes and manner of frames. Wooden. Gilded. New. Crumbling with age. Scorched and melted. Shining and perfect.

On a plinth in the centre of the room a string quartet was playing a haunting, almost familiar melody, but when Sorcha tried to place it she found that it was impossible.

A song from a dream, perhaps, she thought, moving through a crowd of intoxicated, masked creatures who eagerly parted for their king. Sorcha was barely aware of the fact she was following him, so entranced by the scene around her as she was.

That was when she began to notice individual revellers. A burly faerie in the corner with a river nymph on either of his arms, polishing his horns with what could have been wine but was probably blood. A cat-like, winged creature stalking across a trestle table to steal a plate of golden apples. A group of seven impossibly beautiful, blue-skinned faeries lying in a pit of pillows, limbs twisted and entwined together as their faces contorted in pleasure.

Sorcha's cheeks grew red, and she looked away, but then all the blood quickly drained from her face when she focused her gaze on the musicians. They were human, which was not so uncommon at a faerie revel, and they were enchanted, which was even less of a rarity, but it was the condition of them that made Sorcha's stomach turn.

Their fingers were raw and bloody, some of them worked down to the bone, and yet still they continued to play their instruments with mad smiles on their faces and not an ounce of pain in their eyes.

Sorcha caught sight of more humans in the crowd after that; she wished she hadn't. Most all of them were suffering in one way or another, though they were blissfully unaware of their agony. Two mortal men were fighting to the death, one of them bleeding heavily from an ugly gash in his leg even as he tore into his opponent's arm with his teeth. A group of Unseelie surrounded them, cheering and drinking and gambling on who would win.

And there was a small child in a corner crying for his mother, who had been forced to drink faerie wine and was now pleasuring a twisted creature twice her size.

When Sorcha witnessed a girl younger than herself being eaten alive, laughing delightedly even as a faerie with the scales of a snake gorged on her innards, she froze to the spot out of fear she would collapse and never get back up.

Eirian turned to face her when he realised Sorcha had ceased walking. His eyes followed her line of sight, a sigh passing his lips when he realised what had caused such an ashen expression to spread across her face. "We are the Unseelie, lass," he said, taking Sorcha's hand in his own and pulling her towards a table laden with glasses of strange-coloured liquids. "I would have assumed that, given your familiarity with our brethren, you would be aware of our natures."

Sorcha stared at him in horror, then gulped down

her fear and tried her best to put herself back together. She had walked into the proverbial lion's den, except the lion had been replaced with creatures far more dark and dangerous. If she was not careful then she would become their prey before the moon truly rose into the sky that night.

"I am afraid I do not have the *stomach* for such entertainment," she told Eirian, "though I imagine you knew that already."

The grin he gave her was predatory. "I did surmise as much," he said, "though I will eagerly admit to taking much pleasure out of watching you react to said entertainments. Have a drink, Miss Darrow. Our blackberry wine rivals anything the Seelie Court makes."

But Sorcha knew better than to accept the glass of black wine Eirian offered her. Lachlan and Ailith ensured that she never consumed anything made of faerie flora and fauna, for if she did then not only would Sorcha have fallen into a giddy, prone-to-hallucinations state for hours on end, but she would no longer have been able to leave the faerie realm of her own free will.

"Thank you for the offer, King Eirian," Sorcha said, pushing away the glass, "but I must refuse."

"You are clever."

"I am experienced more than I am clever," she replied, glancing around the revel as she did so. The bloody-fingered musicians kept drawing her eye again and again. "You did not think to entrap me here like the other poor mortals attending your festivities, did you?"

"If I did not try then I could not call myself a faerie," Eirian laughed. He swept Sorcha away from the table and towards a group of dancing faeries. Their energy was frenetic, as if they might never stop dancing even if it killed them. Sorcha knew that, for humans, it often did. "But I do have more important motives for inviting you here than to trick you."

Sorcha frowned. "I do not believe that."

"Yet I cannot lie," he countered. His eyes slid across Sorcha's dress in a way that made her wildly uncomfortable, but when she tried to look away Eirian grabbed her chin with a long-fingered hand and held it in place. "You are a bonnie girl, as your folk would say," he began, calculating eyes locked on hers, "but I believe you can be more beautiful still. That dress of yours is too...human. Allow me to rectify that."

"I do not –" Sorcha bit out, but her words caught in her throat as she was enveloped in a wave of magic. The sleeves of her gown disappeared, and the material became diaphanous, trailing behind her in soft waves of silvery, iridescent fabric. The neckline grew lower, too, almost as low as the Unseelie king's shirt, revealing far more of the curves of her breasts than Sorcha was used to.

Sorcha reached a hand up to her hair as it came almost entirely undone, tumbling around her shoulders and down her back in wild, sensuous curls. Her ears felt heavy, and when Sorcha caught her reflection in a mirror she saw that many silver crescent moons now hung from them on impossibly delicate chains. A similarly-designed circlet kept her hair away from her face, and lashings of silver lined her eyes.

All around Sorcha faeries paused from their activities to stare at her with ravenous, unbridled desire. *If I can feel their king's magic working upon me then it must be overpowering to them,* she thought, looking back at

Eirian to see a smug expression upon his face.

"Much better," he murmured. Without turning from her, he waved a hand towards the musicians and the melody changed to something Sorcha most definitely recognised.

I sang this through the streets of London when I was being stalked.

"Won't you sing for me?" Eirian asked, voice like honey as he pulled Sorcha further into the crowd of dancers. She swatted away their greedy hands as they pawed at her and begged her to say yes.

"I will not," Sorcha replied, fighting hard to keep her voice firm and steady. After Lachlan's warning not to give the Unseelie anything she was determined to refuse any and all of their requests, no matter how innocuous they seemed to be.

Eirian looked as if his heart had been broken. "Then won't you dance?" he asked instead, holding out a hand for Sorcha to take.

"If I dance I will not be able to stop," she said, just barely moving out of the way as a faerie covered in wicked-looking spines twirled past her.

But the Unseelie king took her hand regardless. "If I promise you that you can stop at any time, will you agree to dance?"

"I –"

Sorcha frowned. If she was allowed to stop when she wished to then in theory dancing would do no harm to her at all. And it would give her time to work out what to do next, and serve as a distraction from the horrors all around her.

449

Do not do it, the sensible part of her brain screamed, but Sorcha nodded her head at Eirian regardless.

"Then I shall dance," Sorcha said, and so she did.

CHAPTER TWENTY-NINE

Murdoch

Just a flicker. Just a glimpse. That was all Murdoch needed to make out Sorcha through the throng of Unseelie revellers, so why could he not find her?

"Fox, we should split up until one of us finds her," he told Lachlan, who winced at the insult but nodded regardless.

"If you find her first I shall cause a commotion to allow you to get her out of here," Lachlan said, a determined glint in his golden eyes as he scanned the crowd. "I expect you to do the same."

"Of course. May the best man find her first."

Under ordinary circumstances both of them may have laughed bitterly at the ironic comment, but there was absolutely nothing ordinary about a kelpie and a faerie king searching for a mortal at an Unseelie revel.

Lachlan stalked away without another word, leaving Murdoch to prowl around the very edges of the hall to take in his surroundings, ignoring the glazed-over eyes of the unfortunate mortals who had found themselves part of the menu for tonight's revel.

He had been to one other such celebration four hundred years earlier, though entirely by accident. A witch who had done him wrong fled to the Unseelie realm, attempting to hide herself in the throng of hedonistic faeries as they danced the solstice away. What she had not anticipated was just how hungry for violence the Unseelie were, and how eagerly they gave her up in order to witness Murdoch tear her apart limb from limb.

That was the first time Murdoch had willingly done something that a faerie wanted him to do, because it aligned with his own interests.

Working with Lachlan to save Sorcha was the second.

Murdoch spent almost twenty minutes skirting the edges of the revel, growing ever more frustrated that he could not spot Sorcha. Faerie folk were beginning to take notice of him, the lower kinds grinning at him as if they believed him to be mortal prey whilst the more magically-inclined onces inched back when he grew near, intimidated by the sheer power the kelpie possessed.

Good, Murdoch thought as he finally carved a path through the crowd. *Leave me be. Let me find her. Let me see –*

He froze.

For there was Sorcha, dressed all in glittering, flowing silver like an ethereal winter queen. Murdoch's heart throbbed painfully in his chest at the mere sight of her. He was beyond relieved when he noticed her eyes were not glazed over, nor was there a vague smile upon her face. *She is not enchanted,* he sighed. *That is one point in our favour.*

But Sorcha had not noticed Murdoch's presence, too absorbed in the attentions of the silver-haired faerie who was leading her through a dance. He seemed eerily familiar to Murdoch, though he did not know why. And then it hit him: the faerie was the one responsible for cornering Sorcha at the art exhibit. He had been cloaked in a glamour before, but Murdoch could see it clearly now that he was looking at the Unseelie in question.

But that...that can't be right, Murdoch thought, growing increasingly frantic as he pushed through the crowd to reach Sorcha. But the creatures all around him pushed back, keeping Murdoch constantly out of reach and sight of her. *That can't be the faerie who was after her.*

If Murdoch hadn't known any better, he could have sworn the one Sorcha was dancing with was the Unseelie king himself.

Lachlan

"The Seelie king! The Seelie king is here!" a shimmering, naked faerie announced excitedly upon spotting Lachlan – a member of his own race, ventured down to the Unseelie realm alongside a group of other like-minded fae for a night of riotous, violent fun.

He forced a smile on his face. "Of course I am here," Lachlan said. "How would it look if I did not show up to celebrate with my brethren?"

Lachlan did not wait for an answer, instead winding his way through the revel as quickly as he could. But he was stopped at almost every opportunity, claws and nails and fingertips alike dragging at his sleeves to pull him into some game or dance or gamble. When someone forced a goblet of amber whisky into his hand Lachlan poured it down his throat simply to appease them, though under any other circumstance he would have savoured every last drop of the stuff.

"Where are you, Clara?" he muttered, reverting to her false name in case anybody was listening. The last thing he needed was for hundreds of sharp-toothed, bloodthirsty Unseelie to learn even one third of her true name. "Just where are you?"

And then as if on command he saw her, more enchantingly beautiful than Lachlan had ever seen her before. *More beautiful than Ailith, even,* he thought, stopping in his tracks to stare unabashedly at the mortal woman who had stolen his heart. The cut of Sorcha's dress was so daring that one wrong move would have revealed every inch of her skin, but the translucent material somehow stayed perfectly in place as she danced.

Danced.

Lachlan bit back a scream.

Sorcha was dancing with King Eirian.

"Clara!" he called, but then Lachlan was swept away by the crowd, and she disappeared from his sight.

Sorcha

Was that...Murdoch? And – Lachlan? Sorcha thought. *But it couldn't be. Murdoch is back at the winter ball, and that golden faerie does not possess Lachlan's long hair.*

"Something the matter?"

She frowned at King Eirian, who pulled her a little closer in response. "I think I – may have seen someone I know," she said, "but I must have been wrong." *Although Lachlan could well be here. He is the Seelie king; perhaps I am not imagining him.*

Eirian twirled Sorcha under his arm, laughing all the while. "They got here faster than I expected."

"You were...I was not imagining the kelpie and Lachlan?"

"I would not think so given that you are here, Miss Darrow," the faerie said, keeping his tone conversational even as his silver eyes grew sharper and his grin more vicious.

Sorcha began searching desperately for another glimpse of golden skin or Murdoch's dark, curly hair as Eirian spun her around and around in time with the dancers. She was growing dizzy, and her feet were beginning to hurt. "I think I would like to stop and find them," she told him, the words coming out a little breathless.

But Eirian merely laughed again. "Do you know how much effort was put into ensuring that you and your dear kelpie came down to London, Miss Darrow?" he asked, sliding a hand down to the small of Sorcha's back to prevent her from pulling away. He cocked his head to the side, watching her face as a hawk might watch a rabbit. "So much magic was put into manipulating those men who worked with Mr Buchanan into pushing on with procuring the Darrow land, and even more into watching your every move."

A shiver ran up Sorcha's spine from where Eirian's fingertips touched it. "You have been...you planned everything from the very start?"

"Why of course," he said simply. "I could not risk my crown on mere *chance,* could I? Not after what happened last time."

"Last time?" Sorcha parroted back, but then she shook her head in an attempt to clear it. "I wish to stop dancing. You said I could stop dancing whenever I wanted to."

But King Eirian bent his head and chuckled softly against her ear. "I said you could stop, Miss Darrow, but not that anybody else would *let* you. Have fun at the revel."

"I - no, I don't want this!" Sorcha cried, as he handed her off to the faerie with blood-soaked horns she had spotted earlier. The Unseelie king merely threw back his head and laughed, accepting the hand of another partner as Sorcha was spun further and further away from him. She pushed against the burly creature who was now forcing her to dance, but his arms were thick with muscle and refused to let her go.

"You are his now, girlie," the faerie grinned, displaying a mouth full of vicious teeth even redder than his horns. "There is no point in struggling."

And yet struggle was what Sorcha tried and tried and tried to do, fighting against every new faerie she was thrown into the arms of. Her muscles ached, and her feet felt raw and slashed to ribbons, but still Sorcha was forced to dance despite her protests. All around her the Unseelie were laughing at her, but none so loudly as their king.

His voice was in her head, taunting her. Threatening her.

"Let. Her. Go."

This new voice was cold and demanding and familiar, cutting through the noise of the revel like a knife made of ice. All at once the laughter around Sorcha came to stop. Something was awry; there was a darkness upon the air that not a single creature seemed to like. Slowly – very slowly – individual faeries began to stop dancing and fighting and kissing each other. Sorcha recognised the looks upon their faces. They were dying.

Drowning.

The kelpie, Sorcha thought, more relieved than she thought she'd ever be at the sight of burgeoning mass murder. She pulled away from the arms of the faerie who had been dancing with her, for they had stopped in horror, but then Eirian reappeared in front of Sorcha and dragged her into his embrace.

"He cannot help you," the Unseelie king said, a delighted, wicked smile upon his face as he continued the dance. "Nobody can. So won't you sing for me, Miss Darrow?"

A feeling of dread spread through her as Sorcha realised she was getting closer and closer to saying *yes.*

CHAPTER THIRTY

Murdoch

With every faerie laid to waste upon the ground Murdoch's soul filled with dark, vicious, unrelenting pleasure. Back when he had attacked the Seelie Court he'd drowned everyone using the burn that ran around the revel grounds, but here the kelpie had no such external sources of water to utilise.

But he was livid. Murderous. More focused than he had ever been in his entire life.

And so it was that filling the lungs of the Unseelie with their own blood was barely a challenge for Murdoch, though his range was limited to perhaps ten or so creatures at a time. He stalked through the crowd, targeting the monsters who were torturing children and raping mortal women first, and when he caught Lachlan's eye the golden faerie did not stop him.

Rather, the Seelie king acted like a mortal himself and began punching faeries in the face, not stopping until they were bloody and unconscious.

If he uses his magic against them then it could be considered an act of war, Murdoch realised. *Until he knows Eirian's intentions for sure he cannot use his full powers.*

"Useless fox!" Murdoch roared, bodily picking up a naked, blue-skinned Unseelie and flinging her out of his path. He could see Sorcha once more in the arms of King Eirian, her face wet with tears as she cried and begged to be let go.

Her misery only fuelled Murdoch's power.

"Get me to Eirian and you will see how useless I am!" Lachlan growled at Murdoch when they found themselves fighting beside each other. "Just keep slaughtering his people. You're good at that."

"I never expected a compliment from you."

"And I never thought you'd willingly fight alongside me, but there's a first time for everything."

All around them more and more revellers were stopping what they were doing, climbing over each other in their haste to get as far away from Murdoch as possible. But the dancers were still dancing and the musicians were still playing, for King Eirian was spinning Sorcha around and around and they were all eager to please him.

When the two of them passed a table Eirian picked up a glass of vibrant, luminous green liquid and held it up to Sorcha's lips. "Drink from this and all your pain will go away," Murdoch heard the king tell her, his voice so soft and seductive that Murdoch knew Sorcha would only be able to resist his charms for so long.

"Kelpie, her feet," Lachlan growled, kicking a goat-eyed faerie to the ground when it tried to attack

Murdoch. So he turned his gaze to Sorcha's feet, and his eyes grew glassy.

Gone were her slippers, leaving Sorcha's feet bare to everything on the floor. They were torn to shreds; bloody, bruised and blackened, leaving a trail of crimson wherever she danced. She could barely stand, but still Eirian was making her dance. Sorcha's face was contorted in pain, trying in vain to avoid the goblet of faerie wine the Unseelie king held to her lips as he urged her to drink.

She was going to take it. Murdoch knew she was going to take it.

He dropped his human form and charged forward, crushing every unfortunate creature that found its way in front of him beneath his hooves. Murdoch screamed, slashing through bone and sinew with his razor-sharp teeth whenever he grabbed hold of a faerie.

"Let her go!" he demanded, in a voice so loud the silvered chandeliers above his head trembled and the clamour all around him seemed like nothing but whispers.

"Kindly stop murdering my people and I shall consider it," King Eirian said, infuriatingly calm, when Murdoch was but seconds away from him. He tried to move closer to the faerie – to steal Sorcha right out of his grasp – but something kept pushing Murdoch's entire body away whenever he got within ten feet of the king.

"Do it," Lachlan told Murdoch, taking a step through whatever barrier was stopping Murdoch from moving forward as if there was nothing there at all. The faerie gave him a side-long glance. "We may still need your strength, so preserve it. But for now it's my turn, horse."

Murdoch was loathe to listen to him. He wanted to continue thrashing his way through the revel, destroying everything and everyone he came across until Sorcha was his again, but with a deep, trembling breath the kelpie struggled back to his human form.

Sorcha's eyes darted from Murdoch's face to Lachlan's and then back once more to Murdoch's. "I am s-sorry," she sobbed, barely audible over the noise all around her but cutting straight through to Murdoch nonetheless. "I'm sorry I –"

"You do not need to apologise to *them,* Miss Darrow," Eirian crooned, stroking a finger down her face even as he kept the faerie wine dangerously close to her mouth. "It is their fault that you are in this position in the first place."

Murdoch scowled at the comment, though its truthfulness was like an arrow to his heart. "You said you would let her go if I stopped!" he cried.

"No, he said he would consider it," Lachlan said, throwing a warning glare at Murdoch when he tried to move forward and met Eirian's invisible barrier once more.

The Unseelie king chuckled softly. "That is correct, my dear Lachlan," he murmured, "but I would rather not have the kelpie begin another rampage." Murdoch dared not breathe when Eirian shifted the goblet in front of Sorcha's face, but then he pulled it away from her and poured the venomously green wine onto the floor, soaking the stone beneath his feet a dark and dangerous colour.

"Give her back," Murdoch demanded between ragged breaths. "The fox and I are here, which was clearly your intention, so let the mortal go."

"Oh, I think not."

Lachlan exchanged an uncertain glance with Murdoch. There was a frown creasing his brow, telling the kelpie that he was currently thinking very hard of how to get Sorcha out of her captivity without accidentally agreeing to anything King Eirian said.

But Murdoch did not care about being cautious. If it meant saving Sorcha, he would agree to anything.

"What is that you want, then?" he asked, moving out of the way when Lachlan made to punch his face in frustration. "To let Miss Darrow go, what is it that you want?"

The grin that spread across Eirian's face was far more wicked than any Lachlan or Murdoch himself could ever have been capable of.

"Why, I want your lives, of course."

CHAPTER THIRTY-ONE

Sorcha

"No!" Sorcha cried out, the moment the Unseelie king voiced his demand. She pulled on his sleeve, emboldened by her fear. "You cannot kill them! What have they done to deserve that?"

When Eirian snaked an arm around her waist and kissed her forehead Sorcha recoiled, and Lachlan yowled in outrage. "Why, the two of them together murdered my beloved brother, Innis, and my dear little nephew, Fergus," he explained, as if it was obvious. "It is only natural that I have the heads of those that slew them with cold, black iron."

Sorcha froze. She stared at the tense, furious figures of Lachlan and Murdoch as they realised they were fully caught in Eirian's trap. Lachlan took a step forward, for whatever magic the Unseelie king had cast around himself and Sorcha clearly had no effect on him. Murdoch seemed to grow even angrier that he could not break through.

"The kelpie murdered your family," Lachlan said, choosing his words very, very carefully. "You can kill him for his crimes if you have the power to do so."

"Lachlan, you cannot mean –"

"Do not interfere, Clara!" the golden faerie warned. "He is guilty and he knows it – *you* know it!"

"It is all right, Miss Darrow," Murdoch reassured, giving Sorcha a small, reassuring smile before turning his gaze to Eirian. "The one who murdered your Unseelie kin was indeed me, as the fox said."

"And yet you let it happen," King Eirian pointed out, waving lazily at Lachlan as he spoke.

Lachlan bristled. "They had cursed me, as well you know!"

"A matter to be resolved between our two families, *not* at the hands of a kelpie."

"I was hardly in a position to stop him," Lachlan insisted. "Nobody could stop him."

"Nobody?"

Sorcha felt Eirian's hand twitch against her waist, and she realised Lachlan had slipped up. *He just told the Unseelie king that nobody in his Court was strong enough to destroy the kelpie. Now Eirian knows the full extent – or limit – of their power.*

Going by the grin on Eirian's face, he was delighted by this piece of information.

Lachlan looked just about ready to hang himself. It was not like him to slip up in such a manner, which meant he must have been truly rattled. *It is my fault,* Sorcha thought, wincing as she shifted slightly on her bleeding feet. *I was lured here to be used as a bargaining chip, and it is working.*

"You underestimate how strong I am, Unseelie," Murdoch thundered, drawing all of their attention back to him. Several nearby faeries stumbled away, hands scrabbling at their throats as they retched and choked on seemingly nothing at all. When the feeling finally abated they fled the revel, followed by a multitude of other creatures who had not yet left out of sheer interest for the confrontation that had interrupted their celebrations.

Eirian cocked his head to one side. "Perhaps. You are indeed formidable; there is no significant body of water in sight and yet you can kill with ease. It is impressive how strong you are."

Sorcha did not know if that meant the Unseelie king was also too weak to destroy Murdoch, or if he could handle the kelpie with ease despite the creature's strength.

She did not wish to find out.

Behind them the poor, doomed, mortal musicians began to play an unsettling melody that caused Sorcha's heart to beat erratically. She wanted to bolt from Eirian's side – was desperate to – but a subtle slide of his hand against her hip warned Sorcha that she would not get very far if she tried, especially on her injured feet.

"I will not let you kill me for something I did not do and could not prevent," Lachlan said after a tense moment of silence. "And I have not used my powers as the Seelie king against your kind. You have no recourse to demand anything from me."

Eirian shrugged emphatically. "And yet here I am, demanding your life nonetheless. But I am not a heartless king," he said, a hideous smile upon his face,

465

"and I am open to bargains of equal value."

Lachlan and Murdoch stared at each other, then in unison looked at Sorcha just as Eirian turned her head to look at *him.*

"This mortal is dear to you," he sneered. "So dear, in fact, that you have risked everything to come here and save her. For the sake of the Seelie, Lachlan, you should not have come to her aid. And you, kelpie," he glanced at Murdoch before returning his mercurial eyes to Sorcha's, "if you did not wish to be controlled or destroyed you should have abandoned her, too. But you did not. I admit that I am curious as to why..."

When Eirian raised a finger to Sorcha's lips she bit it, gnashing her teeth into his flesh in her desperation to break through to the bone. But she barely left a scratch, and when Eirian pulled his hand away he laughed as if Sorcha had just done something incredibly amusing.

"Do not touch her," both Lachlan and Murdoch hissed in unison.

"I think that is up to Miss Darrow," the Unseelie king said. Sorcha's blood ran cold.

"What is that supposed to mean?" she whispered, though she was beginning to understand full well what Eirian was insinuating.

His smile was so radiant that Sorcha momentarily forgot that she was dealing with a snake. "I believe you have already worked that out. If your life is so important to them, Miss Darrow, then I shall have it. A fitting punishment for the creatures who care for you so much."

Lachlan charged forward, but when his foe raised a hand some invisible force stopped him just shy of being able to touch Sorcha. "Clara, don't you dare agree to this!" he snarled. "Don't you dare –"

"I believe it is up to your lovely human paramour to decide what it is that she wants to do," Eirian said. "So what will it be, Miss Darrow: your life, or theirs?"

Sorcha took several seconds to reply, though in truth she needed no time at all to make her decision. Forcing herself to look past Lachlan, she locked eyes with Murdoch and opened her mouth to speak; he dropped to his knees before she uttered a single word.

"*No*," he mouthed. "Do not do –"

"I love you," she told him. "I love you. I love you. I've loved you all my life, even when I did not know who or what you were. Of course I will save you."

Murdoch did nothing but stare at her. Sorcha had just admitted her love for him in front of everyone, and he was staring at her the way he'd done on the plinth in the Seelie Court. There was no doubt about it: he had always loved her, too, as strongly and as deeply and as desperately as was possible for him to love another living being.

And so did Lachlan. Sorcha could see it now, though she had ignored the extent of his feelings and pretended that they were not truly serious for two years. He loved her, and she loved him.

It was simply a different kind of love than the all-consuming feelings she held for the kelpie.

"You know how I feel about you," she said to Lachlan, whose golden eyes were full of furious tears.

Since Sorcha could not fathom being able to live forever, giving up her life for Murdoch and for Lachlan seemed like the biggest gesture of her love for them that she could make. The biggest sacrifice a human was capable of.

She knew before either of them spoke that they would not let her do it.

CHAPTER THIRTY-TWO

Lachlan

Lachlan could only stare at Sorcha in disbelief. Not only had she admitted to loving the kelpie – a fear that had eaten away at Lachlan's brain for the past two years – but she was willing to give up her life for the monster.

And for him.

I will not stand for it, he glowered. *I will not. She cannot do it.*

"You will not give yourself up for me!" Murdoch called out, voicing his protests before Lachlan could even open his mouth. He turned his gaze to Eirian. "I will die, and gladly. Give me the most horrific death you can imagine, only let Miss Darrow go."

But the faerie merely laughed. "She has already voiced her consent. What can you do, kelpie? It turns out this mortal wields more power to control the two of you than I ever could. Except that her power is now *mine.*"

"You...you have no intention of killing her," Lachlan

469

stuttered, horrified as he realised what was actually going on. "You will use her to keep us in check, not as a means to punish us!"

"Why of course. I would never pass up an opportunity for more control, my poor fox king."

"Half."

Everyone stared at Sorcha, various expressions of confusion, anguish and interest upon their faces. She wiped the tears from her face, straightened her posture, then turned to face Eirian properly. Her eyes were dark and angry.

In all her silver splendour, she looked like an Unseelie queen.

"Half," she repeated. "If you will not kill me, then you can have just half my life. Lachlan had no hand in your kin's deaths and had no way to prevent them, as you have already heard. You have no grounds upon which to punish him."

Lachlan expected Eirian's features to contort in anger at being spoken to in such a way, or to strike Sorcha where she stood for being so bold as to make demands of the Unseelie king. Instead the grin on his face grew larger as he brought a thumb up to his teeth. He sliced it open on the edge of a sharp canine, then smeared the resultant well of blood across Sorcha's forehead.

"No, no, no," Lachlan mumbled, watching in horror as Sorcha's deal with the dark faerie was sealed. *She does not know what she has done. This is bad. This is impossible.*

This cannot be happening.

Behind him Murdoch remained on his knees, too

470

numb to speak. Lachlan hated him for his hand in Eirian's grand entrapment, but there was a small part of him that felt sorry for him.

The kelpie had never wished harm upon Sorcha. His love for her was genuine, and Lachlan could see his heart breaking in two. He could not resent the creature for his feelings – not when they were purer than Lachlan's had been when he'd first met Sorcha Darrow and intended to enchant her to be his forever.

Eirian finally let go of Sorcha, then, and she stumbled on bloodied, broken feet until Lachlan leapt forward to catch her. She was as numb as Murdoch was, face pale and blank but for the streak of blood upon her forehead that sealed her fate forever.

"You would do well to leave my realm now," Eirian said, still grinning his vicious grin. "Miss Darrow, you will hear from me in due time. I do hope you give me that song some day."

And with that the faerie disappeared, leaving Lachlan, Sorcha and Murdoch in the middle of a site of absolute carnage. Sorcha trembled in Lachlan's arms, but then he realised that he himself was shaking her.

"You fool," he muttered. And then, louder, "you absolute *fool*. Do you know what you have done?"

"I have saved both of your lives," Sorcha replied, voice muffled against Lachlan's chest. He pulled away from her enough that he could see her face; Sorcha avoided his eyes. "I would never have let him kill you."

"But now he has imprisoned you and can control us!" he shouted, stunned and infuriated by Sorcha's lack of understanding of the gravity of her situation. "That is worse than the kelpie and me dying –"

471

"Do not dare say that!" Sorcha fired back, a spark of life returned to her lovely, mismatched eyes once more. She glanced at Murdoch, who staggered to his feet, then back at Lachlan. "You may have such little disregard for your own lives, but you are more important that I am. You have the Seelie to rule over, Lachlan. And Murdoch...who else can I rely on to keep Loch Lomond and the Darrow land safe? King Eirian can have half my life – I give it to him gladly – if it means our home is left untouched. If it means the ones I love are free from his grasp."

"Sorcha –"

"And besides," she said, forcing a smile onto her face, "it is only thirty years at most. Thirty years is nothing."

"But those thirty years could be from now until your fifty-first birthday, or spread over every night from now until your death, or any iteration in-between!"

"And I give it *gladly*," Sorcha repeated. "Let me save the two of you for –"

But Sorcha's words were cut off as Murdoch wrenched her from Lachlan's arms, crushing her against him as if he never intended to let her go.

Lachlan did not stop him.

He knew exactly how the kelpie felt.

CHAPTER THIRTY-THREE

Murdoch

Despite the fact they were not alone, and that Lachlan himself was one of their onlookers, Murdoch could not tear himself away from Sorcha. He smothered her against his chest, wishing nobody else was around to lay their eyes or hands upon her.

"Just what have you done, you foolish girl?" he murmured into her hair; his voice cracked before he reached the end of his question.

Sorcha squirmed against him, struggling out of Murdoch's embrace just far enough that she could gaze up at him. It was plain to see that she was terrified by what she'd promised the Unseelie king, but there was something else in her eyes, too.

Determination. Conviction. Murdoch hated how familiar they were to see upon Sorcha Darrow's face.

"I would never have you nor Lachlan die for me," she said, resolute. She glanced at the faerie as he watched the pair of them in silence. A small smile curled her lips. "I've never been one to be saved by others."

"Sorcha –"

She held a finger up to Murdoch's lips. "No. Do not argue with me on this. What's done is done, as well you know."

When Murdoch turned to Lachlan it was clear the Seelie king was already thinking hard and fast about how to undo everything Sorcha had promised Eirian. *I guess we'll have to fight on the same side again...for a while,* he realised, not relishing the idea for even a moment.

When Sorcha kissed him softly Murdoch diverted his attention back to her. "I am all right with this, I swear," she said. "If I was given the choice again I would make the same decision in a heartbeat." She broke away from Murdoch's arms and held out a hand for Lachlan, who immediately took it. Going by the wince on Sorcha's face he was all but crushing her fingers, though she did not comment on the pain. "You both cannot be so eager to save me and not expect me to feel the same way in return."

Murdoch said nothing. Lachlan said nothing. Sorcha was right, and they both knew it. And yet still it hurt, for Sorcha was human and they were not. They had powers she could only dream of. They *should* have been the ones to protect her, not the other way around.

And yet we weren't. We couldn't. And if being a kelpie is not enough to keep Sorcha out of harm's way, then...

"Lachlan."

The faerie frowned at him. "What is it?"

"Can you take us back to the Seelie Court?" Murdoch asked, though he was thoroughly uncomfortable even thinking about being there again. But anything was better than the realm they were currently dwelling in. *Anything.*

With some reluctance Lachlan waved Murdoch over to his side and placed his hand on the kelpie's shoulder. His other hand was still wrapped around Sorcha's; she huddled in closer to the two of them on instinct.

"I suppose this will be much drier than leaping from loch to loch," she murmured wryly. If it wasn't for the situation they were currently in Murdoch might have laughed at her joke. Considering Sorcha's torn and bloodied feet, tear-stained face and unsettlingly beautiful, Unseelie ball gown, laughing was the last thing on Murdoch's mind.

Lachlan wiped the mark of the Unseelie king from Sorcha's brow and kissed the skin there, though no amount of washing away the dark blood would remove its curse. "You'll feel a touch light-headed, but that's it. Hold on tight."

And then, between one blink and the next, the three of them disappeared from the Unseelie realm and the haunting, plaintive music of the solstice revel to land right in Lachlan's bedroom.

Sorcha gasped and staggered; clearly the faerie's magic had affected her far more than it had Murdoch. He swept her away from Lachlan to sit down upon the golden, gauzy-curtained bed. The mere sight of it brought memories flooding back of when he had lain upon the mattress and Sorcha had sung him to sleep. Considering what she did to him the following day the memory was bittersweet; Murdoch was coming to accept that his entire relationship with the human woman he loved was going to follow a similar feeling.

Murdoch froze.

I love her. I haven't told her even once that I love her.

He knelt in front of Sorcha, tilting her chin until their eyes were level. "Sorcha," he began, "I –"

"Miss Sorcha?"

Suppressing a scowl, Murdoch turned to see the blonde-haired faerie, Ailith, standing in the doorway. She held a hand to her heart, eyes wide with surprise at the sight of all three of them. But then she smiled in relief. "I was so worried, Miss Sorcha," she said, closing the gap between them to rest a hand upon Sorcha's head. "Around ten minutes ago a group of Seelie arrived at my door and told me about what was going on – I was just about to leave for the revel myself! Oh, Miss Sorcha, you are in pain. Let me see to it."

Clearly she has no qualms about ordering me around, Murdoch thought when Ailith pushed him out of the way to tend to Sorcha's injured feet. He stood up, backing away until he was by Lachlan's side. The faerie glared at him.

"I still can't believe you let her be taken by the *Unseelie king,* you overgrown –"

"Lachlan, hush!" Ailith called out over her shoulder. "You and I both know fine well you intended to take Miss Sorcha along with you to the solstice revel. I am afraid King Eirian was destined to come into contact with her, no matter what either of you did."

"Ailith, he took *half her life,*" Lachlan muttered, outraged once more. "To save *his* skin –"

"And yours, as I recall," Murdoch countered, feeling very much like he wished to punch Lachlan in the face.

476

"And it's all the fault of your kind, anyway. If Sorcha had never –"

"Will you please stop *arguing*?!" both Ailith and Sorcha exclaimed in unison.

"What's done is done," Ailith said, though her sapphire eyes were endlessly sad.

Lachlan shook his head in frustration. "Why are you on her side? She is mortal. She is –"

"Very brave, and responsible for her own actions," Ailith cut in. "I thought you would have learned that by now, Lachlan. You should be more grateful to her for saving your life."

Ailith's words starkly reminded Murdoch of why he had asked Lachlan to take them all back to the Seelie Court to begin with, though now he was faced with what he had to say next he found his tongue had grown thick and dry in his mouth.

Then he caught Sorcha's eye and relaxed. For who cared if Murdoch had to ask a Seelie for help, if it would allow him to spend the rest of his life with her?

"Lachlan," he said, very quietly. "Ailith. I have a request."

Everyone stared at him; Lachlan's brows narrowed in immediate understanding. "You can't honestly expect us to abide by this request. You can't. Surely you can see that."

Ailith glanced at her king, then back to Murdoch. Then understanding dawned on her face, too, and she stood up. "Kelpie, that is serious indeed. Do you truly know what it is that you're asking for?"

Murdoch gestured at Sorcha, who was watching him

from the bed with the most confused expression he had ever seen upon her lovely, human features. *Of course I know what it is I'm asking for.* "She gave up half her life," he said. "All I want is to live that with her – as her equal."

"No!"

Sorcha had bolted upright and rushed to Murdoch's side despite her injured, bandaged feet, grasping at one of his hands with both of her own. "Murdoch, you can't mean that you want them to strip you of all your powers. You can't –"

"If you are allowed to do what you want with your life for me, then I am allowed to do the same," Murdoch said, smiling. He stroked the side of Sorcha's face; she closed her eyes in a moment of contentment. He locked his gaze on Lachlan. "Make me human. I beg you. I know what I ask is no easy magic to weave. I would not ask if there was some other way to do it."

"Such magic is irreversible, kelpie," Lachlan uttered. "Even if I *liked* you I would be disinclined to perform such a –"

"I love her. You know that."

Sorcha's eyes lit up at Murdoch's admission. Her grip tightened on his hand. "You love me," she mouthed, as if in wonder. "You really do. I do not know why I ever doubted that you did."

He could only laugh in disbelief at such a doubt. "Miss Darrow," he said, "I love you more than anything."

It was bizarre; before, it was Murdoch's use of Sorcha's given name that had caused her heart to accelerate and her cheeks to flush. Now it was her

478

surname. Murdoch knelt in front of her, lowering his forehead to rest it against Sorcha's hands. "All I want is to be with you," he said. "I have lived on this earth long enough to know I would be a fool to give up what we have."

Nobody said anything for a while. And then:

"Five years."

It was Lachlan who had spoken. Murdoch glanced at him out of the corner of his eye; the faerie had a calculated expression on his face, as did Ailith.

She nodded her agreement. "Yes, I think five years is more than fair."

"Five years for what?" Sorcha asked.

"For your kelpie to prove that he can truly live like a human," Ailith explained. "If he can do that, then we shall make him mortal."

Murdoch stood up, ready to protest. "But Sorcha might only –"

"It is precisely *because* she does not have a lot of time left that I'm demanding this," Lachlan said, face grave. "If Eirian makes a move over the next few years – which I imagine he will – then the Seelie Court will need your strength to help us. As a kelpie, not a man. And you *will* help us, or we won't help you."

Murdoch said nothing for a moment. He looked at Sorcha, whose mismatched eyes were a little too bright as she watched his face carefully for a sign of his decision. But of course he had already made it; five years was a small price to pay, after all.

He held out a hand to Lachlan. "Deal," he said, resisting the urge to squeeze the faerie's hand a little too hard when he shook it.

A slow grin crept across Lachlan's face as he broke from Murdoch's grasp to address Sorcha. "And in the meantime, Clara," he said, going back to using her false name simply to infuriate Murdoch, "if you ever get tired of your horse – which I don't doubt that you will – you know where to find me."

"Lachlan!" Ailith scolded.

But Sorcha merely laughed. She closed the gap between herself and Lachlan, stretching up on her tiptoes to brush a kiss against his lips. "I know," she whispered. Murdoch's heart tightened and twisted painfully, but then Sorcha added, "You are wrong about him, though, Lachlan. And me. I will not grow tired of him. And I think *you* have known that longer than even I have."

Lachlan sighed. "Do not make me have to admit the truth *in front of him,* lass."

"But then the two of you could be friends!" Sorcha said, voice full of mischief. "You could –"

"Absolutely not," Lachlan cut in, followed by the sound of Murdoch cursing under his breath at such an outrageous suggestion.

Sorcha giggled. "Far more impossible things have happened."

"In your dreams, perhaps," Lachlan scoffed.

Sorcha raised an eyebrow at him. "More of my dreams have come true than naught."

"Well if that wasn't a filthy proposition then I don't know –"

"Will the two of you be staying the night?" Ailith

interrupted, casting a worried glance at Murdoch in the process. But though Lachlan's relationship with Sorcha was something he could never profess to understand, and though the Seelie king delighted in saying just about anything to get a rise out of him because of it, Murdoch could not be angry with the ease of their flirtations.

Sorcha loved him. She loved the kelpie of Loch Lomond. That was enough.

Sorcha shook her head at Ailith, gave Lachlan a final kiss, then walked over to Murdoch's side. His hand found hers as if it was the most natural thing in the world. "No," she said, "I have a poor, *real* horse named Galileo who misses me. Where we have to be is far more important than the faerie realm."

She didn't have to say it out loud. Murdoch knew exactly where she meant.

In an area full of people who loved and depended on the Darrows. In a handsome, red brick house overlooking the loch. In a small gap between worlds, where kelpies fell in love with humans and mortal girls sang longingly to them through the water.

They were going home.

EPILØGUE

Eirian

The Golden King of the Seelie Court was running on borrowed time, and Eirian knew the faerie was well aware of it. A human had saved him, after all. A *human*. And not merely once, either.

Sorcha Darrow had foiled Eirian's attempts to dispatch with Lachlan twice.

It was supposed to have been simple: his brother, Innis, was already in love with Queen Evanna. That part Eirian had not planned but was instead happy coincidence. Or, rather, a sign from the fates themselves that they wished for the Unseelie king to hold dominion over all otherwordly creatures.

Innis had not taken much convincing to get behind his brother's plot to overthrow the Seelie Court. Evanna's only son and heir would never be ready to rule, he had said. He didn't have the right temperament. His own son was a much better fit for the crown alongside the kind and beautiful faerie, Ailith. Eirian had not argued on this point, merely encouraging his brother to keep Lachlan close at hand once it became apparent that his mother's health was failing.

When Evanna passed away Innis and Fergus' part of the job had been simple: get rid of the Seelie prince. A fox curse had been a stroke of genius – even Eirian could see that. His brother and nephew never needed to hide Lachlan's death, for they would not kill him. All they had to say was that the poor lad, anguished by his mother's death, had run away.

That was supposed to have been it. Fergus would take the throne of the Seelie Court, calm the faeries down after Evanna's death and her son's disappearance, and then...

Eirian would swoop in, kill both his brother and his nephew, and take the kingdom for himself.

So how had it transpired that Sorcha Darrow enchanted a kelpie to her side to kill Eirian's family first, then break Lachlan's curse to put him back on the throne? How had a *human* managed to undo years and years of planning?

And now she had stopped Eirian from getting rid of Lachlan once again, though the Unseelie king knew that the damage he could inflict upon his royal rival by taking half of Sorcha's life would be worth it in the long run.

Eirian had always been in it for the long run.

"*But tho' my despair is past curing,*" he sang, gazing out of his bedroom window as the beginnings of a blizzard obscured his entire kingdom from view. It was the last line of the song Sorcha had sung through the streets of London when Eirian had ordered his ghouls to frighten her right into his arms. He had almost spirited her away then and there out of sheer spite.

But there was something about the girl that was charming. Something that had given Eirian enough pause to not simply destroy her where she stood. She had a kelpie – the most powerful kelpie in all of Scotland – and the Seelie king under her thumb, after all. Though she was a human, she was valuable.

Now Eirian had big plans for her and the delicious fear and disgust he had seen in her eyes when she signed over half her life to him. He knew Sorcha had refused Lachlan's offer of immortality time and time again; when she'd agreed to Eirian's deal she'd clearly thought she was giving him no more than thirty years.

He was going to make that closer to forever.

"*But tho' my despair is past curing,*" he repeated;

"*And much undeserv'd is my fate,*

I'll show by a patient enduring

My love is unmov'd as her hate."

Yes, Eirian had always been in it for the long run, and he was going to drag Sorcha Darrow along for the ride.

KING ØF FØREVER

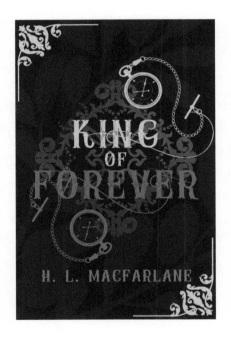

UNDERGRØUND

It's only forever...not long at all.

Underground (D. Bowie; 1986)

PRØLØGUE

Every Unseelie worth their salt knew what was going on. Even the ghoul who had once been called Beira, currently enjoying a luxurious exile in the depths of Loch Lomond, was well aware of the rumblings of trouble between the faerie factions.

Beira's exile had not been quite so lovely back when she'd had to beware of the kelpie. The beast could have easily rent her flesh from her bones if he'd felt that way inclined; Beira had been very careful to sneak around and only risk drowning and devouring her next meal when she was quite certain he was miles away.

One hundred years ago she might have been a match for the kelpie. An intimidating witch by anyone's standards, with particular talents for prophecy and blood magic, in her quest for power and glory Beira had broken most every taboo known to faerie-kind. The Seelie Court had been the first of the factions to cast her out, though eventually even the far more vicious and bloodthirsty Unseelie – her own kin – banished her, too.

And so it was that Beira spent decades skulking from

place to place, stripped of most of her power and influence, until she came upon Loch Lomond. It was dangerously close to the centre of the Seelie Court but, because of the even more dangerous kelpie, Beira knew she would face no problems from the faeries so long as she stayed within the confines of the water.

Beira knew the danger was worth the risk, anyway, for she wanted to be close to the Court in order to keep up-to-date with the ebb and flow of the faerie realm. It was imperative she was immediately informed when an opportunity finally arose for her to break her exile and regain her true and rightful power.

When she discovered that the kelpie was seeking her out Beira had been certain her end was nigh. But then the creature asked for her help. *Her* help. Beira, the all-powerful. Beira, the all-seeing. Beira, the bloodthirsty.

Though the first part was no longer true, no amount of binding faerie magic would ever strip Beira of her prophetic abilities. And she was just as bloodthirsty as she'd ever been; if she could strike up a deal with the kelpie wherein he left her to do as she pleased within his domain then she would gladly help him.

That the kelpie needed transformation magic had been a relief for it was the very limit of Beira's already limited abilities. He used his twelve hours in the form of a man well, going by the fact he had since regained his bridle. And, true to his word, the beast had largely left Beira alone since then.

On occasion he actively sought her out to join him in a hunt. But the kelpie spoke but rarely during these times and, when the hunt was over, would disappear for months on end. In reality he was hardly in the loch at all any more, choosing instead to live as a human with the

Darrow girl who looked after the land.

"The Darrow girl, the Darrow girl," Beira sang in her twisted, ugly voice, though it had once been frightening and beautiful. She scanned the loch with wide, keen eyes, hunting down a human who had fallen beneath the surface. Their fear hung in the water, tantalisingly close by. She continued singing as she swam, the same line over and over again: "The Darrow girl will cause problems for you all."

In truth the Darrow girl had caused many problems *already* for both the kelpie and the golden King of the Seelie Court, but the biggest problems of all were yet to come to pass. It was true that the mortal would also bring great joy to those who loved her across the span of her life, but that joy came at a heavy price.

Beira wondered if that price would - or could - be paid.

"The silver king will come for you, girl," she murmured, eyes flashing in the dark water as she finally caught sight of the unfortunate soul who had fallen into the loch. A young boy, already drowned and sinking down, down, down. Beira wasted no time in darting out to claim him before any other wicked creature could. She placed a gentle kiss upon the boy's forehead as a gesture to his mother, who would despair to discover him lost.

Then she opened her maw wide around his skull and shattered it with one terrifying bite.

"The silver king is coming," Beira sang, long after all that remained of the boy were a few finger bones and the rags of his tattered clothes. "He is coming, and you have all run out of time."

CHAPTER ONE

Lachlan

It was raining, and Lachlan hated it. Under ordinary circumstances he would have deigned not to go outside, but today was different.

The last five years had passed like five minutes, and two months ago Lachlan celebrated his one hundred and fourth birthday. Now that he had lived a full century he could finally stand tall and true beside the older members of the Seelie Court, though by his kind's standards he was still very young indeed.

Especially to be king, as they keep reminding me, he thought dolefully. With the threat of war with the Unseelie simmering beneath the surface of every choice the Court made Lachlan had been subject to ever more criticism from his kin. He had been foolish to face up to Eirian with no way of winning against him, they said. They were right, of course, especially since the Unseelie king now had the worst kind of leverage against him.

That leverage was Sorcha Darrow.

But Lachlan could not find it in him to regret his feelings for the mortal woman, who was the reason he was standing outside in the rain, nor the hold she had over his heart. He loved her dearly, and deeply, in a way he might never admit aloud to anyone. His feelings for her cast a shadow over the love he held for his queen, Ailith, making it feel shallow and adolescent.

Though that may be because of her new consort. Lachlan pushed the thought away.

"Sometimes the mortals really do know how to put on a good funeral service."

Lachlan smothered a flinch of surprise at the voice, which belonged to his adviser, Ronan. The faerie was broad and burly, with curling horns like a ram's upon his head, though at present he was under the glamour of a human. Lachlan was, too, as were the rest of the faeries with him. For they were indeed at a mortal funeral: that of William Darrow.

Sorcha, whose usually wild hair was pinned back and impeccably tidy for once, stood by the edge of her father's grave with her bereft mother and her kelpie lover, Murdoch, by her side. A fine mist of winter drizzle enshrouded them all, causing their silhouettes to waver as if they, too, were made of water. When Margaret Darrow began to weep Murdoch swept her into his arms so that her tears could remain hidden from the rest of the funeral-goers.

Though it frustrated him that the kelpie had integrated himself into Sorcha's family in a way Lachlan could not, he kept his insecurities from showing on his face. He was not the kind of fool to interrupt the family during such a moment, after all, though Lachlan wanted nothing more than to console the woman he loved. No, he remained a polite distance away with his small cohort of faeries who wished to pay their last respects to the kind and loving human that was William Darrow.

The man had been keeper of the land around both the loch and the forest his entire life, protecting everyone from all manner of threats from greedy, selfish mortals. In his later years he had passed that duty onto his daughter due to his ailing health, thus keeping the Darrow tradition alive. The faeries owed a great deal to the family, though they knew humans in general were becoming a bigger and bigger threat against their supernatural way of life.

Sorcha and the kelpie's battle against Murdoch Buchanan's old work colleagues was chilling proof of that.

The beast wearing Murdoch's skin cast his eyes over to Lachlan. A curt nod passed between them, then the man who was not a man returned his attention to Sorcha and her mother. Lachlan reached a hand out across the graveyard towards Sorcha, thinking that perhaps it wouldn't hurt to say a few words to her, but Ronan gently touched his wrist to stop him.

"Leave her for now, Lachlan," he said, not unkindly. "Miss Darrow and the kelpie are coming to the Court this evening, are they not? Save your words and sympathies for then."

Yet Lachlan could not help but take a step or two towards Sorcha until his keen ears could pick up on the muffled sobs of Margaret Darrow through the rain as she cried against Murdoch's chest.

"He would have l-loved to see you two m-married," she wailed. Murdoch stroked her greying hair, keeping his eyes on Sorcha as she fought back tears herself. She could not bear to look at her mother, that much was clear. "A w-wedding and a child," Margaret continued, "wouldn't matter if the bairn was a b-boy or a girl. William was so good with children."

Something inside Lachlan twisted and coiled like a snake readying to strike. Whilst Murdoch was still a kelpie he could not father children with a mortal...but his final five years as a magical beast were up. Lachlan and Ailith had promised to change his very being permanently, and faeries always kept their promises.

There was just one thing Lachlan had to ask of Sorcha before he turned Murdoch human.

Tonight, Lachlan thought, as Sorcha's green-and-blue eyes caught his for just a moment before he turned for the forest with his companions. In them he saw all the anguish she was keeping at bay for the sake of her mother. She would cry later, he knew, perhaps when nobody was around. Lachlan loved her for it – the strength she held for other people in place of herself – though he also despaired because of it. It was the reason Sorcha was currently in such a dire situation, after all.

But Sorcha had long since made her decision to save the Seelie king and the kelpie of Loch Lomond at the price of half her life. There was nothing Lachlan could do about it now, except approach his mortal love with his most demanding request to date.

Tonight, he thought again as Ronan led him back into the cover of the forest. Once well hidden from the mortals at the funeral the faeries collectively let their nondescript human glamours drop, resulting in a whole host of strange and magical creatures left looking more bizarre than usual due to their uncomfortable, sombre mortal clothes.

Lachlan tossed one final glance over his shoulder in Sorcha's direction, though through the dense cover of winter pines he could no longer see her. *I will ask her tonight, whilst there is still time left to fulfil the request.*

He knew that Murdoch would not like what he was going to ask at all.

Ailith had remained at Court whilst Lachlan attended William Darrow's funeral, though the pale-skinned faerie was nowhere to be seen when he returned to the Seelie palace. *Her new lover is keeping her company, no doubt,* he thought, wasting no time in requesting a jug of blackberry wine from a passing servant on his way to the throne room. Lachlan was happy for Ailith – truly, he was – but seeing her with another was not exactly something he'd wished to witness over the past year.

And so it was that Lachlan was somewhere past tipsy when a silent-footed servant crept into the throne room to inform him that Sorcha and Murdoch had arrived. He was still in his mortal funeral clothes – largely all black, a colour Lachlan rarely wore – and his shoulder-length hair was in desperate need of a comb, but he did not care.

For what were appearances, in the face of the woman who could see right through them?

"Send them in," Lachlan said as he waved towards the servant, but in the time it took for him to speak the door was pushed wide open by Murdoch, closely followed by Sorcha. The kelpie was similarly still in the clothes he had worn to the funeral, though against his dark hair and coal-coloured eyes the ensemble did not look out of place in the slightest.

Sorcha, however, had changed into a familiar, forest-coloured dress with an intricately embroidered bodice that Lachlan adored. She had released her hair from its pins, too, and had clearly brushed through it until it shone going by the soft and lustrous way it tumbled down her back. She was a sight to behold, even with the slight tinge of red rimming her eyes suggesting she had indeed cried in the hours since Lachlan left her father's funeral.

Now I feel an idiot for not making an effort with my appearance for her sake, Lachlan thought glumly, rubbing a lock of bronze hair between his thumb and forefinger. *Though I suppose there is naught I can do about it now.*

Murdoch was the first to speak when he and Sorcha stopped in front of Lachlan on his gilded throne. He preferred the thrones that sat on the plinth outside in the revel clearing but given that it was January it was altogether much too cold to host such a meeting beneath the stars.

"What was so important that you had to call us here today, fox?" Murdoch demanded, though his voice was soft and gentle. For Sorcha's sake, Lachlan assumed, though given the kelpie's usage of his favourite insult *fox* he had to wonder what the point was of changing his tone. Either way, it didn't matter; Lachlan had to pose his request to Sorcha regardless of what Murdoch said or did over the next few, all-important minutes.

However, now that he was faced with what he had to ask Lachlan found that he could not look at Sorcha at all. He straightened on the throne, smoothing a hand over his hair and hooking a finger inside the uncomfortably restrictive collar of his human shirt as his brain fumbled for the right words.

496

"What I have to say – what I have to ask of you," he began, very slowly, "is no easy request. I am well aware of that. Yet I have thought on the matter at length over the past five years and find myself in a position where it would be detrimental to delay voicing my request any longer."

Murdoch frowned, deeply suspicious, though Sorcha's previously sad expression changed in a moment to one of curiosity. She closed the gap between herself and the throne to rest a hand over Lachlan's. Her skin was icy cold, sending a shiver down his spine. But the way Sorcha looked at him was warm and familiar and tugged at Lachlan's heart, forcing his request out of his mouth before he could do anything to stop it.

"Have my child."

CHAPTER TWO

Murdoch

The kelpie of Loch Lomond had lived for five hundred and thirty-five years. Five of those years had been spent under the guise of Murdoch Buchanan. They were, without a shadow of a doubt, the best five years he had ever lived.

And now they were over, marked by the impossible request Lachlan had just placed at the feet of the woman Murdoch loved more than anything.

"Have my child, Clara," the faerie said again, falling back on the false name Sorcha had used when she first met him. "I beg of you. Please. I do not ask this lightly."

Sorcha said nothing. She stood inches from Lachlan, utterly immobile. Murdoch wished he could see her face – to know how the love of his life had reacted to the Seelie king's words.

She can't possibly accept, Murdoch thought, shifting his weight from foot to foot as he tried to decide if he should say something before Sorcha did. *What Lachlan*

498

is asking is madness.

"Why are you asking this of her?" he blurted out, no longer able to remain silent. "Why now?"

Murdoch expected Lachlan to scowl or snarl or tell him it was none of his business. Instead, the faerie broke his attention from Sorcha to stare directly at him. "You should know that it is difficult for faeries to conceive a child," he said. "Our women give birth so infrequently, and it is a dangerous process. Having a babe with a human is the sensible option. And if I am to have a child with a mortal, then..." Lachlan returned his gaze to Sorcha, an enchanted smile on his face. "I would give up most anything for that mortal to be you, Sorcha Darrow."

"So you waited until my five years were *up* before posing this question to her?" Murdoch asked, beyond indignant. "Are you really so intent on getting between me and Sorcha that you –"

"It was precisely *because* I did not wish to interfere with your relationship that I had not yet asked," Lachlan cut in, a familiar lashing of venom colouring his voice. Murdoch scowled, intending to thoroughly disagree, but the faerie held up a hand to quell his tirade before it could begin. "I am being serious," he said. "With every year that passed with no interference from Eirian – and barely a word of gossip about the goings-on of the Unseelie Court – I realised all of us were only creeping closer to the moment when he might take her. No matter my opinion of you, horse, you clearly make Clara happy. Who was I to get in the middle your life together?"

Murdoch merely glared at him, for Lachlan *had* gotten in the middle of his and Sorcha's relationship on several occasions. The two of them would by lying in bed together, content to do nothing but listen to the sound of wind and rain battering the walls of the Darrow house. Then, in the minute space between one moment and the next, Sorcha would be fast asleep.

It wasn't difficult to work out who was responsible for her sudden unconsciousness and inevitable, enchanted dreams.

Murdoch never asked Sorcha what she got up to in such dreams, nor had he ever confronted Lachlan about them. He knew it was not his place to pry; Sorcha and her fox had a complex relationship that Murdoch would never understand. But he *did* understand that Lachlan was important to her, and she to him.

He had taken to breaking his human form to go hunting in the loch whenever Lachlan invaded Sorcha's dreams, desperate to wipe the contented look on her sleeping face from his mind. Sometimes Murdoch would run into the Unseelie ghoul who had once granted him twelve hours as a human when his bridle had been stripped from him, thus saving his life as he knew it. They would hunt together, swimming close to the shore in order to lure unsuspecting humans out for evening strolls or midnight trysts to their waiting teeth and the mortals' inevitable doom. They would see who could do it the fastest, or the stealthiest, or with the most flair.

When Murdoch returned to the Darrow house after such hunts he always felt just as guilty as Sorcha looked upon waking up. They both knew they were indulging in dangerous impulses that they were not supposed to indulge. Yet despite those rare nights of madness the two of them had lived five unfathomably happy years, even taking into account William Darrow's increasingly ailing health.

And so it was that Murdoch could not help feeling glad that at least Lachlan's interferences had remained in the realm of Sorcha's dreams, and that their conscious interactions had been purely platonic. It was only listening to him now that Murdoch realised Lachlan could easily have taken things much further purely because he could. Alongside the fact that faeries could not outright lie, Murdoch had to conclude that the Seelie king was currently telling the truth about having not asked his ridiculous request of Sorcha at an earlier date.

"A child," Sorcha murmured, finally breaking her very long silence. She moved from Lachlan's throne to sweep around the room, eyes thoughtful and very faraway. Murdoch resisted the urge to rush to her side. She glanced at Lachlan, who stood as if on command. "You never mentioned wishing to have a child before. You are still very young by faerie standards, are you not?"

He nodded. "I never thought I'd want one at this age, admittedly. But you are twenty-seven, Clara, and in the blink of an eye you will be forty, then sixty, then gone. If I cannot have you happy to live forever then grant me the miracle of a child to remember you by. I would love them more than anything else in the world."

Again, Murdoch knew he had to be telling the truth, though it was plain as day from the look on Lachlan's face that he sincerely meant every word he said. A pang of sympathy ran through him, for of course Murdoch knew that the faerie loved Sorcha. Eirian might have stolen half of her life but at least Murdoch would get to live the other half of it with her, ageing alongside her – *dying* alongside her.

Lachlan would never have that.

The Seelie king fidgeted uncomfortably when Sorcha continued her tour of the throne room in silence, tawny hair flashing copper down her back whenever the flickering light of a torch caught it. When the faerie threw a glance at Murdoch he promptly looked away, for he did not know what to say or do.

"You do not need to make a decision right here and now," Lachlan said, the words spilling out of him so quickly that Murdoch almost laughed at the faerie's uncharacteristic display of nervousness. "Take all the time you need. But please –"

"I'll do it."

"You'll – what?"

Both Lachlan and Murdoch stared at Sorcha as she finally came to a stop in the middle of the room, a determined glint in her eye that was completely at odds with the red-rimmed evidence of her grief over her father's death. "Of course I'll have your child, Lachlan," she said. "I would have done so even without your half-dozen reasons for why you believe I should."

Lachlan's face broke into a gleeful, sharp-toothed grin; he rushed forward and swept Sorcha off her feet, twirling her around and around until she was clinging onto him for dear life and the two of them were laughing. Murdoch took half a step towards the pair before thinking better of it. This was not something he should be part of.

Yet still Murdoch wished he was.

Eventually Lachlan placed a dizzy, stumbling Sorcha back on her feet and kissed the crown of her head. "Can you give me a few minutes with the horse, Clara?" he asked. Sorcha nodded and dutifully exited the throne room, though not before giving Murdoch the smallest of smiles that promised they would talk about everything later.

As soon as Sorcha was gone the atmosphere in the room grew tense and electric. "How bad is she getting?" Lachlan asked, eyes on the grand double doors as if Sorcha were still standing in front of them.

"She spends more and more time simply looking out of the window, but not at anything in particular," Murdoch replied, moving over to Lachlan's throne to lean against its side. All of his energy seemed to be leaking away at an alarming pace, as it always did with he and Lachlan discussed Sorcha's deal with the Unseelie king.

Lachlan finally tore his eyes away from the door and returned to his throne, slumping into it as if he felt exactly the same way as Murdoch, which he likely did. "Have you asked her what it is she's looking at...or looking *for*?"

"Every time. She says not to worry – that she is looking for nothing."

"You do not believe her?"

"Of course not."

A silence stretched between the two of them as they mulled over what this meant. Then, because he had heard no mention of it for a while, Murdoch asked, "Any news from your wizard friend? The one you hoped might be able to help us out of this?"

Lachlan shook his head. "Even knowing that Genevieve is a princess in France has not helped me in locating Julian. I fear we are running out of time."

Murdoch said nothing. To admit to the same fear aloud was to acknowledge that Eirian taking Sorcha away was real.

"If Sorcha does not get pregnant with the next two years then I will give up on having a child," Lachlan murmured, watching Murdoch out of the corner of a golden eye to see how he would react. "I do not wish to take more time away from the two of you than that. Ailith and I can still turn you mortal now, if that is what you wish, or –"

"I will wait," Murdoch said, certain. "If Sorcha is to carry a babe then I need to be able to protect her as best I can."

A flash of approval crossed Lachlan's face. "Good. I was hoping you would say that. Now go find Clara and help her grieve her father in a way that I cannot."

Murdoch did not need to be told to look after the woman he loved twice.

CHAPTER THREE

Sorcha

"You do not have to do this simply because you feel obligated, Sorcha."

Sorcha did not look away from the drawing room window, even when Murdoch perched himself on the arm of her chair and squeezed her shoulder. "I do not feel *obligated*," she said. "I want to do this."

A pause. And then: "I know. I just wanted to be sure."

The drizzle from earlier that day had turned into an all-out storm the moment the sun set. Sorcha peered through the darkness at the turbulent loch, listening to every crash and slap and groan the waves made as they slammed against the shore. She had encouraged her mother to drink several drams of whisky to help drown out the noise and ease her into sleep an hour earlier, and though Margaret Darrow had insisted she would find neither sleep nor solace in the bed she had shared for thirty years with her husband, but fifteen minutes later she had collapsed into an exhausted sleep.

Sorcha sincerely hoped the woman would be blessed with dreams of her husband in his heyday, when William was strong and young and illness did not plague him.

"The storms are not your doing, are they?" Sorcha asked Murdoch, though she knew he could no more control the weather than she could.

He chuckled softly. "It feels that way, sometimes. But I am not in so bad a mood tonight to cause a storm, my love."

"Even after Lachlan's request?"

When Murdoch slid down to sit beside Sorcha she made room for him, resting her head against his shoulder after a moment or two. He began to stroke her hair the way she liked, and she sighed contentedly.

"I cannot pretend that I am happy about what he asked of you," Murdoch said, "but I do at least understand. It is a kind and gracious thing for you to do, Sorcha, even if..."

"Even if you wish it was *our* child I was having," Sorcha finished. She looked up at him, craning her neck until she could graze her lips against Murdoch's jawline. It was dark with a shadow of stubble, but Sorcha enjoyed the sensation of it against her mouth. Murdoch's impossibly black eyes watched Sorcha's every move like a hawk.

She smiled. "We will have a family, I swear it. When I have borne Lachlan a child I will do the same for you – for us – and our little world will be happier for it. And just think!" Sorcha chuckled, more to herself than to Murdoch. "I will then have one mortal and one immortal child. Siblings. What are the odds they'll get on as well as you and Lachlan?"

Murdoch snorted at the notion. "I perish the thought of being more involved with the fox than I already have to."

"You would be brothers, almost."

"Now you are teasing me for the sake of it."

"It makes a difference from *you* doing all the teasing," Sorcha said, snaking a hand around the back of Murdoch's neck to bring his lips down to hers. He eagerly complied, wasting no time in deepening the kiss as he ran his fingers through Sorcha's hair.

A rumble of thunder broke the kiss a moment later; Sorcha immediately shifted her attention back to the window as if Murdoch was not sitting beside her at all. In truth she could see nothing through the pitch black of the stormy night, but it did not matter.

"When you and Lachlan have a child then neither of you will be alone, even when I am gone."

Sorcha was barely aware of what she was saying, nor of Murdoch's grip on her wrist as he tried to regain her attention. When he attempted to turn her back to face him she blankly resisted.

"Sorcha –"

"Carrying on their family lines is the only way mortals can truly live forever," she continued, voice eerie and disturbingly sing-song even to her own ears. "You and Lachlan will be fine. And I will be back before you know it."

"Sorcha, what is it that you aren't telling me?" Murdoch pressed, trying once more to turn her around to face him. He was successful this time, though the searching look he gave Sorcha turned to one of disappointment when it became clear she would not – or could not – answer him.

With a sigh he got to his feet. "Please speak to me," he said. "Or Lachlan. As much as I hate it, if it's him you have to talk to then talk to the Seelie king. Only do not keep what is happening to you inside your head. We want to help."

Murdoch paused then, waiting for Sorcha to reply. It took everything she had in her to say, "I think I would like to be alone, to grieve for my father," before returning to the dark expanse of night behind the windowpane.

She did not hear the kelpie leave the room, but part of her heart stung at his absence. It was her own fault, Sorcha knew. She was pushing both him and Lachlan away, bit by bit, and she could do nothing to stop it. There was an impulse – a voice in her head, almost – urging her attention to somewhere else.

Someone else.

That was when the raven appeared.

The bird appeared like clockwork, using the cloak of night to flit in and out of Sorcha's vision. It had become a regular fixture during the last five years of her life, appearing whenever Sorcha was feeling particularly sad or angry or confused. But it also appeared in moments when she was contented – when her life was easy and relaxed and she had could all but forget her deal with the King of the Unseelie Court.

All around her the shadows in the drawing room began to flicker and change.

Sing, girlie, they said. *Just one song. You are cruel*

to keep it from us for all these years.

Sorcha did not reply, though a song was on the tip of her tongue dying to be released. She clutched her throat with desperate hands, begging the notes and words to stay firmly where they were.

"You are the cruel one," she whispered to the raven. Finally, the supernaturally large bird perched on the window ledge to tap on the glass right in front of Sorcha's face, watching her with eyes of unearthly silver instead of midnight black.

Sorcha touched the glass where the raven's beak had tapped it with the tip of her index finger. "Tell him that if he wishes to bother me here that it is time taken from the half of my life he holds claim to."

The bird cawed as if it was laughing. It sounded disturbingly familiar; nightmarish memories of dancing around and around on bloody, aching feet as mortal musicians played their fingers to the bone filled her head.

A song! the shadows called. *A song to dance to! A song to cry to! A song to die to!*

A single, delicate tear ran down Sorcha's face. "Leave me alone. Please leave me alone."

She knew deep down in her soul that they never would.

CHAPTER FØUR

Lachlan

Lachlan was nervous. More nervous than he'd been when he'd watched the kelpie behead his stepbrother and it did not break the fox curse the faerie had placed upon him. More nervous, even, than when an enchanted mortal woman had been sent to taunt Lachlan with riddles about Sorcha and the danger she was facing in London. Lachlan was, in fact, more nervous about tonight than he had been when he asked the question that directly led to what would transpire in the hours to come.

But the feeling was warranted; tonight was the first time Lachlan and Sorcha would actually go through the motions of trying to conceive a child.

Outside of her dreams Lachlan had not touched Sorcha the way he'd constantly longed to over the past five years. It had been difficult to resist whisking Sorcha away to the Seelie Court whenever he missed her most. But Lachlan was no fool, and he had grown up more in the past seven years than he had in the preceding ninety-seven.

She chose to live a mortal life with the kelpie, who was willing to give up all his power to be with her. That is not a relationship you interfere with.

And yet Lachlan *had* interfered despite this, on nights when the air was restless and everyone was dancing and laughing and losing themselves in each other at revels. He would sneak away from such events to his favourite room in the palace, deep underground and protected by a heavy iron door. There Lachlan would collapse into a pit of pillows and think of Sorcha, and within a matter of minutes he'd fall asleep and there she would be.

Lachlan knew Sorcha never told Murdoch about what the two of them got up to in her dreams, though often all they did was lie in each other's arms and talk for hours upon hours. Five years ago Sorcha's dreams had been full of splendid sunsets and golden lochs and jewel-coloured rain which never quite touched Lachlan's skin; since then, however, cold silvers and flickering shadows and blinding flashes of light had begun creeping in from every direction.

The last time he had been in Sorcha's dreams she'd been as distant as Murdoch had described her being whenever she sat by her drawing room window. It was this one, specific moment that had urged Lachlan to ask Sorcha to bear his child and heir, though he was worried he'd already left it much too late to broach the subject.

By the look in Murdoch's eyes as he watched Sorcha tell Lachlan that she *would* fulfil his request, he could only conclude that the kelpie very much believed there wasn't enough time left for her to have a faerie's child.

Lachlan shook his head; he couldn't afford such

concerns to colour his mood right now. He had to ensure he looked perfect for Sorcha's arrival, and right now he could not decide what to wear.

"It will all come off soon enough," he mumbled at his reflection in the intricately carved, bronze-framed mirror that took up much of an entire wall of his chambers. Lachlan picked at the frilly collar of the white shirt he'd pulled on over his head, wondering if he should abandon it in favour of wearing his favourite green-and-gold robe over his bare chest, instead.

A flutter of nerves and excitement filled his stomach once more at the mere thought of being naked with Sorcha, limbs entwined and drenched in each other's sweat. The handful of times they had lain together in her dreams simply could not compare to the feeling of her skin beneath Lachlan's fingertips in real time. He imagined her cheeks flushing as he unlaced her dress, eyes never leaving his as he cast his gaze from her wild, unruly hair all the way down to her feet.

"Are you really faltering over what to wear, Lachlan?"

Lachlan jumped in fright at the interruption, grabbing his robe from his bed to hide the obvious physical proof of his impure thoughts. Ailith merely laughed her bell-like laugh as she glided into the room and easily folded herself into a chair by the fireplace. Her impossibly straight, pale blonde hair reflected the flames like a mirror, setting every strand alight.

He scowled. "Have you ever heard of knocking?"

"Have you ever heard of having ears with which to listen to your door opening?" Ailith countered. "Come sit with me for a minute."

Lachlan glanced at the door. "Clara will be here soon."

"And you do not wish her to see me in here with you?"

"Not directly before she spends the night, no," he replied, averting his eyes when Ailith snorted into her hand.

"Where did this sense of decency come from, Lachlan?" she asked. "You never cared about her knowing we were together before."

Lachlan leaned against one of his tall bedposts. He closed his eyes for a moment, pinching the bridge of his nose in the process. He was not sure he knew how to vocalise his current feelings. "This is...different," he ended up saying. "I feel uneasy. Nervous. I haven't – Clara and I haven't –"

"Ahh," Ailith cut in, understanding dawning on her fair face. She smiled sympathetically and rose to her feet, smoothing out non-existent creases in her long, silken skirt as she did so. "It was unfair of me to come here without taking your feelings into consideration. But you have kept a lot to yourself recently, Lachlan; it has not been easy to read you."

He shrugged. "You have been busy. I have not wished to burden you with my decidedly mortal woes."

"That is *exactly* what you should do, you fool," she said, closing the distance between them in an instant to gently kiss Lachlan's cheek. Ailith's next words were a whisper against his skin. "No matter how many lovers we take I am your queen, and you are my king. We have always been a good pair. And we will remain a good pair, until the end of time."

Lachlan bent his head, resting his brow against Ailith's as he sighed. "Do you think your consort is the faerie my mother prophesied?" he asked. "The one you were meant to be with in the end?"

"Lachlan –"

"I know, I know," Lachlan interrupted, quickly moving away from Ailith to browse sightlessly through his wardrobe. "It does not matter. But I hope he is, all things considered. For you to find him so soon, when you are both so young and with hundreds of years ahead of you...I am happy for you."

Ailith said nothing. She didn't have to; they both knew what was really on Lachlan's mind.

"Your Majesty. She is here."

Lachlan turned at the sound of the servant's voice, glancing at the door and then at Ailith as he fought against his now desperately beating heart. It was too late to fuss over clothes or Ailith's lover or any other matter that could possibly arise in the next thirty seconds.

"I shall go," Ailith said in hushed tones, reaching the door in three swift, easy strides. She gave Lachlan a radiant smile. "Good luck, my king. Try to remember to enjoy the evening."

As she left his room with the servant Lachlan almost laughed. Almost, but he couldn't force the sound out of his mouth. A vulpine bark was emitted instead, and Lachlan winced. *I shall never be allowed to forget my time as a fox, will I?* he thought, hurriedly running a gilded comb through his hair as the familiar sound of human-heavy footsteps reached his chambers.

"You are early," Lachlan said, taking a moment to collect himself before turning to face the woman who was currently closing the doors of his room behind her.

A pause. "Is being early a problem?"

When finally Lachlan *did* turn he forgot all about his nerves immediately. For there she was, the mortal he loved, dressed in a burgundy slip of a dress that must surely have been crafted by the silk weavers of his own Court. It hardly covered anything at all; Lachlan could see every curve and line of Sorcha's body beneath the fabric. Her hair was all loose tendrils around her face and shining waves down her back; a small smile curled the corners of her lips, which had been stained berry red.

"I thought it would be prudent to dress for the occasion," Sorcha said, not a hint of human modesty to be found in her voice. She took a step towards Lachlan. "But the faeries worked their magic faster than I thought they would, so –"

"Not a problem," he sputtered, too quickly, rushing to close the gap between them as quickly as he could. Lachlan slowly cast his gaze up and down her body just as he had imagined doing so five minutes earlier. "Being early, that is. That dress, however...now that *is* a problem."

Sorcha's mismatched eyes glittered in the low light of the room. When she brushed her lips against Lachlan's it was all he could do not to throw her to the floor in a flurry of mad, reckless lust. "Then how about we rectify said problem?" she asked, very quietly.

Lachlan's hand found hers, and he laced their fingers together. When he moved towards his bed Sorcha eagerly followed him. "That sounds good to me," he said, as he lay upon the bed and pulled Sorcha down on top of him. He kissed the skin below her ear, and along her jaw, until finally he found her mouth.

He bit Sorcha's lower lip. "That sounds very good to me indeed."

CHAPTER FIVE

Murdoch

Over the past five years Murdoch had tried his level best to live completely as a mortal. On nineteen occasions, however, he had succumbed to the primal desire to swim through the loch and search for lost souls to devour. Nineteen evenings of returning to his true skin; of feeling the rush of cold, dark water against every fibre of his being as he called out for prey.

Today marked the twentieth occasion.

"I wonder if the ghoul is about," Murdoch wondered aloud, rolling a crack out of his left shoulder as he prepared to dive into the loch. Three days had passed since Lachlan asked Sorcha to bear his child and Murdoch had later struggled to maintain Sorcha's attention for longer than five seconds as she sat by the window.

He had been concerned that night, as he lay in bed and waited hopelessly for her to join him, that this was the end for Sorcha. That Murdoch would awake the next morning and find her gone, spirited away to live half her life with the Unseelie king. But when the weak January sun rose and half-heartedly flooded Sorcha's bedroom with pale, wintry light Murdoch was relieved to find the woman in question curled up beside him, and when he roused her from her sleep Sorcha had been herself again.

She had not once sat by the window since then, though Murdoch caught her stealing glances at seemingly innocuous objects whenever she thought he wasn't watching. The objects were usually reflective, or cast long shadows, and every time Sorcha looked at them Murdoch's heart grew tight.

Eirian is watching her everywhere she goes. If Lachlan cannot find his wizard friend – or if the man can do nothing to help us – then Sorcha is doomed. I am doomed.

But, for now, the matter of the Unseelie king's claim on Sorcha was not the primary issue taking up all the space in Murdoch's head. For tonight Sorcha was going to stay in the faerie realm, and what she did with Lachlan in her dreams those past nineteen evenings would become very much a reality once more.

Do not be jealous. Do not be jealous. Do not be jealous.

There were faeries who granted wishes when they were recited three times, Murdoch knew; he wondered if any of them were listening to him right now. The relationship between himself, Sorcha and Lachlan could not be judged by mortal nor kelpie standards, for there was nothing simple and monogamous about it. But such a relationship was normal by *faerie* standards.

Though Lachlan loved Sorcha he continued to love

Ailith, too, despite Murdoch recently learning she also had a new paramour. And Sorcha had never had an issue with this – not even when Murdoch had been out of the picture, a prisoner in his own loch. Lachlan may have hated that Murdoch had since managed to win her heart, but the faerie had not once tried to stop Sorcha from being with him.

"Which means I am the only one who needs to get over my jealousy," he muttered. "I am the one who needs to change."

On this particular evening, however, Murdoch had no intention of getting over it. *No,* he thought, as he waded through the frigid loch and gladly leapt beneath the waves when it was deep enough to accommodate him, *tonight is for funnelling all my negative thoughts into a hunt.*

Murdoch swore it would be the final time he did so. But, unlike faeries, kelpies could lie.

*

"Something awful must be filling your head, to have drowned three people tonight so far."

Murdoch was quick to gather his dissipated form back together to face who had spoken: the Unseelie ghoul. The witch, for lack of another word.

He had learned over the past five years that the ghoul was female. She was a bizarre, ugly creature, with midnight-coloured, weed-like hair, disconcertingly large, metallic eyes and silver skin akin to fish scales. Her claws were honed to deadly points, as were her teeth. Even the ones that had broken were sharp enough to rend through flesh and bone.

She flashed those evil teeth at Murdoch. "Hello,

kelpie. Penny for your thoughts?"

"I think not."

"And here I thought we were friends!" she cried, twisting this way and that all around Murdoch with practised ease. He whipped out his tail and hit her in the face, though the Unseelie promptly avoided the attack in a flurry of bubbles.

"That you cannot lie makes that comment even worse," Murdoch bit out testily, annoyed that she had managed to evade him.

She pouted – or, at least, Murdoch thought that was what she was doing with her broken, twisted mouth – then turned herself upside down and swam in front of Murdoch's face. "I don't believe you do not think of me as a friend. I have helped you more than anyone, have I not? And I know you enjoy our hunts together."

"Friends have names, of which you seem disinclined to tell me yours. I thought it was humans who had to be wary of giving their names to faeries, not the other way around."

The Unseelie giggled. It was a disgusting sound. "That may be so, but I am also a witch. There are creatures darker than you or me that could do great and terrible things with my name...if there is any power left behind my name at all."

"Any power left?"

"Oh, kelpie, if only you had seen me in my heyday!" the creature exclaimed, dramatically falling deeper into the loch for several feet before returning to Murdoch's side in the blink of a gleaming, unnatural eye. "What a pair we would have been. I was quite beautiful, before."

"All your kind are beautiful, until they are not,"

Murdoch countered. "And you can glamour yourselves to look however you want, anyway. Superficial beauty matters naught to me."

"That is part of what makes you so formidable. You cannot be charmed or controlled by that which has vanquished generations of mortals and faeries alike."

Murdoch growled impatiently. "If you do not have a point –"

"I do, I do!" the faerie insisted. "I like you, kelpie. I like your home, and that you allow me to live here. It is the only kindness I have known for a long time. So I will grant you a kindness in return, if you only tell me what is on your mind."

Murdoch regarded her carefully. Faeries could not lie, but they could conceal their motives with well-spun words and flowery language. The Unseelie in front of him, however, could ultimately do nothing with the knowledge of what was bothering Murdoch. It was worth the risk of telling her what troubled him simply to see what sort of 'kindness' she would bestow upon him.

He let out a long spray of bubbles in lieu of a sigh. "Miss Darrow agreed to bear the Seelie king a child. She is with him now to...begin the process. I do not want to appear bothered by it for her sake, but it is vexing to say the least."

The silver creature grinned. "I already knew."

"Then why make me say it?" Murdoch demanded, snapping his teeth at her.

"Because we are friends! And now I know you are willing to talk to me. It means a lot, when part of your punishment is silence from your own kind."

Had this been any other day Murdoch would have

been genuinely curious about the faerie's past. Considering his current circumstances, he could not bring himself to care.

He huffed in her general direction. "What is this kindness that you promised me, then?"

"Oh, it is very kind and very good, I swear it," she said, bobbing up and down in the water as she spoke. "I saw something about you and your Miss Darrow."

If Murdoch had been in his human body he would have frowned. Instead he sharpened his form once more until he was large and solid and threatening against the comparatively tiny faerie. "What do you mean, you saw something? As in a prophecy? Or a vision? Or –"

"It is the kind of *saw* that is certain. Would you like to know of it?"

Murdoch could tell from the creature's deformed face that she was enjoying herself. All supernatural beings enjoyed teasing others, after all. It was simply that those 'others' were usually mortal.

He thought carefully about his answer before replying. The Unseelie swore what she had seen was good, and that it was certain, which meant that Murdoch knowing about it would not change fate. "Go ahead," he relented, after a minute of silence.

The faerie's bulbous, metallic eyes went glassy almost immediately. "Eighteen months and a day," she announced, in a voice that took Murdoch starkly aback by how beautiful and frightening it was. "Eighteen months and a day shall pass, and the kelpie will be granted a son from the woman he loves most dearly. Eighteen months and a day, not a second more nor less."

Murdoch struggled to process what he'd just heard. *A...son?* he thought. *A son! Sorcha and I are going to have a son. But eighteen months is not long at all. Will she – could Sorcha possibly bear Lachlan a child in that time frame, too? It does not seem likely.*

The faerie's prophecy changed everything. Knowing he and Sorcha would have a child together – a family together – so soon caused Murdoch to no longer care that she was currently with Lachlan. *Let them try their best for his sake. If Sorcha can deliver a child for him, too, then we will all be better for it.*

"A child for you both, so that you will never be alone," the Unseelie sang in her usual, garbled voice, interrupting Murdoch's train of thought. Her eyes were no longer glassy and faraway.

Murdoch stilled. "What did you say?"

"He has ears with which to hear," she said, propelling herself forward until Murdoch could no longer see her in the dark, murky water even with his exceptional vision. But her voice echoed all around, taunting him. "He can hear her, and then we all know. News like this never stays quiet long in the faerie realm – even for those of us no longer welcome there."

And then the Unseelie was gone, leaving Murdoch with a dozen new thoughts with which to wrestle. He twisted and turned on the spot for a moment, conflicted over what to do, before surging through the loch in the opposite direction to the faerie.

"Just one more soul and I am done hunting," Murdoch said, lying.

CHAPTER SIX

Sorcha

There was something dark and desperate about the way Lachlan touched every inch of Sorcha's body and held her close. She knew there had been more to his obvious nervousness when she'd first appeared in his chambers. A mania lurking beneath the surface, perhaps, or a madness.

Lachlan made no attempt at hiding such feelings now.

"I have missed you," he murmured, the words tickling Sorcha's ear when they brushed past her skin. Their clothes lay forgotten on the floor, their hair in equally wild disarray. When Sorcha rolled onto her back Lachlan rested his head against her chest with a contented sigh.

She stroked the length of his pointed, golden ear. "I have missed you, too."

"So why did you never approach me outside of your dreams to –"

"Lachlan."

There was a warning in Sorcha's voice, but a sadness, too. It wasn't that she hadn't *wanted* to get lost in the arms of the Seelie king in her waking moments. Sorcha imagined she would never be able to stem such feelings. Yet she loved Murdoch dearly. She loved the kelpie with everything she could give him – everything but the love she held for Lachlan. Murdoch had told Sorcha, before, that kelpies loved but once and deeply.

They were completely different from faeries.

Murdoch tolerated Lachlan creeping into Sorcha's dreams, though she could see how much it cost him to do so. Each and every time Sorcha found herself knocked out by the faerie she awoke to discover Murdoch looking furtive and guilty; it did not take her long to work out what he'd been doing whilst she was unconscious.

Does he hate being a kelpie, or does he hate thinking that I might disapprove of what he is doing as a kelpie? Because I could never do that. Or...does he hate how much he relishes returning to his original form?

The last possibility hurt Sorcha the most, and made her feel ever more guilty. *She* was the reason Murdoch was giving up everything that he had been for five hundred years. His power. His proverbial freedom. His identity. And yet here she was, in the arms of the Seelie king.

A silence stretched between Sorcha and Lachlan, then, during which neither of them moved. But then the faerie started tracing circles across her chest, and her stomach, and her thighs, and he sighed.

"I understand," he said. "Of course I do. I only

wish..."

"That Murdoch was a faerie?" Sorcha suggested, a frown creasing her brow. The pleasurable haze that had enveloped the two of them mere moments ago disappeared in an instant, leaving Sorcha feeling irritable and defensive. "That his approach to love and lust was the same as your own people? Or do you wish that he was not around at all, or that I did not love him? Or –"

"Sorcha, Sorcha," Lachlan cut in, the use of her true name causing her to stop mid-rant. He sat up, shaking his hair out of his face before looking down at Sorcha with desperately sad eyes. "You know that is not what I meant. If I had not accepted the horse by now I'd have tried to ruin your relationship long ago."

And then, as if it had never existed in the first place, Sorcha's anger blew away like a dying candle. She rolled onto her front, burying her face in a silken pillow before muttering, "I know. I'm sorry. I do not know what came over me. It was not my intention to ruin this evening for us."

It wasn't, of course. For with Murdoch's acceptance and understanding of the situation, and Lachlan's desperation to have a child, and her keen desire to give them both as much of her as she could *whilst* she still could, Sorcha had been looking forward to tonight.

But something was eating away at her brain.

Sorcha knew what it was even as she wished she didn't.

"He said you have been growing ever more distant," Lachlan said, stroking Sorcha's hair before trailing his fingers down her spine. She squirmed beneath his touch, and though it should have been pleasant the sensation was ruined by Sorcha imagining Lachlan's elegant fingertips belonged to someone else.

"The kelpie, I mean," Lachlan continued, when Sorcha made no attempt to reply. "I can see that what he speaks is true. Where are you right now, Clara? Where is your pretty head?"

"Away with the faeries," she replied, so wryly that both of them laughed despite themselves. She turned her head to peek a look at Lachlan out of the corner of her eye. "It is getting worse. I want to tell Murdoch but... I can't. Something is compelling me not to. It's funny... I've tried to tell you before – in my dreams – but I've never been able to. So why now?"

Lachlan considered this for a moment, scratching at the down-soft layer of stubble that covered his jaw. He chewed on his lower lip – a habit Sorcha was fairly certain the faerie had developed from her – then gasped when he came to a conclusion.

Sorcha pulled herself into a sitting position, deeply confused. "What is it, Lachlan?"

"When you are dreaming...I always thought, because it was an enchanted sleep, that if anything was creeping into them then it would do so here, but –"

"What on earth are you talking about?"

Lachlan grinned, a glint of hope in his molten eyes that Sorcha had not seen in months. "When you are dreaming you are still in your house," he explained. "A mortal house. Still susceptible to the magic and influence of Eirian. But in the Seelie Court – in the palace – my magic is strong enough to keep it out. I cannot believe I did not realise sooner!" He reached for Sorcha, grabbing her shoulders and shaking them out of sheer excitement. "Tell your horse, Clara – the both of you are moving here for the time being!"

Sorcha could only gape at him. Lachlan's solution made sense, of course, especially if she was going to carry his child. But then she thought of the kelpie, and she grimaced.

"Murdoch is going to simply *love* this."

CHAPTER SEVEN

Murdoch

When Sorcha broke the news to Murdoch that they were moving to the faerie realm – the Seelie Court, no less – he had been furious. But after both she and Lachlan explained to him the reason behind the move Murdoch had no choice but to reluctantly accept.

Eight weeks later he could only conclude that the two of them should have moved there years ago, though Murdoch missed the Darrow house and it was very much clear that Sorcha did, too. But gone were her glassy eyes, vacant expressions and long stints looking out of the window with barely a word to say that made any sense.

Sorcha was more *herself* that she had been in at least two years, and for that Murdoch was eternally grateful. So what if he had to live surrounded by creatures he hated? He would gladly do it...for her.

In truth Murdoch did not hate *all* of the inhabitants of the Seelie Court. He had grown more than tolerant of Ailith over the years. Fond of her, even. The faerie was gentle and sensitive in a way far more befitting a human than a faerie, and she always spoke to Murdoch without disdain or fear or hatred despite the fact he had beheaded her once-future-husband. And he liked Ronan, Lachlan's ram-horned adviser to the throne, who was level-headed, liked to drink and held the Darrows in the highest regard.

Though he would never admit it, Murdoch found himself feeling safer within the Seelie Court than he had been outside of it. Seeing Sorcha finally relax and let her guard down only solidified his opinion that living with the faeries was the best thing for them.

At least for now.

"What are you thinking about, kelpie?"

Murdoch glanced up from his dinner – a feast of venison, blackberries and fat, buttered root vegetables that put most mortal meals to shame – to find Ronan collapsing down on the wooden bench beside him. The horned faerie looked exhausted, though his movements were just as agile as ever as he stole the largest chunk of venison from Murdoch's plate. The look Ronan gave him dared Murdoch to object, though he had no intention of doing so.

"I am merely thinking how Miss Darrow living here can only ever be a temporary measure," he said, granting the faerie the pure, unbridled truth. He speared a crisp-edged potato and chewed on it, only continuing to vocalise his thoughts once he had swallowed it in its entirety. "Tell it to me straight, Ronan: how long do you think we can hold off Eirian's attempts at reaching her?"

Ronan drank from a water skin attached to his belt, grimacing at the taste. He indicated towards Murdoch's goblet of dark, heady wine. "May I?" he asked, but before Murdoch had the opportunity to nod his assent Ronan had already begun drinking from it. When a servant passed by they dutifully handed Murdoch another goblet, though the faerie was quick to take that one, too.

"Bring us a jug," Ronan ordered, wiping his mouth before stretching his burly arms above his head. He let out an enormous yawn. "It has been long, exhausting work, ensuring the Court is protected to the standards set out by the king."

Murdoch did not take that as a good sign. "So you are saying we do not have long."

"On the contrary, we have needed to do this for many a year," Ronan said, surprising him. When the servant reappeared with a jug of wine the faerie eagerly took it and poured Murdoch a new measure of the stuff, thrusting it at his chest with brusque efficiency. "The Guard are exhausted, granted – I'm sure you have worked that out already – but we need to be pushed. To be trained. Queen Evanna ruled us for a long and fruitful time, and then she married the Unseelie king's half-brother. Clearly the idea was to unite the factions to maintain the peace she had worked for. However..."

"Eirian does not want that," Murdoch finished. "Do you think he can break through to the Seelie Court?"

Ronan's face was grave. "I will not lie to you, kelpie – even if I could, I would not. Your lady promised King Eirian half her life, so half her life he shall have. All you are doing is claiming your right to as much of the other half as you can whilst she is still young and beautiful."

Murdoch had not thought of it that way before; he had always, somewhat foolishly, believed that he and Lachlan could find a way to circumvent Eirian's claim and free Sorcha from her promise. Now it was looking as if that had never been an option, and never would be.

He stood up.

"Kelpie...?" Ronan wondered, eyeing him curiously.

"If I have but limited time with Miss Darrow then I should be spending it with her," he replied, inclining his head politely towards the faerie before rushing to the rooms he shared with Sorcha as fast as he could. The Unseelie witch in Loch Lomond was inside Murdoch's head again, taunting him with her intoxicating prophecy of a son.

Eighteen months and a day, she said. It has been almost two months since then; if this prophecy is as certain as she claims then I must become mortal and Sorcha pregnant – with my child, not Lachlan's – within the next seven months. What if a year and a half is all I get with her before – before –

Murdoch's manic train of thought was cut off as he became aware of the sound of retching. Anxious and hesitant, he paused outside the door to his and Sorcha's chambers to listen to what was going on, though ended up knocking upon the door before he could think better of it.

"Sorcha?" he wondered aloud. "Sorcha, are you –"

"C-come in," she sputtered, voice muffled by the thick wood of the door. "I am fine."

"You do not sound fine," Murdoch replied as he bowled into the room. By the fireplace sat Sorcha, shoulders hunched and arms curled around a wide metal bucket. A fine sheen of sweat covered her brow.

"I swear I –" she began, but then her eyes grew wide and she threw up into the bucket.

Murdoch rushed over, kneeling beside Sorcha to sweep her hair out of her face. "What have you eaten to cause such a sickness? You were fine earlier on."

When Sorcha finally stopped vomiting she let out three long, trembling breaths. She glanced at Murdoch for but a moment. "I have been like this for days now, though I have been lucky the nausea has hit me when you are in meetings with Lachlan."

"*Lucky?*" Murdoch bit out, incredulous. "Sorcha, what could possibly be lucky about –"

"I'm pregnant, Murdoch."

He froze.

Pregnant? If she is pregnant now, but has just seven months in which to carry the child before she becomes pregnant with mine, then...will she lose this baby? What was missing from the witch's prophecy?

But Murdoch could say none of this to Sorcha. Instead he forced a smile to his face, kissed her brow and said, "We must tell Lachlan. He will be thrilled."

He wished he had no reason to believe the Seelie king's happiness would be short-lived.

CHAPTER EIGHT

Lachlan

As Lachlan stared at Sorcha laughing and dancing away with Ailith he was struck by the realisation that he had never been as happy as he was in that precise moment. Everyone he cared about was close at hand, and safe, and *celebrating*.

I am going to be a father.

Lachlan would never have thought himself the type to possess a paternal instinct before. Even after he'd made the decision to ask Sorcha to bear him a child he hadn't been at all certain that he'd develop one. But now, with the knowledge that a baby was indeed on the way, all Lachlan could think about was being a father.

"My mother would not believe her eyes, to see me like this," he murmured, readjusting the delicately-woven golden circlet he was wearing to keep his hair securely away from his face. Lachlan stretched languorously, revelling in the comfort of the pit of pillows he was currently using as a throne, having ordered the iron-doored, underground room typically used by him in the late, late hours following a revel to be turned into a paradise befitting Sorcha for the evening.

All around soft, glowing lights floated from place to place, lazy and slow as if they were heavy with sleep. The air smelled of lilacs, bluebells and pine, for garlands of flowers and sweet-smelling berries were strung from every nook and crevice in the stone walls, and shelves of rock had been covered in fine cloths and a plethora of food and drink.

Lachlan had worked his own magic upon the bubbling, merry burn that snaked across the room, lending it an internal glow to match that of the phosphorescent mushrooms that grew in clusters alongside spears of gemstones in a multitude of colours.

A small fiddle band played in the centre of the room, having removed the cushions and blankets from the largest pit to turn it into a recessed stage. Around them all manner of Seelie danced and sang; Lachlan felt his entire being relax simply by watching them.

He was content. He was happy. He didn't want the night to end.

When Sorcha caught his eye she beamed, her face luminous in the green-and-blue light currently enveloping her frame. She did not wait for Lachlan to wave her over to break from her dance with Ailith to collapse beside him in the pit. Sorcha made to kiss Lachlan's cheek, though he turned his head just enough that her lips landed upon his own, instead.

"Fox!" came Murdoch's warning cry immediately, as if he had been standing behind Lachlan the entire time waiting for him to do something offensive; Lachlan would not have been surprised if that had indeed been the case.

The kelpie was quick to sit down by the edge of the pit, cross-legged and cross-armed and looking particularly unamused. But there was a flush to his cheeks that suggested Murdoch was tipsy, and his shirt had been undone to his navel.

"You look as if you've been more salacious than I have, horse," Lachlan said, wrapping an arm around Sorcha to pull her in closer. But she merely giggled, sliding out of Lachlan's grasp to sit precisely in the middle between him and Murdoch before grabbing both of their hands.

"The two of you must learn to get on," Sorcha insisted. She glanced at Murdoch. "You have enjoyed living in the Seelie Court, though you would never admit to it aloud. And Lachlan – you feel safer knowing you have a kelpie on your side, and you know it. Murdoch has proven again and again that he is trustworthy. So can't the two of you just be...friends?"

"Absolutely not!" they both bit out, which only made Sorcha laugh harder.

"You cannot say I have not tried, at least. Murdoch, why are you so dishevelled, anyway? Did that water nymph try and seduce you again?"

Lachlan barked at the notion. "Someone other than Clara found your dark and moody countenance attractive enough to proposition you *more* than once? I do not believe it."

"Murdoch Buchanan is a ladies' man," Sorcha said, grinning at Murdoch's murderous expression. "A real Lothario. Clearly even as a dead one he is irresistible to all manner of women."

"I think she hoped I might grant her part of the loch," Murdoch admitted, running a hand through his curly hair as he did so. Lachlan noted it was growing well past his ears again and wondered, not for the first time, if the kelpie himself decided whether his hair and stubble grew or whether it happened naturally.

I truly know nothing of the creature, Lachlan thought. *Perhaps it would not be a terrible idea to at least learn more about Murdoch in the years to come.*

"I thought you had already granted a faerie part of the loch," Sorcha said, starkly removing Lachlan from his own head.

He frowned at Murdoch. "You have? A *faerie?*"

"An Unseelie ghoul hardly counts as a faerie," the kelpie replied, flashing a look at Sorcha that screamed *Why did you tell Lachlan about that?*

Lachlan forced back a shiver at the notion of an Unseelie ghoul. They were foul creatures, and if this one lived in Loch Lomond instead of the faerie realm, then...

"Did they tell you why they were in your abode?"

Murdoch grimaced. "No, but from the little I have learned I do not imagine I want to. She was a witch, though, and a powerful one, so I imagine she performed some kind of unforgivable magic."

"And how have you come to –"

"If the two of you are going to discuss this until it becomes an inevitable argument then I shall continue dancing with Ailith," Sorcha cut in, turning first to Lachlan to kiss his cheek and then to Murdoch, who kissed her brow instead, before leaping out of the pit with a spryness Lachlan would not have expected from a pregnant woman.

Though she is not that far gone yet, he reasoned. *Now that the sickness has passed she will have a few weeks of respite before her belly truly begins to show.*

"Everyone believes it is Ailith who is pregnant, yes?" Murdoch asked the moment Sorcha disappeared, sliding down from his perch to sit as close to Lachlan as he could clearly bear.

Lachlan forced himself into a sitting position, sighing heavily. "Must we ruin this one evening of happiness with talk of the danger all of us are in?"

The kelpie did not answer; his dark eyes said everything Lachlan needed to know, though they were bleary from alcohol and faerie fruit.

He scratched his ear where his mother's bell-like, silver earring used to be. "Only my inner circle knows. Most everyone in this room believes Ailith to be the one carrying my child, yes. Which was difficult to pass off, given that we cannot straight-out lie."

"And you have quelled the rumours for why Sorcha and I are staying here?"

"The entire realm knows about her deal with Eirian, horse," Lachlan said, rolling his eyes. "They believe you are both here to try and stay away from him, which is the truth. What more could you want?"

Murdoch crashed onto his back, falling heavily through a flurry of pillows. When he resurfaced he looked throughly resigned. "For there to be a permanent solution to our problems," he said, so quietly Lachlan almost missed it. "I would live within the Seelie Court forever if it meant Sorcha never had to go to him."

It was Lachlan who did not have to reply with words this time. To have Sorcha live within his home for the rest of her life was all Lachlan had ever wanted. Even if that life was a mortal one. Even if it included a kelpie who had once tried to steal his throne – and his face.

With a long, slow stretch Lachlan got to his feet, then held his hand out to help Murdoch up. "Come," he said. "I fear Ronan will drink all the wine if we do not take some for ourselves."

The kelpie looked at him suspiciously. "We are not seriously becoming friends, are we? I cannot stomach such a thought."

Lachlan grinned a grin full of sharp teeth and devilish intent. "No, but we are comrades whether we like it or not, and as such I intend to show you how easily I can out-drink you."

"That sounds like something I can perhaps agree to," Murdoch said, pushing aside Lachlan's hand in order to stumble to his feet on his own, "though I most assuredly will be the one to out-drink *you*. I am a giant, monstrous horse, after all." He glanced down at his mostly-undone shirt as if considering buttoning it back up again, then shrugged and left it the way it was.

Comrades, Lachlan mused. They passed Sorcha and Ailith, who delighted in the sight of the Seelie king and the kelpie of Loch Lomond in each other's company without a fight breaking loose. *I can cope with comrades. It would make Sorcha happy, too.*

After all, that was all Lachlan wanted, and that was what she currently, undoubtedly was.

He did not want the night to ever end.

CHAPTER NINE

Sorcha

Within the underground revel time stood still, but deep inside Sorcha's bones she knew it was very, very late indeed.

Or early, as the case may be, she thought. *This is the faerie realm, after all.*

The celebrations were beginning to die down, faeries dropping where they stood to collapse across blankets and cushions and each other. Some of them were doing far more than simply sleeping, their soft laughter and sighs of pleasure from the shadows the only hint Sorcha needed to politely look away from their salacious activities.

In one corner lay a drunk and unconscious Murdoch, half-hidden in a mound of cushions with an exhausted but contented smile upon his face. Sorcha bit back a laugh at his dishevelled hair, wine-stained lips and unbuttoned shirt. He had lost his shoes at some point in the evening, and the ends of his trouser legs were wet, suggesting that he'd waded into the ethereal burn winding across the floor like a luminous serpent.

Sorcha had not seen the kelpie so relaxed in months – years, even. It hurt her heart to think of what her promise to the Unseelie king had done to him. But Sorcha could not regret saving Murdoch's life at the expense of half her own. Could *never* regret it.

She loved him more with every passing day. That he was alive because of her was perhaps Sorcha's greatest personal achievement.

"Would you like some sugared plums, Miss Sorcha? Miss Sorcha?"

Sorcha blinked in Ailith's general direction. It took her a while to spot the faerie, for she was nestled in the crook of her consort's arm. He was taller and broader than Lachlan – similar to Murdoch in stature – with soft brown hair and eyes to match. Sorcha vaguely recalled talking to him earlier in the evening and liking him well enough, though she found she could no longer remember their conversation.

She could not even remember his name.

I feel hazy, Sorcha thought. *I must be tired.* But the haziness felt different to exhaustion. Familiar, in a way Sorcha did not wish to acknowledge.

"No thank you, Ailith," she said, remembering to answer the faerie's question a moment too late. But if Ailith noticed Sorcha's obvious distraction she did not comment on it, choosing instead to beam at her before feeding her lover a sugared plum from the woven basket sitting on her lap.

A few minutes later both Ailith and her brown-haired companion fell into an easy sleep, so Sorcha drifted across the room following the path of the burn. It was then that she noticed Lachlan, snuggling a small mountain of cushions as if they were leaves and he was still a fox. His cheeks were rosy, his smile soft and innocent.

He looks so young, Sorcha thought. *Too young to be a father.*

But Lachlan had one-hundred-and-four years of life experience, whilst Sorcha had a meagre twenty-seven. Even taking into account that Lachlan was still a relative youth in faerie terms, she had no doubt that he would make a good parent. In the seven years that Sorcha had known him he'd demonstrated a willingness to learn, grow and compromise that was unrivalled by any human she had ever met – including her own father.

She placed a gentle hand across her belly, thinking of the child growing inside her.

"O can ye sew cushions," Sorcha murmured. A lone fiddler sent her a hopeful glance, lifting up his bow as if to join her song, but Sorcha merely shook her head and he lowered it, disappointed. *I will sing the full song to the babe when I feel their first kick,* she decided.

Sorcha had never imagined herself the maternal type; until perhaps a year ago she hadn't once considered the possibility of having children. But the thought of raising a family with a human Murdoch – to pass on the Darrow name to a new generation – had been too beautiful a dream to pass up. That Sorcha was now in a position to do the same for Lachlan brought her a happiness she could not put into words.

She gazed down at her stomach. Soon she would begin to show, and then the pregnancy would have to be kept hidden from the rest of the Seelie Court. Sorcha was no fool; she knew how important it was to stay safe and protected within the bounds of Lachlan's magic until the babe was born. To be taken by Eirian before then would be immeasurably dangerous.

"If you are a boy I will name you..." Sorcha began, but then she froze. She felt as if something was choking her, forcing her to keep her babe's name secret. Sorcha swung around wildly, wondering what was wrong. Behind her the lone fiddler began to play a heart-wrenchingly sorrowful melody.

That was when the shadows began to flicker.

Nobody else still awake seemed to notice them or, if they did, passed off the strangeness as a side-effect of faerie wine and revel madness. But Sorcha could see them. Could *hear* them.

No, she thought, stricken. She turned this way and that, intending to rouse Lachlan or Murdoch or Ronan and his guards, who should never have fallen asleep but were dozing together against a wall regardless, heads drooped low over their chests.

Leave them, a silky voice ordered, *and follow me.*

It was a voice Sorcha had not heard in five years. A voice she wished somehow to never hear again, despite her promise to the creature to whom it belonged. Though the voice had not spoken aloud, it felt very much as if it had come from behind the heavy iron door that prevented all but the most powerful faeries from entering and exiting the room.

But Sorcha Darrow was not a faerie.

Holding her hands over her ears, Sorcha tried desperately to retreat further into the underground room and away from the door, all the while flashing pleading glances at a group of nymphs who were somehow still awake. But they ignored Sorcha, choosing instead to continue dancing to the fiddler playing his ballad. With every note he coaxed from his strings Sorcha's feet insisted that she should follow the terrifying, seductive voice that had spoken to her.

She stumbled across the burn, feet away from Murdoch. *Just scream,* Sorcha thought. *Scream or kick his shoulder and he will –*

Follow me, the voice commanded once more, and Sorcha dropped her hands. She took a step forward. Another. Two more. Five. Before she knew it Sorcha was unlocking the door, fingers shaking as she fumbled with the lock and slid out of the room without so much as a glance back at Murdoch and Lachlan.

Sorcha tried to yell out but she couldn't make a sound. She tried to drag herself to a halt, or claw her nails across her skin to force a cry from her lips, but she had lost all control of her body. She walked up the heavy, carved stairs that led to the ground floor of the palace and glided down the corridors as if pulled by an invisible piece of string.

Very pale morning light filtered through unshuttered windows, causing Sorcha's eyes to water. She blinked tears away until she grew accustomed to the light, just in time to reach the grand front doors of the palace.

I cannot open them, she realised, a surge of relief washing over her. *They are too heavy. Just so long as –*

The doors swung open.

When Sorcha peeked outside she saw that one of the guards had opened them for her; before her very eyes he grew sleepy, then passed out on the gem-encrusted pathway.

How has he broken through Lachlan's magic? Sorcha wondered, horrified, as her feet resolutely marched her off the path and into the forest. The air beneath the trees was dark, wintry cold and entirely untouched by the morning sun. The grass and moss all around her was covered in frost, and it occurred to Sorcha as the ice stung her skin that she was barefoot.

Closer, the voice said, much louder this time. *Just a little closer.*

Sorcha had no choice but to grit her teeth against the cold biting at her hands and feet and face, the skirts of her gossamer and silk faerie-spun dress trailing behind her like fog rolling off the loch. Along with her wild hair, wide eyes and pale cheeks Sorcha half-imagined herself a ghost as she continued through the silent forest.

If you are a ghost then disappear, she thought, wishing she could close her eyes. *Disappear, and everything will be fine. If he cannot see you then he cannot find you.*

But such thoughts were in vain, and as Sorcha came across a clearing lit by a singular, slanting ray of light her heart grew heavy. For standing there in front of her was her doom, and she was walking right towards him.

He was dressed in regal, smoke-coloured armour shot through with starlight, and sat upon a dappled grey mare with soft eyes, a wavy mane and a calm, pretty face. With his winged, silver helm, braided hair and flowing white cape the King of the Unseelie Court looked every inch a knight in shining armour, the kind of which featured prominently in the stories Sorcha used to delight in reading with her father.

Except the faerie was no knight, and he was not here to save her.

A resplendent villain, Sorcha thought, taking a step towards the faerie despite herself, *but a villain nonetheless.*

"Come," King Eirian said, whisper-quiet. His mercurial eyes never left Sorcha's as he held out a hand to help her onto the back of his horse.

Sorcha had no choice but to obey his command.

The last thing she was aware of thinking before the Unseelie king urged his horse to hurtle through the forest, Sorcha clinging to him for dear, terrible life, was that she had not had the sense to tell both Murdoch and Lachlan that she loved them at the revel.

As a single raven feather fell from the heavens above, something deep inside Sorcha became certain she would never get to say such a thing to them again.

CHAPTER TEN

Murdoch

When Murdoch awoke his body was sore and his head was groggy. All around him the revel had died, with most of the attendants passed out in pits of cushions and silken sheets. He rubbed at his temple, the promise of a headache beginning to creep up on him, but Murdoch pushed it to the side for now.

How long was I out? he wondered, dragging errant curls of hair away from his face as he tried to work out how late it was. The soft, glowing lights that floated through the air before Murdoch passed out had whittled away to next to nothing, and the burn was no longer lit from within, but Murdoch's keen eyes were used to such darkness. The dull light from the phosphorescent mushrooms reflecting off quartz and topaz and tourmaline was more than enough for him to make sense of his surroundings.

Two pits of cushions to Murdoch's right lay a soundly sleeping Lachlan, on his back with limbs sprawled lazily around him. His bare feet were twitching as if he were chasing something through a dream.

Once a fox, always a fox, Murdoch thought, rolling his eyes before sweeping his gaze across the room. He spied Ailith in a corner, curled against the side of a tall, broad-shouldered faerie whom Murdoch now knew was her consort. Two members of Lachlan's guard were leaning against either side of a snoring Ronan, whose horns were stained with blackberry wine and decorated with twisting wreaths of ivy.

All of the musicians in the centre of the room were asleep, bar one, who was playing the softest melody upon his fiddle that Murdoch had ever heard. It was lulling the last of the revel-goers into unconsciousness, though a group of four or five nymphs insisted on dancing to the music even as they yawned and closed their eyes.

Everything was calm. Everything was quiet.

Everything was wrong.

There was no physical evidence to point to such a wrongness but the kelpie did not need any. Murdoch could feel it in his bones. In his stomach. In his heart.

He staggered to his feet, bile rising in his throat that had nothing to do with the excesses of the revel.

"Where is Sorcha?"

Murdoch's question had been quiet, yet there was a thunder in his voice that carried across the entire room, silencing the lone fiddler and halting the nymph dancers in one fell swoop.

A solitary golden eye became visible in the corner of Murdoch's vision; he turned to face Lachlan just as the faerie rolled over and leapt to his feet. The delicate circlet upon his head was at such a haphazard angle that the moment Lachlan took a step towards Murdoch it fell to the floor with a clamour. The sound echoed all around them, reverberating off the stone walls and returning to Murdoch's ears as a distorted, unsettling mockery of the original jingle of metal on stone.

Lachlan sniffed the air, ears pricked up to attention. He narrowed his eyes at Murdoch. "When did you see her last?"

"I do not know," he admitted, waving a hand uselessly around him. "You were still awake when I fell asleep. How long have you been unconscious?"

The Seelie king considered this for a moment, waving over Ronan and the two members of his guard who had been snoring softly but a moment ago. "What time is it?" he asked.

"Close to eight in the morning, going by the sound of the birds above us," one of the guards replied. The creature had huge, owl-like ears; clearly being underground was no barrier to them being able to hear the goings-on of the forest. They inclined their head politely at Lachlan. "You have not been asleep long, Your Majesty. But an hour or so. Queen Ailith was still awake with Miss Darrow at the time."

"And then what?" Murdoch demanded, stealing the words before Lachlan himself could ask the same question. "Where did she go? Why were you asleep when she was still awake?"

"I –" the owl-eared faerie glanced at their partner, then at Ronan, who grumbled as he tore away ivy from his horns.

"We do not know why we fell asleep," Ronan said, answering for all three of them before either Lachlan or

Murdoch had an opportunity to lose their temper. His eyes were bleary in a way that had nothing to do with alcohol.

Lachlan glanced at Murdoch. "He was here. He was *here*. In the Court."

"He might still be," Murdoch said, wasting no time in heaving open the iron door that nobody but Lachlan and Ailith could open.

Lachlan roused his queen with a gentle touch of her cheek; Ailith's eyes opened immediately. "Sorcha is missing," he said. Murdoch hated that he could hear a waver in the faerie's voice. "Search the east side of the palace with Ronan. The kelpie and I will take the west."

Lachlan did not give Ailith a chance to reply before he rushed out of the door with Murdoch in tow. The palace was deathly quiet; all Murdoch could hear was his and Lachlan's heavy, foreboding footsteps as they rushed down corridor after corridor. Early spring light filtered through the windows, painting the golden walls with heartbreakingly beautiful sunshine.

Too beautiful for this particular morning, Murdoch thought. *There should be rain. There should be a storm. There should be darkness.*

When Lachlan made an about-turn and veered towards the entrance to the palace Murdoch stumbled over his feet in shock. "You sense something?" he asked, watching the Seelie king as the faerie darted his eyes in most every direction.

His nose twitched. "I can smell her. She went outside."

"Being a fox is good for something, at least," Murdoch said, the rising panic in his throat turning him towards useless conversation in order to keep his wits about him.

Lachlan threw a raised eyebrow his way before struggling to push open one of the enormous front doors. Murdoch moved forward to lend his weight to the endeavour, and when the door slammed open the sound of it hitting the palace walls awoke a guard, who was strewn across the gemstone-encrusted pathway as if he'd had too much to drink.

Murdoch helped the faerie to his feet. "How long have you been asleep?" he asked.

The guard furrowed his brows against the morning light. "I was asleep? I don't remember...Your Majesty!" he cried the moment he spied Lachlan. He hurried into a bow. "King Lachlan, I do not know why –"

"How long were you asleep?" Lachlan asked, repeating Murdoch's question in decidedly clipped tones.

"L-less than an hour, going by the sun," the guard stammered.

"Did you see Miss Darrow?"

"Miss Darrow? I – yes," he said, very slowly. Horror paled his face as he realised what he had just said. "Something compelled me to open the door for her, and –"

"Damn it!" Lachlan cursed, sweeping past the guard to venture into the forest, Murdoch close behind.

For twenty minutes neither of them spoke a word. Lachlan followed his nose, and Murdoch dipped his fingers into every burn and pond they passed. But the water-dwelling creatures he spoke to seemed to have no memory of the last hour; they had nothing of use to tell

Murdoch.

Close to an hour later the kelpie had to admit that their search was fruitless. He had known, from the moment he awoke, that something was awry. Murdoch did not need a fox's nose or an owl's ears or a falcon's eyes to know what it was he knew.

He could not feel Sorcha anywhere.

When Murdoch came to a stop it took Lachlan a moment or two to realise he was not following him. The faerie paused, turning his head to look at Murdoch with an expression that screamed *do not say it.*

Murdoch said it anyway.

"She is gone, Lachlan. Sorcha is gone."

CHAPTER ELEVEN

Sorcha

The first thing Sorcha noticed about the Unseelie Court was that it was cold. The solstice revel she had attended five years prior had been attended by so many creatures that the bitter, winter air of the ancient ballroom had been kept at bay by a thousand bodies. Now she was surrounded by emptiness, and though it was near the end of March and spring had been upon the air back home Sorcha couldn't stop shivering.

All around her was eerie, suffocating silence as King Eirian slowed his grey mare to a halt in a cobblestone courtyard. Fog rolled across the stones, obscuring much of Sorcha's surroundings, but here and there she could see hints of a gargantuan, intimidating castle rising up to dwarf her very existence.

The horse let out several puffs of air, her muscles shuddering as the Unseelie king gracefully dismounted and held out a hand to help Sorcha off, too.

She did not take it.

"You cannot sit upon my horse all evening," Eirian said, chuckling softly as he removed his winged helm and shook his hair out of his face. "I have no doubt that you are tired, Miss Darrow, so come down and let me show you to your chambers."

For a long moment all she did was stare at him. King Eirian looked even paler and unnatural in the fog than he had done at the winter solstice revel, though Sorcha knew that it was her – not him – who was out of place. A faint sheen of sweat crossed the Unseelie king's brow; it brought out the blue undertones of his silvered skin, reminding Sorcha of fish scales beneath midnight waves.

Eirian frowned. "What are you thinking about, my mortal paramour? You have the most unusual expression on your face."

"I am – I am *not* your paramour," Sorcha bit out, indignant, finally breaking her silence. The words felt odd in her mouth; she had not spoken for hours and hours, though she had been screaming inside her head ever since Eirian stole her away from the Seelie Court.

A small smile flitted across his face. "Perhaps not. Perhaps I am getting ahead of myself. Either way, you must be freezing. Allow me to bring you inside."

Sorcha forced herself not to comment on the Unseelie king's presumption. With a flick of her wrist she swatted away his outstretched hand, gritting her teeth against her frozen muscles in order to slide down from the mare on her own.

The moment she dismounted a ghost of a faerie emerged from the fog to take the horse's reins, gently pulling the creature away until, in the space of a blink, she could no longer see the mare's soft grey hair nor hear her hooves clatter against the cobblestones.

When Eirian shirked off his thick, white cloak to drape it across Sorcha's shoulders she shrugged it off. "I do not need your false kindness," she said, marching forwards in what she hoped was the right direction. "You and I both know I promised half my life to you under duress. You are no gentleman, so do not act like one."

"You are bold, to speak to the King of the Unseelie Court in such a way," Eirian replied, tone entirely pleasant as he wrapped his hand around Sorcha's left arm to lead her towards the entrance to the castle. His talon-sharp nails dug through the sleeve of her dress to bite at her skin, though Sorcha resisted displaying her discomfort of the sensation on her face.

She did not look at Eirian as she said, "I see no reason why I should not say what I think to you. You cannot kill me, for doing so breaks our deal and frees Lachlan and Murdoch to destroy you. I do not imagine they would respond kindly to you torturing me, either."

Eirian's resultant laughter was so loud and gleeful that Sorcha flinched. It echoed all around the courtyard, even through the fog, and when the sound returned to Sorcha's ears it was warped and sinister.

The Unseelie king stopped in his tracks and turned to face Sorcha. His silver eyes flashed like knives, cruel and razor-sharp. "You have no idea what I can do to you, Miss Darrow," he said, tone as silky and dangerous as it had been at the solstice revel. "You are lucky I would very much prefer things remained civil between us. So civil, in fact, that you grow sick of it, and fall willingly into the Unseelie way."

"That will never happen," Sorcha replied, fighting to sound steady and unfaltering when in truth she was terrified. She had seen but a glimpse of the savagery of the 'Unseelie way' at the revel, and it was not something she ever wished to witness again.

Sorcha knew she would have no choice but to experience it again over the course of the next thirty years that Eirian owned.

The Unseelie king's mouth pulled into a smirk. "I am inclined to believe you," he said. "That is, in fact, what makes this entire deal so amusing. Now follow me, and let us get out of this cold."

So Sorcha followed him, for there was little else she could do. Momentarily she entertained the idea of fleeing simply to see what would happen, but ultimately Sorcha dismissed the idiotic notion. For she could finally think – and converse – properly; Sorcha could not remember a single prior encounter with the Unseelie king in which she had been in full control of her senses. She did not want to give him a reason to weave whatever magic was responsible for clouding her mind whenever he was around, or watching her through a raven, once more.

If she was going to spend half her life in the Unseelie Court, Sorcha Darrow would much rather be lucid and fully in control of herself. To lose her senses would spell doom, and it was not only her life that would suffer for it.

The baby, she thought, gulping back a sharp intake of breath as she finally *remembered* that she was pregnant. Eirian glanced over his shoulder at her as they ascended a helical staircase, but did not utter a word.

I have to be careful, she thought, a hundred times more anxious than she had been mere seconds ago. *He cannot find out. But how can I hide a pregnancy? I will begin to show soon. And then – and then –*

Sorcha could only pin her hopes on Lachlan, Murdoch and the members of the Seelie Court working out a solution to her impossible problem. Eirian had no claim to the baby, but he could just as easily kill the child the moment they were born. *But that will incite war. That will –*

"We are here."

When Eirian unlocked a large door made of ash and embellished with silver Sorcha hesitantly peered inside. The room was high-ceilinged and circular, with tall windows punctuating the stone facade facing east and west. Large swathes of the stonework were covered in tapestries; the floor was likewise adorned with all manner of furred and woven rugs.

A four poster bed larger than Lachlan's fit against the curve of the furthest part of the wall from the door. There was an obsidian fireplace built into a recess a few feet away from it; the flames within burned white-hot, chasing the chill from the air. Above the fireplace was a vast, frameless mirror, its edges clouded with age.

The smallest of touches on Sorcha's shoulder was enough to make her stumble into the centre of her new chambers.

Her prison.

"There is a washroom through there," Eirian said, waving almost lazily at a heavy maroon curtain that mostly obscured another ash door, "though the hot springs down below make for a far more pleasurable bathing experience."

Sorcha said nothing. She wondered if Eirian would simply leave her be if she remained silent, though when he turned her around to stare at her it became apparent that he would not.

"I suppose this is acceptable for thirty years or so," Sorcha commented, trying her best to remain unphased by the entire situation.

Eirian cocked his head to one side, silver-white hair flashing in the firelight as if it were made of stars. When he grinned Sorcha caught sight of his wicked canines, which were longer and sharper than Lachlan's. Everything about the Unseelie king was harder than his golden kin. Crueler. Sadistic.

It should have therefore come as no surprise to Sorcha when King Eirian raised an index finger to her forehead – the same one that had marked her with his blood five years ago, thus sealing her fate – and laughed very softly.

"Tell me: do you know what half of forever is?"

Sorcha's insides froze. When she tried to back away Eirian slid a hand behind her back, forcing her to stay put. "What are you talking about?" she asked, though Sorcha was not stupid. She knew exactly what Eirian was insinuating; it was simply that she could not fathom it.

It was the Unseelie king's turn to say nothing. A frown of concentration darkened his eyes, and all the laughter was lost from his lips. But a moment later his expression returned to one of amusement, and he lowered his finger from Sorcha's brow.

"It's said that when a human is turned immortal they steal their new lifetime from a faerie who was doing nothing with their own," he said, retreating towards the door as his eyes scanned Sorcha from her head to her toes. "So I wonder, Miss Darrow, that if there were some truth to the saying, who then might be the unfortunate creature from whom I stole their life to give to you?"

Something warm and faintly ticklish began to creep down Sorcha's inner thigh, followed by a spasm in her womb that she fought to keep to herself. Her heart was beating far too quickly, chest heaving in fear and horror.

No.

Oh, please, no.

Eirian smiled grimly, clearly enjoying the look of blank shock upon Sorcha's face, but he could not see the singular drop of blood that was beginning to run down the inside of her thigh that indicated she had lost something far more precious than her mortality.

"Enjoy forever, Miss Darrow," he cackled, closing the heavy ash door with a resounding slam as he left her new prison.

Blindly Sorcha rushed to the closest window ledge, though she could see nothing but fog through the glass. When another cramp hit her she collapsed, crumpling to the floor as she clutched her stomach and tried her hardest not to cry out. With every passing second more blood escaped her body, crawling and seeping down Sorcha's legs. She could do nothing to stop it; nothing to turn back time.

Sorcha Darrow's unwanted immortality had come at the cost of her baby.

CHAPTER TWELVE

Lachlan

Murdoch had barely made it into the throne room, dripping wet from his head to his toes, when Lachlan asked, "Anything, kelpie? Anything at all?"

The dark-haired man nodded his head, morose and exhausted. He had been jumping from loch to river to sea for thirty-six hours straight, looking for answers concerning Sorcha's disappearance. "A pair of selkies by Liverpool swore they saw Eirian upon the back of a grey horse, a woman in tow," he said. "An Unseelie near London said the same, though they did not wish to." A vicious, humourless grin spread across the kelpie's face, leaving Lachlan in no doubt about how the creature coerced the Unseelie to speak.

He tossed Murdoch a loaf of bread, which he enthusiastically tore into. Lachlan was just as tired and hungry as the kelpie was; he had spent much of the past day and a half scouring the forest and the outskirts of the Seelie Court for any witnesses to Sorcha's disappearance. Unsurprisingly there were none, though a faun claimed to have spied a raven flying overhead for hours and hours before it vanished from sight whilst the revel celebrating Sorcha's pregnancy was going on.

Most likely Eirian himself, looking for a weakness in our defences. My *defences.*

Lachlan leaned against a nearby column of stone, sliding down to the floor as he let out a long, low whistle of air. "So Eirian broached through our defences on a horse. He sent everyone still conscious to sleep and lured Sorcha out to meet him without having to enter the palace or alerting me to his presence. Damn the forest!" he cursed. "I thought we might actually be strong enough. I thought we could keep him at bay until – until –"

"Until your mortal wizard appeared and told us he couldn't help us?" Murdoch cut in bitterly, following suit and collapsing to the floor beside Lachlan. He stole the wineskin from the faerie's belt, gulping down half the contents before unceremoniously flinging it back at Lachlan.

He caught it without looking at it. "He might have had a solution," Lachlan insisted, though his voice was weak and lacked conviction.

"Yet he could not help you with your fox curse," Murdoch pointed out. "I thought you said the wizard admitted to not being well-versed with curses?"

"This is not a curse, though; it's a promise made under duress. There's a marked difference between the two."

The kelpie clucked his tongue. "What could a human do to wheedle out of a faerie promise? Wizard or not, mortals lack the years of experience needed to deal with your kind."

"Oh, but he was very well versed with *my kind*," Lachlan countered, bringing the wineskin to his lips and finishing what Murdoch had left for him. Though he knew the wine was deep and sweet and heady, Lachlan thought it rather tasted of ash and winter in his mouth.

"He had a way with words, my wizard," he added on quietly, thinking of Julian and his companion, Evie, with her hair spun from gold. "He knew what to say and what not to say to me. Do you know I owe him a favour for saving my life? If he can help us now I'll owe him a hundred of them, and gladly."

Murdoch thought about this for a long time. Eventually he said, "What if we can do nothing, Lachlan? What if Eirian's hold on half of Sorcha's life cannot be broken and –"

"She is carrying my *child*, Murdoch," Lachlan snapped, surprising even himself with his use of the kelpie's self-appointed name. "You think I would be able to rest, knowing that silver-skinned monster has – has –"

Lachlan couldn't finish the thought. He was ashamed to feel tears beginning to prick his eyes, so he turned his face away from Murdoch. *How could I have had a mere handful of joyous days before everything was torn from me? Sorcha, our child, our future...*

A silence stretched between the pair, during which time Murdoch wrung out his sodden sleevesr. For a few moments Lachlan listened to the water drip down to the floor. Then, because he realised his previous statement implied he only cared so much because of the babe in her womb, said, "I wouldn't give up on saving her even if Sorcha wasn't pregnant."

"I know."

Lachlan stilled. "You do?"

"Of course I do," Murdoch said, sighing heavily. Lachlan glanced at him; there were dark, purple-tinged shadows beneath the kelpie's eyes, making him look closer to death than to life. He looked haunted and hollow. Hopeless.

He looked exactly how Lachlan felt.

"I would be a fool to deny how much you love Sorcha," Murdoch continued, staring up at the ceiling with irises so black they seemed to absorb all the light from around them. "Just as you would be foolish to pretend my love for her does not run deeper than my love for the water – for my very being. And yet our feelings were not enough to keep her safe. If anything they were her downfall."

Lachlan considered this. *It is true Sorcha would never have become embroiled in all this had I never met her. But I cannot imagine my life without her in it. The kelpie must surely feel the same way.*

"Would you have revealed to her who you truly were, had I not shown up and interfered with your plan to act as Murdoch Buchanan?" he asked, genuinely curious.

The kelpie seemed surprised by the question. He ran a hand along his jaw, which was rough with stubble. "If I am honest I had not thought things through, at the time," he admitted. "I saw the man standing by the shore and acted on impulse. I'd only meant to consume him, not become him."

"But then you did."

He smiled. "I did, because of her. I wanted to meet

her. I'd always wanted to meet her."

"So why *hadn't* you? You could have taken on the guise of most anybody to meet Sorcha."

"Like I said, I did not plan it," Murdoch replied. "I thought I was content merely watching Sorcha from afar. But once I *had* met her...well, I lost all such notions of leaving her side."

Lachlan barked out a laugh. "So we are in agreement, then?"

"In agreement?" Murdoch frowned, confused. "Agreement of what?"

"That there is no situation in which either of us could not have her in our lives. Which means there is little point in mulling over whether things might have been different, once upon a time."

And though Lachlan felt like he might drown in his feelings of loss and helplessness and fear, he knew he was right. Drinking wine and ruing their life choices would not save Sorcha.

He stood up, sending a wave of drying magic Murdoch's way. The kelpie winced as he always did when faerie magic touched him. "Come," Lachlan said, indicating towards the door with a nod of his head. "The envoy I sent down to the Unseelie Court might have returned by now, and Ronan has been hard at work figuring how we might find a way to *fight* Eirian, should we fail to save Sorcha through other means. I imagine such a plan is of interest to you."

When Murdoch flashed the same murderous, blood-drunk grin Lachlan had seen upon his face the night they stormed through the Unseelie solstice revel he knew the kelpie was more than on board with such a plan.

"I am glad I did not turn you mortal back when you first asked, all things considered," Lachlan said as the two of them wound their way through the palace.

Murdoch cracked his knuckles, chuckling softly.

"I am inclined to agree with you, fox."

CHAPTER THIRTEEN

Eirian

Forty-eight hours had passed since Eirian stole away that which Sorcha Darrow treasured most: her mortality. He had been waiting five years to take it from her, and now those five years were finally, deliciously over.

And forever was only just beginning.

The Unseelie king's haunting of her over the past half a decade had successfully isolated Sorcha from most everyone she loved, until she could hardly focus on anything but the foreboding presence of a silver-eyed raven.

When Lachlan had decided to move Sorcha to his Court Eirian had admittedly been irked. The young king's power grew with every year he sat upon his throne, and it had been no easy task for his silver counterpart to infiltrate the Seelie side of the faerie realm. But Eirian had managed it, and now he had the mortal who so foolishly promised half her life away in order to save the Seelie king and the dark, dangerous kelpie of Loch Lomond.

Now that Sorcha had lost her mortality, the unfortunate girl was a hostage Eirian could use until the end of time; a threat to keep both Lachlan and the water horse firmly in their place.

Beneath my feet.

"You have not moved an inch in two days, little bird," Eirian murmured, swirling a fingertip across the surface of the tall, mottled mirror through which he was observing Sorcha in her room. He could only see her back, for the mirror in her chambers was behind her, and though her stillness piqued Eirian's curiosity he had resisted visiting Sorcha during the past forty-eight hours. He had sent no servants to her with food or water or warm clothes, either, in the hopes of forcing the woman to leave the confines of her room of her own volition.

But Sorcha had not moved.

Behind him the crack of a whip and a wretched, high-pitched scream filled the air, curling Eirian's mouth into a cruel smile. He rose from the mirror, smoothing down the front of his shirt before sweeping across the torture chamber to face the source of the anguish.

A torn, bloodied slip of a faerie limply hung from her shackles. Beside her stood a pointed-nosed Unseelie, who sneered at her before snapping his long, leather whip across her chest once more. She was cut to ribbons; Eirian knew the unfortunate creature would be left with no skin at all once her torture was over.

The faerie was an envoy, sent by Lachlan to ensure Sorcha was untouched and in good health. The Unseelie king had no qualms, of course, about leaving him entirely in the dark on the matter of the safety of his human consort.

And flaying the yellow-gold faerie who had been sent to shed light on the matter.

"He should have sent nobody at all, until he had a promise from me that no messengers would be harmed," Eirian said, mostly to himself. It seemed like folly on Lachlan's part, though he reasoned the fox might simply be acting rashly over his fear for Sorcha's wellbeing.

She would be faring much better if she submitted to her fate and dared to leave her room, Eirian thought, leaving the torture chamber to head for the woman's room in question. In truth he expected nothing less from Sorcha than to be hard-headed and wilful; her choosing not to move even for food and drink and rest was not so impossible a decision. But it still felt odd. Wrong. Out-of-sorts.

Something was going on with Sorcha Darrow, and Eirian had grown impatient to discover just what exactly that was.

When he reached the door to her chambers Eirian paused, hand on the carved silver handle as he considered what he might do if the woman inside refused to speak to him. *I could cloud her mind as I have done before,* he reasoned, *though that takes a fair amount of concentration on my part...as well as diminishing how fun it is to tease and torment her.*

But when Eirian finally opened the door and took in the sight of Sorcha by the window all such thoughts vanished. For the pale, weightless material of her dress was bloodied around her thighs, and her expression was so hollow that for a moment the Unseelie king genuinely believed that Sorcha Darrow had killed herself. Then she blinked, and he breathed a small sigh of relief.

"What have you done, foolish lass?" Eirian asked, closing the distance between them to loom over Sorcha. The skin beneath her eyes had purpled like bruises; when she looked lifelessly up at him she looked more a ghost than a human.

"It is none of your concern," she croaked through lips that were as cracked and dry as her throat. Her bottom lip had split open, revealing a flash of scarlet blood.

When Eirian bent down to investigate what she'd done to herself Sorcha flinched away so quickly that he was taken entirely by surprise. He frowned. "I will not harm you" he said. "I merely -"

"Stay away from me!" Sorcha cut in, baring her teeth as if she were a trapped animal. Eirian supposed she likely felt like one, but he had no patience to deal with such behaviour. He grabbed at the skirt of Sorcha's dress, ripping most of it away even as she continued to scrabble away.

Eirian scowled. "All I want to do is heal whatever mess you've made of - oh."

Oh.

He had expected to see welts or cuts across Sorcha's thighs - evidence that she had deliberately hurt herself in retaliation for him spiriting her away and turning her immortal. There had been too much blood soaked into her dress for it to be explained away as the natural bleeding a woman experienced with every turn of the moon, after all.

But there were no cuts. No bruises. The blood had come from within her, spilling down her thighs until it dripped down onto the stone floor. For a moment Eirian did not know what to say, for he was not sure what was going on.

Kelpies cannot father children, he thought, staring hard at Sorcha even as she looked away, eyes too bright with the promise of furious tears. *And it was only just announced that Ailith was pregnant with the heir to the –*

"You were the one carrying Lachlan's child," Eirian murmured, voice soft and very gentle as he let go of the torn, bloodied material of Sorcha's dress to kneel by her side. Inside he was roaring with delight; he could not have asked for a better turn of events. There was no torture Eirian could imagine that would destroy his rival more than the loss of his own child.

But, for now, Eirian kept such gleeful thoughts to himself. Sorcha was one bad day away from madness, and he rather did not want her to stoop to such levels so soon. With a sigh he scooped the woman into his arms and got to his feet, tightening his hold on her when Sorcha struggled and pushed against his chest.

"Do not fight me," he warned. "All I am doing is taking you down to the hot springs to clean you up. You cannot languish like this for any longer."

"I can *languish* however I want," Sorcha choked, throat full of tears but otherwise dry as bone.

Eirian cast a glance at her, though Sorcha's green-and-blue eyes did their absolute best to avoid his gaze. She looked small and insubstantial in his arms, her bloodied, white dress making her look altogether like a sacrifice to the Christian devil, saved from the alter with but seconds to spare.

His mouth was a hard line as he said, "I will not allow you to sit there and wait to die. Either you clean yourself, feed yourself and get some sleep, or I will do all three for you."

Sorcha did not reply; it was clear from the look on her face that she did not like either option. When finally they reached the hot springs, however, a glint of interest lit up her face, and she pushed herself once more out of the Unseelie king's arms.

Eirian smiled as he let her go. "I had a feeling you would like it down here. Now, would you –"

"Leave me alone," Sorcha said, not looking at him. Her eyes were fixed on the scene in front of her: a dark forest, nestled in the very centre of the castle with the midnight sky high above it. Steam filled the air, snaking across the floor and around the trees, obscuring the actual hot springs from sight.

Eirian's temple twitched at Sorcha's insolent tone, though he merely gave her a mocking bow and retreated. "As you wish, Miss Darrow. I shall send someone down with more appropriate clothing for you."

Sorcha did not reply; she had already disappeared into the steam, as if she had never existed at all.

"A strange one indeed," the Unseelie king muttered as he turned and left the forest. "A strange one, and a difficult one, but I shall break her."

After all, Eirian loved nothing more than a challenge.

CHAPTER FØURTEEN

Lachlan

Lachlan did not notice Ailith, even when she bent low to plant a kiss on his cheek. It was only when she spoke hushed, soothing words into his ear that he realised he was not alone.

"I may have a way you can see Miss Sorcha."

He stared at her without seeing her; Lachlan had spent many a sleepless night trying to reach Sorcha in her dreams over the past three weeks to no avail. Not a single envoy he had sent to the Unseelie Court had returned, either, meaning Lachlan had no idea how Sorcha was or she was being treated. He knew that if he went down to speak to King Eirian the Unseelie king would almost definitely refuse to grant him an audience with Sorcha, and would instead likely use the opportunity to torment him.

Lachlan therefore could not fathom how Ailith had possibly worked out a way he could see the mortal woman he loved.

His assurances to Murdoch that they would work out how to save Sorcha and fight Eirian had fast become empty words; with no information coming through on the state of the Unseelie Court Lachlan, the kelpie and Ronan could not construct a sound plan of attack against the silver king. And there was still no word from Julian despite Lachlan's messengers finally locating the wizard's abode, for the man had not been home in some time. Every new blow resulted in a hopelessness seeping into Lachlan's soul which he could do little to quell.

I am running out of what few options I thought I had.

"Lachlan? Lachlan, are you listening to me?" Ailith asked, no hint of scorn or impatience in her voice. Her eyes were soft and gentle as they watched Lachlan's every move, though a frown darkened the lovely blue of her irises.

"I am, as always, open to any and all ideas," he finally sighed, collapsing into the embrace of a velvet-lined armchair that perfectly imitated the ones in the Darrow drawing room. He had grown fond of the chairs over the years; now that Sorcha was gone Lachlan found himself spending more and more time sitting upon his replica instead of his throne.

Ailith chuckled as she perched upon the armrest. "It is gratifying to see how much confidence you have in my idea," she said, "though given the current state of events I am inclined to forgive you."

Lachlan's only response was a pointed look.

Ailith swept his hair out of his face with careful, unwavering fingers. "How would you feel about being a fox for a few hours?"

"I – excuse me? A *fox*?"

"You heard me," Ailith said, a slow smile spreading across her face. "I have been thinking on it for a while – how you might creep into the Unseelie Court unnoticed. King Eirian only seemed able to broach *our* defences in the form of a raven, if the faun in the forest is to be believed."

"But we do not know for sure that the raven was –"

"Ah, but we have another piece of evidence that suggests it was," she cut in.

Lachlan furrowed his brows. "And what, exactly, is this evidence you speak of?"

"You."

His frown deepened. "I must admit that you have lost me, Ailith. What do you mean that *I* am the evidence?"

Ailith shifted from the armchair to stand in front of Lachlan. She placed her hands over his own, squeezing them in barely-contained excitement. "Seven years ago you stalked back into the Seelie Court in the form of a fox, and both Innis and Fergus did not notice."

"But that was because the kelpie was wearing my skin," Lachlan countered. "He –"

"Was still not *you*. That you were able to re-enter the Court without alerting anyone to the presence of a powerful faerie tells us that it is indeed possible to do so. It lends credence to the idea that Eirian was that raven. He only reverted to his true form once everyone powerful enough to stop him had been lulled to sleep. And if he can do that..."

"Then I can," Lachlan finished, no longer frowning.

Ailith's idea was outlandish and dangerous, but it was also the best idea Lachlan had heard in weeks. He bit his lower lip as he thought things through. "I would have to remain a fox whilst inside the Unseelie Court," he murmured. "I do not have the talents someone as old as Eirian has in putting a hoard of faeries to sleep. He will notice my presence if I turn back into a faerie."

"Then it is a good thing Miss Sorcha is very familiar with your fox form," Ailith said. With a tug on Lachlan's hands she pulled him to his feet. "Come, there is no time to waste. Once you are transformed I can transport you to the outskirts of the Unseelie Court. The faster you leave the faster you can reach Miss Sorcha and check on her health...and the babe's."

Lachlan winced. He had tried his level best not to think about his unborn child, though he had not slept for longer than two successive hours because of the difficult subject. He trusted Sorcha to keep her pregnancy hidden as best she could. *But soon...*

Soon she will no longer be able to.

"The hor-Murdoch is still in the loch," Lachlan said, forcing himself to think of more than his own worries and desires for a moment. "Perhaps I should wait for his return in case he has any messages he wishes to pass on."

But Ailith shook her head. "He has been gone almost two days, Lachlan, and he did not say when he would return. I believe he would understand the urgency with which you need to reach Miss Sorcha."

Lachlan did not need to be told twice. "All right," he said, inspecting his gaunt reflection in a mirror before remembering that Sorcha – if he managed to reach her at all – would see him as naught but a fox. "All right. Let's do this. Turn me into a fox, Ailith."

*

Lachlan hardly had time to process Ailith's magic before he found himself unceremoniously dumped on the shadowy outskirts of a thorny, wicked-looking briar of dead brambles. He rolled to his feet – disconcerted to discover how easy it was for him to ease back into having four of them instead of two – and snapped his teeth.

"Twelve hours and counting," Lachlan muttered, the words coming out as half a bark. That was how long Ailith could give him, though he doubted he'd need longer than that to find Sorcha. She would be in Eirian's castle, no doubt, and though Lachlan was not all that familiar with the place he *was* familiar with Sorcha's scent. With the nose of a fox it would be easy to track her.

He simply needed to stay hidden whilst he did so.

I should be glad for this fog, Lachlan thought, taking a few careful steps beneath the dark, twisted trees that surrounded the castle. *It will keep me concealed. But I mislike it nonetheless.* The fog was freezing, even through his fox fur, and when Lachlan tried to shake off the cold he became aware that he was growing damp.

"Wonderful," he growled, before deciding to remain silent for the rest of his search. A wily faerie would be able to sense that another faerie was nearby, after all, though they would have no idea how strong or important said faerie was.

Lachlan thought back to the cursed fox he had met seven years ago; he had been able to intermittently smell a faerie upon the air, because the poor creature was close to losing himself entirely. But Lachlan had only been able to track him because he knew he was searching for a fox that was not a fox; if an Unseelie sensed him now they would have no idea that the faerie they were aware of was hidden in the guise of an animal.

Which I must use to my advantage at every turn.

Over the course of two hours Lachlan traversed the thorny forest until he came upon the castle itself, sniffing at the cold, dead stones until he found several of them that were warm and teeming with life. Steam curled from the cracks between them, intermingling with fog and soaking Lachlan in condensed rainwater. He shook himself as dry as he was able to, nose to the ground as he searched for a weakness in the earth to grant him passage to the castle.

And then he heard it – the sound of running water, almost swallowed in its entirety by the fog. Lachlan skittered towards it, stopping when he reached a narrow burn crawling *out* of the castle through a small grille in the wall. Plumes of steam wafted off the water's surface, and when Lachlan placed a curious paw within it he found that the water was warm.

I can make it through there, he thought, cocking his head to regard the grille before burrowing between two of the bars. It was a struggle, though, and for one horrible, drawn-out moment Lachlan was sure he was stuck. But the sound of two perimeter guards approaching was the panicked impetus he needed to push through, and with a rushed exhalation he squeezed between the metal bars.

Lachlan held in a splutter of relief as he crept along the bed of the burn, keen eyes adjusting to the glum air with every step he took. Black pines and wispy willow trees surrounded him, turned ghostly with ever more steam. When the burn began to deepen Lachlan nimbly jumped out of it and followed its path, veering to the left when it began to widen into a pool. He could hear what sounded, bizarrely, like a waterfall in reverse, and Lachlan realised a moment before he saw it what was responsible for the noise.

A hot spring.

He had never been in this part of Eirian's castle before, though it did not surprise him that the king possessed such a lovely secret within his walls. Even in the height of summer the Unseelie Court was generally cold and foreboding; it made sense that there was at least one warm place in the castle at all times of the year.

Then Lachlan heard a splash, and he retreated into the cover of the trees. But he could not smell a faerie, though all the water around him made it difficult for Lachlan to smell anything at all. Curious despite himself, he edged back towards the water, sniffing this way and that until –

Sorcha. I can smell Sorcha.

Lachlan wasted no time in running around the water, following her scent as it got stronger and stronger until, finally, he caught sight of her. Sorcha was sitting below a willow tree, legs dangling in the steaming pool in front of her with her dress hitched around her waist. Her eyes were closed; her breathing slow. Lachlan wondered for a moment if she was asleep, but then Sorcha sighed and slumped her shoulders.

His heart ached to watch her. Her cheeks were gaunt and pale, and her collarbone protruded outwards more than it had done when Sorcha had been stolen away. Lachlan grew furious thinking about Eirian starving her, then pushed all notions of the Unseelie king away. He was here to talk to Sorcha about herself and their baby, not the villain who had taken her.

Lachlan wondered how to announce his presence to the mortal woman. His bushy tail twitched, and as he shifted his weight from his left paws to his right it occurred to him that he was nervous. *This is not the time for immature, human emotions,* he chastised, taking another step towards Sorcha. He shook out his fur again, causing it to stand on end before the steam curling all around him began to flatten it once more.

But Sorcha did not hear his silent approach, and with her eyes closed she could not see him. So Lachlan swallowed, pushed his nervousness to the side, and did the only thing he could think of doing.

He sang.

"But to see her was to love her;

Love but her, and love forever," Lachlan began, keeping his voice as soft as a whisper in a dream. Sorcha's eyes flew open, looking around wildly until she spied the orange fur and pointed nose of the fox mere feet away from her. She stared at Lachlan in disbelief.

"Had we never lov'd sae kindly," Sorcha replied, singing the next line of the song with a voice full of tears.

"Had we never lov'd sae blindly," Lachlan echoed back.

"Never met – or never parted –

We had ne'er been broken-hearted."

An insurmountable pause. And then –

"Lachlan!" Sorcha cried, crushing him against her chest when Lachlan leapt into her arms. She buried her face in his ruff, sobbing without restraint. "I couldn't –

how did you –"

"I am a fox," Lachlan replied with a confidence entirely put on for Sorcha. "Of course I was going to find a way to reach you. But I fear we do not have long; I cannot risk being spotted. So tell me, Clara, how are you?" When Sorcha lifted her head she looked thoroughly miserable. Lachlan nipped at the end of her nose. "He is not starving you, is he? You look about ready to faint!"

"No, I – I have been given plenty to eat," Sorcha said, wiping away her tears with the back of a hand, "but I haven't had much of an appetite. I –"

"You have to keep your strength up, Clara!" Lachlan insisted. "Eirian wins if you are kept meek and submissive. And the baby –"

"I lost the baby."

"...needs all the – what?" Lachlan stared at Sorcha, not quite believing the last words to have been emitted from her mouth.

He was numb.

He was empty.

He didn't know what to do.

"What did you...the baby?" he said, though the words felt flat and useless. "You lost the baby?"

"I do not think – it was not my f-fault," she wailed, which crushed Lachlan's heart to hear. He could mourn later, on his own. For now he had to support Sorcha through her loss.

"Of course it isn't your fault, Clara!" he said, gently licking her tear-stained cheek and tasting salt. "There are always risks with pregnancy, and for faerie children even more –"

But Sorcha violently shook her head, cutting Lachlan off. "I do not mean it like that. I – Lachlan – *he* took our baby! He stole the child's life to make me immortal. He...he means to keep me here forever."

Lachlan went limp in Sorcha's arms. For most of the past seven years he had longed for his mortal companion to willingly live forever with him – for her to *choose* to strip away that most fundamental part of her humanity so that he could love her until the end of time. But in the beginning he had not intended for Sorcha to be able to choose; he had wanted to use her full name to enchant her to his side.

Now that Eirian had taken Sorcha's mortality from her, Lachlan realised just how villainous his original intentions had been towards her.

"We will work this out," he said, though the words were empty. "There is a solution. We can –"

"But I cannot be turned mortal again, can I?" Sorcha countered. There was a darkness clouding her eyes that Lachlan hated to see. "The process is irreversible one way or the other. That was what you told Murdoch, was it not? When he wanted to be turned human."

Lachlan said nothing. It was true, and they both knew it. But he didn't want this to be how things ended – Eirian winning against him in the most wicked, underhanded way possible at the expense of Sorcha losing most out of everyone.

He rubbed his muzzle against Sorcha's face. "Do not lose hope yet," he whispered. "You saved me from my curse when the situation seemed impossible. Allow me to do the same for you, Clara. Please –"

Lachlan flinched; he could smell a faerie upon the air. Going by the way Sorcha stilled she had sensed the new presence, too.

"Go," she mouthed, kissing the top of his head for but a moment before Lachlan slid out of her grasp and darted through the trees towards the grille in the wall. To his relief the faerie presence did not follow him, and when he escaped the warmth of the hot springs for the bitter chill of the fog outside he could no longer smell the creature at all.

Lachlan ran from the castle. He ran through the forest, and when he reached the bramble briars he ran some more. He did not stop running until his fox form finally dissipated and, even then, he continued on two feet back to the Seelie Court.

Every step away from Sorcha was worst than the last, and the further Lachlan got from her the more her confession weighed upon him.

Our baby is lost.

CHAPTER FIFTEEN

Murdoch

So much for living as a mortal, Murdoch thought as he ploughed through the loch. *I have spent more time in my true form than my human one ever since Sorcha was taken away.*

Murdoch had just returned from a five-day-long trip around the waters of Great Britain, scouring for gossip and scraps of overheard conversation that would give him a clue about how Sorcha was faring and what King Eirian was currently plotting. That none of Lachlan's envoys had returned from the Unseelie Court unnerved Murdoch to no end, and he could not bear to rest on his laurels and wait for news that may never come.

But the kelpie was exhausted from his journey – and starving. It was poor etiquette to hunt in another kelpie's territory, so Murdoch had not eaten for days. Now that he was on his home turf he was determined to fit in a hunt before returning to Lachlan and his Court, where he would doubtless be disappointed by the lack of news concerning Sorcha.

It is hardly as if I found out anything, either, Murdoch thought as he slowed his pace through the loch, drifting upon the lazy springtime currents to listen out for any humans taking advantage of the warm afternoon sunshine close to the shore. The water was still freezing, of course, for the snow sitting atop the mountains had finally melted into the loch, but Murdoch had found that the bite of the water did little to deter those most determined to swim.

A kick somewhere above his head and a squeal of delight alerted Murdoch to the fact that a child had jumped into the loch, closely followed be their complaining elder sibling. They were easy prey; for a starving kelpie there could be no better meal.

But they were children, and Murdoch had gradually lost his stomach for eating them ever since he began living with Sorcha Darrow. Now that Sorcha was pregnant the thought of dragging babes to their doom made him feel sick.

It made him feel monstrous.

"You have lost your touch, kelpie."

Murdoch retreated from the shore into darker, deeper waters before materialising and turning to face the Unseelie witch who had spoken. He expected her to grin her bizarre, twisted grin at him, as she usually did, but the creature appeared uncharacteristically serious.

In her hands was an adult leg – a man's, going by the size of it – which she promptly threw in Murdoch's direction. He snapped and gnashed his teeth at it, devouring every last morsel of flesh and bone in a matter of seconds. The Unseelie watched him do so with gleaming, silver eyes; she nodded in satisfaction when Murdoch finished eating.

"You have been away awhile," she said. "I had a notion you would be hungry."

Murdoch growled softly, though there was no malice behind the sound. "And why would you concern yourself with my appetite, faerie?"

"How often must we attest that we are friends before you trust me?" she asked, visibly affronted.

"Forever," Murdoch replied. And then, with some reluctance: "Regardless, thank you. You are right; I have lost my touch. I cannot bear the thought of devouring a child."

"Understandable, given the circumstances."

Murdoch eyed her suspiciously. "Maybe so. You have no qualms with eating children, I presume."

The faerie merely laughed, insidious and sinister. She swam away from the shore and the children, in the direction of the waterfall pool that connected the loch and the forest, looking behind her every so often to ensure Murdoch was following her. He complied, if only because it was clear the Unseelie either had something she wanted to say or show him.

"What have you learned about the Unseelie Court during your travels?" she asked after a while, genuinely curious. Murdoch recalled that the witch was not supposed to have any contact with faeries – Seelie *or* Unseelie – and that she had to rely on any new information reaching her ears through outlaws, passers-by and unfortunate victims of her insatiable appetite.

Or visions, he mused, thinking of the one the creature had shared with him. Less than six months remained before Sorcha was supposed to become pregnant with Murdoch's child, if he was to believe what the witch had seen, though given Sorcha's current state of imprisonment Murdoch was beginning to seriously doubt the prophecy.

"Eirian has not left his castle since he hid Sorcha within its walls," Murdoch finally replied, voice quiet and insubstantial in the water. "Every creature who isn't a member of his Court that has entered the castle has not been witnessed leaving. That is all I know."

Murdoch wished he had learned more during his scouting mission; alas, it had been difficult enough to find a water nymph who both lived close to the Unseelie Court and had been willing to talk. He could only hope that Lachlan had learned more than the kelpie had during his absence, though Murdoch was not feeling hopeful about this.

"Hmm," the Unseelie witch murmured, carefully traversing the narrow stream that connected the loch to the waterfall pool. When she reached the pool itself she cast a furtive glance all around, then relaxed when it became clear nobody was nearby. She sighed happily. "I have not been so close to the faerie realm in decades, kelpie. And I would not dare to, were you not with me."

"I am glad to be of service, I suppose," Murdoch replied, checking for himself that there truly was nobody around before reverting to his human form. He broke through the surface of the water, shivering in the chilly air beneath the shade of the trees, then hauled himself out of the pool to lie on a patch of grass illuminated by the afternoon sun. His sodden shirt and trousers soon began to dry, and eventually Murdoch began to feel more like a human and less like a monstrous water horse.

"Will you really become mortal for your lass?" the

faerie asked after a long stretch of not-unpleasant silence, as if reading his mind.

Murdoch replied almost immediately, with a surety he had never experienced before falling in love with Sorcha. "Yes."

A pause. And then: "I have a way that you can save her from the silver king."

"You – what?!" Murdoch cried, sitting bolt upright to stare at the ugly, wretched creature who was in turn watching him intently. She reached the bank of the pool, rested her head on silver-scaled arms and closed her eyes for slightly too long to have been blinking. When she opened her eyes again her pupils had contracted to pinpricks, leaving naught but mercury in her bulbous eyes.

"Upon a horse with a king and a babe in tow she went, and upon a horse with a king and a babe in tow she can return," the witch said, voice terrifyingly beautiful and seductive just as it had been when she'd voiced her original vision to Murdoch. "Under no other circumstances can you break her promise with the Unseelie king. But recreate such circumstances exactly, and he cannot demand her back."

Murdoch chewed over the witch's words carefully. He had heard of a tale akin to this before – of a mortal man stolen from his true love by a faerie queen, and his love's quest to retrieve him. In truth he'd thought it sounded ridiculous and over-complicated, but that was exactly how the rules of the fae worked.

And, after all, Murdoch was a horse, and Lachlan a king.

Slowly, surely, a giddy grin began to creep across his

face, and Murdoch rose to his feet. "This is...I can make that work. Lachlan and I can make that work. I – how can I thank you?" he asked, euphoria filling every corner of his body as the Unseelie witch grinned right back.

She laughed. "Oh, you can thank me in due time. Only do not forget me, when you have your lovely lady back."

"I could live another five hundred years and not forget you," Murdoch replied, not caring when a broken branch prodded the bottom of his shoeless feet. He had always returned to his human form by the Darrow house; this was the first time in a long time he had done so within the confines of the forest. He glanced at the witch. "Though I sincerely hope I do *not* live for another five hundred years."

"A pity," the Unseelie said. "A real pity. Well, you best be off to tell the Seelie king the good news. Best of luck to you, kelpie."

With a final nod Murdoch turned and fled through the forest, darting beneath the trees with a grace he had never before experienced upon two feet. He was impatient to reach the Seelie Court; to regale Lachlan and Ailith with his news.

They could save Sorcha. They were *going* to save Sorcha, and Lachlan's baby, too.

But when Murdoch caught a glimmer of golden skin half an hour later he paused in the midst of his mirthful run, frowning at the figure staggering through the forest just ahead of him. "...fox?" he called. When the faerie in question turned to see who had shouted Murdoch called out again, more confidently this time. But something was wrong.

Lachlan was crying.

Murdoch's very blood froze in his veins. "What is wrong?" he asked, fearful of the answer Lachlan would give. The Seelie king's eyes were red-rimmed and terrible; Murdoch had never seen his face so pale before. "Lachlan, what has happened?"

A few seconds of anguished silence. And then: "T-the baby," Lachlan stuttered. "She lost the baby."

CHAPTER SIXTEEN

Lachlan

"No."

"It is true," Lachlan said, which was a pointless thing to say given that he could not lie. But Murdoch was looking at him as if he had spoken nonsense – as if he could not understand the words Lachlan had uttered.

Lachlan hated that he was crying. He hated even more that, upon realising what he was doing, the tears fell heavier than before and Lachlan with them, collapsing to his knees even though he had an audience consisting of the one creature he never wished to display weakness in front of.

The kelpie's pitch-black eyes grew wide at the sight of him. "What happened, Lachlan?" Murdoch asked, surprising Lachlan by using his actual name for the second time in as many minutes. "How do you – did an envoy finally return?"

Lachlan shook his miserable head. Above him the sun filtered through the trees, warming his skin and hair even though his very core was frozen. It was as if he was stuck in the cold, unrelenting fog of the Unseelie Court, never to remember what heat felt like again.

"I saw her, kelpie," he finally said. "Ailith had the idea of turning me into a fox so I could sneak into the Unseelie Court unnoticed. And it...it actually worked. I wish we had thought of the idea sooner. I wish..."

"There is no point wishing for anything now, fox," Murdoch said. He sat down upon the forest floor in front of Lachlan, face constructed into something resembling control. But Lachlan could see right through the veneer; Murdoch was inches away from breaking down just as Lachlan had.

Once he told him what Eirian had done to Sorcha, he imagined the kelpie's control would melt away entirely.

Murdoch's expression darkened at Lachlan's foreboding silence. "For the love of the forest speak clearly," he demanded. "I cannot read your mind. What exactly happened? Do not keep secrets from me now!"

"...immortal," Lachlan mumbled, looking away as he spoke. He could not bear to face the kelpie as he acknowledged the Unseelie king's evil act with his own words – his own voice. "Eirian took Sorcha's mortality away, and she – she lost our –"

The sentence ended in a string of incomprehensible sobs. Lachlan did not think he had ever cried so much; he had not believed it *possible* for him to do so. They wracked through his body, bending him double and stabbing at his stomach like knives instead of tears. "O-our child," he stammered, "the magic took the babe away."

It was Murdoch's turn to be silent. Lachlan was vaguely aware of the man's ragged, accelerated breathing, as if the mere action of processing what Lachlan had said was painful. *That is because it is,* he thought, wishing he could turn back into a fox simply so he could claw away at his own stomach. *I have never been in so much pain.*

"...does he know?" Murdoch eventually asked. "The Unseelie king, I mean. Does he know Sorcha lost –"

"There was no time to ask about it," Lachlan replied, his words more a croak than anything else. He gulped, and forced himself to straighten his back against the tree he was sitting by, and when he wiped away the tears from his eyes Lachlan found that he could discuss the topic at hand so long as he dealt with it in as detached a manner as possible.

"But she is alive and well, save for the fact she has lost her appetite," he continued numbly. "I told her she has to keep up her strength, but now...I wonder if she even wants to. Clara never wanted to be immortal."

Murdoch banged a fist against the earth beneath him. A low, rumbling snarl began in the back of his throat – a sound Lachlan had only heard from him in his true form before. It was thoroughly discomfiting to hear such a sound emitted from the mouth of a human.

Except Murdoch was not human, and Lachlan had never been gladder for it.

"He did not break the tenets of Sorcha's promise by making her immortal, did he?" the kelpie asked, still snarling.

Lachlan shook his head. "Everything she agreed to still holds true. Unless Eirian makes a move to end our lives – directly, irrefutably by his hand, that is – he still holds claim over her. But that does not mean we will not get her back. I do not care what it takes to do so."

It was then that Lachlan noticed a despondence in Murdoch's demeanour that, for some reason, he did not think had anything to do with the terrible news he had placed at the creature's feet.

"What is wrong, horse?" he asked, bending forwards an inch as if intending to console Murdoch before thinking better of it. Lachlan frowned. "You were... happy...when you came across me. What had you learned in your travels?"

Murdoch's eyes were far too bright as he stared at his own hands. "It means nothing now."

That only piqued Lachlan's curiosity more. "Tell me."

"I assure you that you do not want to –"

"*Tell me,*" Lachlan urged, more insistent this time.

With an air of defeat Murdoch collapsed onto his back to stare up at the late afternoon sky. Lachlan followed his gaze, spying a raven. A normal, natural one, rather than a faerie in disguise. He was tempted to kill the creature anyway.

"Sorcha mentioned my 'Unseelie friend' in Loch Lomond the eve she was taken," Murdoch said, very slowly. "Well, I suppose she actually *is* my friend, all things considered."

Lachlan shifted on the spot, impatient with the speed with which the kelpie was speaking. "Where is this going?" he asked, but Murdoch ignored him.

"She is a witch. A powerful one from days gone by, if she is to be believed. She told me how to save Sorcha, though the information is useless now."

"She...how? How could we save her?"

"I told you; it is useless –"

"For the sake of the forest just tell me, Murdoch!" Lachlan spat, anger beginning to thaw his frozen insides. *Trust the kelpie to rouse me to fury even when I thought I was empty.*

Murdoch cast him a side-long glance. "We have to recreate the circumstances in which Eirian took her away. Upon a horse with a king and a babe in tow, the witch said. Well, between the two of us we have a king and a horse, but a child..."

The weight of Murdoch's words crushed Lachlan as he absorbed them. "We could have...and he would not have been able to take her back?"

"Not without unlawfully spiriting Sorcha away, which would give us cause to wreak havoc to get her back. But if Sorcha has lost your baby then there is nothing we can do."

"So submissive," came a voice from behind them, which was entirely unfamiliar to Lachlan. "And here I was convinced by tales of the fearsome kelpie of Loch Lomond and the wily King of the Seelie. Wizard, you have lied to me."

"I did not," replied a tetchy voice that Lachlan *did* recognise. "It merely seems as if the opponent I've been asked to help defeat is more formidable than anyone I've come across before."

Lachlan could not believe his ears. The kelpie cast his gaze all around him, thoroughly confused, slowly standing up and turning just as Lachlan did the same.

And there, accompanied by a raven-haired man with unnervingly amber eyes, stood the wizard Lachlan had spent years searching for.

The man who had saved his life once upon a time: Julian Thorne.

A mad grin crept across Lachlan's face. "You are late, wizard," he said.

Julian raised an eyebrow. "Going by your current circumstances I would rather say that I'm precisely on time."

CHAPTER SEVENTEEN

Sorcha

Several days had passed since Lachlan's miraculous, impossible visit in the form of a fox. Sorcha was still struggling to wrap her head around what had transpired, though that was partly due to how hungry she was. She had hardly eaten in weeks, her grief and anger and abject, intolerable loss eating away at her, instead. But she knew she had to kick herself out of her stupor. Lachlan and Murdoch would never forgive her if she didn't.

More importantly, Sorcha would never forgive herself.

It was time to do something with the immortal life that had been thrust into her arms.

"Miss Sorcha?" came a placid, feminine voice from the door, interrupting her reverie. For a moment Sorcha was thrown back to the Seelie Court, to Ailith and her soft utterances of the same phrase. But there was no affection to be had in this unfamiliar voice speaking her name.

"Come in," Sorcha sighed, immediately regretting giving the voice permission to enter.

The faerie who opened the door kept her silver eyes level with the mirror upon the wall opposite her, entirely avoiding looking at Sorcha curled up like a ball by the fire. She placed a dress protected in a bag of white linen upon the bed. "King Eirian requires your presence for dinner in his private chambers."

Oh, for the love of the forest, no.

But Sorcha's stomach growled horribly, in direct contradiction to her horror. And she remembered what Eirian had said, the last time he'd deigned to speak or see her. *'Either you clean yourself, feed yourself and get some sleep, or I will do all three for you.'*

Well, I have followed the first, she thought, *since I spend much of my time in the hot springs, but I am guilty of ignoring his second and third rules. If I refuse this meal I have no doubt Eirian will plan something much worse for me.*

"Give me fifteen minutes to ready myself," she told the faerie, who merely nodded and retreated from the room. Sorcha imagined she was likely standing sentry outside the door, and would give her precisely the fifteen minutes Sorcha had asked from her – no more and no less.

It took Sorcha every ounce of willpower she possessed to rise to her feet and stumble over to the bed. With some trepidation she opened the linen bag, expecting the dress within it to be just as insubstantial and otherworldly as the one Eirian had magicked onto her at the Unseelie solstice.

She was therefore surprised to find a simple, knee-length dress of soft ivory, with a delicately embroidered bodice and floating, flouncing skirt. The sleeves were slashed and elbow-length; the neckline sweeping but not nearly as low as the ones Sorcha had seen at the revel.

"I think I actually like this," Sorcha murmured, throwing off her current clothes and sliding into the dress. It fit perfectly, though Sorcha had expected it to. It was likely created *for* her, after all, and faerie tailors had some of the best eyes in the world.

Sorcha moved through to the washroom to splash ice-cold water on her face, then grabbed a soft bristle brush and ran it through her hair until it was free of tangles and tumbled over her shoulders in a far less haphazard fashion that it had done moments earlier. She resisted checking her reflection in the large mirror in her room, for she suspected Eirian used it to keep an eye on her.

After a brief search by the bed Sorcha came to the conclusion that the dress the Unseelie servant had brought in did not come with shoes, though she did not mind going barefoot. Sorcha had become used to the practice with all her time in the Seelie Court and her summers spent close to the shore of Loch Lomond, and had ultimately always misliked having to wear shoes in general.

When she heard a knock on the door Sorcha knew her fifteen minutes were up. With a surreptitious glance at the mirror she left her room, dutifully following the servant as she wound her way down the tower and across the grand, sweeping entrance hall of Eirian's castle.

Do not think of Lachlan and Murdoch, Sorcha thought, steeling her frayed nerves. *Do not think of home at all.* She knew the Unseelie king would work out something was awry if she wasn't careful, though Sorcha's general despondency over the past three weeks would go some ways in masking any odd behaviour she might exhibit after Lachlan's secret visit.

But that very thought caused Sorcha's heart to beat altogether too quickly. *Eirian might well know of Lachlan's visit already,* she panicked, fighting to keep her expression as neutral as possible when the servant glanced back at her. *That could be why he wishes to see me tonight. What will I do if he knows? What will* he *do if he –*

"Sorcha Darrow. Please, have a seat."

Sorcha's eyes widened in surprise when she caught sight of the Unseelie king, resplendent in a deep blue tailcoat and matching trousers, his signature, slashed shirt and silver jewellery flashing from his neck and wrists and fingers.

She fought back a gulp. *I was so lost in my thoughts I did not keep track of how I got here.* But then Sorcha looked around Eirian's chambers and realised she was at the top of a tower opposite the one she'd been imprisoned in, going by the view through the tall, arched window behind Eirian. She shivered, for though it was April and no more fog roiled and tumbled around the castle the Unseelie king's chambers were chilly.

Eirian smiled at her expectantly, sharp teeth gleaming in the silvered candlelight that filled the room. "A seat, Miss Darrow?" he said again, indicating towards a high-backed, velvet-lined chair that sat beside a circular table with impossibly spindly legs. Behind it was a large and frameless mirror that took up much of the wall; for a moment Sorcha wondered what Eirian saw within the glass.

I do not wish to know, she decided, closing the gap between herself and the Unseelie king to sit upon the chair he proffered her in careful silence. He nodded approvingly. Then, with the flick of a wrist adorned with chains and heavy, midnight-blue jewels, he dismissed the servant who had shown Sorcha to his chambers.

"The dress is to your tastes, I see," he said, sitting down opposite Sorcha. It wasn't a question, so Sorcha did not answer. Eirian chuckled. "Silence does not become you. You are enjoying the hot springs, I trust? My servants tell me you spend much of your time –"

"Is anything on the table made of faerie food?" Sorcha asked, cutting Eirian's musings short to ask the one question she absolutely needed a truthful answer to. The food and drink presented before her was beautiful, ranging from savoury, rosemary-scented pies to delicate sugared plums to deep, sweet berry wine. Sorcha's stomach clawed at her to reach for the nearest morsel and stuff it in her mouth.

But something grew in Eirian's unnatural eyes in response to her question – a sharpness, perhaps – that Sorcha did not like. His lips fell into a hard line, and he cocked his head to the side to regard her. Sorcha found that she could not maintain eye contact, so she focused on the way Eirian's long, silken hair fell across his shoulder, instead.

"No," Eirian eventually said. "Everything here is safe for you to eat and drink...unless you asked the question with the intention of consuming faerie food?"

Sorcha deigned not to answer the question, for her answer was obvious. Without waiting for Eirian to say anything else, and for fear that he could somehow read

600

in her mannerisms that something was wrong, Sorcha nimbly chose one of the pies sitting on a plate in front of her and began to eat it.

She was painfully aware of Eirian's inscrutable gaze upon her as she ate, even when he finally picked up his knife and fork and began to dine, too. It was in this way that Sorcha had perhaps the most awkward meal of her life, though the food was just as delicious as the food in the Seelie Court – if not more so.

I would never admit that, though, she mused. *Lachlan would be furious if I said such a thing.*

"You are smiling."

Sorcha froze, for the very thought of Lachlan had indeed caused the hint of a smile to cross her face. "The food here is wonderful," she said, relieved to find the half-truth dripping off her tongue in an instant.

Eirian seemed pleased by her answer. He leaned back in his chair, a satisfied look on his face. "You would have learned this earlier, had you deigned to try it."

"I think I had as good a reason as any to have lost my appetite."

That sharpness again. Sorcha forced herself to face it this time, though Eirian's gaze made her deeply uncomfortable. But the Unseelie king's next question caught her by surprise in its gentleness. "How are you faring?" he asked. "It is good to see some colour return to your cheeks."

"I...so long as I do not think much about anything I am faring as well as one might expect."

When the Unseelie king laughed Sorcha's cheeks burned. There was something about having him laugh at her that left Sorcha feeling distinctly humiliated.

"You have a clever tongue, Miss Darrow," Eirian said, taking a long draught of wine without once tearing his silver eyes away from hers. "It is hard to believe you were not always a faerie."

"I am not one now, either."

"You are in all but name, now that you are immortal."

Sorcha bit back a retort. Eirian was baiting her, it seemed, and she was far too easily falling into his trap. *If I am not careful I will let something slip about Lachlan, and all will be lost.*

"You have not once asked for information about the Seelie Court, and your bereft suitors," Eirian said, very softly, though the words hit Sorcha's ears as if he had shouted them.

"You would not tell me anything if I asked...unless to torment me," Sorcha replied, choosing every word as carefully as if she were picking her way across a precipitous mountainside. "I am not wrong, am I?"

Eirian waved a dismissive hand, bracelets and bangles jingling musically as he did so. "Most likely. But you are taking the fun out of this for me, Sorcha. Won't you play the begging, desperate prisoner for me even a little?"

"I do not think so," Sorcha replied, flinching despite herself at Eirian's solitary use of her first name. "But you must have known I wouldn't."

"I am beginning to understand that, yes. You are an interesting creature."

She shook her head. "Not so. I am but a lowly

mort-"

When Eirian cackled at Sorcha's half-sentence she looked down at her hands, immediately on the verge of tears. She had spoken the truth, when she told the Unseelie king she was faring well enough so long as she did not think about anything. But the moment Sorcha dallied with the idea of immortality...

"I have had my fill," she said, not quite succeeding in smoothing a crack from her voice. "May I be excused?"

The look Eirian gave her suggested he hadn't nearly had *his* fill, though he nodded his head. "You may go. But you will return her at the same time in three days. And three days after that, and three days after that, until I see fit to end the arrangement."

Sorcha said nothing. There was nothing she *could* say to get out of such an arrangement, if Eirian himself wished it, and she knew he could easily make it every night instead if he so desired. Without another glance at the Unseelie king she fled his chambers, somehow not surprised in the slightest to find the faerie who had led her there waiting by the door.

"Take me back," she said, allowing the servant to walk ahead of her to lead her to her room.

Forever only grows longer, she thought, morose, when she collapsed beside the fireplace despite the fact her pristine dress became covered in soot within seconds. *Dinner with Eirian every three nights will be torture.*

It did not escape Sorcha that this was most likely exactly what the silver king had intended.

CHAPTER EIGHTEEN

Lachlan

"Your home truly is beautiful, Lachlan of the Seelies."

"It would have been more beautiful with Clara in it, had you shown up when I started looking for you," Lachlan countered as he led the way back to the palace, nerves still too raw from his meeting with Sorcha and Murdoch's devastating news to temper his words.

The wizard's amber-eyed companion snorted. "I think I like you, Seelie king."

"Who is this man, Julian?"

"I second that," Murdoch chimed in, "though it seems as if both of these men know about me already."

Julian Thorne cast his gaze over Murdoch, a small smile on his face. There were a few new lines creasing the skin around his eyes, and there was a hint of grey at the sides of his temples, but all in all Lachlan figured the past seven years had been good to the wizard.

"Of course I have heard of you," Julian told Murdoch. "You are the reason the Seelie king was in dire need of my help all those years ago."

"And is, of course, still in your debt, I would imagine," the raven-haired man added on. He brought a shard of tourmaline out of his pocket, held it up to the dying afternoon light and inspected it with a frown upon his face. "Wizard, this really did take us right into the centre of the Seelie Court. You were not lying when you told me it came from here."

Julian rolled his eyes. "Why would I lie to you?"

"To impress Red, of course."

"How many times do I have to –"

"*Who are you?*" both Murdoch and Lachlan insisted, exchanging an exasperated look that Lachlan had often seen Ailith and Sorcha share when witnessing him and the kelpie arguing with one another. His heart twisted at the thought of Sorcha; going by the momentary wince that crossed Murdoch's face Lachlan could only imagine a similar thought had crossed his mind, too.

Julian's companion bowed gracefully in response. "My apologies. The wizard always brings out the worst in me, you see. We aren't exactly what one would call *friends,* though our better halves decidedly are." When he came out of his bow Lachlan got a closer look at the man, and though he seemed to be at a similar stage of his life as Julian himself there was something ageless about him, too.

It is his eyes, Lachlan thought. *They are not human, somehow.*

The man caught Lachlan staring, and he smiled an animalistic grin that was somehow familiar to him. "My name is Adrian Wolfe," he said, "and I am arrogant enough to believe that you would most sincerely regret using my full name against me, faerie."

Something about Adrian's manner irked Lachlan, though he assumed that was the point. To his left Murdoch was appraising the man with a critical eye and a familiar, intimidating silence. Lachlan found himself appreciating the kelpie's presence, for the creature was able to look through deceptions just as well as he was – if not more.

Lachlan took a step towards Julian. "If the two of you are not friends, as Mr Wolfe so cannily described, then why is he here?"

"He has skills that near no-one else has," the wizard explained, though it seemed to physically pain him to admit it. He glowered in Adrian's direction, though the man deliberately ignored him. He prowled around Murdoch, instead, examining him with the same curiosity the kelpie was showing him.

Lachlan frowned. "Please elaborate."

"Curses," Adrian replied, still circling Murdoch. "The weaving of words. Blood magic. The wizard's strength lies in the physicality of magic – of fire and flesh and gold. My own expertise is far more like your own, faerie, although without the caveat that I must not lie."

A shiver ran through Lachlan despite himself, though it was tinged with excitement. Adrian Wolfe was powerful, of that he had no doubt. That he was on the side of the Seelie Court was an advantage Lachlan could only have hoped for.

If he's on our side, that is.

"Name your price," Lachlan said, bringing everyone's attention back to him. Even Murdoch stopped watching Adrian, an uncertain look upon his face.

"Careful what you promise, fox," he said. "You are not in a position to –"

"I know what I am and am not currently in a position to promise," Lachlan cut in. He turned to Julian. "The Seelie are in panic mode right now. King Eirian's presence looms over us; everyone knows that we are likely not strong enough to defeat our southron brethren. But if we can gain an advantage over him – if we can defeat him – there is not a thing in the world I would not promise you."

Julian's face paled. "What has he done to you, Lachlan? All the news I received was that you required my assistance to take him down, but no reason as to why."

"He took Sorcha."

It was Murdoch who answered. The way he spoke – the way he *looked* as he spoke – was all both Julian and Adrian needed to fully understand what was going on.

Julian nodded. "For saving your life seven years ago and helping you now – that makes two favours you owe me. I ask, for the first, that myself and anyone I would consider family will always be safe and welcome within your side of the faerie realm, and may find room at your table in the Seelie Court."

"Done. And the second?"

"The second I would leave for Evie," he said, smiling. "She would never forgive me if I took a faerie's favour from her. When your war is fought, Seelie king, I would ask that you grant her whatever she wishes."

Lachlan was starkly reminded of why he had put his

trust in Julian in the first place. The relationship he'd had with his golden-haired love was something so rare and pure that he'd instinctively known the pair would do anything for each other.

"Gladly done," he said. "And you, Mr Wolfe? What would you have of me?"

When the man did not answer immediately Lachlan knew he would not like what he eventually said. Adrian ran a hand through his hair, rearranging a solitary streak of white that broke the black in the process. "I have no need of a favour at present," he said, smiling softly. "And, indeed, it seems as if your current problem may take months to solve, given the tricky political position you're in. I would rather have the notion of a favour looming over you, Seelie king. And you, too, kelpie."

Murdoch's eyes glowered like coals. "Your skill set had best be worth such a thing."

"Oh, trust me," Adrian said, "it is. I will prove most useful – on the battlefield as well as off it."

"Then a favour in the future is granted," Lachlan said, "though I am curious as to what you mean by *on the battlefield*."

When Adrian grinned again Lachlan realised why it was so familiar. *Like mine,* he thought. *Vulpine. No... lupine.*

"They do not call me Mr Wolfe for nothing, Seelie king," he said, amber eyes glittering in amusement. He drew back his top lip, introducing a snarl to his smile. "Now, let's get planning."

CHAPTER NINETEEN

Eirian

For three months now King Eirian had been dealing with silence on two very different fronts.

The first was the Seelie Court. After Sorcha had initially been spirited away the entire realm had been pandemonium. There was hardly a corner one could visit without news of Eirian's deal with the Seelie king's paramour. Lachlan had sent envoy after envoy to collect information. Numerous performers and gossip-mongers sought an audience in the Unseelie Court in order to be the first ones to know just what exactly was going on. Eirian had prevented them all from leaving, of course, but he had not expected the Seelies to stop trying to fish for information.

Except that they did. Now that Sorcha had been locked away in the Unseelie castle for thirteen weeks straight the Seelie Court was a wall of silence. Eirian had no way of knowing what they were planning, for in an ironic twist of fate any envoys *he* sent to his northern brethren did not return.

Any Unseelie living beneath the surface of lakes and rivers and lochs were keeping quiet about the wanderings of the kelpie, too, out of sheer terror. Eirian misliked how much independent power he had. The monster was not bound by any of the laws of faerie; if he had an impulse to attack the Unseelie Court Eirian had no doubt that he could indulge it.

Keeping hold of Sorcha Darrow was supposed to keep Lachlan and the water horse under my thumb, he mused. *It feels like they are planning something.*

Eirian almost laughed at the notion. Of course they were planning something, but he doubted very much that it would work. Both the golden king and the kelpie would stay their hand the moment Eirian threatened Sorcha, and that was ultimately all the leverage he needed to keep them in their place. *Let them scheme and sit in silence. It will all be for naught.*

All he needed was a little more time. Another few years and Eirian would bring down a full-fledged assault against the Seelie Court, and take control of the entire realm. He only wished that he was not quite so alone in the venture, for though it had been Eirian's plan all along to be rid of his half-brother and his nephew, now that they had been gone seven years the Unseelie king had to admit that there was a part of him that almost missed his family.

Almost.

The second wall of silence Eirian had to deal with was, of course, Sorcha Darrow.

The former mortal was certainly proving to be a formidable opponent. Even now, as she sat opposite him for their three-nightly dinner arrangements, looking perfectly lovely and innocent in a periwinkle dress of gossamer and spider-silk, Sorcha had refused to respond to any of Eirian's questions and comments for the best part of an hour. She answered only as and when she decided it prudent.

Her behaviour had long since grated on the Unseelie king's nerves.

Sorcha proved immune to Eirian granting her the freedom to roam the castle, and insisting that she be left alone in the hot springs if she wished to enjoy them by herself, and the dresses, jewellery and pretty silver combs he gifted her every week. Sorcha did not care that her captor was doing everything to make her comfortable. It did not make her fonder of the place. It did not make her rage and scream in frustration. It did not make her cry, or outwardly appear to miss her family.

No, it simply did nothing at all.

It therefore stood to reason that the Unseelie king had constructed a new plan of attack...and intended to put it into action that very night.

"You cannot stay silent forever, little bird," he told Sorcha, refilling their wine glasses as he did so. "I can tell how much you are dying to speak and sing and scream."

Sorcha eyed the wine carefully. Every evening the two of them dined together she asked the same question: *is any of the meal made using faerie food?* Every time Eirian had truthfully answered no, and tonight was no different. So Sorcha, after a moment of hesitation, took her glass when Eirian finished refilling it and took a long draught from the golden wine. Seelie summer wine, since it was June, and Eirian felt very much like indulging Sorcha's tastes before setting his plan in motion.

"I am not a bird," Sorcha muttered, a moment or two later.

Eirian almost smiled. "And yet I've heard tell you sing like one, over and over again, though I have yet to hear you myself."

"And you won't." A pause. And then: "Why do you care so much about that, anyway?"

"Why, Miss Darrow, are you asking *me* a question?" Eirian said, holding a hand over his heart in mock surprise.

Sorcha clicked her tongue in disgust. "It does not matter."

"Oh, but it does. You are curious. I knew you must be. I have been asking you to sing for five years now, after all."

When she did not reply Eirian sighed. Sorcha's mismatched eyes glimmered in the dim light of his chambers, one green flame and one blue. He was fond of her eyes, in the way a magpie loved shiny objects. He had no doubt Lachlan and the kelpie were both equally as enamoured with them.

"I imagine you are well aware of how covetous my kind can be," Eirian said, deciding to give Sorcha an answer to her question instead of teasing her. Her eyes widened; Eirian saw her barely suppress a gulp of interest. *She is far more curious than she would have me know,* he thought. *That is good.*

"When we hear of mortals with great skills," he continued, "we doubtlessly want them. We find any way to bring that individual's gifts within our power – compliment them, promise them the world, charm them to join the faerie realm...or use their name to enchant them, if they prove to be resistant." Eirian gave Sorcha a look loaded with meaning, then, though she did not flinch away. There was something in her expression that screamed *you wouldn't dare.*

It was not as if Eirian did not *dare* use Sorcha's name to enchant her, though in truth the Unseelie king did not yet know her full name. It was, rather, that he did not want to. He wanted her as lucid and aware of everything that happened to her as possible, for all the years to come.

A night or two in oblivion, however...

"I do not believe it is as simple as you merely wanting my voice just to have it," Sorcha replied, certain.

Eirian grinned. "You would be correct. I want it because the creatures who love you cherish it. I told you; faeries are covetous creatures. And if it is our neighbour – our rival and enemy – who has something pretty...well, then we want it even more."

"You are so *petty,*" Sorcha replied, indignant enough to forget her rule of silence. She rose from the table, moving over to the fireplace with a sweep of her delicate, feather-light dress. The flames danced in the hearth, painting Sorcha's skin the colour of sunset. "Your entire kind. Petty to a fault."

"You say this as if humans are any better."

"Humans have perhaps eighty years at best to live; it is no wonder they want everything they can reach. Faeries...you have forever."

It was interesting to hear Sorcha talk about humans as if they were a species entirely separate from her. That she did the same for faeries caused Eirian to wonder just how confused she was about what her place in the world now was.

Never far from me, he thought. *That is her place in the world, so long as she holds value.*

"You are taking this too personally," Eirian said, standing up to join Sorcha by the fireplace. He took with him a bowl of sugared plums, which he had learned were her favourite the very first day he met her, in London, when she had gazed at the confections in the window of a baker's shop and realised that the glimmers reflected on the glass were not what they appeared to be.

"And how else am I supposed to take it?" she demanded. "You wish to hear me sing so you can possess my voice, simply to win another victory against Lachlan. That seems rather personal to me."

Eirian popped a sugared plum in his mouth in response, which only irritated Sorcha further. She snarled at the fire, entirely avoiding the Unseelie king's gaze, though grabbed a plum from the bowl he was holding and bit into it with a viciousness Eirian relished.

"I suppose it should make me happy," Sorcha mused, more to herself than to Eirian. "To know that you wish to hear me sing and never will, I mean."

Her lovely hair flashed copper in the firelight, in stark contrast to the blues and purples and silvers of Eirian's chambers. There was something poetic about it; the Unseelie king thought he might have written a song about it, once upon a time.

Another time, long, long ago.

Eirian cocked his head to one side. "You forget that the reason your fox – and your kelpie – adore your voice so much is that it is something truly special."

"And that should matter to me because...?" Sorcha

wondered, blithely eating another plum as Eirian gleefully watched her pupils begin to dilate and her movements become slower and slower.

"Because it means *you* are special, even without their attentions," Eirian said, placing the bowl in his hands onto the mantelpiece above the fire to help steady Sorcha when she stumbled. "Which means I wish dearly to hear you sing, simply for myself. You were correct; this *is* personal. Are you feeling quite all right, Sorcha Darrow?"

She was staring at him, bleary-eyed and confused. Sorcha's cheeks had flushed, though she began to rub her arms as if she were freezing. "What have you...what is wrong with me?" she asked, following Eirian's gaze to the sugared plums with some difficulty. "No...no. You have not –"

"Never turn your back on a meal prepared by a faerie," he said, voice dripping with deliberate danger and seduction fully intended to entrap Sorcha in his grasp. "You might just find he has offered you something you really should not eat."

CHAPTER TWENTY

Sorcha

Sorcha Darrow was dizzy. Sorcha Darrow was confused. Sorcha Darrow could barely see.

Sorcha Darrow did not care.

"So this is faerie fruit," she said, altogether far too happily considering what had just happened to her. There was a part of her brain that was telling her this was wrong, that she had been poisoned, but that part was diminishing by the minute. "I have never..."

"Never?" came a voice Sorcha vaguely recognised as King Eirian. But all the animosity – all the fear and anger and sorrow – that she'd felt towards the faerie mere moments ago had disappeared. His voice affected her differently now. It was inviting. Flirtatious.

Dangerous.

Sorcha always longed for dangerous.

"Never," she repeated, shaking her head in an exaggerated fashion. "I did not wish to lose myself." She flounced from the fireplace to the gargantuan mirror in Eirian's chambers, trying her best to focus on her own reflection with little success. She could make out her wavy, dark auburn hair, and the pretty colour of her floor-length, floaty dress, but that was it. Whenever she tried to zone in on her face it hurt her head, so Sorcha stopped trying.

But when the Unseelie king crossed the stone floor to stand beside her Sorcha could see every detail of his form in the mirror.

His almost translucent white shirt, billowing in some non-existent breeze and begging Sorcha to follow the deep slash in the material all the way down to the faerie's navel.

His skin, which was silver in one light, blue in the next, then back to silver in the space of a blink.

His mercurial eyes and predatory grin, complete with razor teeth that could easily tear out Sorcha's throat.

His long, pointed ears and the jewels that adorned them, reminding Sorcha for a moment of the beautiful silver earring Lachlan had once owned.

The one I broke, to free him.

"You do not lose yourself," Eirian said, voice soft upon the air between them. He reached a hand out to the mirror, so Sorcha did the same. The glass was cold and solid beneath her fingertips, which surprised her; Sorcha had expected that she might fall through the surface. "Faerie fruit merely lowers your inhibitions. Allows you to indulge urges you might otherwise be too cautious to enjoy."

Sorcha considered this for a moment, then discovered her brain was too heavy to understand such a complicated explanation. "Where does the mirror go?" she asked, instead.

Eirian chuckled. The sound was pleasantly musical to Sorcha's ears, and she longed to hear more of it. "Wherever I want...within reason. I cannot reach the Seelie Court through it, for example. But I could reach a winding London street, or an ostentatious art exhibit."

"You..." Sorcha shook her head, then smiled at some notion she could scarcely comprehend but that made her happy nonetheless. "Lachlan is strong enough to keep you out."

If she had been in her right mind Sorcha would have seen Eirian bristle at such a comment. Instead, all she saw was the easy smile of his reflection, and the way the Unseelie king inched closer towards her.

"Your fox would not make a very good king if he was not strong," Eirian said. Sorcha nodded her enthusiastic agreement.

"He is stronger than he thinks, I believe. Nobody would follow him if he were not."

"So you trust in his strength?"

"Absolutely," Sorcha replied, moving over to the solitary, curved window in Eirian's chambers as if she were floating. It was open; she revelled in the cool night air upon her skin as she stared out at the inky sky, wondering how close the summer solstice was. *Have I really been here over three months?* she wondered. *Has it been so long?*

Eirian did not move to join her at first. Sorcha vaguely heard him pacing to and fro across the stone floor, footsteps muffled whenever he reached one of his finely-woven rugs.

"So who is stronger?" the Unseelie king asked, after a moment of silence that could well have lasted hours and hours.

Sorcha turned her head to blink at him. "Who is stronger than whom?"

"Your fox, or the kelpie?"

It was not a question anybody had ever asked Sorcha. In her usual, lucid state it was not a question she would have ever answered. "Murdoch," she said, without an ounce of doubt and a generous measure of pride. "My kelpie is stronger than most any of the fair folk."

"So if Lachlan ever meant you harm," Eirian began, taking another step or two towards Sorcha, "what would your kelpie do?"

"He would drown him whilst he was sleeping," Sorcha replied, matter-of-factly. "But Murdoch would never do that."

A pause. "And why not?"

"Because Lachlan would never mean me harm."

"So you trust the two of them, alone, without you?"

Here was another answer Sorcha had no doubt about. An angelic smile crossed her face as she thought of her dark kelpie and her golden fox. "More than anything."

Again, had Sorcha been in her right mind she would have seen the flash of irritation that crossed Eirian's face. But he hid it behind another heartbreakingly beautiful smile, and when he reached the window and slid his arms around Sorcha's waist she did not pull away.

"You are lucky to be so loved, Miss Darrow," he said, leaning his chin upon her left shoulder. Sorcha's heart was already beating too quickly; something inside her told her that if she turned around to face the Unseelie king it would beat all the faster. So she kept her eyes locked on the stars in the uncharacteristically clear night sky, though part of her wondered why the sky was so dark and haunting when it was already midsummer.

She did not respond to Eirian's statement so, after an insurmountable amount of silence, he asked, "Why are you so focused on the stars?"

"You are made of starlight," Sorcha replied. "Starlight and dark, empty nothingness."

Eirian chuckled against her ear, tickling her skin. "You flatter me," he said. "Would you like to see the real stars closer than you ever have before, Sorcha?"

But before she could respond Eirian tightened his arms around her waist and vaulted the two of them out of the open window. Sorcha let out a yell, terrified, yet in the space of a second it turned into a cry of delight when it became apparent that she was not falling to her death.

She craned her neck to see Eirian behind her, but he merely grinned. With the slightest of tilts of his head they careened up and up and up, until the air grew thin and Sorcha breathless with it.

"How are you..." she began, but Sorcha could not finish the question. For in the nighttime air Sorcha's skin was as silver as the king who carried her through the sky. She matched the stars clustered all around her, larger than she had ever seen them before as they twinkled their hellos. The moon hung fat and heavy just out of reach; the prized jewel in a decadent crown.

It was perhaps the most magical sight Sorcha had ever witnessed.

Though she couldn't see them, Sorcha could hear the beating of impossibly large wings. Once or twice, out of the corner of her eye, she could have sworn she saw a raven's feather, iridescent in the moonlight, but when she tried to focus on it the feather disappeared.

Sorcha could not truly process what she could see and hear and smell and feel as she was wound through the sky. She was aware of Eirian's arms around her waist, ensuring she did not fall, and the rush of air against her face, but everything else that assaulted her senses felt like a dream.

Another life. Another world.

Before she had the opportunity to breathe again, the two of them were back in Eirian's chambers.

The Unseelie king tugged at his shirt, pulling it over his head and dropping it to the floor before shaking out his hair. Sorcha had only ever seen it immaculate and straight; now it was wild and windswept.

She liked it far better this way.

"Your hair," she said, giggling as she stumbled towards him. "It is as much a mess as mine usually is."

His lips quirked into a smile. "And yet, somehow, you like that. Why is that, Sorcha Darrow?"

"Rules are for accountants. Rules are for lawyers. Rules are for –"

"Anyone but you?"

Sorcha stared at him, wide-eyed and full of adrenaline. "Yes," she answered simply. "They are for ordinary humans."

The Unseelie king closed the gap between them, stroking the length of Sorcha's jawline as her breathing hitched in response. "And you are not one of them."

Eirian's cruel lips found hers, and she did not pull away. For though the kiss was wrong – terribly, monstrously wrong – in her current state of mind Sorcha thought that it was just right.

Then the Unseelie king slowly but surely slid her dress from her shoulders to join his shirt on the cold, stone floor, and the night was lost to gasps and sighs and whispers.

In the light of day those whispers were as sinister as curses. Beneath a moonlit sky they were endless adulations of love.

Sorcha eagerly drank up every last word of them.

CHAPTER TWENTY-ONE

Sorcha

Almost a full nine months had passed before Sorcha was truly aware of it, and the winter solstice was looming on the horizon. She wondered if her grasp of time had changed the moment Eirian stripped her of her mortality.

If it had, she truly wanted nothing more to do with it.

To be numb to so much of my life is horrible, she thought, *though I have to wonder if this is how all otherwordly creatures feel.*

Sorcha did not want to dwell upon this, for if it were true then that meant Lachlan, Murdoch, Ailith and even Ronan and the rest of the Seelie Court always felt this disconnected. It was not something she would wish upon anyone.

A spasm ran through her stomach, bending Sorcha double. She had been plagued by aches and nausea for a few weeks now, though she had hidden her discomfort as best she could from Eirian and the servants he sent to spy on her. Sorcha had been very, very careful to avoid the mirror in her room whenever she felt ill, for the last thing she wanted was for the Unseelie king to gain more leverage against her.

"Why do I feel like this?" she groaned, clutching at her stomach. Sorcha contemplated going to the washroom to vomit, or to the hot springs to soak her aching skin in bubbling, restorative water, but ultimately she did not have the energy to move.

Sorcha wished she knew why she felt the way she did. But she had experienced several odd, prolonged bouts of memory loss that she could not explain over the past half a year, and she was scared to address them. With the way time had affected her since she was spirited away to the Unseelie realm Sorcha would not have been surprised if the gaps in her memory were simply to do with her becoming adjusted to immortality.

Something told her this wasn't the answer.

Every three nights she had dinner with the Unseelie king. On the third of each of these three nights she could never remember what she got up to after their shared meal, no matter how hard she tried. Sorcha shuddered merely thinking about what was going on.

She entirely lacked the courage to confront King Eirian about what he might be doing.

Whenever she thought of such unpleasant subjects Sorcha, as if in defence, forced herself to think of Lachlan or Murdoch or lazy days spent braiding Ailith's impossibly long hair as they traded gossip about Darach and the Seelie Court. *They will work out what to do,* she reassured herself, over and over again. *Eirian was not supposed to make me immortal. Though it doesn't void the promise I made to him it most certainly* changes *things. Nobody who cares about me will let this lie.*

She hoped.

"Mama," Sorcha groaned, when another dagger drove itself into her stomach. As a child she had never been that close to her mother, and as a teenager even less so. Sorcha's initial adventure with Lachan had been what changed her attitude towards the woman who birthed her, despite their differences. Sorcha missed her greatly; all she wanted to do was become a little girl again and cry in her mother's arms, her reassuring hands stroking her daughter's hair.

But Sorcha could not have that, nor could she have a fireside story from her father.

Sorcha Darrow had no family left.

When she heard a knock upon her door Sorcha became rigid, then fled to the washroom in a fit of sudden, inevitable nausea. She did not give the knocker permission to enter – she did not tell them to do anything at all – so when Sorcha heard the heavy door open and shut she knew the faerie who knocked could only be one, specific creature she absolutely did not wish to see.

King Eirian.

"Where are you, Miss Darrow?" Eirian called, voice almost sing-song. Sorcha wished nothing more than to hide in the washroom, out of his sight, until the Unseelie king finally gave up and disappeared.

She knew that would never happen.

"I am – wait just a moment," she gasped, before losing the battle with her stomach to keep what little that was inside it *inside it.* Sorcha heaved, and retched, and by the time she was finished the Unseelie king stood in the doorway to the washroom, watching her with a frown on his face.

He almost looked concerned.

"You are not well," he said.

"C-clearly," Sorcha replied, wiping her mouth with the back of a shaking hand before slowly moving to the nearby basin to splash ice water over her face. It tingled so much that it burned, but Sorcha relished the feeling.

Eirian handed Sorcha a towel for her to dry herself. For a moment she considered not taking it, though she found that she did not have the energy to defy such a harmless gesture. "How long have you been ill?" Eirian asked as she dried her face. "I have not noticed -"

"I have been hiding it," Sorcha told him, barely managing to get to her feet to stumble past the Unseelie king. She made a beeline for her bed but then, in a sudden change of heart, collapsed by the fireplace instead.

Eirian seemed inordinately impressed by her statement, which confused Sorcha to no end. "You truly are a stubborn one, Miss Darrow."

She did not care about what he meant. "What was it that you wanted?" she asked, breathing in the smell of burning wood from the fireplace and sighing in relief when she realised it settled her nausea.

"To see how you are, of course."

"How generous of you."

Sorcha thought Eirian was going to laugh at her reply; instead, he crouched low beside her, a look of unmistakable concern upon his face. "How long have you been ill?" he asked, brushing a hand across Sorcha's forehead. She did not bother pushing it away.

"A few weeks. Do you know why I'm feeling like this?"

Silence. Sorcha watched as Eirian struggled with how to answer her question using some form of the truth, which did not bode well for her at all. "Perhaps," he finally said, and then: "Do not make a sound for a minute."

"What do you –"

He placed a finger to her lips. She resisted the urge to bite it as a warning for him to leave her alone. But Sorcha was deathly curious about what the Unseelie king thought might be wrong with her, so she indulged his request to stay silent.

When his mercurial eyes widened there was something akin to disbelief within them. "That hardly seems possible..." he mumbled. Then, before Sorcha could stop him, Eirian bent his head low and placed an ear against her stomach. She pushed at his shoulders to try and get rid of him but the faerie was far too strong for her shoves to make any impact.

"What are you *doing*?" she demanded. Bile was beginning to rise in her throat again; if Eirian did not move soon Sorcha was sure she would be sick all over his silken hair.

Then perhaps he should not move, she thought, grimly satisfied with the notion of doing something so disgusting to her captor.

"You are pregnant."

Oh.

For a moment Sorcha could not breathe. Could not think. It took every ounce of strength she had in her to process what the Unseelie king had just said to her.

"I cannot be –"

"You are *pregnant,*" Eirian repeated, so obviously delighted that Sorcha was taken entirely aback. The faerie got to his feet, pulling Sorcha along with him. He squeezed her hands so tightly she winced. "For something to happen to the same woman for *two* kings is…impossible. Improbable, at the very least. Some witch or ghoul or seer must have foreseen this. Why have I heard no news of it before? I must search for –"

"How?" Sorcha asked, cutting through Eirian's self-possessed ramblings as she forcefully pulled her hands away from his. "How am I pregnant with…"

Then the Unseelie king's words truly set in. *Two kings, he said. One was Lachlan. The other…*

"No," she gasped, beyond horrified, but when Sorcha tried to take a step away from him Eirian merely grabbed both her wrists in a vice-like grip.

His eyes shone with an excitement she had never seen before. "This changes everything, little bird," he said. "It seems it is time I expedite my plans."

Sorcha did not want to know what those plans were. Going by Eirian's face, however, she had a fairly good – and awful – idea about what he was intending.

"I am afraid I shall have to rearrange tonight's dinner plans, *my love,*" he said, enunciating the final two words with sick and frightful glee. He broke away from Sorcha, quickly making his way to the door before she had a chance to breathe.

He flashed a grin at her. "I have a war to start, you

see."

Sorcha did not make it to the washroom in time to vomit once more.

CHAPTER TWENTY-TWO

Lachlan

A rumbling filled the air. Lachlan was startled from his morning doze, shivering back into consciousness in response to the sounds.

"Just what is going on?" he wondered aloud wincing at the weak morning light that hit his eyes when he opened them.

Then Ronan crashed through the doors to Lachlan's chambers, ruddy-faced and panicked. "He is here."

Lachlan frowned. "Who is here?"

"The Unseelie king," the faerie replied, falling over the words in his urgency to utter them. "He is here with an army. He is here to attack us!"

Lachlan leapt to his feet, tense and deathly alert. "He was never supposed to attack us. Not now – not for years, even! I thought no information had leaked out about our planned ambush. So how –"

"I do not know," Ronan cut in, giving Lachlan just

enough time to pull on a pair of leather trousers, a shirt, a green-and-gold overcoat and knee-high boots before corralling him out of his chambers towards the strategy room. They met Murdoch on their way there; deep shadows lurked beneath his eyes, making the kelpie look entirely haunted.

"There is a disturbance," he said as they rushed through the door. Ronan cleared the large, central table until all that remained was a detailed map of the Seelie Court and the surrounding forest. "I felt it in the air. What is going on?"

"Eirian," Lachlan muttered. "He is here...with an army. How large, Ronan?"

The horned faerie frowned for a moment. "Scouts say several hundred, but I'm inclined to believe that may be a glamour. If Eirian is leading the army himself I'd say the number is fewer than a hundred...but all well-trained, vicious creatures which are happy to do anything to fulfil their king's desires."

Lachlan considered this for a long moment, just as Julian and Adrian rushed through the door. Julian looked haggard, as if he had been unhappy to find himself roused from sleep; Adrian, on the other hand, looked as if he had been up for hours.

"I guess our winter solstice ambush is no longer happening," the amber-eyed man said, stating the obvious. "So what's the plan?"

Lachlan glanced at the map, thinking hard. It had not rained or snowed for days. The forest was dry and brittle. If they could catch Eirian's army before they reached the central part of the Seelie Court then they could well defeat him.

After all, the silver king had no idea his opponent had the best fire wizard in Europe on his side.

"Burn them," he said, staring at Julian as his mouth widened into a humourless grin. Out of the corner of his eye he saw Murdoch share a similar reaction, though Adrian looked somewhat hesitant. "Do you have an issue with this?" Lachlan asked the man.

He shook his head. "It is a fine plan – and the best we could hope for on such short notice. I simply have... bad memories...of fire."

"I can keep the fire under control," Murdoch chimed in. "That was supposed to be the plan for the ambush of the revel, anyway, to distract the Unseelie. Burn and drown. Only on a much smaller, less noticeable scale. But I can handle a large fire."

Julian glanced at him. "It could very easily grow out of control in a dry forest like this. Are you sure?"

"Positive."

"Then let's do it." Lachlan indicated towards the entrance of the palace. "Ronan, we need soldiers at every entrance. Guard the revel clearing as best you can, though if you have to choose between the two then prioritise the palace. But keep a small number of soldiers within the underground passages to the clearing, just to keep them protected. Is Ailith awake yet?"

"Being woken as we speak. I've requested she organise the healers."

"Good. Now go."

Ronan nodded, then silently left the room to organise his troops. Lachlan watched as Julian cracked his knuckles, one at a time, and Adrian stretched his back in a slow series of pops.

The two men stared at him. "Better to limber up now than in the field," Adrian said, explaining what they were doing. "Can't be stiff when performing magic."

"I admit to being curious as to just how *wolfish* you are in battle," Lachlan replied.

The man laughed. "I am just as curious to see the kelpie in action."

"Good thing Eirian has brought the fight to us, then," Murdoch said, before moving towards the door. He glanced back over his shoulder, lingering his gaze on Lachlan. "Will this work?"

"It must. It has to."

"Then let's do what we must, because we have to."

As the four of them rushed out of the palace and entered the bitterly cold, dimly lit forest, Lachlan could not help thinking how bizarre the creatures around him were. *Two mortals with magic and a kelpie, of all things. But I would not be strong enough without them. I would be destroyed without them.*

Lachlan did not know if the notion was a good one or not, though he did not have time to dwell upon it. For now he had to rely on the men he had placed his trust in to help him rescue Sorcha and save his kingdom.

He simply never imagined the latter would come before the former.

CHAPTER TWENTY-THREE

Sorcha

Sorcha paced around the Unseelie castle for so long she felt sure she would erode the stone floor beneath her feet. The place seemed almost empty, devoid even of its usual ghostly whispers, stretching shadows and glimmers of silvery light. She knew why this was, of course.

Eirian had left to attack the Seelie Court.

But three days had passed since he had made the decision to preemptively strike his northern brethren. Sorcha was still struggling to come to terms with *why*, not least because the Unseelie king had not answered any of her questions – nor indeed spoken to her at all – since laying the revelation that she was pregnant at her feet.

With his child.

A sudden urge to be sick rolled over Sorcha. If she was being honest the baby-induced nausea and stabbing pains had entirely subsided over the last two days, which meant the only reason Sorcha felt sick at all was because of the situation in which she became pregnant.

In my bouts of memory loss he touched me, she thought, close to tears. Sorcha had either been on the verge of tears or full-on sobbing ever since she found out what had happened to her. *He perverted my mind and violated me. And now...*

She gulped down a fresh wave of tears, though the lump in her throat made it difficult for Sorcha to breathe. But she could not cry – not anymore. The baby growing inside her was *hers.* She had to cling to that even as she wished to violently reject the foreign life in her womb.

"My child, my child," she mumbled, over and over again. "My child, not his."

Sorcha knew Eirian would never let that be. The babe was his heir and, going by the way he'd reacted to the news of Sorcha's pregnancy, the Unseelie king had never reasonably expected such a thing to happen. *Lachlan did say it was difficult for faeries to conceive,* she thought. *But I did not realise it was as hard as this. And if it is so hard...*

Why was it so easy with me?

Before she knew it Sorcha found herself wandering through the hot springs, folding her legs beneath her to sit by the edge of the steaming water. She breathed in deeply, feeling her heart rate finally begin to slow to a far less tumultuous rate. But the sight of the water made her deeply unhappy, for it made her think of Murdoch.

"My second child I swore to you," she whispered, gazing at her hazy reflection in the hot springs. "Just as I failed Lachlan I have failed you."

Somewhere deep inside Sorcha knew that neither

Murdoch nor Lachlan would have deemed her a failure. Their love for her – her love for *them* – was far too strong for a string of broken promises to destroy. But with Eirian descending upon the Seelie Court even as Sorcha bit back another round of tears she could not help the thought that both the kelpie and the Seelie king would have been better off if they'd never met her.

They would tell me I am foolish to believe such a thing. But it was foolish of them to love me in the first place.

It was foolish of me to love them.

"But I love you anyway," Sorcha said, swirling a finger through the hot water. It made her realise how cold her own skin was, for it stung her like a thousand needles. But she put up with the pain, drawing patterns through the water akin to the way Murdoch's form stretched and receded whenever he willed it to within the loch. Sorcha wished for nothing more now than to be enveloped in his embrace, when she was cold and frightened and felt very, very small. The kelpie of Loch Lomond had always looked out for her. Always protected her.

Sorcha had tried to return the favour – sacrificing her life for his – and now he could no longer look out for her.

She had never felt so miserable.

"*From ev'ry joy and pleasure torn,*" she whispered, still swirling the water. The song had been in her head for months now. The one she had sung to Murdoch, the night she'd tried and failed to betray him. If she squinted she could almost see dark shapes forming around her fingertip, so she sang to them.

"Life's weary vale I'll wander thro';

And hopeless, comfortless, I'll mourn,

A faithless woman's broken vow!"

Sorcha stared at the water beneath her, unblinking, imagining through her bleariness that the dark shapes she thought she could see through the steam were Murdoch himself. But then she frowned.

She *could* see Murdoch. In his true form.

With a gasp Sorcha realised the steam all around her had begun to dissipate, and the water right in front of her had become mirror-clear despite her breaking its surface with her finger. She lowered her hand further into the water, fruitlessly trying to grasp at strands of Murdoch's midnight-coloured mane before a heavy object knocked him to the ground.

He let out a scream, though it was tinny and insubstantial through the water, then with some effort shoved whatever had hit him off his back. There were glints and flashes around him as he ran that were not silver, like the Unseelie, but orange and red and *burning.*

There is fire around him.

Sorcha did not know what she was seeing. She had never witnessed a prophecy before – she was not sure she even believed them. And if her vision was wishful thinking then why would Sorcha have imagined Murdoch running through a wall of flame?

"Murdoch," she said, very quietly, then louder she repeated it. "Murdoch. Murdoch. Murdoch."

The kelpie paused in his tracks. "...Sorcha?"

She could not believe it. What Sorcha was seeing

was not a prophecy, nor a fantasy created by her brain.
She was seeing the present.

CHAPTER TWENTY-FOUR

Murdoch

"Lachlan!" Murdoch coughed, shifting a fallen tree off his back with a sharp twist of his shoulder. "Julian! Where are you?"

All around him was smoke and steam and cloying, burning soot. It filled Murdoch's lungs, stealing his very breath as he pushed away the tree trunk and struggled to his feet. Julian had not been joking when he said his fires could get large; for the first time Murdoch entertained the notion that they were perhaps too large for even him to quell.

No, he thought, shaking out his mane as he fled through the burning forest, willing the loch and its tributaries to douse the fires behind him. *I cannot lose faith now. Our plan is working.*

Though Murdoch had not seen the Unseelie king even once, he had torn apart dozens of his ghouls and twisted, ugly soldiers over the past hour. He only extinguished the fire around him when he was sure the

639

area was empty.

All he had to do was listen to his enemies' anguished screams as they burned to death. When they, too, were extinguished, so too was the fire.

But Murdoch was tiring. He would go on – *had* to go on – for as long as it took, but such a broad-ranged attack was draining beyond belief. The kelpie had never had to deal with such vicious fires before.

He hoped never to have to do it again.

"...doch. Murdoch. Murdoch. Murdoch."

He froze. Was he imagining things? For through the haze of the burning fire – the cracking of wood, the screaming of faeries, the rush of the flames – Murdoch almost thought he could hear...

"Sorcha?" he wondered aloud, thinking he must be going mad.

Out of the corner of his eye Murdoch noticed a flash of silver just a moment too late. A bug-eyed, grotesque monster of an Unseelie had taken advantage of his momentary distraction to aim their cavernous maw right at his throat. The kelpie steeled himself for the blow, but the attack never came.

A blur from the right came crashing into the creature, snarling and snapping at their twisted skin until the Unseelie grew silent. When Murdoch spied a pair of startlingly amber eyes he relaxed.

"A wolf in more than name," he said, taking a few careful steps towards the hulking, long-limbed wolf that stood before him. Wordlessly the two animals that were not animals gently touched their noses together, blood dripping from Adrian Wolfe's wicked teeth as he smiled at Murdoch.

There was a wound on the wolf's left flank, though Adrian did not seem to mind it. He stalked around Murdoch the way he had done the first time they met, clearly searching for injuries upon the kelpie, then stopped in front of him then it became apparent his search brought up naught.

"A tree fell on me," Murdoch said, "but such a trivial thing cannot harm me. How are you faring, Wolfe?"

But Adrian did not reply, tongue lolling from his mouth as he stared at the kelpie. It occurred to Murdoch that the man may well not be *able* to speak in his animal form. He was a mortal, after all.

With no warning but a flick of his bushy tail Adrian bolted back through the forest the way he came, following the scent of blood that was pervasive upon the air. Murdoch allowed himself to admit that he need a minute to gather himself together again so, after a final glance at the ugly remains of the Unseelie Adrian had felled, he headed for the nearest burn that ran into Loch Lomond.

The water was a welcome slash of icy coolness against the suffocating, dry heat of the smoke. Murdoch dipped his muzzle into it, gratefully gulping down mouthful after mouthful of the stuff before treading his hooves through the bed of the stream. But as he moved an odd detail in the water caught his eye.

"No, it can't be..." he murmured, darting his head around to check that he was defiitely alone before peering down into the burn. "There is no way that –"

"Murdoch! Oh Murdoch, can you hear me?" came a voice that was unmistakably, impossibly Sorcha's. But before his eyes was her watery image, hair wild and

641

tangled around her pale, astounded face.

Murdoch slipped into his human form in an instant, not caring for the way the water of the burn nipped at his naked skin to remind him that human flesh burned just as badly through ice as it did flame. He reached a hand out to Sorcha's face. He felt nothing but water, of course, but when she closed her eyes and cried out happily he could almost imagine the sensation of her cheek beneath his fingertips.

"How are you...is this real?" he asked, not daring to believe that it was.

But Sorcha nodded. "I spoke your name to the hot springs in the depths of the Unseelie castle, and sang you a song, and there you were! I thought you were a figment of my imagination but you're not, are you?"

"Not unless we are both imagining each other," Murdoch said, feeling a giddy urge to laugh.

A smile grew across Sorcha's face, mirroring the one Murdoch found his own lips curling into. "Murdoch, I have missed you so! It has been a torment unlike any other to be without you – to fall asleep in an empty bed, and sit by the fire alone, and keep songs within me instead of singing them for you."

"We will save you," Murdoch insisted. He leaned his face closer to the stream, wishing he could reach through the water and steal Sorcha away when nobody was watching. "*I* will save you. Just wait and see."

Sorcha's face softened at his words, but then quickly grew hard and serious. "What is going on in the Seelie Court? Eirian –"

"We are handling it," he insisted. "We are winning. Lachlan's fire wizard finally came through for us. We are burning the vile Unseelie to ash."

To his surprise Sorcha did not look happy at all. Rather, a fleeting moment of heartbreak crossed her face, looking for a moment as if she would cry. "The forest," she murmured. "All the creatures within it. They will die, too."

A pang of sympathy and pure, unadulterated love hit Murdoch. He let out a short laugh. "Of course you are worried for the forest. But I am minimising the harm that comes to it, I swear it. The forest will regrow – Lachlan and Ailith will see to it that it happens as quickly as possible. So do not worry, Sorcha. We will best Eirian and then we will –"

Murdoch paused. He could hear a scuttling upon the earth to his left, and a soft stalking on his right. He had spent too much time focused on his impossible communication with Sorcha, and if he did not cut it off now then he would be in serious trouble.

"I must go," he said, hating every word as he rose to his feet. "I have to fight. I love you, Sorcha. I love you, I love you."

Panic crossed her face even as the very lines of it began to ripple and fade away. "I have to tell you something!" she cried. "Eirian, he – I am –"

But the rest of her sentence was lost to the sound of snapping teeth as a cat-faced Unseelie launched itself at Murdoch. He bodily kicked it away, still in the form of a man, and in the second it took the creature to recover Murdoch became a kelpie once more and trampled the faerie to death.

When the source of the scuttling – a grotesque, many-legged, scarlet-horned imp – came upon Murdoch he made quick work of it, too. But then another Unseelie came through the trees, fully engulfed in flame, aiming an attack at him even as their flesh was burned asunder. Several more followed, and before Murdoch had a chance to process where each enemy was coming from he was overrun with opponents to destroy.

Mustering all the concentration he had, he began to fill the Unseelie soldiers' lungs with their own blood, using the same trick he had used at the winter solstice revel five years prior. They choked and gagged, but still their attack did not relent.

It was therefore to his relief when Adrian leapt from the trees, pinning down a faceless, burning faerie despite the wolf's proclaimed fear of fire. Julian Thorne was not far behind, his scarlet robes stained black with soot and smoke. He looked exhausted beyond belief, as if a gentle push to his chest would knock him to the ground. But still he joined the fray, blasting the Unseelie with balls of fire so hot they burned blue.

"Thank you," Murdoch mouthed, before returning his attention to the stream of monsters intent on destroying him.

So absorbed in the onslaught was he that the kelpie did not have the time to think, even once, about what Sorcha had been trying to tell him.

CHAPTER TWENTY-FIVE

Lachlan

All around Lachlan was smoke and fire and death. It permeated the air, leaving him blind and deaf in a torrent of danger. He had to find a way through it.

He had to reach the Unseelie king.

"Where are you, silver bastard?" Lachlan bellowed, taking one of his favourite mortal curses as his own. "Come and fight me! That is what you're here for, isn't it?"

He did not expect Eirian to reply, of course, but the screaming and goading fired up Lachlan's fury until it burned hotter than the forest around him. He wiped away a fine sheen of sweat from his brow before it could reach his eyes; when he pulled his hand away it was black with soot.

"If only Clara could see me now," he coughed, almost laughing. "This is most definitely a sorrier state than being a fox ever was."

Fuelled by anger and a desire to steal back Sorcha

once and for all, Lachlan powered on through the forest. When an Unseelie attacked – a beautiful faerie, dressed in silver armour engraved with fine scroll work and shards of diamond – Lachlan wasted no time in felling him with the blackened iron sword which had, once upon a time, been used by Murdoch-as-Lachlan to murder King Eirian's brother and nephew.

Lachlan felt it only fitting to use the same weapon to extinguish the final member of the Unseelie king's family.

When another equally beautiful faerie attacked him – a woman, this time – Lachlan kicked her in the stomach and commanded her to become one with the earth. His voice dripped power; the Unseelie, horrified, realised too late that she did not possess the ability to defy him. With a wretched scream she collapsed to her belly and dug and dug and dug at the ground, filling her mouth with soil until her scream was quelled. Lachlan watched with sickening satisfaction as the light from the creature's eyes disappeared.

"That was impressively cruel, fox king," an echoing, magically enhanced voice said.

Eirian.

Lachlan's long ears struggled to pinpoint the origin of the voice. But he followed his instincts and, though it involved fighting through the thickest licks of flame that enveloped the forest, he blindly clawed his way through to a clearing in the trees.

When he reached it, the space was completely devoid of smoke and carnage.

The pine trees circling the clearing were lush with green needles so dark they were almost black, and there was a fine layer of frost upon the ground that had covered the entire forest but two hours ago. The air smelled of cold, and winter, and life put on pause, and was startlingly, completely silent.

Beneath the empty boughs of an oak tree that was waiting for spring stood the Unseelie king himself, dressed in armour even more impressive that the kind his soldiers had been wearing.

The faerie smiled at Lachlan, all sharp teeth and ill intent. "Why, it appears you have found me alone and unarmed. Whatever will I do?"

Lachlan did not need his fox nose to smell a trap. His hand tightened around the leather-bound hilt of his sword, testing its weight as he took careful step after careful step towards Eirian.

The Unseelie king's smile only grew wider. "It seems your Court mislikes the fire as much as my poor army does. Tell me, Lachlan, how much energy will it take to restore your home? Far too much to employ a counter-attack against me, I would presume. Too much to even think of stealing back your unfortunate mortal love."

Lachlan bristled at the comment, though it relieved him to know that Eirian seemed to have no idea he managed to meet with Sorcha earlier in the year. But then he realised what the Unseelie king's first comment meant.

This entire attack was meant to maim us, not destroy us.

It made sense, of course. Eirian's numbers had been few, as Ronan predicted, and next to no direct attacks had been made on the palace. Most of the fighting seemed to be taking place directly in the forest; Lachlan himself ran into scarcely a handful of foes.

"If you think to injure us then you underestimate us," Lachlan said, using a touch of magic to clean the soot and sweat from his skin and clothes. His grip on his sword tightened as a result, though Eirian merely laughed.

"You are not even wearing armour, my dear Lachlan," he chided, throwing his arms open wide as if inviting an attack. "Are you even *trying* to best me?"

Lachlan dashed forwards to slash at Eirian's right hand, so quickly that it was all the faerie could do to just barely avoid the attack. "Armour slows me down," Lachlan snarled. "I have no doubt that I am faster than you."

"But are you stronger?"

Before Lachlan could strike another blow Eirian blasted him back with a burst of silver-rimmed magic. His eyes twitched, smarting at the sensation of the Unseelie's magic on his skin, before shaking himself out and attacking his opponent once again.

He was met with another blast.

"Your physical assault implies that you know your magic cannot beat me yet," Eirian said, gleeful as he stood and watched Lachlan fruitlessly try to reach him again and again. "And here I was, thinking you might have actually been some kind of match for me, after what dear Sorcha said about you."

"Do not speak her name!" Lachlan roared, furious. But it was true that he doubted the strength of his magic; that he could control Eirian's armoured soldiers was a good sign, but the Unseelie king was hundreds of years old.

Lachlan knew in his heart that he needed Murdoch.

"Your kelpie cannot help you," Eirian said, silver eyes catching Lachlan's almost imperceptible look around him. "You will find that most all of your friends are, quite deliberately, otherwise engaged."

Damn it! Lachlan thought, stalking around to Eirian's left as he uselessly tried to find a weakness in the faerie's defence. It was clear that the Unseelie king had known exactly what he was doing from the start.

"You are making a direct attempt on mine and Murdoch's life," Lachlan said, aiming for a different tactic.

Eirian raised an eyebrow. "And? What of it?"

"You have broken the tenets of Sorcha's promise. By law you must release her!"

The laugh that was emitted from Eirian's mouth was manic. He threw his head back, near incapable of breathing through his mirth. "You are funny, fox king," he gasped. "You do not seriously believe that I will give her back, do you?"

"I have every right to rain fire upon your castle if you do not!"

"I would love to see you try." Eirian's laughter abruptly stopped, and his face grew serious. He took a step towards Lachlan, then another and another, crunching through frost with deliberate, slow movements. "Give her up, Lachlan. My claim on her is endlessly stronger than yours. I must profess my sympathies for your lost child, however. I would never rest in my quest for revenge if I were in the same position."

Lachlan froze. He was not supposed to *know* that

Sorcha had lost their child. It was not difficult to feign horror and desperate disbelief at what he was hearing, much to Eirian's obvious enjoyment. "D-do not talk to me about family, you silver snake," Lachlan growled. "You know nothing of it."

He did not like the way Eirian kept coming closer, not a hint of fear in the faerie's eyes. He knew that Lachlan was not a threat to him. Not on his own. Not without back-up.

It had been his plan all along.

But when Eirian stood close enough to Lachlan to deal a killing blow, he paused.

Lachlan bared his teeth. "If you do not kill me now, I will strike back and destroy you in your sleep."

"How amusing," Eirian replied, eyes glinting as if they were made of the frost that covered the clearing. "Sorcha told me that if you ever meant her harm her kelpie would drown you in yours. The beast must be rubbing off on you, for you to have the same ideas of vengeance."

"Do not talk as if you know her – as if you regard her life as more than a bargaining chip against those that would otherwise destroy you!"

Eirian chuckled. "That is where you're wrong, my dear Lachlan. You are still so green. So much to learn. I think that, for her sake as well as your suffering, I will keep you alive for now. It would be a mighty shame if you did not see the events of the future unfold before your very eyes. This has been fun, fox king."

And with that he was gone. Lachlan hardly had the chance to blink before the Unseelie king disappeared, replaced by little more than a raven's feather.

Which means the defences are down around the Court, if he could magic his way out, Lachlan thought, too numb to process anything else Eirian had said as he stumbled back to the palace. Most of the forest around him was no longer aflame, but the damage had been done.

Everything was dead. It would take years to recover.

Lachlan forced himself to head towards the throne room instead of his chambers, though he was desperate to sleep. But he had no time to sleep – not when his entire kingdom was at stake.

He drowned his sorrows in half a pitcher of wine before Ronan showed up to stand in front of the throne, closely followed by Julian, Adrian and Murdoch. The entire group was covered in burns, soot and blood, blood, blood.

Lachlan could not tell if it was their blood or their enemy's.

"An ambush," Murdoch heaved. Julian was leaning heavily against his shoulder, barely conscious. "We might have lost, had Ronan not shown up in time."

"Four-and-ninety Unseelie ghouls, not afraid to burn and die," the horned faerie said. His eyes were blank; Lachlan had never seen him look so hollow. "They did not stop. They were mad. They were –"

"Enchanted, to stop the lot of you from helping your poor king."

Lachlan stilled. He did not recognise the voice. Nobody did.

Except Murdoch.

The kelpie turned to face a caped, shadowy figure

lurking in the doorway. "In what world would you dare show your face in the faerie realm?"

"An opportunity arose that benefits both myself and your sorry group," the figure replied, stalking across the gilded floor of the throne room and parting the group standing before Lachlan in order to bow before him. "You have more need of what I have to say than you could ever know, King Lachlan."

He frowned. "Who *are* you?"

When the creature drew down their hood Lachlan was faced with silver, bulbous eyes, broken teeth and hair like seaweed. There was something familiar about them that he could not quite place; a memory of a story, perhaps, or a picture in a book.

And then it clicked.

"Beira," he said. "You are Beira."

The witch grinned a crooked, hideous grin. "That was my name, before. I would like it to be my name again."

CHAPTER TWENTY-SIX

Murdoch

"Beira?" Murdoch asked, more a question than a statement. It was a name he had not heard in quite some time. A name that wrought fear in faerie kind, and the humans who were unfortunate enough to cross her path.

"My mother cast you out," Lachlan said, frown deepening as he leaned forwards on his throne to inspect the wretched creature standing before him. "And then your own kind did, too. *Eirian* banished you. Someone get Ailith – she knows the history of this witch better than I."

Beira cackled. "I do not need a reminder of what I have done. Trust me, my former proclivities are where they should be: in the past. I am a changed witch, and I can prove it."

"I do not believe you."

"I cannot lie."

"And yet you are lying," Lachlan insisted, a fury rising in his eyes that Murdoch suspected had little to do with Beira herself and everything to do with the loss the Seelie Court had clearly just sustained. For if the tumultuous attack Murdoch, Julian and Adrian had faced was indeed an ambush, then...

That meant Eirian intended to face Lachlan alone.

And Eirian is still alive, which means Lachlan was not strong enough to defeat him on his own. But Lachlan *is alive, which means –*

"Why did the Unseelie king not kill you, fox?" Murdoch asked, cutting through the tension in the room with his question. He had no reason to distrust Beira, after all; she had only ever helped him. He did not mind getting answers from Lachlan in front of her.

The golden faerie stared at Beira, then at Murdoch. "This witch is your *friend*, isn't she? The one who told you how to –"

"To save your lovely lass," Beira said. "That was me. See? I want to help you; truly I do."

"You have never helped the Seelie before."

It was Ailith who had spoken, breathless in her rush to reach the throne room. There was blood on her hands and sapphire dress, though it did not belong to her. She shook her head sadly at Ronan. "Frederick will be fine, as will Jonas. Saoirse, on the other hand..."

The blank look on the horned faerie's face somehow got worse. Murdoch knew the Seelie Court had not been forced into fighting since before Lachlan's birth; though Ronan had been glad for the excuse to strengthen their defences Murdoch somehow doubted the faerie had all that much actual combat experience.

"My role in the realm was never to help anyone – not directly," Beira said, responding to Ailith's first comment. "I was crucial in the building of our world. Our mountains. Our rivers. Our forests. I could see what others could not –"

"And used that to destroy what you saw fit!" Ailith snapped. Murdoch had not often seen the faerie irritated. It was an odd look upon her fair face. "You consumed mortals who were promised to members of our kind, transformed changelings into trees when you had no right to them, made moves to –"

"As I said before you appeared, Seelie queen," the witch said, her ugly voice masking all other noises in the throne room, "I do not need to be reminded of what I did in the past. More than a hundred years have passed, and I have learned my lesson. I truly am here to help, as the kelpie can attest to. All I want is a chance to return to the form and power I once possessed – that which is rightfully mine."

Against Murdoch's shoulder Julian had fully lost consciousness, and was beginning to fall to the floor. Adrian caught the man before he hit his head, easing him down to rest between them. It was bizarre to have Julian simply lie there, in the middle of the throne room, but for now it would have to do. Nobody wanted to miss part of the conversation, after all; that much was clear.

For a moment nobody said anything, then all eyes went to Lachlan. In this room – in this Court, in this kingdom – his word was law. Even Adrian Wolfe, who seemed inclined to follow his own rules as and when he liked, maintained a respectful silence instead of making a sly comment, though he glanced at Murdoch as if insinuating he expected the kelpie to say something.

But Murdoch had asked his question. It was up to

Lachlan to answer it.

Eventually the Seelie king sighed, and slumped against his throne. "Eirian has something he wishes me to be alive to witness. Something for which I will *suffer,* it seems. I should not be surprised; that is his way of doing things. But he also..." Lachlan ran a hand over his face, then stared sightlessly at the ceiling. "He gave me his sympathies for the loss of my child. His sympathies! I am trying to see the jibe behind his words but I cannot. He said that there is nothing he would not do to get his revenge, were he in the same position as I am. What was his point in saying such a thing to me?"

"Because he is expecting an heir," Beira said, so matter-of-factly it took Murdoch entirely by surprise.

"You cannot mean that," Lachlan scoffed. "Surely not. Is this in the future? Is it something you have seen?"

"It is something I have seen but it is also something that is current. The Unseelie king is indeed going to, finally, become a father."

"And who is the mother? Who is -"

"*No.*"

The word came out of Murdoch before he could stop it, for now that he was no longer facing an assault on all sides by vicious, murderous foes he remembered his conversation with Sorcha. She had tried to tell him something.

Something important.

Something to do with Eirian.

When Beira nodded Murdoch collapsed to his knees. But Lachlan was still a few seconds behind

Murdoch's revelation, so the kelpie was witness to every moment it took the fox to understand what Beira was insinuating.

"No!" he shouted, so loudly Julian groaned from his position sprawled across the floor. Lachlan got to his feet, a terrible expression on his face as he closed the gap between himself and Beira. He towered over her hunched, decrepit figure, yet she did not seem at all perturbed by the menace presented before her.

"Clara is not carrying his child. That is not what you are saying. There is no –"

"But this is good, isn't it?" Adrian chimed in, entirely unwelcome on all fronts.

"How *dare* you say that!" Lachlan snarled, just before Murdoch could say the same thing.

The amber-eyed man shrugged. "Did your witch friend's solution to taking Sorcha Darrow back not involve her being pregnant? Or did I misremember that?"

Murdoch stared at the man, then at Lachlan. He was right. To hear that Eirian had laid hands on Sorcha was an unimaginable nightmare. Murdoch could not fathom the pain she must be in. But the fact that she was carrying a child was the miracle he and Lachlan had been waiting for.

"You wish your form and power restored, you say?" Lachlan said, very quietly.

Beira grinned. "This information is surely worth it, fox king. Or have I overestimated the lass' value?"

"You have not. But –"

"Lachlan," Ailith said, voice full of warning.

Murdoch watched as the two of them exchanged a meaningful look.

"Trust me," Lachlan said, before turning back to Beira. "I will grant you what you wish, but on two conditions."

The witch nodded. "Name them."

"We must successfully take Sorcha Darrow back from Eirian and, once we do, you must help protect her from him. This naturally involves you helping the Seelie Court as and when we need you."

"I am happy to agree to such terms, so long as helping the Seelie Court never interferes with the safety and wellbeing of the kelpie and his loch." She cast her bulbous gaze to Murdoch. "We are friends, after all."

An unexpected surge of affection hit Murdoch. Clearly he had underestimated how much the witch had valued his company over the years. He would be sure not to make the same mistake again; it was a good feeling to have someone fighting in the same corner as him... even if it was an Unseelie.

"Then we have reached an agreement," Lachlan said. "Somebody please take Julian to a bed and heal his mental trauma. Everyone else...sleep well. You will need all the rest you can get." Though Lachlan's voice was solid and determined Murdoch could not mistake the distress he saw in his eyes. The faerie would not sleep tonight, he knew. He would only think of Sorcha, and the child growing inside her that was not his.

Or mine, Murdoch thought, growing despondent in a moment. *Though Beira said Sorcha would have my child, that will not come to pass. It is impossible. I fear it means Beira's plan to save her will not work.*

But the kelpie did not vocalise his fear. They *needed* Beira's plan to work, after all.

He could deal with her being wrong about his son if it meant they saved the woman he loved.

CHAPTER TWENTY-SEVEN

Sorcha

Sorcha didn't know what was making her stomach roil and twist more – her pregnancy or the sight of Eirian torturing a broken-winged Seelie messenger in front of her.

"Does he really think I will communicate with him right now?" Eirian crooned, before stabbing the Seelie's stomach with a scalding hot iron. The creature screamed; their eyes cried red, red, red.

Sorcha wished she could put them out of their misery.

"His fire wizard may have successfully kept my ghouls at bay, but the fox could not best *me*," the Unseelie king continued, as if nothing out of the ordinary was happening whilst he spoke to Sorcha. "He is not strong enough. And your horse was not there to help him, nor his mortal friends. Rest assured Lachlan will not get a second chance to face me."

Eirian twisted the iron in his hands, pushing it

further into the messenger's stomach. With a final, guttural cry the Seelie collapsed to the floor. Whether they were dead or simply unconscious, Sorcha could not tell.

"Why are you making me watch this?" she asked the cruel, silver king as he dropped the iron poker, removed the leather glove he'd worn to hold it, and turned his back on his prey.

He stalked towards Sorcha, sliding a hand across her stomach when he reached her even as she tried to flinch away. "Our child must see what their kind are capable of," he said. "They must grow used to the screams and cries of their enemies, for in the blink of an eye they will be ruling alongside me."

"I will *never* let that happen," Sorcha growled, once more attempting to move away from Eirian. But he grabbed at her cheeks with a grip of steel, preventing her from leaving.

"I do not see how you can stop me," he said, soft and sinister. He let go of her face, but with the Unseelie king's mercurial eyes so close to hers Sorcha found she no longer had the power to walk away from him. "Like it or not, lass, you are the mother of my child," he continued. "My heir. That makes you important above all others, and I would never dream of parting you from the babe. But mark my words, Sorcha: if you dare attempt to flee, I will hunt you down. I will scour the realm, and every corner of the earth we walk upon, until you are mine again, and you will be imprisoned in a corner of my kingdom until the end of time."

Silence. Sorcha could do nothing but return Eirian's stare.

"But we will not let it come to that," he said an

interminably long time later, sickeningly cheerful again in the blink of an eye. He placed a gentle kiss on Sorcha's lips – a mockery of an affectionate gesture. "You will be my queen, if you only let me crown you. You need not suffer forever."

Considering what being Eirian's queen entailed, Sorcha rather preferred the option of being locked up until darkness permanently shrouded the earth and snuffed out her life for good.

Save me, she thought, feeling entirely hopeless when Eirian finally gave her leave to return to her chambers. *Somebody save me.* It did not matter who. If Sorcha could save herself she would, but she had no options left to her.

Eirian had proven he was stronger than Lachlan, and the Seelie Court was in ruins. Sorcha had witnessed but a fraction of the damage the fire had caused through her communication with Murdoch; it would take many years to restore its power.

Sorcha had to entertain the idea that the kelpie may well not be strong enough to battle head-on with Eirian, either, though now that the Unseelie king had attacked him he was free to respond in kind. She dearly did not want to lose Murdoch to Eirian, regardless if that meant Sorcha had to spend the rest of her life imprisoned by the faerie.

When she reached her room Sorcha spied one of the numerous hair pins Eirian had gifted her, laying innocuous on an ash table by the bed. Lilacs and bluebells and fronds of ivy, immortalised in silver and painted enamel. The sharp end of the pin gleamed wicked and inviting in the firelight.

"No," she murmured, trembling fingers grasping at

the beautiful ornament as she stared down at her stomach. "I always have a way out."

But then she dropped the hair pin, numb to the sound of it clattering against the floor. Sorcha could not do it - could not even fathom the notion of taking her life when she held another within her.

The babe might have been Eirian's, but it was also hers.

Her child. *Her* responsibility. *Her* joy.

Nobody would take that from her...not even the creature who had forced his warped version of love upon her and taken away every choice Sorcha ever had in the matter of becoming a mother.

CHAPTER TWENTY-EIGHT

Lachlan

"We will only have this one shot."

"Yes, and you will succeed."

"You really think so?"

"I could not say it if I thought it were false, could I?"

Ailith's hand slid over Lachlan's and squeezed his fingers. In the darkness, beneath the sheets, with but a glimmer of light accentuating his queen's startling eyes and ice-blonde hair, Lachlan was reminded of a time gone by. All he'd had was Ailith. All she'd had was him.

Things were endlessly more complicated now.

Lachlan did not think either of them would change the circumstances of their current relationship even if they could. Ailith had Tomas – a soft-spoken, curly-haired faerie who provided Ailith with a settled love Lachlan could have never given her. And Lachlan...

No matter where she was, or who else she loved, Lachlan had Sorcha Darrow. The girl with the mismatched eyes. The girl with the voice of a silvered bell, or water over stone, or the wind through the trees.

The girl who was once, and always would be, Clara.

"We will save her," Lachlan said, to assure himself as much as Ailith. He kissed her brow when she closed her eyes. "The horse and me both. We will bring her back."

Ailith smiled. "Then be gone, my king. Do not return without her."

Lachlan did not waste much time in getting dressed before leaving his chambers. He spent more time searching for the kelpie, who did not seem to be anywhere in the palace. He spared a moment to check in on Julian, who after spending five solid days asleep was finally conscious once more.

"What are you doing, lurking within your own abode?" the wizard asked when he spied Lachlan by the doorway through a slitted, curious eye.

"I did not wish to rouse you from your rest," Lachlan replied simply.

Julian snorted. "I have slept quite enough, thank you. Evie would kill me if I slept through your rescue attempt. She will demand a minute-by-minute recount the moment I return to her."

"There won't be much to tell her about the hours you will have to sit here, waiting to see if the kelpie and I return empty-handed."

"Then I guess I can while away my time asking Wolfe to tell me everything I have missed," Julian said, wincing at the notion of talking to his not-quite-friend. Then he pointed behind Lachlan, smiling slightly. "You should not tarry much longer, Lachlan of the Seelies. Save Miss Darrow, so that I may finally meet her."

Lachlan nodded, turning from the room without saying goodbye. Upon the advice of a guard he left the palace and passed through the revel clearing. The space had, miraculously, been saved from the fire, though just a few feet out of the clearing everywhere was a mess of burned, broken trees and blackened ferns.

It will take a lot of magic to encourage quick regrowth, he thought, pausing a moment to lay his hands upon the scorched earth. He could feel a pulse within it – a sign that it was not quite dead. He smiled grimly. *It will take a lot, but we can do it. The Seelie Court is strong. The forest is strong.*

Lachlan would not let Eirian destroy everything he held dear.

Almost two hours passed before Lachlan reached the waterfall pool where Murdoch Buchanan had first revealed himself to be a kelpie. He was lying beside the water in his true form, seemingly deep in silent conversation with Adrian, who was a wolf.

"I thought he couldn't speak in that form?" Lachlan asked, announcing his presence.

The kelpie whinnied softly. "He can't, but we understand each other anyway."

"Are you ready?"

"If I wasn't it would not matter; we need the distraction of the solstice revel in order for this to work."

With a shake of his head Murdoch got to his feet, intimidatingly tall and fearsome beneath the midnight moon on the darkest night of the year. Adrian stood, too, giving Lachlan a wolfish grin before loping off into the forest on silent paws.

"Has he told you how he can become a wolf?"

Lachlan asked, when he was sure the man was well out of earshot.

"Something to do with the remnants of a curse he can now activate at will," Murdoch replied. "It does not harm him the way it did before, so he no longer has to worry about losing himself to the beast. What is wrong?"

Lachlan realised he was grimacing at the kelpie, and had taken a step away from the creature. "I do not like it when you talk in this form," he admitted. "It is... unnerving."

Murdoch grinned, though it was all impossibly sharp, gleaming teeth and entirely terrifying. "Good," he said. "I am supposed to be unnerving. Now get on my back before I think better of this plan and buck you off."

"You could lower yourself to the ground to make this easier..." Lachlan muttered as he struggled to reach the kelpie's mane. Murdoch merely flicked his ears in response and, when Lachlan finally had but a tentative grip on the kelpie, hurtled off to the shore of Loch Lomond.

"Are you trying to kill me?!" Lachlan gasped, just barely managing to keep hold of Murdoch's mane. With some difficultly he launched himself onto the kelpie's back, kicking his heels into the creature's haunches in deliberate protest.

"You would know if I was trying to kill you."

"Drown me in my sleep?"

Murdoch glanced back at Lachlan, who could see himself reflected clearly in the kelpie's huge, coal-black eye. "What makes you say that?"

"Apparently Clara told Eirian that you would kill me in such a way, if I ever meant her harm. Was she speaking the truth?"

"I do not deny it," Murdoch replied, somewhat amused. "Though I would also consider crushing you beneath my hooves or ripping your throat out with my teeth."

"Charming. How did Clara know of this?"

"Because I told her, of course."

Lachlan all but choked in disbelief. "Is that what the two of you discussed in the Darach house, in your never-ending conversations by the fireplace?"

The briefest of hesitations. "I may have promised Sorcha I would kill you if you hurt her by the fireplace once or twice."

"And she simply *let* you?"

Murdoch snorted. "Hardly. It is gratifying to hear she remembered what I said, though."

"For you, perhaps."

"Perhaps. Are you ready?"

Lachlan realised they had reached the shore of the loch the instant before Murdoch stopped before it. He gritted his teeth, for he did not relish the thought of storming through lochs and rivers and seas with the kelpie.

In order to reach the Unseelie Court unseen, he had to.

"I am always ready for Sorcha," he said, reverting to her real name. "You remember what you need to do when we get there?"

"Focus on finding her," Murdoch replied, taking a few steps into the loch as he did so. The night air was freezing upon Lachlan's face; he shuddered to think of how cold it would be beneath the surface of the loch. "Do you believe Beira spoke true, when she said Eirian would focus solely on your presence?"

Lachlan nodded. "As far as anyone knows he does not realise there is a way for us to permanently take Sorcha from him, otherwise he would most definitely have killed me when he could. Better I distract him than the other way around."

A pause. "And what if he kills you, fox? Then there will be nothing stopping him following me and Sorcha and taking her back whenever he pleases."

"Do not consider me that weak. And besides...I trust you. To keep her safe, at least."

Another pause. "Likewise. But let's not have it come to that."

Lachlan barked out a laugh. "Yes, I would rather not die tonight. Now come on; let us save Sorcha Darrow."

CHAPTER TWENTY-NINE

Sorcha

Something woke Sorcha abruptly from her unsettled sleep. A noise. A disturbance.

A crash.

"I thought the revel didn't take part in the east wing of the castle...?" she wondered blearily. Stumbling slightly Sorcha got out of bed and made her way to the west-facing window – the one that looked over at the tower containing Eirian's chambers. There was light coming from his room, which seemed strange given that the Unseelie king was supposed to be at the revel.

Sorcha had declined to go, of course, and though it was clear Eirian was not pleased by this there was nothing he could do to force Sorcha to go without risking hurting the baby growing inside her. It was an unexpected, welcome perk to being pregnant with the heir to the Unseelie throne; Sorcha could not be harmed or drugged or otherwise put in a physically compromising situation.

"What is he doing in his chambers instead of the revel, then?" she wondered, concerned and curious. The winter solstice was the most important date in the Unseelie calendar, and after their apparent loss at the hands of the Seelie it was more vital than ever that Eirian demonstrated his strength and reliability as a king to his subjects.

They did not know his true intentions behind his attack on the Seelie Court, after all. They did not know that their king had done exactly what he intended to do...even if that came at the cost of a hundred Unseelie lives.

With a sigh Sorcha wandered over to the mirror in her room, staring at it with every intention of being noticed by the watcher on the other side. "What is going on?" she demanded. And then, because he was more inclined to answer her if she framed it in such a way: "I will not have revellers anywhere near my baby."

It was to Sorcha's immense surprise when a long-fingered hand with nails filed to points – Eirian's hand – appeared through the glass and pulled Sorcha through its surface. She flinched for but a moment, expecting to hit it, but then the moment passed and she found herself in a room entirely unfamiliar to her.

"So you were not in your chambers, then," she said, somewhat dazed. She looked around the barely-lit room, though aside from the aged and cracked mirror she had been pulled through there was nothing inside it.

Eirian was holding a candle in his other hand; he held it up to illuminate his face as he pulled Sorcha close. "It seems we have intruders, though they should not have made it this far without being noticed."

Sorcha hardly dared to acknowledge the spark of

hope that lit up her heart.

"Are you sure they aren't simply revel-goers who have lost their way?"

The look on Eirian's face suggested he was in no mood for such questions. In the candlelight she could see that his pupils were dilated, suggesting he was not in the least bit sober. A dark stain upon his shirt could have been wine, though Sorcha reasoned it could just as easily have been blood.

"So you *were* at the revel," she mused, ignoring the way Eirian's grip on her wrist tightened. "The light in your chambers – a ruse, then? What could you possibly be expecting to happen after you so decidedly decimated the See–"

"The gravity of your situation escapes you, it seems," Eirian cut in, turning from Sorcha to pull her along a corridor she had not been able to make out in the darkness. "If anyone has come to try and *save* you, mark my words, Sorcha: I will kill them. I will kill all who helped them."

Sorcha gulped despite herself. She had no doubt Eirian would do such a thing, and for the most part she sincerely wished the disturbance in the castle had been exactly what she suggested it might be: a lost reveller.

Yet somehow she could not find it within herself to feel truly fearful. The idea that Lachlan and Murdoch had so swiftly gotten back on their feet to launch an assault against Eirian was gratifying.

Encouraging.

"You will remain here for now," the Unseelie king said, letting go of Sorcha to light several torches set into sconces. With a glance at a grey-stoned fireplace the hearth burst into silver flames, taking the edge from the chill of the room in an instant. Below her feet the floor was covered by a threadbare rug, though the bed in the corner looked far newer and well-maintained.

"I am underground, aren't I?" Sorcha asked, certain.

"What does it matter where you are? You will not be able to leave."

"Then perhaps you underestimate me."

Eirian dropped the candle in his hand; its flame stuttered out of existence at his feet. Sliding a hand to the small of Sorcha's back, he pushed her against him until she had to crane her neck upwards to see his face. Without the candle's flame the faerie's pupils dilated even further, leaving but a sliver of silver around them.

Like an eclipse, Sorcha thought. *But the moon never hides the sun for long.*

"If you think I would so easily give you a chance to escape then *you* underestimate *me*, my foolish queen," the Unseelie king murmured. He bent his head, first placing a kiss upon Sorcha's brow, then the tip of her nose and, lastly, her lips. She went rigid in his grip, trying desperately not to taste anything on his tongue when Eirian forced her mouth open to accept it, lest he had been drinking faerie wine. But the kiss was insistent and brutal; Sorcha could do nothing to reject it no matter how hard she struggled.

When Eirian finally broke away a smirk pulled at the corners of his mouth. "I do not need faerie wine to keep you in here," he said, making for the corridor that led back to the crumbling mirror he had pulled Sorcha through mere minutes ago. "For you are without magic, and without magic you have no chance of breaking through a wall of stone."

Sorcha frowned at him. "A wall?"

His smirk became a grin. "Like this," he said, and clicked his fingers.

The opening to the corridor vanished and Eirian with it, though Sorcha could hear him cackling from behind the blockage. "I will enjoy our time together, once I have dealt with this *disturbance,*" he called through the stone. "You had best get some sleep whilst you still can."

When the sound of his footsteps receded into silence Sorcha threw herself against the wall with a roar of frustration. "I will not wait here for you to violate me as you see fit!" she screamed, banging her fists against the cold stone in front of her before collapsing to her knees in front of the silver fireplace. She stared into the flames, imagining Eirian within them, burning.

A rescue, she thought, after her rage had finally subsided. *I must have faith. I will wait for a rescue.*

There was nothing else she would willingly wait for.

CHAPTER THIRTY

Murdoch

"Sorcha, Sorcha, Sorcha," Murdoch uttered under his breath, over and over again as he searched wildly around for her. The Unseelie castle was cold and empty, since most all of its usual inhabitants were at the revel. The deluge of noise coming from the celebration had covered Murdoch's tracks as he carried Lachlan to the exact spot the faerie guided him to – a grille in the castle wall, where steaming water escaped into the cold, unforgiving forest behind them.

Lachlan had hoped Murdoch would be able to melt into the water, and him with it. But the stream of water had been far too small for him to properly utilise so, without thinking of the consequences, Murdoch had merely bowled straight into a fault in the wall once, twice, three times, until the stones gave way and he galloped through the resultant opening into the middle of a steam-filled underground forest.

The noise the kelpie made in entering the castle this way had been tumultuous, but neither he nor Lachlan had the time to be angry with his approach. Without a word Lachlan had slid off Murdoch's back and vanished into the darkness in search of Eirian.

The kelpie changed into his human form, the better to navigate tunnels and stairwells. But after fifteen minutes of searching he found he could not make heads nor tails of the place, and had no hints as to where Sorcha might be.

I need her scent, he thought, shaking himself back into a kelpie once more. It made traversing through the castle far more arduous, and eventually Murdoch grew so frustrated he was tempted to simply bowl through every wall he saw until he found the room where Sorcha was hidden.

But he couldn't do that; a series of crashes and loud, furious gallops across hard stone floors would be far more of a distraction than Lachlan could ever be. Murdoch would be found and, with it, any chance he had of finding Sorcha.

"Where are you, Sorcha?" he whispered, creeping along a ground floor passageway after investigating a tower in the east wing. It had been full of Sorcha's scent, yet she was not in it. There was no trail from the tower, either, which meant Sorcha had been removed from the tower by other means.

Magical means.

She has to be here, Murdoch thought, growing ever more desperate as he rather inelegantly made his way down to the first basement level of the castle. The smell of the food stores overwhelmed his nose, so Murdoch retreated from them to travel further downwards. But the passageways were getting narrower and narrower; soon he would have to turn back into a man, and he would lose his acute sense of smell.

"A clue," he mumbled, nosing at the stones beneath him as he traversed a dark and dingy corridor. It ended at a gnarled door, which stood ajar, so with a butt of his head Murdoch pushed it open. Inside was a room that was just as sparse and dark as the corridor, but upon the wall...

There was a mirror.

And Murdoch could smell Sorcha.

The doorway was far too small for a kelpie to walk through, so Murdoch shifted back to a man as his pulse raced faster and faster. "Sorcha!" he cried, not caring when his voice reverberated back at him a thousand times louder than his initial shout. He was so close; he would not let Sorcha slip away by staying silent. "Sorcha, where are you?"

But the only reply he got was his own voice, then silence, so Murdoch stalked around the room searching for any sign of Sorcha's presence. When he realised a further corridor led off from the room he wasted no time in sprinting down it, knowing in his heart that Sorcha must surely be at the end of it.

It was a dead end.

"Damn it all to hell!" Murdoch yelled, slamming his hands against the wall. "Don't keep her from me, you snake! Give her back!"

"...Murdoch?"

He froze, listening intently. Murdoch had been sure he'd heard his name, just as he'd heard it back in the forest when everything was on fire.

"Sorcha?" he called, staring at the wall in front of

him as if he could somehow see through stone.

"It's me!" she cried, filling Murdoch with relief. "You found me!"

"Where are you?" he asked, relief quickly replaced by urgency when he remembered he likely had very little time left before Eirian realised Lachlan had been naught but a distraction. "Behind the wall?"

A pause, then: "Yes! Yes, behind the wall. I actually nodded in answer first. How silly is that? I –"

"Oh, I love you," Murdoch said, a wide smile on his face for nobody to see but the wall. "I love you more than anything. Did Eirian magic you into there, Sorcha?"

"There was a door, at first. He walked me through, then removed the door when he left – or turned it into a wall. Does that make a difference?"

"All the difference in the world," Murdoch said, tapping upon the stone where a door might be. And, sure enough, the sound his knuckles made was not what he would have expected from a solid wall made of two feet of stone. "A wall this thick with no faults in the stone is difficult even for me to break," he murmured, continuing to tap across the wall to determine the dimensions of the door. "But one which is no true wall at all...stand back, Sorcha."

With a savage grin Murdoch backed away from the door, steeling himself for the tight fit of the corridor before transforming once more into a kelpie. He pawed at the ground, shifting his weight from one leg to the other, then hurtled down the corridor with all the speed he could muster.

When he hit the wall a resounding crack filled the air, but it did not come down. Murdoch pushed against it again, then retreated down the corridor to charge a second time. The cracking grew louder, and the air filled with dust. One final shove and the wall crumbled, sending stones of all sizes skittering across the wall.

Murdoch could not see anything through the debris at first. He returned to his human form, coughing as dust filled his lungs. But then the air cleared, and a figure became visible in front of him.

"*Fair and lovely as thou art,*" Murdoch recited before he could stop himself, the words belonging to a song Sorcha used to sing to him. He kicked away the remaining stone that stood between him and the woman he had spent every day and night over the last nine months longing for.

"*Thou hast stown my very heart;*

I can die – but canna part,

My bonnie dearie."

Silence. The air completely cleared, and she came fully into view.

"You grew out your hair," Sorcha said, tears in her eyes as she stumbled into Murdoch's arms.

He could not believe she was here – that *he* was here, with her. Murdoch could not stop his hands from trembling, no matter how tightly he grabbed onto Sorcha. "You will have to cut it for me," he said, laughing. "But first – but first –"

Murdoch broke away from Sorcha just enough to tilt her chin upwards, marvelling at her green-and-blue eyes staring right back up at him, and kissed her. He kissed her like it was the first time he had ever kissed her, and the last time, and all the times in-between. If he could have his way Murdoch would have remained in that moment, kissing Sorcha Darrow until the end of forever.

A certain someone would never forgive him if he did.

He pulled away from the kiss and gently took Sorcha's hand in his, pulling her down the corridor as he did so. He flashed a grin at her she eagerly returned.

"First we have a fox to save."

CHAPTER THIRTY-ONE

Lachlan

"Do not dare take her from me, Lachlan."

"I wondered when you'd find me," Lachlan said, turning to face King Eirian as the silver faerie approached him. He pointed upwards. "I was going to look for you in your chambers, but of course you would not be there. The light in the window was a ruse."

"Which you were clearly too clever to fall for," Eirian replied, eyes glittering dangerously as he stalked around Lachlan even as Lachlan did the same to him. He gestured around them. "The courtyard seems as interesting a place as any to destroy you. Tell me: what did you expect to achieve by coming here?"

Lachlan chuckled. "Why, to prove that I am not too weak to best you, of course. And to tell you that I know."

The Unseelie king froze. "Know what, exactly?"

"Everything. I knew Sorcha lost our baby months and months ago."

"You are –"

"Lying?" Lachlan cut in, continuing to prowl across the courtyard. He had to clear a path for Murdoch; he did not want to risk the kelpie bowling into Eirian on the off-chance the faerie was strong enough to cling onto him. "I am lying, you think? I do not have time to twist my words into half-truths and jibes like you do. No, I am being honest. I crept into your Court – into your castle – and spoke to Sorcha. She told me about the babe. About the fact you turned her *immortal*."

His final word was a snarl.

Eirian composed himself within the space of a blink. An easy smile spread across his face, and he flicked his hair over one shoulder. "It does not matter that you already knew. It does not matter at all. Your child is gone, Lachlan, and your mortal love, too."

"That she is not mortal may be true, but she is not gone," Lachlan replied, daring to take a step towards Eirian. With his keen eyes he could see the silver king was not in his complete and lucid mind. His pupils were far too dilated; his movements but a fraction too slow.

We were right to use the solstice as cover, he thought, viciously happy. *If his actions are slower then I can only hope his mind is slower, too.*

"You cannot have her," Eirian insisted, as if that was that and the matter was closed. "I have taken a liking to her. So leave, before I kill you for a girl you will surely forget in a hundred years or so."

"I know she's carrying *your* child, Eirian."

A flinch.

"You cannot know that."

Lachlan could only cackle the way Eirian always did. "A woman becoming pregnant at the hands of both faerie kings? You thought I could not know? Did you not consider that there must surely be one witch or sightseer or another who saw this happening?"

That Eirian did not immediately reply meant that he most certainly had. But that Lachlan had been the one to hear the prophecy, not him, was a blow against the Unseelie king's pride.

"And who, if you would care to divulge, was this visionary behind this auspicious event?" he asked, almost through gritted teeth.

Good, Lachlan thought. *Get angrier. Get sloppier. Get so involved in your rage you do not notice the kelpie thundering out of your castle until it is too late.*

"I think you may have heard of her, once upon a time," Lachlan said, thoroughly enjoying himself despite the gravity of the situation. "She was truly formidable. Terrifying. And she will be, again, because of me. It is most certainly a boon, to have Beira the Bloodthirsty in the service of the Seelie Court."

Eirian's eyes grew wide. "You are *lying.*"

"You seem fond of saying that, when it seems as if others know things that you do not. Are you really so arrogant as to believe not a single soul out there can outsmart you?"

"You have not *outsmarted* me, damn fox," Eirian said. He looked around the empty courtyard. "You came here alone, with the blind courage that you could somehow defeat me. But you can't, Lachlan. You are not strong enough."

"You are right," Lachlan replied, feigning sorrow. A

rumbling beneath his feet told him it was time to leave. He took another step towards Eirian, then another and another, with fury in his eyes and a growl upon his lips. "I am not strong enough to defeat...yet. But I am not alone."

Finally, too late, Eirian took notice of the stones below him vibrating as if they were abuzz with energy. "What –" he began, but then the kelpie came crashing down the stairs, screaming and roaring as he seemed to all but fly across the courtyard.

Lachlan used Eirian's momentary distraction to push him away with a surge of magic, sending him tumbling backwards and well out of reach of Murdoch.

A hand extended down from the kelpie's back.

"Lachlan!" Sorcha cried. With the moonlight in her wild, copper hair, and the wind billowing the gossamer material of her dress, and the luminous look upon her face as she reached for him, Lachlan thought she looked altogether unreal. But she *was* real.

Lachlan took her hand.

"I'm sorry it took so long," he said, crushing Sorcha against his chest and clinging to the kelpie's mane in the process.

She let out a barely discernible sob. "You were just in time."

"*Bring her back!*" Eirian screeched, razor-sharp teeth bared and silver eyes flashing as his gargantuan raven-feathered wings unfurled into existence. "*Bring her –*"

But Murdoch ran faster than the Unseelie king could possibly contend with, and the end of Eirian's demand was lost to the wind.

Lachlan indulged the urge to pat the kelpie's neck as if he were a horse and not a monster. "Take us home, horse."

Murdoch snorted. "Do that again and I –"

"Shall drown me in my sleep," Lachlan said.

"Shall drown him in his sleep," Sorcha replied, at the same time.

And then, because no other words could describe what they had just gone through – what they had been going through for years, ever since Lachlan was first turned into a fox at the hands of his Unseelie stepfamily – Murdoch said, "Home it is."

CHAPTER THIRTY-TWO

Sorcha

Sorcha was barely given time to exhale before she was thrust into the overwhelming brightness of the Seelie Court. Lachlan and Murdoch blithely led her to one of the many drawing rooms, where several people already resided.

"Miss Sorcha!" Ailith cried, bodily throwing herself at her before Sorcha had an opportunity to respond. But she returned the embrace, feeling her throat begin to clog with tears when the faerie stroked her hair and openly wept.

"I am – I am here, Ailith," Sorcha said, choking on a laugh as she pulled away from her and saw her lovely face dripping with tears. "I made it back safe and sound. Well, sound, but are we safe?"

She turned her gaze to Lachlan, then Murdoch. "What is to stop Eirian from coming after me?"

Lachlan grinned. "We copied the circumstances upon which he stole you away. He has no right to claim you, now."

Sorcha considered this. It seemed ridiculous, to have been saved in such a way, but many faerie laws and customs seemed ridiculous to a mortal.

Not a mortal.

Her sudden ashen appearance was noticed in an instant by Murdoch. He reached for her, and pushed towards the fire. One of the two men who were sitting in armchairs by the hearth - both of them strangers - politely stood up and offered his chair to her. As he moved Sorcha caught a flash of amber, and she realised he was not a stranger at all.

"You," she said, losing all coherent speech for a moment. She forced her brain to work once more. "London. The coffee house. You told me to be careful, but not of Murdoch. Just who exactly are you?"

Lachlan, Murdoch and the remaining stranger stared at the amber-eyed man.

"You never told us you *met* her!" the stranger complained. "Not once, the entire time we were travelling to the faerie realm, did you mention this. Did you not think it prudent to tell me you had once run into Sorcha Darrow?"

The man shrugged. "What of it? It does not matter now. She was not careful, and she paid the price, but she is safe now."

"I would hold your tongue if you wish to keep it," Lachlan hissed. "Do not talk of -"

"Will you all calm down?" Sorcha demanded, exasperated but happy in equal measure. This kind of argument felt familiar. It was something she could deal with. "The man is right; I *wasn't* careful. I should have heeded your advice when you gave it to me, Mister...?"

"Wolfe," the man replied, bowing deeply. "Adrian Wolfe."

She smiled at the remaining stranger, who was still glaring at Adrian. "Which makes you Julian, the wizard. Please accept my deepest gratitude for saving Lachlan's life, seven years ago."

When Julian stopped glaring and granted Sorcha a smile she was taken aback by how handsome it made him. "It is a pleasure to meet you, Miss Darrow, though I wish the circumstances were better. How are you feeling?"

It was a strange question to be asked, though it was the most normal question in the world. "I - do not know," Sorcha replied. "Nine months ago I was mortal, and I was..." She gulped, flashing a look at Lachlan before staring into the fire to keep back her tears. Now that she was sitting down, and warm, and safe, Sorcha was beginning to find the circumstances of her life altgother far too overwhelming.

Behind her Ailith began stroking her hair once more, crooning softly as she often did when the two of them spent time together. It set Sorcha at ease, which she gratefully assumed was the point. She set a hand across her stomach. "Now I am pregnant once more, but it is not the babe I chose to have."

"We will get rid of it," Lachlan said, rushing to her side with eager eyes. "We can magic the babe away, Clara. You will feel nothing. No pain. We can -"

"*No!*" she cried, beyond horrified. "This is my baby. *My* baby. You will not take them away from me!"

"But Sorcha," Murdoch said, kneeling down in front

of her, "you cannot have the baby. Eirian will –"

"You said I was safe!"

"Not if you have the baby! You cannot –"

"Do not tell me what I can and cannot do, after all that has happened to me!"

Sorcha began to hyperventilate; even Ailith's fingertips on her head could do nothing to calm her down. "I will not –" she gasped, "I cannot – to lose my mortal life and my baby – I will not let that stand!"

The look in both Lachlan and Murdoch's eyes was tragic. But they could not understand; they were not the ones carrying the life within her. It had been the only thing stopping her from ending her *own* life to escape Eirian's torment. She would give the child all the love in the world, to replace the entirely loveless way in which they were conceived.

"You would dare tell a woman to give up her child?"

Sorcha turned her head to face the door. A faerie she did not recognise stood there, impossibly beautiful and statuesque. Her hair was the colour of moonlight, and flowed down to her feet like a river. Her face seemed carved from marble of a similar colour to her hair, and her hands were elegant and long-fingered. Startling blue eyes shot through with silver gazed around the room in fury.

Lachlan frowned. "Who are –"

"You ask me to protect this girl from the Unseelie king," the faerie interrupted. "Do you doubt my powers to keep him at bay? She is carrying a babe who will one day *rule*. Sorcha Darrow will have her child and they will both be safe. You have my absolute word on the matter."

Out of the corner of her eye Sorcha saw a flash of recognition cross Murdoch's face. "Beira?"

The faerie nodded. "Returned to my true and rightful state, as promised by the Seelie king."

"You said...rule?" Sorcha asked the faerie.

"My visions do not lie. Your child will rule a faerie throne."

Sorcha still had no idea who the faerie was - her name meant nothing to her, and the accuracy of her visions even less so - but she was pleased to have such a commanding presence on her side. "If you would mean to protect me and my baby then I gladly accept your offer, Beira."

"As is only right," Beira said, satisfied. "The babe will need all the help they can get, with the fox and the kelpie around."

Both Lachlan and Murdoch looked as if they wanted nothing more than to complain, but found that they couldn't.

Murdoch sighed. "You are right, and I am sorry. Sorcha, I did not mean -"

"I know," Sorcha said, She turned her gaze to Lachlan. "Both of you. I know you only want to protect me. But this baby is not a threat to me; their father is. And I will *never* let Eirian near them, not for as long as I shall li-"

"Of course!" Adrian burst out, much to the surprise of everyone currently discussing Sorcha's baby. All attention diverted to the magician.

He grinned a wolfish grin at Sorcha. "...I think I've worked it out."

"What do you mean, you *think you've worked it out?*" Lachlan asked, narrowing his eyes at Adrian. "Worked what out?"

"Your mortality issue."

"Which part of the conversation was about that?" Murdoch asked, deeply confused.

But to his right Julian cocked his head, a wave of understanding crossing his face. He turned to Adrian. "Like with the Greek girl and the king?"

Adrian nodded. "A counter-curse. A balance."

"What do you mean?" Sorcha asked, not daring to trust the excited gleam in the man's amber eyes. "What would you do to me?"

"Mortality to immortality, and immortality to mortality, can only happen once, am I correct?" the man asked Lachlan, who nodded. "Could you take someone else's opportunity to switch between the two?"

"The legend goes that when a mortal is made immortal, they steal the life from a faerie who was not using it, but I believed it to be nonsense," Lachlan said, "until Eirian cast the magic on Sorcha and she lost her half-faerie child. But that could simply be awful coincidence."

But Adrian shook his head. "Blood magic is never coincidence. Your legend may only hold true for women who carry another life within them."

Sorcha rushed to her feet immediately, heart racing in fury. "I will not give up my –"

"You will not lose your baby," Adrian said, very patient. "But your baby will lose their ability to become mortal."

Sorcha faltered. "They – you can do that?"

"If you wish it to be so, I can do it."

All around her were murmurs of excitement. Murdoch in particular looked ecstatic by the prospect.

"I knew there was a reason I brought you with me, Wolfe," Julian muttered, which caused Adrian to roll his eyes.

"I can't," Sorcha said, causing gasps of disbelief all round.

"Sorcha," Murdoch said, taking her hands in his and squeezing them slightly too hard. "You cannot mean that. You –"

"I will not take my own child's right to choose away from them," she insisted, knowing it was the right move. "To do so would make me no better than *him*."

Adrian considered this. "Once the babe is born I cannot work the counter-curse. If we wait for the child to make the decision of their own accord it will be too late."

"But does the counter-curse have a time limit?" Julian asked. "Is it immediate, or can you –"

"Ah, I knew there was a reason I brought *you* with me," Adrian chuckled. "Miss Darrow, how about this: when you child comes of age – whenever that may be. When they are ready to rule, when they are ready to choose. When they are ready to forsake their chance for mortality. Then, and only then, will that chance be given to you."

"I..." Sorcha mulled the man's words. They were imbibed with magic, washing over her with their power and their promise. "Yes," she said. "Yes, I can agree to

692

that."

"Oh, thank the forest," Lachlan breathed out, looking almost ready to collapse in relief. He ran a hand through his hair. "But they will *rule*? You are sure, Beira?"

The faerie gave him a look that suggested his question was an affront to her powers, which Sorcha imagined it was. "I am never wrong, as I have said at least once or twice before."

"I do not care if my child wears a crown or not," Sorcha said. "But what I do care about – what I want more than anything – is to get to my bed. *My* bed, in *my* house."

Without a word of warning Murdoch swept her up into his arms. "Then bed it is. Ailith, I don't suppose you could spare some magic to –"

"No need to ask," she said, smiling. "Simply take a step outside this room and you will be back in the Darrow house."

Sorcha grinned at Murdoch, then glanced at Lachlan. "If you go near my dreams tonight –"

"Murdoch will murder me."

"No, *I* will. I need to sleep for at least three days."

The faerie chuckled softly, for he understood what Sorcha was saying. *Not tonight, but sometime soon.*

Tonight was for Sorcha, and Sorcha alone.

She could deal with the beginning of the rest of her life in the morning.

CHAPTER THIRTY-THREE

Murdoch

Murdoch could only watch as Sorcha rubbed a hand against her growing belly and sang softly. She was singing nonsense – made-up words and riddles with no answers – but her voice was so lovely that Murdoch's heart ached to hear it. There was a tenderness to it that he'd rarely heard before, in fleeting moments where she'd sing to Galileo when she thought nobody was listening. He wondered if the baby would inherit her voice.

He would be a dangerous faerie indeed, to inherit such a skill.

He had not once told Sorcha that he knew the baby would be a boy. That would involve telling her about the vision Beira had recited to him – that Sorcha would grant him a son within eighteen months and a day – and Murdoch did not want to put such pressures on the woman he loved. If Sorcha wished for Murdoch to help her raise her baby as his own child then it had to be *her* choice, not because of something a faerie witch had proclaimed.

To think Beira meant I would have an Unseelie son, of all things, Murdoch thought, edging closer to the fire to warm the ends of his fingers. It was a bitterly cold February evening; Murdoch and Sorcha were curled up in their favourite armchairs by the drawing room hearth.

Murdoch caught Sorcha watching him warm his hands with a slight smile on her face. She indicated towards one of several blankets covering her lap. "Take one of these if you are cold, Murdoch," she said. "I do not need them all." Going by the rosiness of her cheeks she was telling the truth.

But Murdoch shook his head. "Those are for the babe," he insisted. "We cannot risk h-them catching a chill." He just barely stopped himself from saying *him*; Murdoch inwardly cursed.

Be careful. Do not make Sorcha's pregnancy more stressful that it needs to be.

Murdoch suppressed a humourless snort of laughter. It was hard to imagine anything more stressful that being impregnated by the Unseelie king by way of faerie-fruit-induced hallucinations. It didn't help that Sorcha couldn't involve her mother with the baby's birth, either – not until the boy was born and Lachlan could work a glamour upon him to look truly human.

"What is on your mind?" Sorcha asked, catching the dark, troubled look that crossed Murdoch's face with practised ease.

He moved over from the fire to perch on the arm of Sorcha's chair, squeezing her shoulder before gently kissing her forehead. "It is nothing," he said. "Just the usual worries."

"You are lying."

"I am not."

"You are!" Sorcha pressed, looking up at Murdoch with a frown on her face and a pout on her lips. It was so endearing that Murdoch found himself leaning down to kiss her properly before he could stop himself. Sorcha eagerly welcomed the kiss, wrapping her arms around Murdoch's shoulders to pull him insistently closer. Her mouth tasted of sugar and lemons – a remnant of the tart, sherbet-filled sweets Mrs Ferguson had sent up from London after Sorcha had requested them a fortnight ago.

When their lips finally parted Sorcha leaned against Murdoch's chest, sighing heavily. "Please tell me what it is that is troubling you so. You have had the same conflicted expression on your face for weeks now."

Murdoch hesitated for a moment. "I sincerely do not wish to push such matters on you when you –"

"*Murdoch.*"

It was his turn to sigh. "Fine," he said. "I give in." With gentle hands Murdoch pushed Sorcha away from his chest so he could look at her properly. Her green-and-blue eyes were bright and intent on his; Murdoch loved those eyes more than he could ever say. His grip tightened on her shoulders. "I – we have not discussed this yet, because I did not think it would be fair to do so, but –"

"You have never hesitated to say *anything* to me before," Sorcha cut in. "After knowing each other for so long just what is stopping you from saying what you think?"

Murdoch's gaze fell to her stomach. "The baby."

"What about the baby?"

"I..." Murdoch took a gulp of air and closed his eyes.

696

His heart was hammering in his chest, making him feel altogether sick with nerves. "It is your baby and therefore your choice," he said, opening his eyes once more to find that Sorcha had cocked her head to one side and was biting her lower lip in curious confusion. "After everything you have been through – after every choice that has been torn from you – you have every right to tell me you do not want this."

Murdoch took another deep breath. "Sorcha Darrow, will you allow me to love and raise this child as my own? I know this was not the way we planned to have a baby together – that we may not get to have the family we wanted for a long, long time – but all I want is to raise this child with you. As *our* child."

An achingly long moment of silence stretched on for what felt like an age. Murdoch could read nothing from Sorcha's face, which only caused his heart to hurt even more. But then her eyes grew altogether too shiny, and she began to cry, and she ran a hand through Murdoch's hair to pull his lips back to hers once more.

"Of course, you idiot," she said, voice full of tears as she kissed him again and again and again. "I was beginning to think you would *never* ask me. Was so worried you wouldn't. I didn't want to push any responsibility onto you."

Murdoch wrapped his arms around her in delight. "We are both as bad as each other," he laughed. "We could have felt a whole lot better about this situation had we merely talked about it long before now."

"I did not know if you could love an Unseelie child," Sorcha admitted, the words muffled against Murdoch's lips. "Considering the circumstances in which I found myself pregnant –"

"Sorcha, it is *because* of those circumstances that I will love the babe more than anything," he interrupted, grazing his teeth along Sorcha's jawline as he did so. When Murdoch reached her earlobe he gently bit it. "How could I not love a child borne from the woman who means the world to me?"

The two of them said nothing for a while, content to plant lazy kisses on each other and embrace within the confines of Sorcha's armchair, but then the booming crack of the front door opening drove Murdoch immediately to his feet.

Sorcha looked at him with wide eyes before grabbing his hand. "Who on earth could it be at this – Lachlan?!"

Murdoch's shoulders slumped as the golden faerie opened the drawing room door and stood, breathless and dishevelled, before them. "What do you want, fox?" he scowled, turning from Lachlan to rearrange the blankets on Sorcha's lap as he did so. "Surely nothing is so important it could not wait until morning."

A pause. And then: "I want to raise the baby."

Murdoch whipped back around to face Lachlan so quickly he almost lost his balance. "You *what?*" he exclaimed, releasing his hold on Sorcha's hand in order to storm over to the Seelie king. Murdoch was taller than him; he was gratified when Lachlan had to tilt his chin up slightly to meet his gaze.

The faerie's golden eyes narrowed. "I did not come here to talk to you, horse. I am here to talk to Clara about being the babe's father."

"Too late, useless vermin," Murdoch grinned, glee washing over him as he realised Lachlan was going to get

698

thoroughly rejected. He even took a few steps back to allow the faerie to approach Sorcha, get down on his knees and hold both her hands in his own, so sure in her answer as he was.

"Clara," Lachlan began, an eager smile on his face that implied he'd thoroughly ignored what Murdoch had just said. "Clara. *My* Clara. The wolf said that you would regain your mortality on the day your child was ready to sit upon a throne, but he did not specify which throne that must be. So let us raise this baby together, and prime him for *my* throne. I will happily give it up so that you can return to the life you wanted as fast as possible."

Sorcha's eyes widened in surprise; so did Murdoch's. *Lachlan has a point,* Murdoch thought, though it irked him to admit it. "That does not mean you have to be the baby's father," he told the faerie, who threw him a dismissive glance before returning his attention to Sorcha.

"But I *want* to," Lachlan said, squeezing Sorcha's hands as he did so. The same unreadable expression she had worn earlier had returned, which unnerved Murdoch to no end. Lachlan continued: "Clara, I have been thinking about this ever since we got you back from Eirian. We lost our child because of him. Let us raise this one together, instead."

Oh.

Murdoch's heart twisted at Lachlan's words. They were full of a raw, painful grief that the Seelie king had revealed to Murdoch only once before, immediately after he first learned of the loss of his child. It was impossible for Murdoch not to feel for him. *He has more claim than I to this child. But I cannot...*

He shook his head. Murdoch wanted to raise

Sorcha's baby with her more than anything. And then:

"Both."

Murdoch blinked, turning his gaze to Sorcha's determined face in utter confusion. "What do you mean, both?"

"I mean that you can *both* be a father to my baby," she said, a flash of amusement lighting her eyes when Lachlan pulled away from her hands with an outraged yowl.

"You cannot be serious, Clara!" the faerie complained. He pointed at Murdoch. "You wish me and him to – to –"

"Sorcha, are you sure this is wise?" Murdoch cut in. He waved a hand uselessly in front of him. "To raise a child in such a way..."

"And how else would you suggest I raise my half-Unseelie, half-human baby, who needs to be protected from their sire's own people, prepped for the Seelie crown *and* be able to live some semblance of a happy life all at once?" Sorcha darted her eyes from Murdoch to Lachlan then back again. "I need you both in my life. I *want* you both in my life – for me and..."

When Sorcha lowered her gaze to her belly and ran a hand across it Murdoch softened immediately. "We will surely be no ordinary family," he murmured, reaching out to place a gentle hand over hers, "but if this is what you truly desire, Sorcha, then I am only too happy to oblige."

Sorcha beamed at him, the smile lighting up her face as if it was on fire. When she turned her head to look at Lachlan, Murdoch followed her gaze. The faerie stood there, watching them, a conflicted expression twisting his brow. But when Sorcha held out her other hand for him Lachlan immediately took it, and squeezed her fingers as if his life depended on it.

He threw a molten glare at Murdoch. "I won't be bested by a water horse. Just see, kelpie, I shall leave you in the dust. No father will be as great as I w–"

"Lachlan!" Sorcha scolded, though she was giggling. "I thought the two of you had finally reached some kind of understanding after all these years."

Murdoch snorted. "It would take a hundred years and more for things to change between us, my love."

"Well it's a good thing we have such a span of years," she replied, momentarily sober and serious.

When Lachlan reached forward and kissed her brow Murdoch did not stop him; he was impressed that he didn't even flinch at the display of affection. "We will do everything we can to raise the child good and true, Clara. And then..." He threw half a glance at Murdoch, who smiled.

"And then we can have the mortal life we want together," Murdoch finished. He smoothed Sorcha's wild hair away from her face, tucking an errant strand behind her ear as he did so. Her skin grew hot against his touch, and the way she traced her fingertips across his hand told Murdoch that they would perhaps not fall asleep quite as quickly as he had originally imagined they would once Lachlan left the Darrow house.

Sorcha let out a somewhat shaky sigh, then pulled away from both Murdoch and Lachlan with a smile. Her eyes flicked to the bay window, though the curtains were drawn. It did not take Murdoch long to work out what she was thinking of, though it was Lachlan who spoke first.

"He will never touch you again," he swore. "You or the baby. If there is one thing the kelpie and I can agree on, it's that. And we have Beira on our side, who I must admit terrifies me."

Murdoch nodded. "The fox speaks the truth."

"As if I can speak anything but."

"Oh, but can you say each others' names?" Sorcha teased, a wicked smile painted on her lips.

The kelpie of Loch Lomond and the King of the Seelie Court looked at each other. Murdoch could see his reflection in Lachlan's eyes: dark-haired, broad-shouldered and pale-skinned. A stark difference from the faerie himself, with his bronzed hair, golden skin and narrow frame. They were opposites of each other down to their very cores. But one vital thing they shared, and it was the most important thing of all.

They both loved Sorcha Margaret Darrow.

"No," they said in unison, chuckling when Sorcha rolled her eyes and collapsed into her armchair in exaggerated exasperation.

"It is not my fault if my child grows up calling you both *fox* and *horse* instead of father," she warned.

Lachlan grinned. "Then we shall have to offer a trade to the bairn for the right ones: a name for a name. It is the faerie way, after all."

Murdoch resisted the urge to argue with Lachlan. For the child *would* be a faerie, whether he liked it or not. It was up to himself and Sorcha to ensure the boy grew up to be a good one.

And, at the end of the day, not all faerie customs

were bad ones.

Murdoch gave Lachlan the barest of smiles. "A name for a name."

EPILØGUE

Eirian

Sorcha Darrow's baby was born on the day of the summer solstice.

By the time news of the child's birth reached the ears of the Unseelie Court the sun had already dipped as low on the horizon as it would go that evening. So, in the everlasting twilight of midsummer at midnight, Eirian took on the guise of a raven to circle the realm of the Seelie. For he knew Sorcha would not be in the Darrow household – not when she needed to ensure the safety of her baby's birth.

His baby. Eirian's child and heir.

Even as a raven Eirian found it difficult to trick his way past the charms and spells Lachlan had woven over the Seelie Court. Bitterly he conceded that the young faerie truly was more powerful than he'd given him credit for, and would only grow more so with every passing day sitting on his throne as the golden king.

Eirian had been foolish to assume Evanna's son –

despite being barely more than a boy in terms of years – would be green and inexperienced. He had brought Beira to his side, after all. Beira, whom even Eirian was wary of.

Lachlan was crafty. He was sneaky. He found solutions to problems where there should have been none.

He was a damn fox.

Eirian allowed air to fill his wings like sails, slowing his lazy, spiralling flight to a near-halt in order to survey the Seelie Court below him. All around him were trees and bushes laden with colourful faerie fruit, filling Eirian's nostrils with their heady, dangerous scent. Bright torches of orange and blue and flickering green flames lit the gemstone-encrusted path that led to the golden palace, which glittered even in the blanket of night. It was a beautiful place, the Seelie Court; Eirian had always appreciated its splendour.

"Where are you, my lovely queen?" he murmured, voice silky upon the warm nighttime breeze despite coming out of the beak of a raven. Eirian liked to think of Sorcha in such terms despite the fact he had made the fatal mistake of *not* marrying her whilst he had the opportunity to. But Eirian had taken Sorcha from Lachlan and the kelpie as a means to control them; marrying a human had never been something the Unseelie king would have considered doing.

But that was before. Before Sorcha became the mother of his one and only child – a rarity amongst his kind. Eirian was closing in on nine hundred years old, during which time not one of the babes he had put inside of faeries and mortals alike had survived past the first few months of pregnancy. That Sorcha had made it through childbirth with both her and the baby alive and well made her endlessly valuable in ways the girl likely could not yet fathom.

Once Eirian got his hands on Sorcha he would not make the same mistake again; whether through enchantment or blackmail he *would* make her his bride. That doing so would forever torment Lachlan and the water horse was a delicious bonus.

Off in the distance a fiddle was playing, and the sounds of laughter and dancing could be heard. *Celebrating my child's birth,* Eirian thought as he descended towards the ground. It was a good sign, for if most everyone in the Court was outside celebrating then there would be few creatures currently residing in the palace.

A lone faun on spindly legs glanced at Eirian as he flew past it to settle on the low boughs of an ash tree, close to an open window of the Seelie palace. He cawed at the animal, peeved that it did not immediately run away, before ignoring it in favour of peering inside the palace.

The window he'd stopped by looked in on the king's chambers; Eirian was pleased that his memory of the labyrinthine Seelie palace remained pinpoint accurate. Despite the heat of the evening a fire was roaring merrily in the intricately carved hearth, filling the room with the pleasant smell of woodsmoke. The flames were the main source of light, casting long, dark shadows into the far corners of the room.

Lachlan himself was nowhere to be seen, but the dark-haired human form of the kelpie was sitting cross-legged on the floor with his back against the bed. A painfully fond smile was painted across his face. In front of him, lying upon a pile of silken cushions and thick, woven blankets was a woman with wild, tangled hair, pale skin and rosy cheeks, clutching a bundle to her breast with the utmost care.

Sorcha and the babe.

"You are sure about the name?" the kelpie – Murdoch – asked, so softly that Eirian had to risk clambering over from the ash tree to sit upon the windowsill to hear him. "Lachlan might protest to it being far too...human."

Sorcha let out a gentle snicker, bending her head low to plant a kiss upon the baby. Eirian turned this way and that to try and catch a glimpse of the child from his vantage point but to no avail, which frustrated him beyond belief.

Move an inch to the left, he thought, willing Sorcha to do as he wished. *An inch, for just one look.*

"If Lachlan is concerned about the human nature of my *half-human* child then he can take it up with me," Sorcha told Murdoch, an exhausted but amused expression upon her face as she spoke.

It was his turn to laugh. "Take it up with you and lose, you mean."

"Exactly." She kissed the baby again. "If the name was good enough for my father then it's good enough for my son."

Eirian stilled. *A son. I have a son. Sorcha has given me everything centuries of women could not. But what was her father's name?*

Murdoch shuffled closer to Sorcha, sliding an arm around her waist to pull her against his side. She eagerly leaned her head against his shoulder. "I like William," he said. "It's a good name. Most of the *Williams* I ate over the years were honest, decent men."

"What a horrific thing to say!" Sorcha gasped, appalled, but then she giggled. "I suppose he'll have to get used to you saying such things, though. Do you think a half-human, half-Unseelie child has ever been raised by a kelpie father? *And* a Seelie father? The King of the Seelie Court, no less."

"I'm inclined to believe that the definitive answer to that is *no*," Murdoch replied. He kissed the crown of Sorcha's head and smoothed her hair back. "How are you feeling? I can hold little Will so you can rest."

But Sorcha declined with a shake of her unruly hair. "I am happy just the way I am," she said. And then, after a moment of contemplation: "I don't suppose I could convince you to find me some wine, though? Given the fact I gave birth just this afternoon I'd say I deserve it."

Murdoch chuckled as he stood up, giving Sorcha a half-mocking bow. "But of course. Your wish is my command, as it were."

Eirian watched as the man who was not a man left Lachlan's chambers. For a minute or two he did nothing but watch and feel and listen from his spot on the windowsill; Eirian could sense no faeries nearby, nor any other creature of consequence. It was just him in the form of a raven, Sorcha...and the baby.

With a final glance behind him Eirian took a risk and flew into Lachlan's chambers on silent wings. He landed on top of a handsomely carved wardrobe out of Sorcha's line of sight, pleased to see that she had not noticed him.

William, she named him, Eirian thought, when he

was finally granted a view of the son she had given him. *It is not a bad name as far as human names go.*

He was every inch as beautiful as Eirian could have hoped. William's skin was a fainter silver-blue than a full Unseelie faerie; it shimmered and caught the flickering light of the fire in the most breathtaking of ways. His hair was just as starkly silver as his father's, but it had a slight curl to it that suggested the baby had inherited the same wildness of his mother's hair.

Eirian would have to wait and see if William's teeth and nails grew sharp like the Unseelie or rounded like a human's, though he did not care for such things right now. No, all he wanted was a glimpse of the boy's eyes.

Sorcha shifted William in her arms, cooing down at him as he gurgled back with eyes held tightly shut. Though she was clearly exhausted – barely five minutes away from falling into unconsciousness, Eirian reckoned – her expression grew bright when she gazed at her son. "Will you be a singer too, my love?" she asked him, gently touching the end of Will's nose with her index finger. "Would you like to sing with me now? I have a song for you."

Eirian cocked his feathered head to one side, wishing he had his own ears with which to listen as Sorcha began singing. She had thus far avoided granting him a song, after all, and though this one was not strictly for him it *was* for his son. Eirian would take it, and gladly.

"*Oh can ye sew cushions,*" Sorcha began, tickling William under his chin as she did so. "Your father – well, the kelpie one – loves this song. I hope you will love it too, little Will. *O can ye sew cushions,*"

"*And can ye sew sheets,*

And can ye sing ballalloo when the bairn greets?
And hee and haw birdie,
And hee and haw lamb,
And hee and haw, birdie, my bonnie wee lamb.
And hush a baw baby and balilly-loo,
And hee and haw birdie my bonnie wee doo."

Even though Eirian hated that the song belonged to the kelpie, he was enraptured. Sorcha's voice was lilting and lovely; he could listen to it for forever. *Would* listen to it for forever, when he found a way to lure Sorcha back to the Unseelie Court.

The lullaby should have sent William to sleep. Instead, the child slowly blinked open his eyes to stare at his mother as he continued to babble incoherently. And so it was that Eirian finally saw what colour they were: one green and one blue, like gems cut from the land and sea themselves.

His mother's eyes, he thought, swiftly flying out of the room when he sensed someone walking down the corridor towards the door. He did not want to leave – wanted to stay and watch his son grow from this very moment onward – but Eirian knew better than to risk being caught in such a place. He had seen what he needed to see, and had to be satisfied with that.

His mother's eyes, Eirian thought again, ascending into the starlit sky in ever-widening circles. He was pleased with that. More than pleased. Little Will would look like both of his parents, as was only right and proper. It would tie Sorcha to Eirian and his kingdom whether she wanted it or not.

William Darrow was perfect. All Eirian had to do

was wait a little longer to claim the boy and his mother as his own. It was something the Unseelie king could do, and do well; he'd practised patience for close to a millennium, after all.

Eirian had always played the long game, and now the end was finally in sight.

THE STORY WILL CONTINUE...

Just how long will it take for Will Darrow to ascend a faerie throne and grant his mother her longed-for mortality? Find out in the Dark Spear duology...soon.

• • •

Read on for an excerpt from *Intended*,
H. L. Macfarlane's brand new
mythology-soaked fantasy!

A long silence stretched out, then, save for the twittering of a handful of morning birds which remained in Mt. Duega for the winter. Charlie tuned into the sound, breathing in the crisp air in an effort to reassure herself that she was not all that far from home – not really. She was still surrounded by her beloved woods. It *sounded* like her woods. It *smelled* like her woods.

Daniel Silver was staring straight at her.

Charlie flinched, then hated herself for doing so. The last thing she needed was for the man to think she was intimidated by him, though in truth she was. So when he beckoned with a finger for her to come closer Charlie bit back her nerves and walked towards him.

I feel like he's trying to work me out in one fell swoop, she mused, when Silver's gaze swept from her feet to her head, back down again, then settled on her eyes. For a moment Charlie genuinely believed that he *could* get her measure so quickly, and pushed out her Influence on instinct in order to direct him elsewhere.

But before the tendril of magic could reach Silver, Charlie coiled it back in. Her father would hate it if she Influenced her new employer – and she agreed with him. *It will only make my life harder,* she concluded. *I'd have to keep my magic active at all times to stop him from realising someone is working it upon him in the first place.*

For Charlie had no doubts left in her mind about just how powerful Daniel Silver was now that she was finally in close proximity to him. Her father hadn't lied; the raw magic emanating off him was staggering. The urge to Influence him returned, just for a moment, when Charlie's curiosity over how much of her own magic she'd have to use to break through Silver's defences overwhelmed her.

Once more Charlie had to reign herself in. *Focus*

on something else. Like his glasses. They're definitely prescription, she thought, tilting her head to see the slight distortion the lenses caused to Silver's face.

"Just what is it that you're thinking, Miss Hope?" the man asked, noting where Charlie's attention was with passive interest.

"That a magician as strong as you shouldn't be wearing glasses."

"Coming from a young woman who didn't deem it necessary to brush her hair nor tuck in her shirt for her first day at a new job?"

Both quips left their respective tongues in close succession of each other, leaving Charlie in no doubt what the man's first impression of her was. *So he's obsessed with image,* she concluded, glancing down to see that her shirt was indeed untucked. She made no attempt to fix it nor to tidy her hair, which was always unkempt when Charlie left it unbound.

Her decision not to tidy herself up was clearly noted by Silver. His nose wrinkled in distaste, causing his glasses to slide downwards. When he pushed then back up Charlie couldn't help but say, "That wouldn't happen if you fixed your eyesight."

"My personal preferences aren't of your concern. Are you always this rude upon meeting people for the first time?"

"Rude?" Charlie blinked her eyes innocently. "I'm merely making an observation."

"Yes, with the intent of being rude."

Oh, you have no idea, she thought, resisting the

714

urge to say something else that would most definitely be construed as such. Instead, Charlie crossed her arms over her chest and attempted to stare down her new employer. When he remained silent she asked, "So where am I staying, anyway? Or are we going to stand out here all day?"

In lieu of answering her question Silver took a step towards her and mirrored Charlie's crossed arms. Another frown furrowed his brow, causing his glasses to slip once more.

Behind the lenses Charlie noted his eyes were very, very blue.

"Are you a Mind or Matter magician?" Silver demanded, clearly discomfited by the fact he hadn't been able to work it out yet.

Charlie resisted the urge to smile at this invisible victory, then replied honestly, "I'm useless with Matter."

"Mind, then. Any specific strengths?"

"I don't know. I guess you'll have to find out for your-"

"Miss Hope, I'm warning you. I don't have the patience to deal with this attitude of yours."

"I guess you'll have to fire me, then."

For the briefest of moments Charlie was certain that Silver was about to explode. His temple twitched, and his hands gripped his forearms with tense, barely-constrained irritation. She prepared herself for a shout. A curse. An immediate dismissal.

Instead Silver closed his eyes, exhaled, then

turned back towards his expansive house. "Uthesh give me strength, I understand exactly what you're doing. Follow me, Miss Hope."

Well that didn't work out the way I wanted it to, Charlie sulked, nonetheless dutifully following Mr Silver into his abode. *I suppose Da would never forgive me if I deliberately got myself fired.*

The man strode far too quickly through his house for Charlie to make out much of her surroundings, but since the morning sunlight hadn't reached the corridors yet she knew it was pointless to try and memorise the layout, anyway. When a tawny cat leapt from a shadowy windowsill into Silver's arms moments later Charlie jumped in fright.

But then Mr Silver smiled, and all she could focus on was him.

Gone was his detached demeanour and barely-contained temper. Faint lines creased the sides of his eyes, which lit up at the mere sight of the animal. He looked happy. Normal.

Like a mortal human being, not a man who was going to live forever.

"Kit," Silver said to the cat, scratching its chin before bopping its forehead with his own. "Just where have you been hiding all these weeks?"

The cat – Kit – mewed in response before turning its impossibly green eyes on Charlie. She took a small step back in shock.

It's from the woods. Daniel Silver is friends with an animal kin of the Immortal Folk?

Charlie supposed she shouldn't be surprised. Silver's estate was right on the boundary of Duega woods and he was immortal himself. It *shouldn't* have been a surprise.

Except that it was.

Never in all her twenty-four years had Charlie known another soul who fraternised with creatures from the woods.

When Kit meowed at her Charlie was brought starkly back into the present. Silver was staring at her staring at his cat, who jumped from his arms to slink down the corridor. Charlie turned her head to watch Kit leave until he disappeared around a corner.

"Miss Hope."

"Yes?" she murmured, attention still on the tawny forest cat.

"In here," Silver said, opening a door on his left and indicating inside when Charlie finally focused on him once more. All signs of his previous easy smile were gone.

Numbly Charlie entered the room, careful to give Mr Silver a wide berth as she did so. Her Influence magic was exacerbated by close contact; for years now she had barely touched another soul, save her father.

Inside the room was sparsely furnished with high-quality, oak-carved pieces: a high-backed bed, a wardrobe, a chest of drawers, a desk, a full-length mirror and a chair.

"My Chief-of-Staff will deal with you shortly,"

Silver said when Charlie perched upon the bed, testing the spring of the mattress with splayed fingers. "Don't treat her with the same disrespect you have thus far shown me."

Charlie clucked her tongue, keeping her eyes averted as she muttered, "I wouldn't dream of it."

The shudder of the door not-quite-slamming closed was all the reply Charlie got. But when she strained her ears she just barely heard Silver lament, "Just what have I agreed to?"

She threw herself onto her back with a smile. Silver may have worked out that she was trying to get fired but that didn't mean he *wouldn't* fire her.

After all, if Charlie was the most incompetent employee Daniel Silver had ever taken on then he'd have no choice but to dismiss her...or risk the wrath of his political sponsors who had all so desperately wished to have their children taken under the man's wing.

A small, mischievous laugh left Charlie's lips. "I give him a week."

• • •

H. L Macfarlane's *Intended* is an enchanting adult fairy tale ideal for fans of Uprooted, Howl's Moving Castle, and Shadow & Bone.

ACKNOWLEDGEMENTS

King of Forever concludes the Bright Spear trilogy, but as you've seen from the way it ends this is not the conclusion of the story for Sorcha, Lachlan, Murdoch and Eirian. No, it is merely an appropriate pause before the second half of the story is explored in the Dark Spear duology!

I have loved every minute spent working on King of Forever and its predecessors, even when I was in the midst of procrastinating (which was often). Writing my own Scottish fairy tale was a dream come true; nine-year-old me would be very proud.

So which team are you all on? Team Lachlan? Team Murdoch? Or, shock horror, team *Eirian?* The obvious point by the end of King of Forever was that Sorcha did not really have to choose between her fox and her kelpie, because their love for her – and her love for them – was too strong to be constrained by typically human notions of monogamy. Also, they're supernatural creatures. If they want to have a twisted polyamorous thing going on then I say we let them. It's definitely working for Ailith, after all.

I am very excited to bring William Darrow to life. I think you'll either love him or hate him, which is always a good thing.

As usual I would like to thank my partner, Jake; our lovely bunnies; my best friend and editor, Kirsty and, of course, my fans. The reaction to the Bright Spear trilogy has been huge, and I am truly amazed and grateful for it.

Until the next one!

Hayley

ABOUT THE AUTHOR

Hayley Louise Macfarlane hails from the very tiny hamlet of Balmaha on the shores of Loch Lomond in Scotland. After graduating with a PhD in molecular genetics she did a complete 180 and moved into writing fiction. Though she loves writing multiple genres (fantasy, romance, sci-fi, psychological fiction and horror so far!) she is most widely known for her Gothic, Scottish fairy tale, Prince of Foxes – book one of the Bright Spear trilogy.

ORIGIN OF POEMS

Fox Sleep (W. S. Merwin; 1992)

A Vision (Robert Burns; 1794)

O Can Ye Sew Cushions (Robert Burns; 1787)

Home (Robert Burns; 1786)

The Kelpie (Nick Baker; 2010)

Lost is my Quiet (Henry Purcell; 1698)

Flow My Tears (John Dowland; 1596)

Underground (David Bowie; 1986)

Ae Fond Kiss (Robert Burns; 1791)

Home (Robert Burns; 1786)

Ca' the Yowes (Robert Burns; 1794)

O Can Ye Sew Cushions (Robert Burns; 1787)

Ingram Content Group UK Ltd.
Milton Keynes UK
UKHW011813020523
421120UK00005B/182